Unchained
Lightning

Unchained Lightning

LYNN MICHAELS
ANITA MILLS
PATRICIA POTTER
VIVIAN VAUGHAN

St. Martin's Paperbacks

UNCHAINED LIGHTNING

"Whirlwind" copyright © 1996 by Anita Mills.
"Pride's Way" copyright © 1996 by Patricia Potter.
"Storms Never Last" copyright © 1996 by Vivian Jane Vaughan.
"Once Struck" copyright © 1996 by Lynn Michaels.

ISBN: 0-312-95928-1

Printed in the United States of America

St. Martin's Paperbacks edition/August 1996

10 9 8 7 6 5 4 3 2 1

Contents

WHIRLWIND

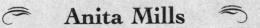 Anita Mills

Western Kansas: July 1877

The only living things he'd encountered all morning were a lone rattlesnake and a couple of buzzards circling over the bloated carcass of a cow an hour or so earlier. He had to have come twenty or more miles without a sign of a sod house—or any other kind of house, for that matter. And he'd followed the dry riverbed, just like Matheny had told him. He couldn't have missed it. The old man had misjudged the distance, that was all. Yeah, before long he'd be finding the Mitchell soddie.

Sweat soaked his hatband and his hair and ran down his forehead, dripping off him like rainwater. By nightfall, he'd be smelling like a polecat, stinking up his bedroll until he wouldn't be able to stand it, and there wasn't enough water for washing. Pretty soon there wouldn't even be any left to drink.

Damn, but it was hot—not the dry kind of heat a body would expect in Kansas, but rather the sultry kind, more like what one'd find in Louisiana. It lay over the prairie like a thick, suffocating blanket, smothering him. Right now, if hell had any other name, it'd be Kansas.

Tired, thirsty, and maybe lost, Ben Haley reined in the weary chestnut horse and reached for his canteen. It was three-quarters empty, and before long he'd have to share what little there was with Rebel. He sat there a moment, wishing he were just about anywhere else. Wishing he hadn't taken Jack Matheny's money.

As he tipped the tin container against his lips for a sip, he took stock of the strange sky. It was the color of a half-ripe peach. A foreboding stole over him as he turned in his saddle to scan the nearly flat land, the fine, almost feathery clouds flying along the horizon, seemingly chased by a roiling, rolling bank of dark thunderclouds. Lightning flickered like a flame in the wind, yet the air was so still that not a blade of grass stirred.

If he'd had any sense, he'd have stayed a few days either at Hays or Ellis and waited for the godawful heat to break. Instead, he was going to get caught out in a damned gulley-washer. He stood in his stirrups, letting the muggy air between his body and the sweat-soaked saddle, and craned his head, looking for anything they could use for shelter. A couple of sickly cottonwoods. No, a man'd be a fool to stand under a tree with clouds like that up there. It'd be like inviting lightning to strike him.

Under his breath, he cursed Jack Matheny roundly, wishing he'd never met the man. And never heard of Preston Mitchell either. But he had, and he'd taken the money, so now he was obligated to earn it. Resigned, he eased his aching body back into its wet cradle, replaced the lid on the canteen, and looped the canvas strap over the saddle horn.

"C'mon, fella. Might as well make as much time as we can before the storm hits," he decided, sighing. "I know you're plumb tuckered out, and you're probably thirstier than I am, but before long there's going to be plenty of water everywhere." He nudged the big horse with his knee. As Rebel eased into his slow gait, a sudden burst of wind hit, whipping the pages of the book Ben had tucked into the top of his saddlebag. He reached back, securing the leather flap over it.

Famed Gunmen of the West by Henry Hempstead Hill. He had his chapter just about memorized. "With cold, killer eyes, and a steel nerve, Ben Haley has twenty-seven notches carved in his walnut pistol grip, one for every year of his life.'' That first line under the scowling sketch was an attention getter, but the only thing Hill had right was his age. The rest of it was riddled with lies.

The artist who'd sketched him had obviously never laid eyes on him. In the ink drawing, he looked downright sinister, with a shock of dark hair, a drooping moustache, and a squinty cast to dark, almost beady eyes. And although only his head and shoulders were portrayed, there was a sense that he was small. In reality, he was clean-shaven, wore his blond hair short to keep it from turning up like a girl's, and had eyes that were an almost startling blue-green. Like the sea on a summer morn, a girl in Abilene had described them. And there was nothing short about him, either. When a Mexican tailor down in San Antonio had measured him for some new clothes last fall, he was six foot one. Bat Masterson, when he saw the book, had busted out laughing.

''Hell, you ought to like it,'' he'd said. ''Maybe if you're ever a wanted man, they'll use this picture, and you'll never get caught.'' Then, as he read the story, the smile faded, and he'd grown downright serious. ''I wouldn't worry about the law, Ben, but those twenty-seven notches might get you the wrong kind of attention around Dodge.''

Not that he wasn't a hell-raiser and didn't deserve at least part of his notoriety, Ben admitted. But he hadn't killed twenty-seven men, and he didn't need nicks in anything to remind him of those he had. He'd been nineteen that first time, and he still remembered it like yesterday. A big, bullying fellow had called him a cheat and slapped leather, giving him no choice but to go for his own gun. When the smoke cleared, Big Ike Thompson was lying in a pool of blood, staring upward, pretty much to the surprise of everyone, including Ben. But it was the beginning, the birth of a reputation that took on a life of its own.

Ben looked down, seeing the same old .44 he'd carried back then. The carved ivory handle might be yellowing a little with age, but other than that, there wasn't a mark on it. He didn't have to look at it to see Ike—or any of the other ten, either. On a bad night, they all haunted him, even though every one of them had forced the fight. And he'd never been a man to back down in a quarrel.

Now there seemed to be no end to it, or none that he wanted to think about, anyway. Since the damned thing came out last fall, it seemed like every town had some wet-eared kid eager to try him out. Like the one in Ellsworth who'd lain in wait, hoping to ambush big, bad Ben Haley. The kid had surprised him, all right, and Ben had shot him. He'd never forget the blank bewilderment, or that little bit of down on that kid's face. The young fool hadn't had his first shave when he died. And the only name he'd made for himself was painted on wood over his grave. *Danny Hayes, 1859–1876.* He couldn't forget the kid's mother spitting on him, calling him a murderer. That still haunted him.

The coroner's jury ruled the killing self-defense, but that hadn't eased the regret, the self-loathing he'd felt every time he thought of Mrs. Hayes. Even drifting over to Dodge, drowning the memory of that kid's face in cheap whiskey and cheaper women hadn't helped either. Drunk and down to his last two bits, he'd been pretty desperate when Jack Matheny found him.

You're Ben Haley, ain't you? I reckon you and me got a little business.

Anymore, those were words that sent a shiver down his spine and his hand for his gun. If Matheny hadn't been an old man, he might have been dead for starting a conversation like that. As it was, when the cattleman laid a copy of the book in front of him, saying he had a little business to conduct, Ben should've got up and left. He probably would have, but he wasn't thinking right at the time. And the two hundred dollars Matheny'd put on the table was a whole lot of money. Easy money, the old man said. All Ben had to do to earn it was steal another man's tomorrows.

When he'd finally sobered up, he was nearly broke again, and he knew he'd sunk about as low as he could get. Having spent Matheny's money, he had to earn it. For two hundred dollars, he'd obligated himself to kill a man he didn't even know. For two hundred dollars, he'd sold what was left of his soul. With one stupid word he'd become something he despised. He was a hired gun.

He could smell the rain on the wind now, and the sky was dark and ugly behind him as he crested the only hill in miles. As he looked down on the squat, ugly soddie and the sheep pens, he reined in. It was as though every muscle in his body tautened. If it was Preston Mitchell's place, he'd get his dirty business over, then try to lose himself in Colorado.

His eyes took in the brown patches that still marked the man's futile attempt at farming. Drought had long since taken his crops, but Mitchell was too damned stubborn to give up. No, instead of selling out to Matheny like everybody else, he'd brought in sheep to graze on the dying grass. He didn't know it yet, but he'd made a fatal mistake.

There was a girl down there, and she was hurrying to get the rest of the flock in before the storm hit. With that poke bonnet on, he couldn't see her face, but by the looks of that little waist and those slender arms, he could guess she had small, delicate features. For a moment, he allowed himself to imagine she was pretty, then he caught himself. It didn't matter—by the time he left the place, she'd be hating him.

Matheny hadn't told him there'd be a girl. He'd thought all he had to deal with was Mitchell. He didn't much like the business, anyway, but she was going to complicate everything. Even if Mitchell went for a gun, Ben didn't want to kill him in front of his wife or daughter.

She stopped to look up, then froze in horror. The wind

caught the front of her bonnet, lifting it off, tearing at a thick coil of auburn hair. He had to stare. His imagination wouldn't have done her justice—she was about as pretty a female as he'd known, and he'd been acquainted with more than his share. He wanted to shout over the wind, telling her she didn't need to be afraid of him, but she suddenly broke into a dead run for the sod house. And about that time, he heard what she'd seen.

The roar sounded like a cross between a stampeding herd and an overheated locomotive going downgrade at full steam. Turning in his saddle, he looked up, and his blood ran cold. That boiling black cloud was dropping a tail, and dust devils were spinning off it before it even touched ground. The thick, whirling column, and the wide swath of dust rising to meet it, were coming right for him. *Tornado.*

He yanked the reins, jerking Rebel's head, turning the animal at an angle to the funnel, then dug in his spurs. The horse bolted, racing headlong down the slight incline, taking him right back into the path of the storm. The twister was gaining on him, sucking up the air, while water and debris fell on him. And yet thick dust was everywhere, blinding him, choking him. A bolt of lightning struck nearby, rocking the earth, sending a flare of fire streaking across dead grass. As the water drowned it, smoke joined the dirt in his throat.

He closed his eyes and tried to pray, but the words were alien, forgotten too long ago. *God, deliver me . . .* As though the Almighty could care whether he lived or died. But Rebel deserved better than this. *Our Father, who art in Heaven . . .* No, he couldn't concentrate enough to re-member. This was the end. There wasn't any bullet out there with his name on it. It was a tornado blowing him to hell.

Wet foam flew back from the horse's shoulders as it threw all the energy it had left into one last burst of speed. It was heading straight for the girl, who was fighting desperately to stay on her feet, straining against the screaming, howling wind. There was no mistaking the terror in her face.

"Get down!" Ben shouted. "Hit the dirt—dammit, hit the dirt! Get your head down!"

She couldn't hear him—hell, he couldn't hear himself. Unable to stop the frightened horse, he dragged his leg over the saddle and jumped, throwing his body into hers. As the impact knocked the wind out of him, they hit the ground in a tangle of arms and legs and wet clothes.

He couldn't see, he couldn't hear, but he could feel her fighting him, clawing at his arms, trying to get free. Rolling over her, he pinned her down and shielded her head with his arms, then buried his face in her bosom. As the full brunt of the storm hit, she quit struggling and gripped his shoulders, digging her fingernails into his flesh.

The spinning air tore at his clothes and grated against his skin like sandpaper, while the vacuum literally pulled the breath from his chest. Limbs, rocks, pieces of metal fell from the sky, hitting him, but he held onto the woman as though she were an anchor holding in boiling sea. Just as he thought he could take no more, that they'd both be dead in seconds, an abrupt calm descended. Now there was no sound beyond the rain.

It sank in slowly that he'd survived. He was numb, but he was alive. He turned his head carefully, Just enough to see the water coming up from cracks in the now-bald earth. It didn't look like there was a blade of grass left anywhere around him. Pieces of twisted iron, broken wagon wheels, cottonwood limbs, and rocks the size of boulders littered the ground. He was alive—by some sort of miracle, he was alive.

Still locked in the woman's embrace, he lay there for a moment, savoring the discovery. Then he dared to look down at her. Blood trickled from her hair down her forehead, turning pink as it mingled with the rain. Her eyes were closed, and she was too white, too still. His first thought was that something had hit her, that she was dead. Twining his hand in her wet, muddy hair, he tried to turn her head slightly, hoping he could see the wound. No, he could feel her chest rise and fall beneath his. She had a heartbeat. Relief washed over him.

"You're all right," he croaked hoarsely. "It's over, and we made it—I don't know how, but we made it. You're all right now—it's over."

His hands moved from her hair to her shoulders, then down to her elbows, feeling for broken bones. She still wasn't moving.

"Can you hear me?" This time, he shouted. "Hey, I'm telling you we made it! It's gone—it's over! You're alive—we're both alive!"

She opened her eyes slowly, then blinked blankly a couple of times, as though she didn't believe him. Her eyes were a soft, pansy brown, but they looked almost black against that white face. She stared mutely, uncomprehending, obviously in shock. Not knowing what else to do, he slapped her wet face.

She came out of it gasping, "I can't breathe—I can't breathe!"

"Oh . . . yeah. Sorry." He rolled off her self-consciously. "I . . . uh . . . I was just holding you down so you wouldn't blow away." It sounded stupid, even to him, but it was the truth. "There wasn't anything else to do— we had to hit the ground or take a ride in that funnel."

But she wasn't looking at him. She was crawling away on her hands and knees, then scrambling to her feet. Before he could stop her, she was running toward the sod house, screaming and sobbing.

"Sam! Sam! Oh, God—*Sammy!*"

He managed to catch her from behind and hold her by her elbows. "Whoa now—hey—"

"You don't understand—I've got to find him—I've got to!" she cried, twisting and ducking, trying to escape. "He's in there! He's inside!"

"Don't be a fool!" he shouted, shaking her.

"Let me go! Please—I've got to find Sam—I've got to! Sammy! Sammy!"

He could see where the cottonwood lattice had caved in, dumping some of the sod roof into the house. His arm slid around her shoulder, pulling her back against him, but she kept fighting him. She kicked backward, getting his shin.

"Hey, that's enough," he warned her.

"Let me go!" In desperation, she sank her teeth into his forearm.

"Ouch! Listen to me, dammit, you can't go in there!" With his free hand, he yanked on her hair and pulled his arm free. "Boy, I'll say one thing for you—you sure as hell aren't much for gratitude, are you?"

She gulped air, and for a moment, he thought he'd calmed her down. "Look, you can't go in there," he tried to explain. "From here, it looks like a good part of that roof is gone, and you sure as hell don't want to be buried under mud when the rest of it falls. Well, you don't, do you?" She seemed almost docile now, making him think he'd gotten through to her. "Yeah, that's better. Come on, let's just sit down." He backed away from the house and eased his hold on her. "Now—"

Before he realized his mistake, she slipped under his arm, then darted for the door, where she pushed and pounded, trying to force it open.

"Sam! Sam! Where are you, Sam?" she shouted. "Sammy! Sammy!"

There was no answer beyond the steady beat of the rain on the soaked sod. Finally, she dropped to her knees and began clawing at the door frame with her hands. Watching her shaking shoulders, Ben felt about as helpless as any time he could remember. All he could think was that he'd missed the Mitchell farm, that he'd come to the wrong place.

She stopped to wipe her streaming face with muddy

hands, then looked up at him through a tangled mass of wet, dirty hair. "You've got to help me, mister—he's inside. Please—he's scared," she choked out.

He'd been too numb to realize what she'd been telling him, but suddenly it dawned on him. She had a kid trapped in there, and that changed everything.

"All right. I'll do what I can. I guess if it falls on me, I'm not much of a loss, anyway. But you've got to get out of my way." When she didn't move, he snapped impatiently, "Look—I said I'd try to get in."

"He won't come to you! He'll be scared of you!"

"If he's under that mess, he's probably out cold." Grasping her arm, he pulled her up, then thrust her out of his way. "Stand back in case that wall decides to fall down—you hear? If you want me to do it, stay put—all right?"

She started to protest, then didn't. "All right."

"That's better." He took another look at the damaged sod house, trying to figure the best way in. The lintel over the doorway sagged, pushing the door into the dirt, making it too low to clear the plank and puncheon floor inside. He'd have to scale the wall and drop through the hole in the roof. Deciding on a place where he thought he could make a handhold, he unbuckled his gunbelt and handed it to her.

"Here—hold this for me, will you?" As she took it, he explained, "I'll try getting over, then work my way back, but there may be a lot of mud in there. If I can get to it, I'm going to try forcing the door open from the inside. Maybe I can get it to swing out."

She shook her head. "The hinges go the other way."

"Then maybe I can break 'em. If I can't . . . well, then I guess it'll just be me looking for Sam." He tried to force a smile, but couldn't. "Look—I don't know what I'll find, but I'll do what I can."

"But he won't come to you," she insisted. "He'll hide somewhere—I know it. He doesn't like strangers."

He didn't want to point out there was no sound coming from inside. It wouldn't do any good right now, and he had her halfway calmed down. "I'll find him," he declared grimly.

Leaving her standing there, his holstered gun in her hand, he walked around a corner, then came back. "Yeah, looks like this is about as good a place as any," he decided. Grasping a tuft of dead turf sticking from one of the sod blocks, he forced the toe of his boot into a crack near the door, then tried to pull his weight up. On the first attempt, he lost his footing and slid down the slippery mud. The second time, he went hand over hand, digging his hands and heels into the baked dirt, then heaved his shoulders and torso over the top, catching his head in a web of broken lattice. He hung there, his legs dangling, trying to catch his breath.

"Can you see anything?" she called up anxiously.

"No, but I've damned near poked my eye out," he muttered.

"You'd better be careful. There's a cupboard under you."

Looking down, he couldn't see anything but hunks of dead sod and the sharp ends of cottonwood poles. And the storm had dropped so much rain that the dirt surfaces would be slicker than bacon grease. With an effort, he managed to straddle the thick wall with his body.

"Any idea which part of the house he'd be in?" he yelled down.

"When it thunders, he always gets under something!"

Cupping his hands around his mouth, he shouted into the muddy interior, "Sammy, if you can hear me, give a holler!" Damn. The kid wasn't even crying. "Sammy, I'm coming in!" Parting the grid that had held the roof, he slid feetfirst down the inside of the wall. "All right, kid, be where I can find you," he said softly. "Be somewhere where I can get to you." And, he added silently, *Be alive. For the sake of that woman out there, be alive.*

"Can you see anything, mister?"

"Not here, but I don't think it's as bad as we thought. Looks like there's a lot of roof left! Yeah—I see the bed!"

He slogged his way through the worst of the damage and emerged into the open room. Dishes, clothes, and furniture were thrown around as though some mischievous giant had discarded them, but once he got past that gaping hole in the roof, everything not under it was pretty much dry. His eyes scanned the room, looking for something a kid might hide under. In the mess, there were a lot of places. Finally, he climbed over pieces of turf to find the door. He'd need a shovel to clear a path before he could open it, but there were two broken windows, one on each side, that had been shuttered against the sun. Moving toward one, he pulled the piece of wood back.

"I've been across the room, but I don't guess I know where to look," he admitted. "Maybe if you'd tell me where you think—" Before he could finish the sentence, she was climbing through the hole, then picking her way gingerly through muddy debris. "Guess you're determined to do it yourself, but if it was my kid, I suppose the Devil himself couldn't keep me out."

She dropped to her knees and started crawling over the rough puncheon floor, calling, "Sammy! Sammy! Here, kitty, kitty, kitty . . . here, Sammy! It's all right, Sam. You can come out now . . . you can come out," she crooned soothingly. "Come to Jessie—come on, Sam."

"Kitty? *Kitty?*" Ben almost choked. "You mean to tell me I dragged myself over that wall for a damned *cat?*" he demanded angrily.

She'd disappeared under the bed, leaving only the soles of her shoes exposed. Her answer, if there was one, was lost in a bout of hissing and spitting, then an angry howl. She backed out, dragging an outraged ball of fur, then sat up. Cradling the indignant creature, she began smoothing its ruffled orange hair, trying to calm it. The thing regarded Ben suspiciously through a pair of round, green eyes that reminded him of an owl's. Sam was definitely a cat.

Just when Ben's temper was about to explode completely, the girl looked up through tears, and her mouth twisted as she tried to smile. "Thank you," she whispered. "I don't know where you came from, mister, but I know God sent you."

He felt foolish now. She was sitting in the middle of what was left of her house, crying over a damned cat. It didn't make sense to him. She didn't seem to care that half the place was ruined, or that she'd nearly been killed. All she was concerned about was that ugly orange cat. Now that it had settled down, she was holding it like it was a baby. And its purr was louder than the rain hitting what was left of the roof.

"You better put that thing down and get some of that blood off you," he said finally.

"Where?"

"I don't know—it was running down your face. I guess it's from the top of your head."

Still holding the animal with one hand, she felt her head with the other. "I've got a few lumps, but I can't find any place where the skin's broken." She looked up again, then stood to get a better view of him. "I think it must be your blood—you're all cut up." Letting the cat jump down, she moved closer. "You've got a real gash on the side of your head. It's a wonder you weren't knocked senseless."

He touched the area above his right ear and felt the sticky place in his hair. When he drew his hand back, it was wet with blood. "I'm all right," he muttered. But he wasn't. Now that the crisis was over, the numbness was leaving him, and all of a sudden it felt like every inch of his body had been beaten with a fair-sized log. By nightfall, he was going to be black-and-blue all over. The euphoria he'd felt when he found himself alive had turned to pain.

"That head needs tending, mister, maybe even some stitching up."

"It'll be all right."

"Not that place. You'd better sit down and let me take a good look at it."

He shook his head, then wished he hadn't. He was seeing stars, but he couldn't give in to weakness, not now, anyway. He needed to find Rebel, maybe to bury him. "You've got better things to do, and if my horse's not out there somewhere, I'll have a helluva walk ahead of me."

"If that head festers, you could get brain fever," she pointed out. "This won't take long, and besides, I feel like I owe you this much for what you did. If you hadn't come along, I'd have blown away, and Sammy'd be here all alone."

"A cat can survive without much help."

"You didn't get a good look at him, did you? Ever since a coyote caught him and tore off a back leg, he's afraid of everything. He doesn't even go outside except to do his business, then it's right back in again. If he had to hunt on the three legs he's got left, he'd starve."

She was determined, he could see that. And the way his head was bleeding, he knew she was right.

"Yeah, maybe you'd better clean it up some," he conceded.

While she'd been talking, she'd turned over a chair and set it out for him. "If I can find my medicine box, this won't take long," she promised. "Go on—sit down." When he didn't, she sighed. "Look—there isn't an animal on the place that I haven't doctored, mister, and nearly all of them have survived."

His head hurt, all right, and he was more than a little dizzy. If he sat down, he was afraid he wouldn't get up, but he knew she couldn't see much if he didn't. She was nearly a foot shorter than he was. Taking the chair, he watched her rummage through an old chest. The thought crossed his mind that she could be Preston Mitchell's daughter. Or his wife. And he didn't much like either notion.

"You always bossing folks around?" he asked, finally taking the chair.

She'd found her medicine kit and gone to the water bucket to wash her hands. She had the dipper full when she turned around. For a moment, she considered how to answer, then decided on caution. "There aren't folks—there's just two of us."

"You don't seem too worried about your man," he observed casually.

"He's not here. He . . . he went into town." Surely God could forgive her for the lie.

It begged common sense to think she'd been left to run a farm alone, even for a few days, and it'd take a man that long to get anywhere and back. With the dangers of wolves, coyotes, renegade Indians, and prairie fires a constant, it wasn't right. But he knew a lot of men who wouldn't think twice about it.

"When do you expect him back?"

She couldn't answer. Instead, she rinsed her hands, then picked up the battered box, holding it tightly. When she turned back to him, she was fairly composed. She considered him, wondering how many lies she'd find herself telling. One lie breeds another, her father had always said.

The stranger was a big man, but in those torn clothes, with his hair dripping bloody water, he looked more like a little boy after a fistfight. And those eyes—anybody with eyes that pretty just couldn't be bad, she told herself. Still, as desperately as she needed somebody to trust, she had to wait. She had to know why he'd come.

"It'll be a while," she answered after a time.

That could even mean a week or more. "You can't stay here like this."

"I have to. He wouldn't want me to leave."

"He doesn't have much sense, then," he told her. "How the hell does he expect a little bitty thing like you to survive out here alone? What are you supposed to do now that a tornado's ripped the place to pieces?"

"I'm not 'a little bitty *thing*,' mister," she retorted. "I'm a five-foot-two-inch woman, and I can probably shear a sheep better than a big ox like you." Then, realizing how rude she sounded, she added more matter-of-factly, "However, since they've already been sheared, all I have to do is move them around on what grass there is, carry water to them, and put them up at night so coyotes and wolves don't get at them. I've been managing just fine," she finished untruthfully.

"Look, I just meant there's a lot of heavy work in farming. I know—I lived on one when I was a boy, and we worked from first light to sunset." He cast a significant look at the rain coming in the hole in the roof. "I'd sure like to know how you plan to fix that by yourself. Unless my eyes are dead wrong, I'd say a number of those cottonwood poles are broken beyond repair."

"People learn to do all kinds of things out here. If they don't, they don't survive."

"That's a damned platitude, not an answer."

"Well, whether you believe it or not, I helped cut and drag those sod blocks, and every one of them weighs more than a hundred pounds. As for the roof, I cut almost all of that willow brush up there, and I'm the one who tied it to those poles. I can do hard work when I have to, and right now I have to."

He should have kept his mouth shut, but it riled him to see a woman living like this. In a few years, she'd look like the rest of them—dried-up and worn-out way before forty. She'd be like his ma, a thin, broken-toothed woman, with too many babies hanging on her. It wasn't a life, it was an existence. But she hadn't realized that yet—she still had some fire left in her. As he looked at her, he found himself smiling.

"I guess I didn't realize you were a midget Amazon."

Counting to ten silently, she told herself it wasn't his fault she was alone, and if he hadn't shown up when he did, she'd have died in that storm. "I'm sorry, too," she managed, somewhat mollified. "I don't know what got into me. I must sound ungrateful, when I owe you for my life."

"You might say that." He leaned back, watching her.

"And you don't have to stare either. I know I'm a mess, but right now I don't much care how I look."

"I was just thinking you're pretty in spite of all that mud and blood. But I reckon your man's told you that a hundred times."

"No," she said shortly. "Are you going to sit still and let me look at your head, or do you intend to keep spouting foolishness?"

"He ought to take you to town, get you some nice frilly things, show you off some, you know. If it was me—"

"Talking about what he should or shouldn't do isn't proper conversation," she declared, cutting him off.

He'd been set down, and he knew he'd deserved it. "Sorry. Guess I'm just used to dance hall palaver. Maybe I've forgotten how to talk to a decent woman." When she didn't respond, he sighed. "Look, I didn't mean anything by it. For all I know, when your man's around, he's downright good to you, and it isn't any of my business, anyway."

"No, it isn't. Here—hold this, will you?" she said, setting the case on his lap. The thought crossed her mind that it wasn't fair for a man to look like this. With those pretty eyes and that ruffled hair, he could make a woman yearn to hear more. Dance hall palaver, he'd said. He'd probably been in a lot of those places. "I'm not as green as you seem to think me, you know," she said severely. "Whether you believe it or not, you're not the first man who ever tried to soft-soap me. But if you want me to do this, you'll have to behave yourself."

"I am behaving myself."

"Maybe I ought to be glad I don't know you any better."

"Those that do don't complain—least not the women, anyway."

Before she got the rusty hasps on the leather-covered box open, Ben caught a glimpse of the words neatly engraved on a tarnished brass plate. *Major J. M. Power, Surgeon, 16th Mass.* He felt an almost instant relief. The name wasn't Mitchell.

"This is going to burn, by the way, but it'll kill any infection." As she said it, she took out a clean rag and a green glass bottle. "It's potassium permanganate, which isn't pleasant, but it does the job." The stopper was stuck, but she wasn't about to let him know it. Instead, she kept twisting it while she talked. "You've probably never been doctored with it."

"My ma believed in turpentine for everything that ailed a body, inside or out."

"I'm out of turpentine . . . and iodine, too. We used them up at sheepshearing, and we haven't been anywhere to get any since."

"I don't suppose there's any whiskey around?" he asked hopefully.

"No. We gave the last of it to the dog for a rattlesnake bite."

"I'll bet it didn't help much, did it?"

"I don't think it really helps anything, mister. Most of the time, it just gives men something to blame when they get into trouble."

"A man's got to blame something. I'll bet your man drinks when you're not around."

"He doesn't. He's a fine, upstanding Yankee from Ohio, who's never had more than a Christmas toddy in his life."

"Grant was from Ohio, and he drank like a damned fish. If he hadn't been drunk most of the time, he couldn't have stomached all those Yankee boys dying."

"I guess I should expect that from a Southerner," she murmured as she finally popped the little rubber cork.

"I never said I was from the South, did I?"

"No, but you didn't have to. As soon as you opened your mouth, there wasn't much doubt. I've already decided you must be from Texas."

"Yeah, I was born down by the clear fork of the Brazos, but that was a long time ago. I left when I was fourteen, and I haven't been back since. There might be one Haley down there, or there might be fifty now, for all I know or care."

"That's your name—Haley?"

"Yeah. Ben Haley." As soon as he said it, he wished it back. He looked up, halfway expecting her to recoil. But she didn't. Nor did she complete the introduction. "I've been gone a real long time."

"You make it sound like you're so old." Taking care not to spill the contents of the bottle, she saturated a folded corner of the cloth with it. "You might want to close your eyes, Mr. Haley."

"I'll be twenty-eight next month. How about you?" he asked, trying to divert her.

"I was twenty-one in May—the twentieth, to be exact."

Suddenly self-conscious, she hesitated. It had to be done, she knew that, but until now, she'd never been familiar enough with any man other than her father to stand that close to his body. Now she'd be running her fingers through his hair, touching him in a way that seemed almost too forward, too intimate when all she knew about him was that he was a Texan named Ben Haley. And he was at least a head taller than Preston Mitchell.

Even though he didn't really want her to put the damned stuff on him, he could sense the change in her. She had everything ready, but she wasn't using it.

"What's the matter? Afraid I'm going to come out of my seat at you?"

"No. I . . . uh . . . well, I don't want you to . . . uh . . . think I'm . . . well, you were trying to flirt with me earlier, weren't you? I don't want you to think you can, that's all."

He crooked his neck to look up at her. "I always flirt with pretty women, but I know where to draw the line. I've never sunk to seducing another man's wife."

"Then that's settled, at least." Taking a deep breath, she began parting his hair with her fingers, searching for the worst cuts. "You've got a bloody mess up here—a real bloody mess. You must have about the hardest head anywhere between here and Texas." He flinched when she touched the wound above his ear, making her feel guilty for what she was about to do to him. "You'd better hang onto something, Mr. Haley," she warned him.

"It's Ben—not mister. I'm not a preacher, a banker, or an undertaker."

"Ben, then."

"And seeing as how you're not an old lady, I'm not much for ma'am either."

"Neither am I."

"So what's your name?"

"Jessamine. *J-E-S-S-A-M-I-N-E.* I don't know why, but I seem to have to spell it for everybody. Usually, I'm just Jessie."

"Jessamine," he repeated, trying it out. "It's unusual, but I like it. It's a flower, isn't it?"

"A flowering vine," she acknowledged. "And since I'm already stuck with it, it wouldn't matter if you didn't. It's my mother's fault—she loved the scent of jasmine blooms, but it's a Southern flower, and with my father's Yankee upbringing, he wouldn't hear of it. So they compromised on Jessamine, which means the same thing, anyway. Four or five years later, when I was struggling to print it out, I think he felt a little sorry he'd been so stubborn over jasmine."

"If it was up to me, I'd call you Jess."

Her hand tensed in his hair. "My father did."

"It's like you—short and sassy."

"Look—are you going to close your eyes, or not? I'm telling you this will blind you. And it's quite painful."

"It can't be any worse than having a bullet dug out, can it?"

She didn't answer. She just pressed the wet cloth over the gash, soaking it, and he knew immediately he was being punished for every sin he'd ever committed. And this time there wasn't any chloroform or opium to take his mind off the pain. The potassium permanganate solution touched a raw nerve, igniting it, then as Jessie warmed to her work, the fire spread across his scalp, taking his breath away, bringing tears to his eyes. He bit his lip hard, trying to counter one pain with another. He could taste his own blood. His hands gripped the chair seat so tightly his knuckles hurt.

"There," she said finally, stepping back. "Are you all right?"

"Oh, I'm just dandy," he gritted out through clenched teeth. "Next time I'm feeling flush, I'll be sure to go out and buy some of the stuff just to have it on hand."

"I see you held onto your seat, after all."

"If I hadn't, you wouldn't be standing up."

"Anybody ever tell you how funny you are, Ben?"

"Nobody alive." He allowed himself a deep breath, then exhaled it fully before he wiped his wet eyes with the back of his hand. "Damn. That's potent stuff."

"It seals off the wound."

"I think I'd rather let the damned thing fester."

"And you just might wind up like Billy Travers, you know. Right before his folks decided to move back to Topeka, he died from a bad cut on his hand. Nobody thought much about it until dark red streaks ran up his arm. According to Doc Sanders over at Fort Hays, it was blood poisoning."

"What happened to Doc Power?"

"Doc Power? Oh—you're looking at this field kit, aren't you?"

"Uh-huh."

"It belonged to my uncle James, who died during the

war.'' Peering more closely at the skin above his ear, she decided, ''Now that I can see it better, this has to be stitched, Mr. Haley. Otherwise, you're going to look kinda funny.'' Seeing that he obviously didn't like the notion, she assured him, ''I can sew it—I did Sam's leg, you know.''

''Yeah, and he's only got three of 'em now.''

She sighed. ''Have you always been like this or did something awful happen to you?''

''If it was me sewing up your head, you'd be clawing your way out that door before I could say Jack Dandy.''

''All right, I won't do it,'' she snapped. ''Just don't cry when you look in your mirror. When scar tissue fills that in, you're going to have a bare spot there. It'll look like there's a part in the wrong place.''

He reached up and touched the area gingerly. While it wasn't oozing anymore, he could tell the skin didn't meet. It felt like there was a gap about half an inch wide that ran for a couple of inches. And there wasn't much flesh underneath it.

''I'm done with the permanganate,'' she assured him. ''It'll just be like sewing a rip in your shirt.'' Moving directly in front of him, she replaced the bottle, then searched for the tin of needles first. She took out one, looked at it, and discarded it in favor of another. Holding the eye end in her mouth, she found the spools. ''Black or white thread?''

He glanced toward the hole in the roof. The rain was slacking off. ''You sure you've got enough light for this?'' he asked uneasily.

''It's a little dark for threading a needle,'' she conceded. ''I'll try to find the lamp. Maybe the wick's still dry enough to light.''

The sky over the hole was brightening, and the sun was trying to come out, affording him a better look at her house. It wasn't much—just the usual one-room sod building with a rough-sawn, uneven puncheon floor. But as crude as it was, it still showed a woman's care. Under the part of the roof that remained, a pretty quilt and fancy crocheted pillow covers were undisturbed on the bed, while a small table with fancy-turned legs had fallen over, spilling a lace-edged cloth onto the floor. No, it wasn't much, but it was better than anything he had, he realized with a pang. It looked like a place a man could come home to.

"There's a big, showy chestnut outside, and he's eating what's left of my flower bed," she announced, returning with a lit lantern. "I'd say your horse survived better than you."

"He's a smart horse—the smartest horse I've ever owned."

She couldn't entirely hide her own anxiety. "I just hope the sheep made it. The pens are down, and there's not a sign of them. Once I'm finished with this, I'm going to have to go looking for them. I need those sheep, or I'm not going to eat this winter."

"They'll probably show up before dark."

"You obviously don't know much about sheep, do you? You must be a cowman."

"Not since I left home. I wasn't much of a cow-puncher."

"Well, sheep are even more stupid than cows—they won't come in from a snowstorm if somebody doesn't lead them. They'll just sit out there and freeze. But maybe I can find them before the coyotes do." Righting a table, she set the lamp on it. "All right, just lean over, so I can see what I'm doing."

"If it was me, I'd look to my roof before I did much else."

"I make my living with sheep. This is going to feel like something's crawling on your head," she said, examining the area for a place to begin.

"I usually kill anything I find crawling on my head,"

he muttered. "By the way, what did you do with my gun?"

"I don't think I want you to have it right now," she murmured. "But I put it on the floor when I was trying to get Sam out. You'll have to clean it, anyway."

"Yeah. Where is the damned cat, anyway—back under the bed?"

"He's drinking cream off the floor, but since the crock's broken, I'm not going to scold him. It'd just be wasted, anyway."

He felt the jab of the needle, then the thread going through his skin. After the first prick, it sort of tickled. She worked deftly, saying nothing. It wasn't until she finished the last stitch and tied a knot that she spoke again.

"You'll have to pull these out when it looks like this has healed. You'll probably want to get somebody to do it for you."

He opened his eyes, staring directly into her breasts. Her wet gown clung to them, showing taut nipples, setting off his imagination. His mouth went dry with the thoughts that filled his mind.

"If you're not a cowman, what are you?" she asked suddenly.

"Huh?" he croaked.

"What do you do?"

Reluctantly, he forced his gaze elsewhere. "Whatever takes my fancy, I guess. Why?"

"Well, we don't have many strangers stop in, so I thought maybe you might be looking for work—or something."

"Somebody. You don't know Press Mitchell, do you?"

"I might." Keeping her head down, she put away her supplies and closed the hasps with unsteady hands. Buying time by moving away, she hesitated, torn between the truth and more lies. Finally, she said, "I'd have to know what you want with him."

"I was going to look him up . . . for old time's sake."

"He's a friend of yours, then?"

He'd hoped she didn't know the man, but in an area as sparsely settled as this one, it stood to reason she would. "Yeah," he lied.

"From Ohio or Illinois?" she asked without turning around.

She'd kept answering with questions. If he weren't careful, he'd be digging his own grave and stumbling into it. Now she not only knew his name, she knew he was looking for Mitchell. If anything happened to the sheepman, he'd just invited the law to come after him.

"I reckon it's not all that important," he said, standing up. "I was just aiming to stop by, maybe chew a little fat with him, talk about . . ." He hesitated, then decided on, ". . . old times in Illinois."

"That's where you knew him?"

"You're damned nosy—you know that, don't you?" he complained.

"Maybe I've got a right to be."

He couldn't see her face, but her words gave her away. He could feel his gut tauten. "I had it right from the beginning, didn't I? This is his place, all right, and unless I miss my guess, you're Preston Mitchell's daughter."

She spun around at that, daring to meet his gaze. "You still haven't answered much, Mr. Haley. Nobody comes out here just to chew the fat, as you call it."

"All right—it's about a debt," he answered, inventing a reason. "It's your turn to answer."

"You've come to collect money from him?" she asked carefully.

The hole was getting wider, deeper, yawning in front of him. If he said yes, he'd be taking her money. If he said no, he'd be owing her something he didn't have.

"No."

She felt the first surge of hope she'd had in three weeks. He owed Press money. He hadn't said how much, but if he felt obligated enough to cross Kansas to pay a debt incurred years ago, he had to be an honest man. But right now she needed something more than money. She needed someone to stay there, someone to help her fix her house and find her sheep. Her heart pounding so loudly she could scarce hear her own thoughts, she took a deep breath, then told him the truth.

"This is his place, but you're just about three weeks late. Preston Mitchell's dead, Ben." As he stared, she nodded. "I know he'd have liked seeing you, because he didn't have any friends left. Once Matheny came out here, they all gave up and sold out. But Papa was as stubborn as I am—I guess I inherited it from him."

He didn't know what to say now, but it had to be something. She was waiting for him to respond. "I'm real sorry," he managed. "It must've been hell for you."

"Yes." She took another deep breath, then expelled it. "Maybe I could have stood it better if he'd been sick, but it was too sudden. He was just making a supply run, but I guess one of the wagon's wheels hit a rock or something, turning it over. I wasn't there when it happened, but it looked as if he tried to jump free, got himself tangled up in the traces, and fell beneath the wagon shaft. There was blood there, anyway. He was dragged to death, Ben." She stopped to wipe her eyes. "I'm sorry," she said huskily. "I'm not usually a crybaby."

"You don't have to talk about it," he responded quietly.

"There's been nobody to talk to—nobody, Ben!" She had to get it all out, to tell him everything, then maybe she could bear it better, she told herself. "When he didn't come home, I thought there'd been more trouble with Matheny, so I went out to look for him." Keeping her voice as toneless as possible, she continued, forcing herself to relive the awful moment when she'd found her father. "I couldn't recognize him, but I knew him from what was left of his clothes."

"God."

"But at least I was able to bring him home before the

coyotes found him. The ground was so dry and hard I had to use his pickax to break it up," she recalled, her voice dropping. "I couldn't let Matheny's men know, so I kept the hole covered in daylight, and I only dug at night when they couldn't see me. I hid his body in the barn until I had everything ready."

"You should have gone for help."

"I couldn't. Around here, it's all Matheny's land and Matheny's men," she said bitterly. "If they'd known he was dead, they'd have run me off."

"You think this Matheny had something to do with it?"

"No. They've just been trying to scare us out. He'd send people over, warning us about renegade Indians or bad water, saying Papa ought to sell out and take me someplace safer. It was all threats, but how do you prove it? The way he did it, it could sound like he was being neighborly. There wasn't anybody here to see the smirks when Vaughn Hacker warned us our sheep might die from the water, but we knew he was talking about poisoning the well. Papa had to make up a cover and a lock, so now I have to carry water to the pens instead of using the pipe we had before."

"Hacker works for this Matheny?"

"Yes, do you know him?"

"I might, but go on. I'm listening."

"Since last spring, we've been finding fresh-butchered sheep. And somebody poisoned Beau—he was our other herd dog. Yet when Papa filed a complaint with the sheriff over the sheep, he was told it was probably coyotes getting them. They didn't even bother trying to explain away the dog. Nobody came out to look, Ben, because we were accusing Mr. Matheny. Everybody thinks he's wonderful, you know—there's even talk he may run for governor. But there's nothing wonderful about him, Ben. He thinks everything ought to belong to him, and if it doesn't, he'll do anything to get it—anything. The man's evil, just plain evil!"

"Yeah."

He felt awkward now, like he ought to run before she found out who he was, why he was there. But as he sat there, he knew he couldn't just go off and leave her in such a fix. She couldn't stay alone in a place that had a big hole in the roof. Besides, he owed her something for stitching him up.

"I don't want your money, Ben. I want your help repairing my house so I can live in it. I don't know how much you owed my father, but if it'd cover that, and maybe some work on the pens, it'd be a big help. Earlier, I said you were a godsend, and I was right. You saved my life in that storm, and now I'm asking you to save Press's place. I lied to you. I can't do it alone. I just can't, Ben, but I can't give Papa's dream away, either."

The last time he'd seen such intense appeal in anyone's eyes, his ma had been begging him not to run away, not to leave her to his pa's mercy. It had been fourteen years, but that look still haunted him. Only this was different, he argued with himself. He hadn't even known Preston Mitchell. But his reason for being there pricked his conscience.

"Yeah. I reckon I can work on that roof," he said aloud. "I reckon I owed Press that much."

"Thank you," she whispered.

"And maybe I can fix the pens. After that, I'll have to move on."

"It'd sure be a help."

He was a man walking in quicksand, and he knew it. If he stayed too long, he'd sink in it. He carried too many dead men on his shoulders to stay afloat. And there was no place, not even a sod house in Graham County, Kansas, where he could hide from that damned book—or from Jack Matheny. But right now, the prettiest woman of his memory was standing there, declaring her gratitude. As he stared into those brown, almost copper eyes, he felt an aching loneliness, a painful sense of what he'd missed, what he'd never have. He wasn't anybody's savior. He was a destroyer.

"Looks like it's about done raining," he said finally. "I'd better see how bad things are out there."

"I'll clean all this up—make you a spot you can call your own," she said hastily, afraid he might change his mind.

"I'd rather keep my bedroll outside, Jess. I think it'd work better that way."

"I wasn't offering to—"

"I know," he said, cutting her off. "I wasn't talking about you—it was me. A man doesn't need any help with the wrong ideas, Jess. I'd have to be reminding myself all the time you were Press's daughter."

"There's nothing but mud out there, Ben. I can string a rope between a couple of those poles," she said, pointing across the room, "and you can hang up a blanket between us. That's all I was meaning. At least your bedroll will be dry in here. I won't be looking at you, and you won't be looking at me."

"I'll find a place. Besides," he added, dropping his gaze, "it'd be damned hard *not* to look at you. There's no sense in putting yourself out for just a couple of days."

"You don't have to go, if you don't want to. Before I'd lose everything I have, I'd be willing to take on a partner. We cleared over six hundred dollars last year," she declared proudly.

"Look, if I couldn't be a cowman, I wouldn't be much of a farmer, either. I'm a saddle tramp . . . a drifter. I'll do what I can for you, but then we're dead even." What he wasn't telling her was that once Matheny found out he'd helped her, his life would be worse than ever. It'd be more than crazy kids coming after him—it'd be every hardcase looking for a reputation. Starting with Vaughn Hacker.

"If you'd even stay until fall, I'd pay you to stay until I get ready for winter."

"No. I'll work off my debt to Press, that's all."

"How much was it?" she asked, trying to figure how much work he'd be doing.

"Forty dollars."

"And you came all the way out here for that? I'll say one thing for you, Ben Haley, you're an honest man. In that respect, you're like Abe Lincoln."

"And you saw what that got him, didn't you?"

"Whether you liked it or not, he was President of the United States."

"And some damned fool shot him."

"It wasn't because he was honest. You don't look like a man who'd have a lot of enemies," she said, smiling at him.

"Lady, you don't even know me."

"I know enough to know you are a man of character, and you were a friend of my father's. That's all I need to know, and nothing else matters, Ben."

"I'd better check on Rebel," he told her, heading for the gaping window.

"It's past noon," she protested. "Don't you want me to see if I can find anything to eat first?"

"No. I've got some jerky in my bag, if I can find the damned thing. Besides, you've got enough to do around here."

She watched him climb through the window frame, then turned her own attention to the mess around her. She could spend all day just picking up things and putting her small world back together, but she didn't have much time. As soon as she found a dry dress and her other pair of shoes, she'd have to go looking for the flock.

In spite of the storm, she felt a lot happier than she had when she got up this morning. Since then, Ben Haley had ridden in, and for a little while at least, she wasn't alone. As she dug in the old chest of drawers, looking for a clean petticoat, she could still see those beautiful, blue-green eyes of his. If only he'd decide to stay. And if wishes were pigs, she chided herself, she'd be rich.

*   *   *

He'd never seen anybody work as hard as Jessie Mitchell had in the week he'd known her. And he'd tried to keep up with her, cutting and dragging cottonwood limbs from down by the creek, stripping the smaller branches for later tinder, then fashioning new poles to replace the damaged ones. Between the two of them, they'd interlaced the new with what they could salvage of the old. And when the willow brush was gathered, lashed to the grid, and covered with strips of dead and living sod, they'd made a decent roof. And while she'd shoveled mud and scrubbed everything she could save inside, he'd wired together broken boards and nailed them to posts to secure the pens behind the house.

They'd even managed to find most of her sheep. Seventeen had died in the storm, and another eleven were missing, but eighty-nine had survived. Skinning and gutting the dead ones was a nasty business, something he'd not done in nearly fourteen years. He'd hated it then, and he hated it now, but he wanted to make sure she had meat laid by for the winter. And she did—some sealed in brine, some cured over smoke, and some still drying on iron racks in the hot Kansas sun.

Everything was mutton, something he'd never eaten before Jessie made a stew of it with potatoes and dried peas that first night. But after a day spent plodding through mud and mire looking for carcasses and stragglers, and after carrying more than twenty buckets of water from the well, it had tasted damned good. Since then, she'd fed him mutton pie, mutton chops, mutton hash, and roasted lamb, and there didn't seem to be any end to what she could do with it.

He'd already stayed too long, he knew that. And yet there was still so much to do, too much for Jessie alone. As it was, she was up every morning before the sky was even pink, and she wasn't falling into bed until well past dark. By the time he smelled the coffee boiling, she'd already done half a day's work. No, he didn't know how she stood it. As much as he'd come to admire all the things she could do, he didn't know how she was going to survive alone. It would break her heart, but she'd have to sell out.

Damn, but it was hot. It'd only been a week, but the creek that had flooded during the heavy rain was down to a running depth of six or seven inches and within days would be going dry again. And the ground was already baked, turning the mud brick-hard. He could feel the sweat running from his shoulder to his navel, and his shirt was too wet to soak it up. But he couldn't quit.

"I've brought you a dipper of water, Ben."

He looked up at the sound of her voice. She had that rich auburn hair tied up in a knot atop her head, but a few strands had come loose, and they curled against her damp, flushed forehead and neck. He had to keep his eyes on her face, he told himself, his mouth as dry from looking at her as from thirst.

But he couldn't do it. As a concession to the weather, she'd dispensed with her petticoats and tied the hem of her skirt in knots to keep it from dragging on the ground. The result afforded him a glimpse of slender ankles. If that wasn't enough to make a man take notice, he could make out the picot edging of a chemise through her thin cotton' waist. And in the absence of a corset to restrain them, her rounded breasts stretched the bodice, straining the row of buttons there.

"Well, do you want it or not?" she asked, betraying exasperation. "Or are you just going to stand there gaping?"

Yeah, but he knew he'd have to settle for water. He forced his attention to the dipper, taking it and downing the warm liquid. Handing it back with one hand, he wiped his mouth and dripping forehead with the sleeve on his other arm. "Thanks."

"It's hotter than Jerusalem out here, isn't it?" she observed. "Maybe you ought sit down awhile."

"I'm about done. When I get these rocks laid, I'll make the marker."

"I just couldn't make the hole any deeper, Ben."

"Yeah, I know." He took another swipe at his head with his arm. "Well, you don't have to worry now. There's not a coyote living that can dig him up now."

"You didn't have to do this, you know," she said softly. "You must have thought a lot of him."

"Yeah."

She stared at the mound again. "You know, those were hard times for him back then. He'd left Mama and me with her folks while he went to Illinois looking for work. Even though I was only eight, I still remember when he left. It was the only time I ever saw him cry."

"I reckon it was hard to leave a wife and kid behind."

"She died before he came back for us." Turning back to him, she asked, "Did he tell you how pretty she was? She was, you know."

"Yeah." Before she could ask more, he turned the subject to the grave between them. "If you've got a chisel, I reckon I can chip out the name on that piece of limestone over there. I thought I'd just lay it here in front—maybe set it against the mound so it kind of stands up."

She cocked her head to study the spot, then nodded. "That'll look real nice."

"I hope so, anyway."

She ought to go inside where it was cooler and start fixing the midday meal, but she didn't want to. She wanted to talk, to know more about him. She wanted his company.

"How about you? Did you leave a wife behind somewhere, Ben?" she dared to ask him.

"No. I never stayed in one place long enough to do much courting—not the right kind, anyway." Picking up Preston Mitchell's rusty pickax, he swung it, breaking a flat rock into pieces. "Sometimes all a man's got is his name, Jess. I never wanted to share mine with the kind of woman who'd have me." Leaning down, he found a small

piece and forced it into a crack between two larger ones.
"Why?"

"I don't know. I just thought . . . Well, you said you
were nearly twenty-eight . . ."

"My pa was thirty-five when he found my mother," he
said, straightening. "And it would have been a damned
sight better for her if he hadn't."

"But then the world would have missed knowing you,"
she said quietly.

"There's a lot of people around who wouldn't count
that a loss, Jess."

"I would."

"Yeah, but you don't know me," he countered. "You
don't know anything about me." Moving to the other side
of the grave, he used the toe of his boot to wedge a chunk
of limestone into place.

"I know my father thought a lot of you. He wasn't a
man to trust lightly."

There she was, turning everything back to Mitchell. He
didn't want to think about the man. He didn't want to
remember why he'd come there. "I told you—it was a
long time ago. Maybe I was different then."

"A person's strength and inner character don't change.
I expect you're as good now as you were then."

It had always been one of the mysteries of life to him,
but every woman he'd ever known wanted to find her own
softness in a man. None of 'em wanted to recognize him
for the animal he was. "Look, Jess—"

"He worked hard for forty dollars," she said suddenly.
"When he was in Illinois, he took every job he could get.
Sometimes he worked fifteen hours every day trying to
earn enough to send for us. I remember watching Mama
hoard every dollar he mailed her, saving them up in an old
green jar, taking them out to count every time a new letter
came. The last time she did that, there were thirty-one, but
it was too late. By then, she had what the doctors called
galloping consumption."

"I don't reckon he knew how bad she was," he said uncomfortably.

"You had to have known him afterward—after she died. Otherwise, he'd never have had any money to loan you."

"I guess that's right."

"It must have been important," she decided.

He'd missed something somewhere, or she wasn't making sense. "Huh?"

"The reason you borrowed from him."

There it was again, that yawning chasm about to pull him into it by his lies. "Yeah."

"Well, I'd like to know what it was. There were years in there when I never heard a word from him, that I don't know what he did. You were a part of those years, Ben. I'd like to know how you came to know him, how you came to borrow so much money from him."

"Yeah, well, I was down on my luck, real down," he answered evasively. "About as down as a man can be."

"And?"

"I needed a stake, I guess. I was wanting to . . . stake myself a claim . . . in Colorado. Hell, I was just a kid, Jess. I reckon I thought maybe I'd get rich. A lot of folks did, you know."

"But you didn't."

"No." He was telling so many lies he couldn't look her in the eye. "A lot of folks went bust, too."

"I guess it made him feel like he was worth something just having that money to lend you," she decided. "He didn't have much going for him back then, what with Grandma and Grandpa Power always telling me he was a worthless dreamer. They hated him so much they didn't even let him know when Mama died."

"I reckon a man's got to follow his dreams, and sometimes they work out, sometimes they don't. Maybe they just didn't understand his dreams."

"Exactly."

"Maybe they blamed him for leaving you and your ma like that."

"He didn't have a choice, Ben. If he'd stayed there, he'd have been working for Grandpa and listening to how he wasn't good enough for Mama. He wanted to make something of himself. But you were right—Grandpa didn't understand. All he could see was his Ellie'd married a ne'er-do-well who couldn't take care of her. And when she died, he tried to fix it in my mind that Papa was no good."

"It didn't take."

"Of *course* it didn't. I stole a dime from Grandpa's pocket so I could write Papa that she was gone, that he didn't need to send any more money, that he could save it to come after me."

"And you think I got money he could've used for that, I guess."

"No. He knew he didn't have any way to take care of a nine-year-old girl." Thinking maybe she'd lost him with her logic, she tried to explain again. "I think he probably needed to feel like he could do something for *somebody,* don't you see? And when you came along, he probably saw himself in you, only you were young enough and free enough to follow your dreams. I think he felt useful giving you that money."

"Maybe. But back then, I'd figure it was hard for a little kid to understand, though. Most kids would've hated him for leaving like that, Jess."

"I just clung to the notion he'd come for me," she said simply.

"How long did it take him?" he found himself asking her.

"Well, he waited until I was nearly fifteen to come back to Ohio, and then it was only supposed to be a visit. Grandpa said he could only stay an hour, then he'd have to go—I heard him say it to Grandma. So I packed up Mama's old carpetbag and hid it under my bed. Then,

when the hack pulled up in front of the house, I was all
ready to go. I wasn't about to be left behind again, Ben.''

"I reckon you gave old Press a real surprise along about
then.''

"A real surprise," she acknowledged, smiling. "When
we were in the hack going back to his hotel, he tried to
talk me out of it. He'd never be a rich man like Grandpa
Power, he said, but I told him it didn't matter. I didn't
want to be reminded anymore about how grateful I ought
to be for the roof over my head, anyway." She looked at
the crude grave and her smile faded. "Poor Papa—when
he staked out this farm, he finally felt like he was amount-
ing to something.''

"Some men are just drawn to land, I guess.''

"He was proud of having his own place. He wasn't
working for somebody, and that meant everything to him.''

And she was living on dreams, just like her old man.
She was deluding herself into thinking she could keep the
place, but he knew better. He'd learned early on in his life
not to cling to anything. Possessions were to be gained and
lost, and people were put on earth to disappoint each other,
then die. It was going to be a hard lesson for her.

"He's gone, Jess. One of these days you'll have to sell
out and move on.''

"No, he's here forever now. And hell will freeze before
I let even one of Matheny's cows walk across this grave.''

"He's dead, Jess, you're alive. You've got to take care
of yourself now. Press doesn't know whether you're here
or not," he argued. "It's all over for him.''

"*I'll* know. I'm not going to sell Papa's land. I'll die
on it first.''

He could imagine it coming to that. If Jack Matheny
had two hundred dollars to give him for killing Press
Mitchell, he probably had that much again to pay someone
else to get rid of her.

"Jess—" He stopped. There wasn't any use saying it.

"Haven't you ever had anything worth fighting for,

Ben? Haven't you ever loved something too much to just give it up?" she demanded passionately. When he didn't answer, she shook her head sadly. "No, I guess not. A lot of people live their lives without ever feeling like that, but I don't guess I'm one of them. I *have* to stay here."

"How are you going to take care of the place?" he countered again. "What are you going to do when I'm gone?"

Her eyes widened for a moment, then she recovered, "I'll manage." Her chin came up. "I guess I'll do what some of the men out here do," she said evenly.

"You're not a man, Jess."

"No, I'm not," she conceded. "But since worse has already come to worst, I guess I'll just have to advertise back East for a husband. Everybody around here is too afraid of Jack Matheny to give me a second look, anyway."

"*What?* Are you crazy?" he demanded. "Any lunatic with a penny for a paper could answer! You don't know who might show up here!"

"Well, I'd want some references from him. I'd have to know something about him before I actually married him. I'd have to know he was committed to hanging onto the place with me."

Thunderstruck, he could only stare at her. When he could speak, he nearly strangled on his own words.

"*References?*" he choked out. "What in hell could pass as a reference for being a husband?"

"That would depend, I suppose."

"On what?"

"I don't know—letters from a minister, from former employers, from a banker maybe. And, if the applicant is a widower, perhaps it will be possible to discover how well he treated his first wife."

She couldn't mean it. She had to be toying with him, teasing him. "This is your idea of joking, isn't it?" he decided. "You're not really serious about this, are you?"

"Well, I'm not leaving. I'll do what it takes to keep my land."

"Whether it's now or later, you'll have to face leaving, Jess. Look—you don't want some stranger coming out here, sweet-talking you, then running off with everything you've got, do you?"

"I'm not a gullible person," she responded stiffly.

"What kind of man do you think's going to answer an ad like that? Some damned fortune hunter wanting to live off you, that's who—that's all you'll get."

"You don't listen much, do you?" she retorted. "I said *I'm not leaving*. If I have to sit out here with Papa's shotgun on my lap, I'll do it. I'll do just about anything to stay. I don't have a fortune, Ben, this place is all I've got." Taking two steps past the rock mound, she pointed at the ground. "I'm going to be planted right here, Ben. When Judgment Day comes, I'll be waiting here. Right next to Preston Mitchell."

"I hope it doesn't come to that," he said soberly. "You've got a lot of living left to do."

"What good is life if you lose your principles?" she asked, her voice rising. "If you have to give into somebody like Jack Matheny? It's not worth much if you let him steal years of hard work from you, is it?"

"A sod house and a few sheep pens aren't worth dying for, Jess."

"Maybe they are to me!" Realizing she was shouting now, she tried to calm herself. "Didn't he ever tell you how much he wanted something he could call his own? His money let you follow your dream, even if it didn't pan out. Well, he finally got his land, Ben. If he shared any of his dreams, then you have to know what this place meant to him."

"I don't remember." Rather than tell her more lies, he leaned down to pick up one of the heavy rocks, then swung it across to the grave. "I'm hoping to finish this up today," he told her. "That way I can cut his name into the stone tonight, and be ready to move on tomorrow."

"You're leaving tomorrow?" she echoed, her heart sinking.

"Like you said, I've about worked off the forty dollars. I think it's time I headed out. I can fix things up for you, but one man's not going to make much difference. If the meanest, orneriest cuss alive answers that ad, he won't be able to stand off Matheny. Then all you'll be left with is a bad husband."

"I see."

She felt foolish now. Whether she'd meant to or not, she'd halfway thrown herself at him, and he hadn't even tried to catch her. She'd been deluding herself ever since he'd been here. She'd thought after seeing him work so hard on the house, that maybe he was deciding to stay awhile. It'd only been a week, but she'd already gotten herself into the habit of thinking in terms of what they'd do about fall planting, of how many sheep they'd need to sell to make it through the winter. Now she knew it was just fanciful, wishful thinking.

Her disappointment was written on her face, in those pretty, almost copper eyes. He felt guilty for deceiving her. "Look—I'd stay if I could, but—"

"I would have made it worth your while, Ben."

The way she said it sent a shiver down his spine. "You're too green to know what you're saying, Jess," he said harshly. "You don't know a damned thing about me."

"I know my father liked you." Then, realizing what he'd been thinking, she felt her face go hot. "I was talking about money, Ben, I told you Papa left a little money," she stammered out. "I can pay you to keep working— that's all I was saying."

He should have felt relieved, but he didn't. Instead, he

felt more than a little disappointed himself. "I've just got to move on, that's all," he muttered.

"But what's in Colorado that's not in Kansas? What's so important that you can't take a job with me?"

"Mountains."

"Mountains." She digested that, then exhaled heavily in defeat. "Well, that's something I can't offer." She looked at the cloudless sky for a moment, then settled her shoulders. "I'll manage," she said with determination. "Well, I guess I'd better be fixing something to eat, hadn't I? The sun's pretty high already."

"Yeah."

She was walking back toward the house, had reached the door almost before he called out, "I'm nothing but a saddle tramp, Jess! You're better off without me hanging around!"

She whirled around at that, and the sun caught the flash in her eyes. "Don't you say that, Ben Haley, don't you *ever* say that again! Nobody's nothing—do you hear me? You are what you think you are!"

Before he could answer, she'd gathered up her skirt and run inside. If he'd been like anybody else, he'd have gone after her, but he wasn't. He had too much blood on his hands to touch a woman like Jessie Mitchell. When he wanted a woman, he'd just have to lay a dollar down on a dresser somewhere. Then it'd be for something they both understood. He could rut on her like the animal he was, and when it was over, he wouldn't even have to know her name. And she wouldn't have to know he was Ben Haley. That way they'd both get what they deserved, not what they wanted.

He felt a deep, impotent anger boiling up inside him, ready to explode on the world. Even if he wanted to be what Jessie Mitchell thought him, he was too late. Casting a baleful look at the white-hot sun disk overhead, he wanted to curse it and everything else on this damned planet. But as a string of oaths paraded through his mind, he knew the fault was his.

He pulled off his wet, stinking shirt and flung it to the ground, then picked up the biggest rock he could find. He'd said he was going to finish sealing off Preston Mitchell's grave before he left, and right now he was in one helluva hurry to go. And the first town he came to, he was going to buy himself a soaking bath, then find the fanciest painted whore money could get him.

Jessie sat down just inside the door and leaned her head back against the cool sod wall. She wanted to cry, but couldn't. The past three and a half weeks had taken every tear she had. No, she had to look past him to what lay ahead. She closed her eyes and tried to think of everything that needed to be done, then she figured out how to do each task alone. All except the fall planting.

Her two draft horses had survived the tornado, but without help that wouldn't make much difference. Unless the sky opened up and it rained for a week instead of several hours, the ground would be too hard for the plow. Last year, before Jake Reynolds sold out, he'd come over to help her father, and it had taken both of them as well as Jake's son to break the ground.

She wouldn't plant this year. She'd raise sheep and hope there was enough rain in the spring to give the grass a good start. With mutton and vegetables from her garden plot, she'd at least eat.

As for Matheny, well, she'd just have to stay on her guard all the time. No matter what Ben said, she didn't think the rancher would actually kill her. No, he'd just try to scare her, and it wouldn't work. He'd find out he couldn't budge her.

Feeling a little better, she stood up. She still had a noon meal to make, and then there was the mending. She'd been planning to darn the hole in one of Ben's socks, and it'd have to be done today or not at all. And he ought to leave with clean clothes—she owed him that much. He'd worked harder than she had a right to expect on a place that wasn't his. If she boiled the water now, she could have everything washed, dried, and ironed before sundown. And if she stayed busy enough, maybe she could hide how much she was going to miss him.

Going to the window, she opened the inside shutter, letting the hot sun into the dim, cool interior. "Ben!" she shouted to get his attention. Her next words died on her lips.

He was half-naked. She stared, fascinated by the sight. Muscles rippled over his shoulders as he swung a piece of the yellow limestone around, then lowered it to the mound. She'd lived in this one room with her father for almost five years, and yet she'd never seen much of his body. No, he might have given her a glimpse of flannel underwear now and then, but nothing more. Out of modesty and consideration, he'd always undressed and dressed in his bed with the covers pulled up. It wasn't until she was readying him for burying that she'd seen all of him, and then she hadn't wanted to look.

"Yeah?" Ben answered, turning around.

Her voice almost deserted her. "Get your things together, and I'll wash them up for you." She sounded like a cross between a squeaky wheel and a nail on slate, even to her own ears. She had no business looking at him, but as he stood there, his chest bared to her eyes, he didn't seem to know it. "I'm putting on the water now. It'll take a while to heat up."

"Can you spare enough for me to wash up?"

"Yes, if you don't mind the wait."

"That's all right," he decided. "I'll just use the pump, and you can save a towel. It's hot enough out here to dry myself without it."

"What about soap?"

"You can hand it out." Wiping his hands on his pants, he walked toward her. "Otherwise, I'll ruin your appetite before you get to eat."

As he came closer, she tried to look away, but couldn't. All that bare skin made him seem twice as big as before. Moving away to break the spell, she picked up the irregular chunk of lye soap. When she dared to turn back, he was at the window, waiting.

Suddenly shy, she kept her eyes on the soap in her hand. "It looks a little funny," she managed apologetically. "I shaved a corner of it off into a jar of water. That way it'll dissolve and be ready to put in with the clothes."

"My ma used to do that."

"Did she?"

"Yeah. Well, am I going to have to climb in and get it, or are you going to give it to me?"

"Oh. Yes, of course." Wiping a wet palm against her skirt, she stepped forward. "Here—"

If she'd meant to say anything else, she couldn't remember it. She was staring into his chest, seeing the flat, hard nipples, the smattering of blond hair curling above them. Her gaze dropped to his outstretched hand. Cuts, broken blisters, and half a dozen splinters could be seen beneath the streaks of dirt. The whole palm looked as if it had been scraped raw.

"Your . . . your hand needs tending before it—"

"Yeah, well, don't go getting out the medicine box. I'd rather take my chances with soap than that stuff you put on my head."

"I've got a salve I made when we sheared last spring. There's a healing oil in the wool, you know."

As he took the soap from her, his fingers closed briefly around hers, and she felt the tremor pass through her body, making her acutely aware of his masculinity. He had strong, warm hands. She looked down, seeing how small hers seemed against his. As if one squeeze could break her bones. And yet what she felt was excitement, not fear.

He felt it also. And yet as desire washed over him, he was filled again with that intense yearning, that wish that he could've met her earlier, under far different circumstances. He looked down, seeing not the cuts and blisters, but only the invisible blood on his hands. And he knew if she even guessed at the life he'd led, she'd recoil in disgust at what he'd made of himself.

"Ben—"

The whispered word jarred him from those thoughts. Raising his eyes, he met the wondering discovery in hers. His mouth was suddenly too dry, his tongue too thick for speech. With an effort, he forced himself to remember that she wasn't a dance hall girl, that she didn't really know what she was offering with those copper eyes. That she was Preston Mitchell's daughter. That he'd come to kill her father.

Taking possession of the soap, he backed away. "Thanks," he rasped out. "I'll go wash." Before she could say anything, he turned and fled for the safety of cool water.

It wasn't until she heard the almost frantic squeaking of the rusty pump handle that she was able to pull herself away from the window. Trying to shake herself free from what had passed between them, she told herself it meant nothing. He was just the first man she'd ever seen like that, that was all. No, she was lying. More than anything, she'd wanted a great deal more than his hand on hers. She'd wanted him to hold her, to touch her, to whisper words a man would say to a woman. But he hadn't, and he probably wouldn't. And now the emptiness within her was unbearable.

She was better off without a man like that, she argued. By his own admission, he was a saddle tramp, a drifter, and in nearly twenty-eight years of life, he'd planted roots nowhere. She could throw herself at him, but she'd probably regret it later. Or even worse, he might spurn her, making her feel like the lowest creature on earth. And either way, he would be leaving tomorrow for Colorado.

She was twenty-one, a spinster by frontier standards, and she'd never been so much as kissed by a man. Nor was she likely to ever get much of an opportunity again. And now the thought of giving herself to some stranger brought out by a newspaper advertisement seemed pretty ludicrous. No, she didn't want that. What she really wanted was for Ben to stay, to love her.

Moving to the chest of drawers, she picked up the ivory-handled mirror she'd brought with her from Ohio. Peering into it, she felt her spirits sink. The girl staring back at her looked sweaty and disheveled, like some old washer-woman over at Fort Hays who'd already done a full day's laundry in the sun. No wonder Ben had taken the soap and run.

But not before she'd glimpsed that one moment of hunger in his eyes, she reminded herself. There'd been a spark there. And maybe, just maybe, she could make it a fire. It was a sinful thought, one that ought to give her pause. What if she threw herself at him, and he left anyway? What if he rode out tomorrow, and she never heard from him again? What if he thought her cheap and foolish, no better than those dance hall girls he'd spoken of? Those were chances she was going to take, she decided. She had one night to make him want to stay. She had one night to pretend he loved her.

Having made up her mind, she went to work with a purpose. Prying open the lid to her father's worn trunk, she took out the green silk dress that had been her mother's. As yellowed tissue fell away, the cloth shimmered in the faint light of the still-open window. Shaking it out, she smoothed the folds with her hands, then carefully laid it over her bed. Taking a clean chemise and drawers from the chest, she draped them over her arm.

She didn't have much time. Going back to the trunk, she took out the pretty lavender sachet and the small, round cake of precious French-milled, lavender-scented soap she'd saved since childhood. If there was ever a time to use them, that time must surely be now. When he came in, she was going to smell so good that he'd forget about food.

Going to the washbasin, she dipped lukewarm water from the bucket into it, then found a cloth. Peeling her clothes down from the top, she stepped out of them, and began washing her damp skin with the fancy soap. The fresh, inviting scent of lavender seemed to fill the room. She would have liked to linger, savoring it, but she had to have herself fixed up before he came in to eat.

At the side of the house, he was buck-naked, trying to drown his desire in the cool water, splashing it over his hot skin, then soaping every inch of his body, including his sweat-soaked hair. The strong, clean smell of Jessie's lye soap made his nose itch and his eyes water. As he scrubbed his head, he could still feel the lumps on his head and the stitches she'd taken in his scalp. When he got the salve from her, he'd have to ask her to take them out.

But then she'd be touching him, and he didn't know if he could stand that. She was too innocent, too pure to understand the effect she had on him, the thoughts that came to his mind every time he got close to her.

He didn't want to leave, but the sooner he put distance between himself and Jessie Mitchell, the better it'd be for both of them. He wasn't fool enough to think he could stay, anyway. Right now, his name meant nothing to her, but someday, some time, somebody'd tell her, and she'd despise him. Now she'd just be sorry when he went. As much as he was going to regret it, it would be better that way, he told himself over and over. That way she'd still have a little regard for him.

Yeah, she'd go on, maybe not the way she wanted to, but she'd go on just fine without him. She'd get married someday, probably have some redheaded kids, and forget she ever knew a Ben Haley at all. But everything would work out for her. While he was lying in the ground somewhere, she'd be living a decent, respectable life.

She couldn't be serious about that stupid advertisement.

Yet in his mind's eye, he could see some tenderfoot hope-
ful stepping off the train, thinking he would be getting a
nice little sheep farm by marrying her. And he wouldn't
be any match for Matheny. She'd just have another body
to bury. Or worse yet, her mail-order husband might just
defraud her. Once married, he'd own the place, and he
could sell it right out from under her, and she wouldn't
have a damned thing to say about it. She'd just be betrayed.

As the rinse water dripped off him, Ben straightened and
reached for his last clean shirt and his spare pair of pants.
Out of the corner of his eye, he caught a quick glimpse of
the sheep pens he'd repaired for her. Turning away, he
glanced up at the roof. It wasn't exactly a thing of beauty,
but it wasn't bad, considering he was a gunslinger, not a
carpenter or a farmer.

And in that moment, he knew what held her there, because he felt it. Pride. Not the stiff-backed, stubborn kind
that he'd thought it was. Pride in having something, in
seeing the result of one's labor, in watching over the flock
of sheep, knowing they wouldn't survive without being
taken care of. Pride in accomplishing something, and in
being needed. Right now, he could feel it, and the place
didn't even belong to him.

It all came back to the same thing, to knowing in his
heart it was too late for him. But right now, he'd give
everything he had and everything he would ever own if he
could just hold Jessie Mitchell, if he could hear her whisper a woman's words of love to him. But he couldn't.
There was Matheny. There was his past just itching to
catch up with him. There was blood on his hands.

He dressed slowly, thinking it was a waste to be cleaning up in the middle of the day. In a couple of hours, he'd
be dirty and sweaty again. But right now, he smelled of
Jessie's strong soap, and it smelled good.

He looked across the yard toward the three walls of sod
and grass that passed for the barn. There was a lot of work

that needed to be done before it was ready for winter. And there was prairie grass to be cut and brought in, or the sheep would starve once the snow was too deep to find it on their own.

But time was running out on him. And on her. In his nearly twenty-eight years, he'd survived a lot of broken dreams. And she would too, he told himself. Squaring his shoulders resolutely, he tucked his dirty clothes under his arm, picked up his boots, and headed for the house.

It was so bright outside, so dim in there, that he had to blink several times to adjust his eyes. At first, he didn't see her, and when he did, his breath caught, and his heart paused. She was standing by her bed, her back to him.

The pins were gone from her auburn hair, and it was tumbling down her back in waves and curls almost to her waist. She had her arms up, brushing it, drawing her thin lawn chemise up, exposing the lace-edged hem of her drawers, her lower legs. Her skin, where the sun hadn't shone on it, was pink and pale. Pure. Untouched.

He had no business standing there, watching her. Any gentleman would have silently backed out the door and waited for her to finish dressing. But he wasn't a gentleman. And right now he wanted her more than he wanted his life.

"Jess—" It wasn't a word—it was a croak.

Startled, she spun around and instinctively crossed her arms over her chest, but not before he'd seen the dark circles of her nipples through the thin lawn. All thoughts of Matheny, all the reasons why he couldn't have her deserted him, replaced by the impossible notion that maybe she wouldn't have to know, maybe when she found out it wouldn't matter. Feeling like a kid in love for the first time, he tried desperately to smile. He was going to put his life on the line and take his chances.

When she'd been bathing, it all seemed so reasonable, so possible, but now—now she almost couldn't meet his

eyes. Now she just felt awkward. She felt more the foolish
spinster rather than any kind of seductress.

"You don't need to write out an advertisement, Jess,
I've decided to apply for the job," he said softly.

He was standing there like a little boy, a lopsided smile
on his face, watching her eagerly. "Oh," she managed,
her heart pounding.

He didn't know what he'd expected, but it was more
than that. He took several steps toward her. "I don't have
much in the way of references, Jess, all I've got are these."
As he spoke, he held out his sore hands. "They're yours,
if you'll have me. I'll work 'em to the bone for you."

She could feel the rush of blood to her face. Stalling to
master her own tumultuous feelings, she took a deep
breath, then let it out slowly to no avail. He was so close
now that his face blurred through her tears. As she looked
up at him, her chin quivered, and she had to fight to keep
from weeping outright. All she could do was nod.

"Oh, Jess." His arms closed around her shaking shoulders, pulling her against his chest. "Just let me love you,
and I'll stay forever," he whispered against her soft, shining hair. "I want to stay, Jess."

Her heart was so full it ached. Rubbing her cheek
against the stiff cotton of his shirt, she admitted, "I've
loved you since the day you got here. I'd rather d-die than
lose you, Ben."

"Hey, are you crying?"

"Y-yes," she sobbed.

"Here now . . ." Still holding her in the circle of his
arm, he tried to wipe at her wet face with his free hand.
But as he looked into her brimming eyes, she smiled.
"God, Jess," he groaned, bending his head to hers.
"Sweetheart, you've got no notion of what you do to me,"
he breathed against her soft lips. "You make me want to
love you, Jess."

Her arms tightened around his waist as she gave herself

up to his kiss. It was new, it was heady, as intoxicating as her father's Christmas toddy. He was teasing, nibbling at the corners of her mouth, tasting her lips with the tip of his tongue. And no matter where he was leading her, she didn't want him to stop.

"I want you to love me, Ben," she whispered.

His tongue slid between her teeth, touching hers, momentarily shocking her, as his hands moved from her shoulders, down her back to her hips, smoothing her chemise over her drawers. An instant heat overwhelmed her, blocking everything beyond the nearness of his body from her mind. She was on fire, she was drowning, and yet she hungered almost desperately for more.

Her eager, unpracticed response surprised him. As he felt his own desire rising, he had to remind himself she didn't know what she was doing, where he was leading her. She wasn't some two-bit whore he could just tumble onto the bed, take, then leave. She was Jess, and he had to make it good for her, he had to take his time loving her. But as her breasts pressed into his chest, as her thighs touched his, he could feel the searing heat through his clothes. If he didn't slow down a little, he wouldn't be waiting for her.

As his mouth left hers, her eyes opened in bewilderment. She swallowed, trying to hide her disappointment. "I didn't want you to stop, Ben," she whispered huskily. "I wasn't afraid."

He searched her face, wanting desperately to believe her. "You're sure, Jess? You're not going to be sorry tomorrow?"

"No."

Drawing her into his arms, he held her close, savoring the sweet scent of lavender on her warm skin. "You don't know anything at all, do you? You don't know what to expect."

"No."

"I'm going to try to go real slow, and anytime you don't

like what I'm doing, you tell me, and I'll try to stop,'' he promised.

Bending his head to hers, he kissed her, and as her arms returned his embrace, he forgot everything but the woman he held. There was no place, no time beyond here and now for him. And as the heat rose again, turning his blood to liquid fire in his veins, nothing beyond her mattered.

In the heat of his desire, she forgot all modesty, answering him kiss for kiss, caress for caress, until nothing in the world mattered beyond him. She might not know what she was wanting, but she was sure she wanted all of it. And this time, when he raised his head, she was ready for whatever he wanted.

Her copper eyes, darker now with desire, told him more than words. He slipped his hands beneath the narrow cotton shoulders of her chemise, pulling it down over her arms, baring her full, pale breasts. Her eyes closed again as she sucked in her breath, holding it as he looked at her. She felt him push the chemise lower, down over her drawers, then his fingers fumbled with the ties at her waist, loosening them also, and both garments slid to the floor.

As warm as it was, gooseflesh covered her body, and she shivered beneath his gaze. His eyes on her, he unbuttoned his shirt, then pulled it off, letting it fall at his feet. His fingers worked the buttons at the front of his pants, freeing him. Blood pounding like a drumbeat in his temples, he backed her against the bed, then followed her down, sinking into the depths of the soft feather mattress over her. As his bare skin met hers, he felt her tense beneath him.

Easing downward, he touched her nipple with his tongue, feeling it harden in an instant. Her hands caught in his hair, opening and closing as he sucked, first on one breast, then on the other. He could feel her belly tauten as his hand slid downward over it to find the wetness below. And with the discovery, he could wait no longer. Her flesh resisted, and she stiffened in shock, then tried to pull away, but by then it was too late. Her cry of protest died in a low moan as her body closed around his.

He'd meant to go slow, to make it good for her, but as her fingernails dug into his back, he forgot everything beyond the feel of her woman's body, beyond the driving need of his own. He rode hard, scarce aware that she bucked and writhed instinctively beneath him. And when the exquisite release came, and he was floating back to earth, he wasn't even sure whose voice he'd heard crying out. Sated, he rolled away to catch his breath.

He lay there, afraid to look at her, wondering if he'd disgusted her, if she thought he was no better than a rutting animal, if she regretted what they'd done. More than half-expecting either disappointment or anger, he forced himself to turn his head toward her.

His gaze took in her closed eyes, her fine profile, her pale complexion, and he was again overwhelmed by how pretty she was, and by the tenderness he felt for her. If a woman like this could somehow love him, he had to be the luckiest man on earth.

She'd turned away in silent mortification. Now that the all-consuming heat of desire was gone, she was utterly embarrassed and terribly afraid. She knew no decent woman would ever do what she had just done, and for all her contempt of those dance hall harlots, she'd just shown him she was no better than they were. She couldn't open her eyes, she just couldn't face the condemnation she'd surely see in his.

Unable to stand her silence any longer, he took a deep breath, then let go of it. Rolling against her, he reached around her, drawing her close. For a moment, the scent of lavender threatened to rekindle his desire, but her still, unresponsive body quelled any notion of that. Instead, his hand sought hers, possessing it.

"You know, Jess," he said finally, "if I hurt you, I'm sorry for it."

Her throat was tight, so tight she could hardly speak.

She swallowed. "You didn't," she managed to whisper. "Not much, anyway."

He'd never been a man for pretty words, and now he was regretting it. They weren't coming easy right now. He cleared his throat and tried to say what he felt, anyway. "You're probably thinking I'm some kind of an animal for wanting you like that, and maybe I am, but I never wanted anybody in my whole life as much as I wanted you today. And I know I've never felt anything near what I feel for you."

"You don't have to say this, Ben."

"I don't know how else to tell you I love you, Jess. Maybe I didn't make it plain when I said I'd stay, but I was asking you to marry me. I'm still asking it, Jess."

Afraid she was going to burst into tears, she bit her lower lip to stop its trembling. Turning over, she buried her head in his shoulder and lost the battle.

His arms closed around her shaking shoulders. Smoothing her hair with his sore palm, he said helplessly, "If you're too disgusted now to want that, I'll still stay on. All you've got to do is say what you want."

Her arms tightened around him, clinging to him as if he were life itself. Still trying to master the overwhelming flood of emotion, she finally choked out, "I want to marry you, Ben, more than anything."

Relief washed over him, followed by the most happiness he'd felt in years, maybe in his life. "Then, Jessamine Mitchell, you've got yourself a husband," he said softly. "Now all we've got to do is find the nearest preacher and someplace where I can buy you a wedding ring."

She looked up at that. "I've already got the ring, Ben, that is, unless you mind it, I've got Mama's. She wanted me to have it when she died, but I've never worn it." Turning away, she pulled up the corner of the quilt to cover her, then leaned over to find the small porcelain box beneath the bed. Sitting up, she held it out to him. "Go on—look at it."

He opened the little box carefully. Inside, nestled in the center of a lock of golden hair, lay a circle of embossed gold. "It's pretty—real pretty," he decided.

"Those are roses going around it," she pointed out.

It looked awfully small. "Does it fit?"

"Yes. I just never wore it because of what it was. It didn't feel right for a spinster to wear a wedding ring. And I don't see any sense now of wearing two of them."

"You sure you don't mind not getting one of your own?"

"It's enough that you love me," she answered simply.

"That's your ma's hair, isn't it?"

"Yes. She cut that for him when they were married. She said she wanted him to have it to remind him of what it looked like when she was old and gray. Only she never lived long enough to turn gray, Ben."

"Yeah. I wouldn't mind having a red one for my pocket watch," he admitted. Out of the corner of his eyes, he saw a lump moving under the covers, coming up from the bottom of the bed. "What th—?" Before she could answer, an orange head emerged next to him. "Oh, it's the damned cat. I was beginning to think he was lost somewhere."

"No." Scooping Sam up, she nuzzled the back of the animal's head. "He's been hiding under the bed ever since you got here, just coming out at night to eat. I guess he knows now you're going to stay."

The huge cat wriggled free, then sat there, regarding Ben owlishly. Finally, he rose on his three legs and came closer, purring, while Jessie leaned over to retrieve her chemise from the floor. Letting go of the quilt, she pulled the undergarment over her head, covering her body, then stood up. Moving to the foot of the bed, she picked up the green silk dress and shook it out.

"That's real fancy," Ben murmured appreciatively.

"It's my wedding dress," she decided. Now that she had a safe distance between them, she dared to smile at him. "I just want you to know I wasn't disgusted. I was more afraid of what you were going to think of me.''

"I think you're the best thing that ever happened to me, Jess.''

Ben had seen a lot of Kansas towns like this one: a few blocks laid out along a dusty road facing the railroad tracks, with three or four saloons, a general store, a little bank, the train depot, and a drugstore that he could see. And while he didn't actually find a sign, he was pretty sure one of those buildings was a boarding house. He guessed if everybody in town lined up facing the tracks, there'd probably be several hundred.

Behind Main Street, there was a string of little homes mixed between several more substantial houses under construction. His gaze strayed the other way, across the railroad tracks where, separated from more respectable citizens, two tents and a "hog ranch" were clearly visible. Yeah, that was something the army and the railroads had in common—everywhere either of 'em went, whores followed.

"You know where we're going?" he asked, turning in his saddle to look at Jessie.

"If you take the first corner, the Methodist minister has the house in back of the bank building. The meetings are held in the drugstore.''

He squinted up at the bright sun, observing, "The sky'll probably cave in.''

"How's that?''

"I haven't been to a church service since I left home, unless you want to count a couple of graveyard funerals.''

"Then it's about time you went, don't you think?''

"My pa was a preacher," he admitted soberly. "He was kinda like some apples that fool you—all nice and shiny until you cut into 'em—then rotten to the core.''

"What an awful thing to say.''

"Yeah, well, he preached against drinking and cussing and talked about God's love and forgiveness on Sunday, but when he was home he didn't follow his own preaching."

"I'm sorry."

"It's not your fault—it was his. He had a temper quicker'n a hair trigger, and just about as deadly. Only he didn't kill anybody outright—he just made us die inside."

It was the first time she'd ever heard him mention anyone in his family other than his mother. "He must have been pretty hard on you."

"It was Ma that took the worst of it. He was harder on her than any of us," he went on. "Everything we did wrong got her a beating, because she'd get between us and him, trying to stop him from hitting us with anything handy. I left because I couldn't stand watching him turn on her." Nudging Rebel to turn, he exhaled heavily. "She had six kids, so I guess she couldn't leave—but I could. The night before I ran off, he knocked out a couple of her teeth, and she still wouldn't go. And you want to know the hell of it? I gave him the thrashing of his life that night, and she turned on me. Yeah—she turned on me. 'You've got to honor your father,' she cried, begging me not to hurt him. Well, I hurt him all right. When I was done with him, it was his teeth he was spitting out on the floor. I got out of there before he woke up the next morning. If I hadn't, I figured one of us was going to die."

"Then you were right to go."

He pulled up in front of the house and swung down, dropping the reins beneath Rebel's nose. He hesitated a moment, then tried to flatten his unruly blond hair by slicking it back with both hands. Now that they were there, he was acutely conscious of the fact he wasn't nearly as dressed up as she was. He just had on a collarless white shirt without a tie, and when he pulled it down, his black frock coat stuck out over the butt of his Colt.

"You look fine, Ben," she said, smiling.

He knew he didn't, but there wasn't much he could do about it now. He just wished she'd seen him all fixed up fancy the way he was when he was flush from winning at poker. But he was forgetting where he'd been leading himself earlier, what he'd been wanting to say before they went inside. Moving to where she still sat sideways on her horse, he looked up, sobering again.

"I just want you to know I'll never be like him, Jess. There's nothing you can say or do that'll ever make me lay a hand on you in anger. And when one of the kids gets into trouble, I swear I'll never do more than take my hand to his backside. If you want him whipped with anything else, you'll have to do it yourself." Having said his piece, he felt more than a little awkward. "I just had to say it—that was all," he said, reaching for her.

"I never thought you'd hurt me, Ben," she said softly, leaning into his arms. "I don't think you could ever hurt anybody if you didn't have to."

As he lifted her from her horse, he almost couldn't meet those pretty copper eyes. He was afraid she could look into his face and see his guilt. And if the time ever came when he had to tell her what he'd done, he didn't know how he could ever explain eleven dead men to her. He set her down and turned toward the little white house.

"You're awfully solemn this morning, Ben," she chided lightly. "If I didn't know better, I'd think you were going to a funeral, not a wedding."

"It's not something I take lightly, Jess." Reaching for her hand, he placed it in the crook of his other elbow. "I'd always kind of expected to die a bachelor."

"You still can, you know."

"No." His expression lightened. "You just watch how I come out. I'll be grinning ear to ear, whooping and hollering like a drunken cowboy, telling everybody around I've got me the prettiest wife in the state of Kansas."

"If you don't mind, I think I'd rather have something in between. A little happiness in your eyes will suffice."

"You've already got that," he said, smiling.

"You know, Benjamin Haley, when you smile, you

have the prettiest eyes I've ever seen on a man. They're almost the color of seawater.''

''When have you ever seen the sea, Jess?''

''Grandpa Power leased a cottage on the shore every summer.''

It was another reminder that she hadn't been born poor like him. That no matter how hard she'd struggled to survive in Kansas, she wasn't really like him. He was going to have to rise to her level; he didn't want to bring her down to his.

She was about to take the biggest step in her life, and as she looked at the minister's house, she felt the enormity of what she was doing. From this day forward, she was going to belong to Ben Haley, she was going to give her life and property into his control. She had to look up at his strong, even profile and tell herself it was right. Her fingers tightened on his arm.

''If I wasn't in the middle of the street, I'd ask you to kiss me for luck, Ben,'' she whispered.

''I'd be proud to do it, anyway.'' Turning into her, his other arm went around her shoulder as he bent his head to hers. ''I'm not going to let you be sorry, Jess.''

She slid her arms around his neck and lifted her face for his kiss, then stepped back shyly when it was over. ''I'm not going to let you be sorry, either.''

''Ahem.''

Both of them spun around guiltily and saw the man in the doorway. There was a brief, awkward silence, then Ben declared baldly, ''Name's Haley—Benjamin Haley—and if you're the preacher here, I'm asking you to marry us.''

Jessie held out her hand. ''Jessamine Mitchell—Miss Mitchell.''

''John Wright—Reverend John Wright.'' The corners of his eyes crinkled as he smiled at her. ''If you're wanting to get married, I hope it's *Miss* Mitchell,'' he added, shaking her hand. ''If you're not, you'd better be a widow—otherwise, it's bigamy.''

"You'll have to forgive me, sir, I'm more than a little nervous."

"No need to be. Just come on into the parlor. Mary," he called into the house, "take off your apron, and come witness a wedding." Once inside, he looked them up and down. "Either of you of the Methodist persuasion?"

"No, sir," Ben answered.

"And you?"

"I was raised Episcopalian," Jessie murmured.

"Close enough." Turning his attention to Ben, he snapped, "As for you, young man, it wouldn't hurt any for you to show yourself in a pew come Sunday morning. And, by the way, I don't allow guns in the church or in my house."

"His father's a preacher in Texas," Jessie interposed quickly.

"What kind?"

"Baptist." As he answered, Ben unbuckled his gunbelt, then bent to untie the leather thong that secured his holster to his thigh.

"Hardshell?"

"All I know is he said he got the call behind the plow. I always figured he must've been hungover when it happened."

"Uh-huh. I've known a few of those myself. But I guess what they lack in schooling, they make up for in zeal."

"He had a lot of zeal, all right."

"Raised on a lot of fire and brimstone, were you?"

"You could say that. A lot of 'spare the rod and spoil the child,' too," Ben added.

" 'Bend the sapling the way it should go, and you'll get a straight tree,' eh?"

"Something like that."

"Did it work?"

"No. I'd say it made me bend the other way."

The man was smiling again. "Then why didn't you go to the justice of the peace? We've got one, you know."

Ben held out his holstered gun. "I only aim to get married once, sir, so I'd just as soon have the right words spoken."

"I reckon that's a fair answer," Wright decided.

Mrs. Wright came out to witness the short service in her parlor. It was a simple ceremony—two questions asked and answered, and the proper words repeated. Once the ring was slipped on Jessie's finger, the pronouncement was made, and Ben self-consciously brushed his lips against her cheek, while the minister's wife clasped her hands and beamed at him. Then he dug into his coat pocket for his wallet.

"How much do I owe you?"

"That depends," the reverend answered. "Three dollars if you want me to write it up in one of the Bibles I keep for the purpose. Otherwise, I just sign the certificate, and you give whatever you feel like to the church building fund."

"A certificate will be fine," Jessie assured him.

"I'd kinda like to see the Bible," Ben decided.

Mrs. Wright produced a large black book stamped with gold letters. Opening it, she showed him where there were records in the middle. As she held it closer, he saw the ornate bridal record across from an equally ornate listing of birthdates for children born to the union. The next page included marriages, baptisms, and dates of death of subsequent generations.

"He doesn't make any money on these," the woman insisted. "The church pays two ninety-five apiece for them, but we started having them because a lot of couples want to save them for their children and grandchildren."

"Yeah. What do you think, Jess?"

"I think it's beautiful."

"We'll take it."

As Ben counted out the three dollars, Reverend Wright wrote in all the details in a pretty, flowery hand, stopping occasionally to check the pertinent facts. And in black and

white script "Jessamine Rose Mitchell, born May 20, 1856
in Cuyahoga County, Ohio, was united in Holy Matrimony
with Benjamin Wilson Haley, born August 27, 1849 in
Shackleford County, Texas, by the power invested in Rev.
John Wright, a Methodist Minister, by the State of Kansas,
county of Trego, on this 29th day of July, in the Year of
Our Lord 1877." When he finished, he handed the Bible
to Jessie, while Ben strapped on his gun and tied the holster down on his thigh.

"May the Lord bless you and your husband, Mrs. Haley," Mrs. Wright gushed.

Ushering Jessie out of the parsonage, Ben overheard the
woman whisper to her husband, "Did you see the way he
wore that gun?" And the good reverend replied, "It's done
that way for 'slapping leather.' "

"What?"

"Didn't you recognize his name? That was Ben Haley—the gunfighter, Mary," he added, trying to jog her
memory.

"Oh, my, but if you knew, why on earth did you marry
them?"

"Because he obviously loves her," he answered. "And
he wouldn't be the first gunman to redeem himself for a
good woman."

But Jessie was too absorbed in her new Bible to hear
them. It wasn't until they were standing on the street that
she looked up, giggling. "Ben, did you see this? There are
fifteen spaces for children!"

"Yeah, well, if it's all the same to you, I don't want
that many," he said abruptly.

Her smile faded. "Is something wrong? You don't
sound happy."

"No, nothing's wrong."

His gaze dropped to the Bible in her hand. She was his
wife now, he told himself, and that was all that mattered.
But it had just occurred to him that within the week his
marriage would be listed in the newspaper, and then all

hell was going to break loose with Matheny. But he didn't want to think of that now. Right now, he wanted to share her happiness.

"I'll be happy with a couple of little redheads like you, that's all."

"I expect we'll take what God gives us, don't you?"

"Yeah. Listen, I was thinking maybe you'd like to eat before we go home, maybe even do a little shopping at the store. You don't get many chances to get out and about, so maybe you'd like to do something you like today." His smile warmed, reaching his eyes. "Besides, as fine as you look in that dress, I'd kinda like to show you off some."

"I don't know of any place to eat around here," she protested.

"What about a boarding house?"

"I don't know . . ." she said doubtfully, "unless it'd be Nellie Brown's place."

"Anything wrong with it?"

"Well, no, but—"

"But what?"

"Can we afford it?" Then, afraid she'd hurt his feelings, she added hastily, "Besides, it's a long way home, and even though they're penned up today, the sheep still need food and water."

"We can make it by sundown. Look—I've got seventeen dollars, Jess, and it's your wedding day."

"Oh, well, then—I hear she has real good fried chicken. But I'm not exactly hungry yet."

"Then why don't you go find yourself something in the store," he offered, taking out his wallet. "Here—" He pulled out five dollars and handed it to her. "Don't spend it on something you have to have anyway, Jess. Get yourself something you'd like with this."

Her eyes misted, and her smile twisted. "You know, Ben Haley, before I met you, I almost never cried. Now I'm getting choked up all the time." .

"Here now—none of that," he said gruffly, brushing at

her cheek with his knuckle. "You go on, and I'll catch up."

"But where are you going?"

"I reckon I got a little business, but it won't take long."

"With whom?"

"I'm thinking about subscribing to the newspaper, if they've got one anywhere around here."

"It's just a single sheet, Ben. I don't think you'd want it."

"I said I wouldn't be long, Jess."

"All right, but you'll find there's nothing much beyond farm prices in it. Unless you want to know what everything's selling for, you won't care much about reading it."

"I'll meet you over at the store."

Mystified, she watched him pull his coat back over his holster before he walked down the dirt street. Just when she thought she might know him, he got harder to figure out. Clutching the five dollars in her hand, she turned toward the general store. While she was there, she might as well price some good white cotton suitable for a man's shirts.

She was right. It wasn't much of a newspaper. The lone occupant of the office was laying out type when Ben walked into the small, narrow building. Wiping ink-stained hands on a blackened apron, he turned around.

"Morning, mister. Anything I can do for you?"

"Yeah. I've got five dollars that says you don't put something in your paper."

"Well, I've been paid for putting things in, mister, but not many folks pay to keep 'em out. What is it, anyway?"

"A wedding announcement." Ben opened his wallet. "Might as well give me a subscription, too. Send it to the Mitchell place up in Graham County."

"Whose wedding?"

"Mine."

"That's not much help, mister."

"The name's Haley—Ben Haley."

He could have sworn the man took a couple of steps backward as his eyes widened. "You're Ben Haley? You're not funning me?"

"Yeah. Think you can do it for me?"

The printer looked him up and down, taking in the raw-hide tie that wrinkled Ben's pants leg below the leather holster, before he found his voice again. "You don't need to pay me anything, Mr. Haley. Way I look at it, you don't give me no trouble, I don't print it," he said quickly. "And you got your subscription—compliments of the editor."

"Thanks."

His business concluded, Ben headed for the store, relieved. He wasn't ready to let Matheny know what he'd done. He wanted to take his time telling Jess, he told himself. No, he was lying, and he knew it. He didn't ever want her to know. And while he wasn't fool enough to believe he could hide his past from her forever, he at least wanted to keep it from her as long as possible. Maybe by the time she found out, she could believe he'd changed.

"Ben! Ben Haley!"

The hairs on his neck stood on end. His hand dropped as he spun around, coming up with his gun cocked, ready. Standing in front of him was Vaughn Hacker, both hands empty and in plain sight.

"Jesus! Kinda jumpy, aincha?"

"I'm alive." Easing the hammer down, Ben jammed the gun back into the holster. "I wouldn't do that again, if I were you, Vaughn. Next time, we might both regret it."

Hacker looked at the Colt, then at Ben's hand. "Damn, but that was fast." Then, recovering his composure, he said, "I heard you'd be coming out, but I didn't know when."

"I wasn't exactly planning to shout it to the world."

"No, 'course not. I was just meaning we didn't know you were around yet. But I can tell you for sure that Matheny's going to be damned glad."

"He wouldn't want it spread around either," Ben said tersely.

"No, but I can tell him. He's coming in today from Kansas City, and I'm meeting the train. He'll want some way of getting in touch with you."

"I'll be the one that makes the moves. Until then, I don't want anybody in my business."

"He's going to want to know when."

"He'll know."

"I'll tell him you're real close-mouthed. I reckon he'll like that."

"You do that, Vaughn."

Retracing his steps toward the store, Ben heard Vaughn Hacker say under his breath, "I ain't afraid of you, Haley. Maybe you can get by pulling that on a lot of folks, but not on me."

Ben stopped, but didn't turn around again. "How's that, Vaughn?" he asked softly.

"I didn't say nuthin'," the man muttered.

"Like I said, don't startle me again, Vaughn."

He found Jessie feeling different bolts of cloth while the proprietor hovered over her. Coming up behind her, he caught her elbow. "Get something with a little color in it, Jess."

"I was thinking of making up some shirts, Ben. Somehow I can't see you in calico."

"No. Buy for yourself."

Her face fell. "But I was wanting to make something for you. I've got more clothes than I need, but you—"

"I didn't give that to you for me."

"But I wanted to do something nice for you," she protested.

He realized then that he'd spoiled her plans, and he felt sorry for it. "I'd say you already have—about fifteen minutes ago. I'm real proud of you, Jess."

In the end, she bought five yards of plain white cotton and a dress-length of a pretty print, satisfying them both.

By the time she added
dollars and fifteen cents.
stepped past him, looking u

"I'm going to order the pa
don't mind the wait," she said.

"Well, if it isn't Miss Mitche
voice boomed. "I ain't been seeing
while, so I was figuring maybe you
Comin' a hard winter, way I hear it."

"I wouldn't know, Mr. Hacker," she r

"Pity the rain didn't last. Another coupl
the grass'll be tinder-dry again. No tellin' ho
we'll be fighting before winter, huh?" Hacke
tip his hat, then saw Ben holding the door from th

"Well, if you don't get around—"

"I don't like your manners, Vaughn," Ben said si
stepping outside.

Moving back apace, the other man blustered, "No har
in talking to the lady, is there? All I was doing was warning her about how dry it gets in August."

"She's my wife."

It took a minute for Hacker to digest that, then his eyes
narrowed. "Where's Mitchell?"

"He's dead—but I'm alive," Ben said significantly.
"You got anything to say, say it to me now."

"I got nothing to say, but I reckon Mr. Matheny's going
to have plenty."

"You be sure to tell him, will you?" But even as he
said it, Ben had that sick, tight feeling in his stomach.

As Hacker walked off, Jessie laid her hand on Ben's
arm. "What was that all about?"

"I didn't like the way he was talking to you."

Her gaze followed Matheny's man for a moment, then
she decided, "I'm still not hungry. If you don't mind too
much, I'd just as soon go home."

"So would I."

She looked up at him. "I was real proud of you, Ben,"

in the findings, it came to three
As he held the door for her, she

terns from Butterick, if you

,'' the already familiar
that pa of yours in a
all was moving out.

esponded coldly.
of weeks and
w many fires
started to
e inside.

o Vaughn
down.''
s invite
orrying
t's go

hat
re-
en
g

kily,

_____ call his own, and
_____ the work or even the smell
_____ to him, he could close his eyes
_____ waiting in his mind. He could watch her un-
_____ for him, see that auburn hair fall over her shoulders,
dark red against the white of her chemise. She'd be looking
up at him with that half-shy, half-seductive smile of hers,
that light in those coppery eyes. One look at her and he'd
forget how tired he was.

This morning, she'd reminded him to come in early, that
it was the twenty-seventh of August, the twenty-eighth an-
niversary of his birth, and she'd have a big supper waiting
for him. And probably a couple of shirts, but she hadn't
said that. He hadn't even seen her working on any, but
there'd been a few telltale scraps in the sweepings, so he'd
guessed it.

She was teaching him a lot about himself, putting some
real sense back into his life. She didn't preach at him, she
showed him. Every night since he'd been married, she'd
gotten out that Bible and read a chapter from it. At first,
she'd done it silently, but when he'd asked, she'd shared,

and now it seemed right to listen. There was a lot in it about forgiveness.

He wasn't *the* Ben Haley anymore. He didn't have to look over his shoulder at every corner—out here a man could see anybody coming. His gunbelt hung on a peg inside the door, because a six-shooter and a quick draw were pretty useless here. Now it was the Henry rifle lying on the ground next to him. Sixteen shots and distance made it more useful, because when Matheny and Hacker made a move, it wouldn't be one against one.

His gaze swept the prairie, taking in the flatness. All he could see were miles of golden grass rippling in the wind. And that bright, cloudless sky, that sun with its relentless heat. He hadn't brought his watch, but he guessed it was about three o'clock, a couple of hours before he usually headed in. But today home was beckoning early. No matter how hot it was out here, inside those thick walls, it was as cool as a cave. And Jess was waiting.

Heaving himself up, he shouted at the sheep. "Come on, girls. Let's go home." Moving around them, he waved the Henry, and they began to move, bleating feeble complaints at leaving the water, but he wasn't having any of that today. "Get a move on. Let's go!"

One of the ewes, a small, spotted one, lagged. He hadn't noticed before, but it seemed to be going lame. And he couldn't afford any stragglers—left out, she'd be a coyote dinner. "Come on," he coaxed. It wasn't going to catch up. Exasperated, he went back, picked her up, and threw her over his shoulder. Her matted wool had a strong smell to it, and where it touched him, it was greasy. "All right— let's go, girls! Keep moving!"

The window shutters were half-closed when he got home, but he didn't think much about it. She did that sometimes to keep out the afternoon sun. Herding the flock into the pens, he set down the little ewe. Later, after supper, he'd come out and get a better look at her foot, but right now, he was hot, greasy, and tired. Right now, he was going to strip off his shirt and drown his head under the pump.

He came in, still dripping, murmuring apologetically, "I'll mop up after myself, Jess."

She was sitting at the table, her back to him, and he didn't smell any food cooking. He blinked several times, trying to adjust his eyes to the lack of light, then walked around to face her. Her mother's ring was lying on the table next to *Famed Gunmen of the West.* As dim as the room was, he recognized that godawful picture. It felt like his stomach dropped into his gut, leaving him sick, hollow. Her first words were like a death sentence.

"Mr. Matheny was here."

"Yeah." His eyes on the book, he groped for words, knowing there was nothing in there she could understand. "Jess—"

"I didn't believe him, you know. I pulled your gun on him and told him to get out," she went on, her voice flat, toneless. "Then, when I was putting it back, I thought you were the only man I knew who wore his holster like that. He said you were a gunfighter, Ben—a hired killer—and he was just wanting to warn me."

"Jess, don't—"

She didn't look up. "I looked through your things after he left, and I found this book. I read what it said about Ben Haley."

"It's not true—not all of it," he said desperately. "There's a lot of lies in there, Jess."

"When were you going to tell me? When you sold this place out from under me?"

"It wasn't like that. I don't want to sell out."

"You never knew Preston Mitchell, Ben. He never hung out with any killers," she declared, raising her head. "You were looking for him, all right, but it wasn't money you were going to pay him."

Now he couldn't meet her eyes. He took a deep breath, then admitted, "Matheny paid me two hundred dollars to run him off, and if he wouldn't go, I was to kill him. But before I even got here, I'd pretty much changed my mind.''

"Then why did you ask for him? Why, Ben? Why didn't you just ride on out? Why didn't you just keep going on to Colorado?''

"I was going to warn him that I wouldn't be the last man Matheny hired. So, help me God, Jess, I wasn't going to kill him.''

"You don't even believe in God, Ben. Anybody who'd kill twenty-seven men can't believe in God.''

"It wasn't twenty-seven. It wasn't anything like that, I don't care what the damned book says.''

"You let me think you were so kind—so wonderful— I was such a fool,'' she whispered brokenly. "You let me believe you loved me.'' Pushing away from the table, she stood up, and her voice rose again. "Why, Ben? Weren't there enough harlots out there for you? Did you have to make me one?''

"Don't say that! It wasn't that way at all, Jess. I wanted to marry you, Jess.''

"You seduced me!'' Even as she cried it, she knew better. "No, that's not entirely true, I suppose,'' she admitted. "I was asking you to do it. I was wanting you to love me.''

"I do, Jess.'' He reached out, wanting to somehow make her understand. "I never lied to you about that. I wanted to marry you more than anything. No matter what else you believe, I'm asking you to believe that.''

She backed away. "Don't put your bloody hands on me, Ben! If you touch me, I'll fight!''

"Don't, Jess, don't—''

Tears were scalding her eyes, nearly blinding her. Clenching her hands tightly at her sides to control herself, she choked out, "I want you to get out of my house, Ben—just go.''

He stood there, hesitating. "You're my wife,'' he said

finally. "I can't just walk away from that."

"There isn't a court in Kansas that won't give me a divorce from Ben Haley," she responded bitterly.

"I'm sorry, Jess."

"Just go. Please."

The pit had swallowed him up all right. He'd gone straight to hell without dying. He could see all he was doing was upsetting her. Maybe if he gave her time, if he wrote from Colorado, maybe he could at least make her understand. But not now. Not yet. Defeated, he walked over and lifted his gunbelt from the peg by the door.

"You forgot your damned book, Ben Haley."

The way she said his name, it sounded like a cuss word. He swung around to face her. "Just burn it."

He took a long, last look at her, trying to photograph her in his memory. She had on that old-fashioned, fancy green dress she'd worn to her wedding, telling him she'd dressed up for his birthday before Matheny came. It crossed his mind that dying would come easier than leaving her, but that wasn't his choice. Right now, she was tearing his insides out, and he couldn't even blame her.

"Good-bye, Ben," she said, her voice making it final.

Stalling for time, he buckled the gunbelt at his waist, then tied the thong around his thigh. Adjusting the Colt so it rode the way he liked it, he said quietly, "It wasn't twenty-seven men, Jess. It was eleven, and not one of them gave me a chance to walk away from him. Until now, I never wanted to kill anybody. I'm asking you to believe that."

She could almost feel her heart breaking under her breastbone. "Where are you going?"

"What difference does it make?"

"In case I have to send you any papers."

He took another deep breath, then exhaled fully. "After I kill Jack Matheny, I guess I'll be heading where I should have gone in the first place. There's a boarding house in Denver—The Prospector. I probably won't stay long there, but put 'em in care of Mattie Daniels, and she'll forward 'em to me. And, no, she's not what you're thinking,'' he added. ''She's plump and gray and old enough to be my mother. She just doesn't ask any questions, and she doesn't answer any, in case the law's after me.'' He tried to smile, but couldn't. ''Good-bye, Jess.''

She waited until she heard him take Rebel from the shed, then she flung herself onto the bed and let everything go. Her sobs shook the slats below the feather mattress, and her tears soaked her best quilt, but she didn't care. She had to cry him out of her.

As he crossed onto Matheny land, Ben looked back at the one hundred sixty acres he'd come to think of as his own. When one considered the thousands that made up the Lazy M, it wasn't much, but it stuck in Matheny's craw like one of those big cactus spines he'd left behind in Texas. The old man was too greedy, wanting to own every inch of ground in the county. But he'd made a mistake going after Jess's farm, and now it was going to cost him.

Ben reined in, deciding that early morning would be the best time to do it. He'd be cooler then, his nerves and hands steadier. Right now, he didn't even have a clear head. Jess's words were still ringing in his ears, accusing him, damning him.

You never knew Preston Mitchell, Ben. He never hung out with any killers . . . Don't put your bloody hands on me . . . There isn't a court in Kansas that won't give me a divorce from Ben Haley . . .

He needed a drink. He hadn't had anything stronger than water in a month. That's what he was going to do. After he killed Matheny, he'd head for the Colorado border and someplace where he could drink himself into a stupor. And if he stayed drunk long enough, maybe he'd get to where he could stand himself.

Or maybe he wouldn't make it. Maybe after Matheny was dead, Hacker or somebody else would get him before he could get out of there. Then Jess would be a widow, and he'd be out of his misery. She'd have her place, and she'd be free to find another husband, someone who deserved her. The thought, while noble, wasn't much of a comfort to him. Right now, he'd be better off just thinking about Matheny.

Dismounting, he unrolled his bedroll, pulled off his saddle, and made himself a cold camp on the hot ground. He couldn't risk a fire, not with the wind up and the grass as dry as tinder. It was early, the sun still up, forming a blazing ball just above the western horizon. When it dropped down, and the moon came up, he'd be exactly twenty-eight. His ma'd said he'd come squalling into the world just past eight.

Using the saddle as a headrest, he lay down and leaned back. Kansas. The only damned place a man could stand knee-deep in mud and have dust blow in his face. The only damned place where the wind blew three hundred and sixty days a year. Whoever'd said that had been here, that was for sure. Only now there wasn't any mud, just wind coming across Matheny land, headed for Jess's place.

He'd just closed his eyes when he smelled it. *Smoke.* Jerking himself up, he looked around, trying to see the source. There was nothing, only a faint haze along the southern horizon. For a moment, he thought his mind played tricks on his senses, but as he kept his eyes turned toward the Lazy M, the haze looked a little like sunset. And he wasn't looking west.

There was a fire over there, and the way the wind was, it'd come galloping across that tall grass like a herd of wild horses. Even as he looked at it, the sky seemed redder, the dark haze rising above it. He rolled out of his bedroll and threw his saddle back on Rebel, wasting only enough time to tighten the cinch. Leaving his blankets behind, he headed back to the sheep farm.

"Jess! Jess!" he shouted, coming over the little hill. "Jess!" There was no mistaking the smell of smoke now.

As he turned in the saddle for a quick look over his shoulder, the southern sky was red. "Jess!" he yelled, spurring Rebel. His throat raw already, he dropped from the saddle and pounded on the door. "Fire! Get your things together—fire's coming!"

Turning around, he glanced at the sheep in the pens, at the three-sided, grass-roofed barn, then back at the house. It was all going to go—everything. "Jess, for God's sake, come out!" Grabbing a shovel from the barn, he didn't wait for her. He started digging, turning under a row of dead grass around the pen, working frantically. In less than an hour, the wind would bring the fire right into the yard.

She came out, and whatever she'd been going to say died on her lips. She turned white, then ran inside. Coming back, she had the water bucket. Moving to the pump, she worked the handle, filling the bucket. Carrying it to where he dug, she shouted, "I'm going to try to save the sheep!"

They'd caught wind of the smoke and were milling, bleating. Taking the pail from her, Ben splashed the water onto the roof of the barn. It'd take a bucket brigade to save it, and there were only two of them. And he couldn't dig fast enough to get a wide enough path around the house and pens.

"Don't worry about the animals! Pour that on the ground!" Pointing out about fifty feet from the house, he repeated it. "Pour that on the ground—over there!"

Not waiting to see if she did, he went into the barn and harnessed the draft horses to the plow. As he led them out, she was carrying more water, pouring it where he'd directed. She looked up, her eyes frantic.

"It's going to go, Ben! I can't save it!"

"Keep the water coming!"

There wasn't enough time to get the ground wet enough to take the blade. After she'd struggled for about ten buckets, he decided to try something else. "Lead the team, and I'm going to stand on the blade, Jess. There's not time to go around everything, but maybe if we can make a line fifty feet long, we can make the fire burn down the sides instead. You can lead the team, can't you?''

"Yes, but—"

It was about the only hope he had. By the time they'd made the first furrow, the smoke was billowing across the prairie, filling the air, choking them. Taking off his shirt, he wet it down and tied it over his face below his eyes. There was a roar to the flames as they shot skyward.

"It's no use!" she cried. "That wind'll blow right across it. My sheep are all going to die!"

"All right—let's move 'em out. Open the pens, and get on Rebel. Drive as many as you can—take 'em west.''

"You can't stay here, Ben!"

"I'm going to try to wet the roof again, then I'll be right behind you. I can ride your horse bareback.'' When she didn't move, he grabbed her waist and threw her up into his saddle. "Get going, Jess! Keep 'em moving!''

The stupid animals milled in the pens even after he opened the gates, forcing him to literally go in and shoo them out. Then he thought of Sam—the damned thing was probably under the bed. "Wait!" Running back to the house, he crawled over the rough puncheons to look for him. When he found the cat, he grabbed one of its legs and pulled. It came out hissing and scratching. Catching it behind its neck, he raced outside to thrust it into Jess's arms. "Now get going!"

"You've got to come, Ben!"

The air was full of crackling, blowing coals, making the place seem like a fireworks display on the Fourth of July, only this one was deadly. He looked up, taking in her sooty, dirt-streaked, sweaty face.

"I'll be along," he lied. "Now, for the last time—go on!" He slapped Rebel's rump, and as the horse bolted, he shouted, "I've always loved you, Jess."

Places were already catching fire. Choking, he took off his wet shirt and beat what he could out. When that didn't work, he retreated behind the area he'd plowed and took stock of it. The only thing left to do was to set a backfire in front of it and pray while he wet the ground in back of it. Going to the team, he pulled off the harness, letting them go. Then he turned Jessie's horse loose, giving it a chance to escape.

He worked feverishly, carrying buckets, dumping them, carrying more as new flames licked the grass beyond the pitiful barrier. He couldn't breathe, he couldn't see, but he was going to do his damndest to save her place for her. Turning around with an empty bucket, he stumbled into her.

"What the hell are you doing here? I told you to get out!"

"I couldn't leave you. You've got to come or die, Ben."

"I'm not leaving the house."

She stared at him, choking back tears. "It's a thing, Ben. You're a man—save yourself."

Flying tinder landed almost at his feet, setting a new fire. As he tried to stamp it out, Jessie grabbed his arm, pulling him away from it. "I can build a new house, Ben. Please, listen to me. I don't care about the house."

"Look, I don't have much, Jess, I've got to keep trying."

"I don't want to lose you. You've got to come now, Ben," she cried. "*Please!*"

"All right."

He looked down at his hands, scarce seeing the dirt and soot on them. All he knew was he'd lost the battle for the house and barn and probably the sheep. Numb in defeat, he followed her to where Rebel waited nervously. With an effort, he caught the saddle horn, stepped into the stirrup and swung into the saddle. Before he could lean down to help her, Jessie was pulling herself up behind him.

The horse didn't need any urging. Stretching its neck in the smoky air, it raced for the nearly dry river, where the sheep milled and bleated in shallow pools of water. The bed was wide, sandy, and pretty much bare of vegetation, making it as good a place as any to wait and watch Jess's whole life go up in smoke.

The ewe Ben had carried earlier bumped against him as he dismounted. Tired beyond bearing, he slid to the ground and sat there, his head in his hands. Jessie came up behind him and stood there, stroking his hair.

"Why'd you come back, Ben?" she asked, her voice hoarse from shouting.

"I had too much to lose—my house, the animals—my wife. If you hadn't made it out of the fire, I wouldn't want to live."

Her hand stilled in his hair. "I was wrong to listen to Matheny, Ben."

"No. I'm not much good, Jess. If anybody was wrong, it was me, thinking I could have myself a decent woman to love."

"Maybe I'm not entirely decent."

He leaned forward to pick up a rock and toss it into the water. "If you're meaning that first time, you didn't know where I was leading you."

Dropping down beside him, she said softly, "I wasn't meaning that. Before you came pounding on the door tonight, I was fixing to write you already. I was going to tell you it's not right to bring a little one into the world without a father, that maybe you'd better come back." As he turned to her, his expression thunderstruck, she admitted, "It's too early to know that, but I figured if I worked at it, maybe I could make it happen before you found out I'd lied to you." Unable to meet his eyes now, she studied the burned holes in her sooty skirt. "I threw you out, but I couldn't let you go, Ben. Once I had my cry, I got to thinking if you hadn't lied to me, I'd have been worse off. And I *know* you're a good man."

"I was going to kill Jack Matheny for you."

"You didn't, did you?"

"I was waiting until morning. I was going to ride in there, figuring he'd expect to talk to me, and then I was going to kill him. I didn't think I had anything left to lose.''

"But you do, Ben. Even if we have to rebuild everything, we've got land, and—'' She stopped suddenly and raised her head. ''Do you feel that?''

''What?'' Straightening his shoulders, he sat stock-still. A lump formed in his throat, making it almost impossible to speak. ''Feels like a crosswind,'' he choked out. Forgetting his aches and misery, he all but jumped to his feet. And as he looked back over the farm, he could see the flames blowing the other way. ''My God, Jess, do you see it?'' he cried. ''Look at that! That's Matheny's land, not ours!'' Throwing his arms around her, he buried his face in her sooty, smoke-filled hair. ''We've still got the place.''

She clung to him for a moment, then stepped back enough to tilt her face and look into his eyes. ''Let's go home, Ben.'' Her hand brushed his hair back from his forehead. ''Together.''

By the time they reached the house, there wasn't much fire left. The roof was singed, but otherwise intact, and down by the place he'd plowed, most of the flames were burning out. Before he knew what she meant to do, she ran into the house, then came back with *Famed Gunmen of the West* in her hand. Marching to a small, isolated patch of burning grass, she threw it down and watched it catch fire. As the flames flared, and the pages curled, she looked across at him.

''I never knew that Ben Haley, anyway.''

''I reckon he's gone, Jess. Forever.'' The soot on his face cracked with his smile. ''I reckon it'll be enough just making an honest woman out of you.'' Watching her eyes widen, he added softly, ''I want to be around to look after that little one you were going to write about.''

''The mail rider came,'' Jess said, handing him the folded newspaper. ''I guess you're finally getting your subscription.''

"What? Oh, yeah." He glanced down, seeing the column of prices for cattle, sheep, eggs, and skins. And then his eyes found the boxed article in the center, and he read it twice to himself before repeating it aloud. "Listen to this, Jess. Deceased: The charred remains discovered on the Lazy M Ranch have been identified by Sheriff W. D. Mason as those of John R. Matheny, prominent area cattleman; V. J. Hacker, Lazy M foreman; and Wm. E. "Bill" Davidson, ranch employee. Apparently all three men died fighting last week's prairie fire. We extend our condolences to the families. Mr. Matheny and the others will be sadly missed."

"Not by me," she declared. "I think it was an act of God's justice."

"I figure they set the fire."

"Exactly."

"You see the hand of God in everything, Jess," he teased her.

"Well, He blew you in on a whirlwind, didn't He? And He brought you back in a fire, didn't He? The way I look at it, He was telling both of us you belonged here."

He pulled her onto his lap, and the paper slid to the floor. "I'm not arguing at all with that," he murmured, reaching for the pins in her hair. As it tumbled in lavender-scented waves over his arm, he whispered wickedly, "How are we doing on the little one?"

"We're still trying," she answered, smiling.

PRIDE'S WAY

 Patricia Potter

☞ *Chapter One* ☜

Colorado, 1870

The sudden mountain storm was both a blessing and a curse. But given the option, Pride Gideon knew he would rather die by nature's hand than by the hands of the men hunting him.

He felt like a wounded animal—alone and surrounded by predators he no longer had the strength to fight. His shoulder was bleeding badly, blood mixing with the pelting rain that slowed his progress to a near halt. His duster was soaked by both.

How far back were Jack Keegan and his bunch?

Pride readjusted the collar of his coat and pulled down the rim of his hat, but the rain came at an angle, and water dripped from his face down his neck.

God, he was cold. And weak. And hungry. He couldn't remember when last he'd eaten a decent meal or slept a night through. The pain in his arm kept him from resting even in the saddle, and brush tore at his face and legs. Sticking to the trail would have made things easier.

But he couldn't afford to use the trail.

Lightning flashed ahead, illuminating the forest for several seconds, its blinding forks crackling as it struck the ground. The sound of crashing trees merged with thunder that roared across the sky like stampeding buffalo.

The earth lit again with eerie brilliance, an arrow of the

lightning striking so close he thought he could reach out
and touch it. Too tired to bolt, his horse whinnied with
fear and trembled under him. The animal couldn't last
much longer.

And neither could he. He had to find shelter which
seemed damned unlikely. These mountains were rugged
and sparsely populated by any but the hardiest and most
determined of placer miners. The nearest town was Breck-
enridge, and that was too far—and too dangerous.

A cave? An abandoned miner's cabin? Pride knew it
would take a miracle to find either. And his life had held
precious few miracles. Nightmares, yes. Miracles, no.

What would King do?

King had always been there for him from the time their
parents died. He'd been six and King thirteen. But King
Gideon—brother, parent, friend—was dead, leaving him
more alone than he'd ever been in his life.

Loneliness crushed down around him, deeper than the
darkness, more agonizing than his wound. He was a man
without family or future. He had nothing left—except his
honor. He would keep his promise to King if it killed him.
Which it probably already had.

Pride leaned over the neck of his horse. "Just a bit
longer," he murmured just as a bolt of lightning blinded
him. A tree a dozen yards ahead split in two and burst into
flames. His horse reared with fright, and Pride's head hit
a thick low-hanging tree branch. He registered a second of
new pain, then everything went black.

Susannah O'Callaghan cursed the rain as she heaped the
last shovelful of mud onto the grave. She had suffered
through mountain storms before, and she knew the rain
might last days. She couldn't wait to bury her father.

"Pa," she whispered. "I'll miss you."

She would miss everything about him: his extrava-
gances, his bragging, his irresponsibility and, above all, his
heart. He had loved her and never let her forget it.

Elijah snorted nearby. The mule was now her only companion, though other animals had come and gone: a hurt wolf cub, an orphaned fawn, several squirrels that had thrust fear aside to eat from her pa's hands. Her father had been a regular pied piper of animals—and could have been of men had he devoted any energy to the pursuit. But he had been a man of dreams who'd followed rainbows, moving from one adventure to another, finally stopping here at a gold claim whose yield he'd embellished—as he embellished everything. To him, one grain of gold became a nugget, a promise became reality.

Her hand trailed over the mud. She wished she had a flower, but she'd had no heart to search out any in the storm. Tomorrow perhaps, or the next day. He would like mountain wildflowers.

Susannah stood, suppressing the ache in her back after digging so long in the mud. What now? Her father's killers might be near. Pa had ridden in hours ago, barely able to sit Elijah's back, falling off at the door.

She'd rushed to his side, cradling his head in her lap as he died. "Who?" she'd asked through tears mingled with rain. "Who?" she'd asked again, though she already knew who. Dave Gallagher had been threatening them for months if her father didn't sign away his claim.

"Gallagher," he'd gasped. "I shouldn't . . . have tried . . . to fight them. Leave. Leave now. They'll come after you."

But she couldn't leave. Wouldn't leave. Her father had fought for the claim, died for it. She wouldn't just run away and leave it for Gallagher. She wouldn't reward a killer.

So she'd lied. "I will, Pa."

"Swear it on your mother's name," he'd demanded, even as his voice grew weaker.

He knew her too well. She'd lied before. Hell's bells, he'd taught her that. But she wouldn't desecrate her mother's name.

"Swear it, Susannah Kathleen." His voice was growing fainter, and the light was fading from his bright blue eyes, eyes that usually laughed with devilment.

"Pa. . . ."

His hand had slipped from hers before she could finish the sentence, his eyes going vacant, staring at her. She'd used the palm of her hand to close them, and she sat, holding his hand as cold mountain rain pelted down on them.

She didn't know how long she'd sat there before, finally, she'd roused herself to bury him. She'd wrapped him in a sheet she'd laundered days ago. He was a small, slight man, though he'd always seemed very big to her, and she'd been able to drag him a few yards away to a proper burying place.

"You and me, kid," he used to say. "We don't need anyone else."

She hadn't. He'd always been enough for her, Pa and his dreams. But he had needed others. He'd loved to drink and gamble and tell tall tales. Daniel O'Callaghan liked to be the life of the party, which was what had brought him to this end. But she wouldn't have exchanged him for anyone else.

And now . . . now she was alone. She had no one.

Looking at the muddy grave, Susannah wished she had a cross. Perhaps she could find some wood tomorrow, or the next, when the storm ended. For now, thunder rumbled, shaking the earth, and lightning lit the grave like a halo. The angels would welcome a fast-talking, giant-hearted Irishman, she thought, smiling a little at the thought that Daniel O'Callaghan would simply talk his way into heaven if nothing else worked.

She said a prayer for him, then turned to Elijah, who, moments ago had been braying in dismay. But Elijah was gone!

She put a muddy hand up to her face, wiping the rain from her eyes, and looked around again. The storm had strengthened and, in the last few minutes, late afternoon had turned to evening. Dark was descending like a curtain.

She had to find Elijah. Aside from being her only transportation, Elijah was a friend. Her father had loved the dang mule. In fact, Elijah had followed her father around like a puppy in a distinctly unmulelike fashion.

Susannah hurried to the cabin and lit a lantern. She pulled on her father's rain slicker and headed outside, toward the steep trail they always took to the spot where her father had panned for gold. Urgency hurried her footsteps up the steep path that wound around a rise, then fell to the stream below. Elijah had traveled it often and she thought he might have gone looking for his master.

Susannah's tears started again as she pushed blindly ahead, ignoring the lightning flashing around and the growls of an angry god.

A flash of lightning illuminated the body sprawled across the ground. Elijah stood protectively above it.

Susannah's first thought was that the man might be one of her father's killers. Perhaps Pa had gotten off a shot before being wounded. She shone the lantern down toward the man's face. She didn't recognize him, and she thought she knew all the ruffians who rode with Gallagher.

Mindless of the mud, she kneeled down, flashing the lantern toward the prostrate figure. With her other hand, she laid her fingers on the pulse in his throat. He was alive. Then she saw the pink staining his duster. He'd been shot sure enough. If he rode with Gallagher, she figured, they would have taken him with them.

Susannah hesitated only a second. No matter who he was, she couldn't leave him out here to die. Despite the summer month, these mountains were often freezing at night, especially in a storm like this. She tentatively reached out a hand and shook his shoulder. "Mister."

Nothing.

She shook harder. "Mister," she shouted, the noise

mixing with a new roar of thunder. God's displeasure, her
pa had said. She unbuttoned the man's duster. He was
soaked through and through, and his body was shivering.
Her eyes went down to his hips. No guns. That was rare
out here. Perhaps someone took them.

"Mister," she said again. The rain pelted harder, and
lightning lit the sky at the same time she heard a movement
behind her. Elijah gave a warning, a sharp barklike sound,
and she whirled around.

The flickering light of the lantern revealed a woebegone
bay anxiously pawing the ground, seeking human com-
panionship in its misery. With a nod toward the unconscious stranger, she asked the horse, "Does *he* belong to
you?" Elijah would probably have answered; she sometimes thought the mule nearly human. But the bay merely
looked at her, exhausted.

"Aye, I think so," she answered herself, hoping the
sound of her voice would chase away her own fear and
the loneliness that was seeping through her as the shock—
if not the pain—of her pa's death receded.

She leaned down to the stranger's face, wishing she
knew what to do. He would die of exposure if she left
him, bleed to death probably, as her father had. Maybe
even by the same hands.

Well, dang it all, Gallagher wouldn't claim another life
this day.

She slapped the man's face, once, twice. Then she shook
him. She couldn't possibly move him without his assis-
tance. He was much too large, so much larger than Pa.

But she wasn't going to let him die. "Wake up, dammit," she demanded in a harsh, frustrated tone. "Wake
up."

Much to her surprise, he responded. She heard a groan,
weak but discernible. She held her lantern next to his face.
As much as she tried to shield its opening from the rain,
she knew the small faltering flame would soon be
quenched. She had to get them back to the cabin. And fast.

The stranger's eyelashes fluttered open for a moment, closed, then fluttered again. The groan, coming from deep in his throat, was louder, stronger.

"Mister," she said urgently.

The eyes opened again, tried to focus against the light of the lantern as a crash of thunder seemed to split the very heavens. God must be very upset, indeed.

"You have to help me get you up on your horse," she commanded. "I can't do it alone."

"Go away," he whispered.

Stunned at his ingratitude, Susannah rocked back on the balls of her feet. Then she started to get angry. Pa hadn't had a chance to live. This man did, and by God, he was going to take it.

"I'm not leaving, and you're going to get up on that dang horse before we both freeze to death," she said angrily.

He blinked a moment, then his mouth seemed to curve into the smallest smile before it turned to a grimace. "You don't . . . understand. I'm trouble. You don't want . . . to get involved."

"Hell's bells," Susannah said impatiently. "I know you're in trouble. No angel put that bullet in you, and no one in his right mind would be riding alone in this storm unless they're being hunted. But I can't leave you out here. Now get your hide moving before this lantern goes out and we never get back."

The stranger moved his head as if searching for someone else. "You're . . . alone?"

"You don't see anyone else, do you?" she said, trying to keep her anxiety to herself. Perhaps it wasn't a good thing bringing a stranger to the cabin. Even a wounded stranger. But she still couldn't bring herself to leave him to die.

"My pa will be around directly," she said, hoping the lie sounded like truth, wishing it *were* the truth.

The stranger tried to sit, putting a hand to his head for

a moment as if to hold it still. Then slowly, painfully he rose to his knees. She held out a hand to him, not knowing whether or not she was strong enough to support even a portion of his weight.

He looked just as dubious.

The light in the lantern flickered out. "Dang nab it," she cursed.

"The . . . reins," the stranger said. "Find the reins of my horse."

Susannah wasn't so sure about fumbling in the dark on the steep path, but she didn't see any other way. Carefully, very carefully, she put one step in front of the other, testing the ground as she moved toward the spot where the spooked horse had been standing.

"Now, sweetheart," she crooned. "Everything will be all right. We have a nice shelter for you . . . and even some oats Elijah will share." She felt the horse's breath, heard the frightened snort, but the animal didn't move away. Her hands found the reins, and clutched them in her soaked gloves. "I have them," she said.

Lightning flashed again, and she saw the stranger. He was on his feet, leaning against a tree for support. Elijah had not moved, though his ears were straight up.

"Dammit," the man said. "You're just a kid."

Susannah's temper nearly exploded. She knew she didn't look like much, especially mud-covered and tented by her father's coat, but she wasn't a kid, hadn't been for a long time. She thrust the horses's reins into the stranger's hands and went to Elijah. "Come, Elijah," she said, "we'll go back alone."

The stranger swore under his breath, but she sensed the meaning of his words and closed her ears.

She muttered to herself about ingrates. Well, she'd done her bit. He had his horse, and he had the reins.

And *she* had Elijah. If nothing else, the mule could pick his way down the mountainside blindfolded. And he might as well have been blind unless mules could see through the night a dang sight better than humans.

"Wait," the stranger said, his voice weak but determined. "You can't go alone . . . in this . . ."

"How do you think I got here?" Susannah demanded, thinking it loco for him to be worried about her rather than his own sorry condition.

The only response was the sound of labored breathing barely audible above the rain. She sensed he was about to fall; he'd hardly been able to lean against the tree. She sighed. The stranger obviously couldn't mount his horse by himself, nor could he move alone in this darkness.

"Dang fool," she said under her breath, including herself in that description as well as him.

She wished for the lightning again, even though it scared the living wits from her. As if summoned, an arrow of light illuminated the sky, then another, and the second caught a nearby tree, exploding in flames that would quickly be quenched by rain. It was enough, though, to see the stranger still slumped against the tree, his hand holding loosely to the reins of a horse half-mad with fright.

"You take the mule," she said, pulling a reluctant Elijah toward the man while the last flickering flames from the tree lit the way. "Just lean over his back, and I'll help you get a leg over." She prayed that Elijah would be cooperative.

The man let out a heavy sigh, so heavy it stabbed through the darkness to pierce her heart, which was already sorely wounded.

"I thank you, but . . ." His voice faltered.

"But nothing," she said angrily. "I can't go off and leave you like this, and I'm nearly drowned already. Now get on Elijah. He'll lead us down."

She prayed her voice held enough authority to convince him.

Apparently, it did. She heard surrender in his voice even as he uttered one last protest. "My . . . horse."

"Doesn't seem much good for anything, but I'll lead him and hold onto Elijah's tail. He knows the way."

"There're men . . . after me."

"Well, they won't get far in this weather," Susannah said. dismissing the fact. Hell's bells, with Gallagher after her, a few more men didn't scare her. Not nearly as bad as this weather at the moment, anyway.

The last flickering light from the flaming tree was gone and they were plunged back into total darkness.

"Mister?" she ventured.

There was only the sound of the pounding rain again.

"Mister?" she said louder. "Dang it, we can't stay here all night."

"All . . . right," he said. "But when we get . . . down from here . . ." His voice was growing weaker, whether from exhaustion or loss of blood she didn't know. She kept remembering Pa, how he bled to death.

She took the horse's reins from the stranger who was only a wavering blob in the darkness. She waited as the blob merged with the larger one of the mule, and she heard a groan, then an "oomph" as he hoisted himself across Elijah's back. Susannah prayed again that Elijah wouldn't buck as he usually did when a stranger neared, but the animal seemed to sense her urgency—or else he simply longed for shelter as much as she did.

Firmly clutching the reins of the horse in one hand, she was able to help the stranger get a leg over Elijah's back. "Go home," she yelled to Elijah through the rain, hoping like the blazes he understood her as well as he'd always seemed to understand her pa.

The mule started moving, and she held on to its tail for all she was worth, hoping he was heading for home and not the stream. She had lost all sense of direction.

Thunder rolled across the sky again, followed by forks of lightning, and she saw the stranger slumped low over Elijah's neck. The rain was coming faster than ever, and the ground seemed to slip away under her feet. She closed her eyes and prayed as she set one foot in front of the other.

That was all that mattered. One step, then another. She would worry about Gallagher later. She would worry about the stranger later.

Just one step, then another.

Chapter Two

The last thing Pride wanted was to draw a kid into his troubles. But he had damned little choice. An instinct for survival flamed in him, undeniable and inexorable. Once he was off this cursed mountain, though, he would push on. The storm should wipe out all traces of his trail.

A few moments rest, some food. Perhaps even some oats for his exhausted horse. So little.

So much.

How long had he been running now? Seemed like forever. This night seemed like forever, the storm endless. He was so cold and wet and tired . . .

He felt himself slipping from the mule. He could barely stay astride a damned animal. He thought about the kid on foot behind him. Gutsy as hell, but damned foolish for helping a stranger. Particularly one named Pride Gideon. He couldn't even remember when last anyone had offered him help, and he sure as hell didn't want the boy to suffer for it.

Concentrate! Concentrate on remaining conscious. Concentrate on remaining on the mule's back. Concentrate on living.

But why?

To run into another Keegan?

Because he owed it to the kid, who was traipsing behind

him, risking a fall from a mountain to save his sorry neck.

And then, thankfully, the mule stopped. Pride stayed seated on the animal, unsure in the blackness whether they had reached whatever destination the kid intended.

"We're here," he heard the boy say. The kid had a throaty voice, husky, and Pride wondered how old he was. He also wondered whether the father had arrived. If he had, Pride knew he would be quickly sent on his way. Everyone knew the name Gideon. And he damned well was not going to lie about it. Not ever.

"Mister?" the voice queried.

"I'm still alive," he acknowledged. Damn, it was black. Thunder still rolled around the heavens, but the lightning had moved on, leaving a drenching darkness.

"Figured as much since you're still on Elijah," the boy said laconically. "Can you get off?"

Good question.

He tried to move his leg. Nothing worked. He swore to himself, then tried again. This time his leg came over, and he slipped down, his legs buckling under him. He lay there for a moment, in the rain and mud, and thought about closing his eyes. If he did, he knew he wouldn't open them again.

He tried to move, and new pain raced down his arm. His limbs refused to obey his commands. He could only lie there, helpless.

"Take my hand."

The words drifted in and out of his consciousness. Fingers intertwined with his, and he felt an unexpected strength in them.

"You can do it."

The intrusive voice wouldn't stop. It demanded. But it also beseeched. The latter gave him will.

His hand tightened around the lad's, and he struggled to his knees, then to his feet, and stumbled to a doorway, a thin arm half-supporting him. He was conscious of a door opening, then entering a dark cabin and being deposited on a narrow bed.

Pride lay there, exhausted, his breathing hard, ragged; his body shivering; his arm throbbing with pain. The sound of the striking match echoed in the room, then light flickered. He heard logs drop, another match struck.

He registered the sounds and their meaning even as the gray fog in his mind grew more intense, darker, and pain began to fade. . . .

Susannah finished fueling the fire, looking on with satisfaction as red embers glowed, sparking a larger blaze that would soon warm the room. She pushed the pot of stew she had started earlier over to a corner, then huddled closer to the new struggling flames. The warmth was pitifully small.

Shivering, she turned to the stranger. His eyes were closed, but she heard his rough breathing. He lived, and that was something. She'd doubted his prospects, had expected him to fall along the trail.

Susannah sighed. She would have to see to Elijah and the horse before she could change to dry clothes. Hurrying outside, she took both animals into the small lean-to, quickly dried their coats as much as possible and poured grain into buckets for them. Then she returned to the cabin, shedding her pa's slicker and the hat she'd worn, shaking out her long hair. She was soaked through. And so was the stranger. They both needed dry clothes. And he was in no shape to undress himself.

Susannah had often undressed her pa, when he came home drunk, but only his outer clothes. A stranger was a different matter altogether.

She went over and peered at him. His face was covered with bristle. His hair was dark, almost black and wet tendrils clung to his forehead. If he'd had a hat, he'd lost it when he'd fallen from his horse.

She inched the duster from one of his arms, then rolled

him over onto his back. He groaned but didn't wake. She managed to disengage the rest of the soaking garment and, once more, took stock. He wore a plaid wool shirt, as many miners did, and denim trousers. Most of the shirt was dark with blood, and she saw bright red oozing from a hole ripped in the garment. Now she was sure he'd been hit by a bullet.

Even in the dim light inside the rough cabin, she could see he was pale. She would have to stop the bleeding, and she knew only one way to do it: cauterize the wound.

She unbuttoned his shirt, only to find a wool undershirt beneath. She would have to cut both away to reach the wound. As she tried to tug the outer shirt off his shoulder, she felt a wad in one of the pockets, and she took it out, smoothing out the wet paper.

The fragile paper curled, but she could decipher the picture and some of the writing.

WANTED DEAD OR ALIVE, it said. She bit her lip as she tried to read the blurred writing: *King Gideon, Wanted for Murder. One thousand dollar reward.*

Susannah couldn't make out the rest. Probably a description. She didn't need it, though. The picture was unmistakable. The cheekbones, the firm chin, the deep-set eyes.

Even *she* had heard of King Gideon, one of the most notorious gunfighters in the West. She stared at the man lying on her pa's bed. He looked younger than she would have thought, though pain had burrowed lines in his face.

Why had he kept the poster? Had Gallagher hired him? Had he been the one who killed her pa? The thoughts flashed through her mind as fiercely as the lightning streaking across the sky. She swallowed hard. Was she helping Pa's killer?

Then reason took over. Gallagher couldn't afford a gunman like King Gideon, and he wouldn't pay good money to hire someone to do his dirty work if he didn't have to.

A shot in the back was more Gallagher's style, and her father had offered little challenge.

Her mind raced onward. If Gideon didn't work for Gallagher, perhaps he would work for *her*. She had a few ounces of gold dust, and if she saved his life he would owe her. He would owe her big.

Hope glimmered in Susannah's heart. She wanted Gallagher dead. She wanted him to pay for her father's death.

But first she had to keep the gunman alive.

She shivered, wishing the cabin would warm faster as she found a knife. Returning to the injured stranger, she thought again that it was strange he didn't wear guns. She wouldn't have thought someone as notorious as King Gideon would ever be without them. She shrugged the thought away. There had to be an explanation.

She hoped he had some other clothes in his saddlebags because her father's clothes would never fit him. She tried to think of that—and other things—as she pushed and pulled him onto his side. With both sides of his shoulder visible, she sliced her knife through the undershirt. Two wounds. So the bullet had passed through. One blessing at least. But while the bleeding had slowed at his back, the wound in front was still bleeding steadily.

She knew she had to work fast. She wanted to cauterize before he regained consciousness. The thought was horrifying to her, but she knew it had to be done, and she'd stopped being squeamish years ago. Living alone in the wilderness with only her pa had forced her to do a lot of things she hadn't liked. She knew how to use a knife, how to skin an animal, and how to administer basic care for illness and wounds. She even knew how to cauterize a wound, having done it once on Pa.

As she heated the knife in the now roaring fire, she washed the wound, praying the man wouldn't wake. As usual, her prayers weren't answered; she saw him move, his eyelids fluttering. He jerked away from her hands, sitting halfway up, balancing himself on his good arm.

"Mr. Gideon," she said disapprovingly. "You must stay still."

His eyes flew open, and she saw alarm in them.

"You know . . . my name?" The question was part exclamation, part groan.

Susannah bit her lip, not wanting to tell him she had snooped in his pockets. "Please stay still. You're still bleeding."

He looked at her then, his face creased with weariness and pain, his eyes alert, searching. His gaze became puzzled. "The kid . . . ?"

"That was me," she said defensively. "My pa's slicker and hat . . ."

His gaze moved from her around the cabin. "Where . . . is he?"

She wasn't ready to tell him that Pa had died hours earlier, that she was alone. He looked too much the brigand, and his reputation was too fierce. *Wanted . . . Dead or Alive.* Had she been completely loco to bring him here?

But she'd had no choice. And she could only hope—pray—that he could help her. She wasn't sure either her pa or God would approve of her trying to use a gunman to exact vengeance. But then, God hadn't been much help lately, and maybe the appearance of the mysterious stranger was a sign of some kind. She didn't want to think that maybe the devil had interceded.

"Pa's . . . gone for a little while," she said, finally.

"You're alone?" His tone was disbelieving.

"I can take care of myself. Better than you, it appears."

He grinned weakly. "You might be right." Then, he struggled to move, a gasp coming from his throat as he did. Blood gushed from the two wounds.

"You're lucky. The bullet went through your shoulder. But you're still bleeding and . . ." She couldn't finish the sentence, seeing the pain evidenced by his tightly clenched jaw.

"Do it," he said.

She stared at him.

"I see the knife in the fire," he said. "If you can do it, I can take it. I have to get out of here."

"What . . . what happened to your guns?"

His eyes narrowed. "Why do you care?"

She *did* care—desperately—but she sensed that if she told him why, he'd try to get to his feet and scat, then and there. She'd have to wait until the debt was stronger.

"No reason," she said. "Just that most men carry them out here."

He stared at her for a moment with hard green eyes, but he didn't answer her question. Instead, he said roughly, "You going to use that knife or not?"

Susannah stared back at him, trying to decipher his answer. He was a gunman. Of course, he carried guns. Was he trying to protect his identity?

He fell back on the bed, evidently exhausted. His heavy breathing mixed with the sound of crackling flames and pelting rain outside. He grimaced, then nodded. "Go ahead."

She hesitated.

The thunder rumbled and, through the cracks of the boarded window, she saw lightning light the sky. The storm hadn't passed, after all. How many more days would it continue? Summer mountain storms often seemed endless, terrifyingly violent in the wilderness. Especially now that she was alone. All alone.

Except for a gunman.

And other gunmen waiting to attack.

But they would wait until after the storm. Nothing could move in this weather.

The stranger's body was tensed, ready for additional pain. She reluctantly took the few steps to the hearth, picked up a rag and plucked the knife from the fire's heated core. Then she retraced her steps.

His eyes were green, very green—dulled with pain but still startling. They were deep-set, framed by thick dark lashes and bushy eyebrows and they bore into her, willing her to do what had to be done.

"Do it," he commanded as she hesitated.

Her hand tightened around the rag-covered handle. She handed him another rag. She didn't have to explain its use. He put it into his mouth and bit down on it.

She touched the knife to the exit wound first, held it there several seconds as the skin sizzled, the smell of burning flesh nauseating her. His body went rigid, then relaxed, and she knew he had lost consciousness. Quickly, she turned him and cauterized the entrance wound, then, swallowing hard, went to look for a bandage.

He was riding hell-bent toward Leadville. Dammit, he should have known, should have realized that the errand King had sent him on was a diversion—an excuse to keep him from town.

King had told him Shep Reynolds was interested in buying four of the wild horses they had captured and broken— the first of a herd that King hoped would free him from a lifetime of killing. Reynolds wanted the horses, all right, but then one of his men asked Pride why he wasn't in Leadville to back King.

Shep Reynolds had looked away, and suddenly Pride knew his brother was facing yet another challenge to his supremacy as one of the West's top guns.

He also knew how tired King Gideon was. The last five years had been hell for his brother—always moving, always knowing someone seeking to make his reputation would be in the next town, waiting.

"They don't know," King once had told him. "They don't know the hell they seek. . . ."

Pride's horse panted and wheezed as he raced back toward town. Foam flecked his mouth but Pride dug in his spurs. He saw the buildings ahead, the street . . . the men standing in the street . . . two men on the ground.

He jumped from his horse and ran to his brother, lying

prone in the dust. "King!" he yelled. "King!"

Blood everywhere. No movement in his brother's body. But then, lips moved. "Promise . . . me you won't use guns," he said. "Promise," and a hand lifted to grip his own.

Stricken, he grasped his brother's hand. "I promise," he said. "I swear it."

Life faded then from the intense dark eyes he knew so well.

"King!"

The shout woke Susannah. She had changed to dry clothes, brushed her hair dry and seated herself next to her patient. She must have dozed . . .

King! Why would he be shouting his own name? She must have misheard.

She reached over and touched the bristled cheek. It was cool. No infection. Yet. Hopefully no pneumonia, either, though she hadn't been able to take off his wet trousers. He was just too heavy to lift, and she hadn't wanted to cut them for fear he had no others. Instead, she had piled blankets on him and kept the fire going.

He *was* going to live. Her pa had died, but this man wouldn't. He would live, and he would protect her—and the claim—from Gallagher. Gallagher would run from a man with King Gideon's reputation. He *had* to.

Her hand lingered on the gunman's brow. She wondered how he would look washed and shaven, whether his face would be as appealing as the rest of him. He was tall and rangy, but muscled. His arms were strong, and his chest like a piece of century-old oak. She already knew he had strength and courage. He hadn't flinched once when she'd cauterized his wound before losing consciousness. And, given the condition of his horse, it appeared he'd gotten a long way before loss of blood had beaten him.

Her hand seemed to soothe him. His restless movement

ceased, and his breathing became more regular. Finally, his strangled cries stopped.

He looked unexpectedly vulnerable, this stranger. Yet he was an outlaw, a gunfighter. But who was he running from? From what she heard, King Gideon never ran from anyone.

And where were his guns?

Pride woke to burning pain and ravenous hunger. He was warm, though. For a moment he took refuge in the pile of blankets over him, but then he remembered. Jack Keegan. The girl.

He couldn't lead Keegan here. Keegan was a killer who wouldn't draw the line at hurting a woman. He had to get the hell out, if it wasn't already too late.

He tried to move his arm. Thank God, it worked. The bullet must have missed doing major damage to his shoulder, though a vein had to have been clipped, given all the bleeding he'd done. Next, he tried to sit. His head spun. Dammit, but he was weak.

The storm was still raging outside. Rain pounded against the roof, and thunder rolled in the distance. The weather should keep Keegan pinned down for a while. Horses couldn't move in this weather, and by now his trail would be wiped away. Still, Keegan knew the general direction he'd taken, and there weren't that many trails heading northwest.

Pride's gaze surveyed the room. The woman was sitting in a chair near him, her eyes closed, her hands clutching the cloth she'd given him to bite on. A long braid fell over her shoulder and between her breasts. Tendrils of tawny hair framed an interesting and attractive, though not precisely beautiful, face.

Her cheeks were smudged, streaked as if tears had recently fallen. She was dressed in a miner's shirt, one big enough to make it impossible to determine much else about her body, and a pair of trousers. She looked small and helpless and alone.

And she had probably saved his life.

He recalled the unexpected strength in her hand. She might be small, but she certainly wasn't helpless. She could have left him, *should* have left him, but instead had risked her life for him. She could well have fallen off that slippery trail.

The best thing he could do for her now was skedaddle. As fast and far as he could.

He tried to swing his legs off the bed. His trousers were still damp, and his feet were encased in his boots; the rest of him was bare. The floor seemed to move under his feet as he tried to stand. He wavered back and forth like a willow tree in a hard wind.

Waves of pain radiated from his shoulder, nearly swamping him, but he maintained his stance and tried a short step. That was too much. He crumpled slowly downward in a spiral like a child's top.

Halfway to the floor, he felt his arm being caught, breaking his descent, keeping him from landing on his wounded shoulder. Again, he felt that unexpected strength as he slid to the floor.

"Dang fool thing to do," the woman said.

She had a husky voice, but it was also musical despite her blunt words.

"Can you help me to my horse?" he managed, biting his tongue to keep from yelling out in pain.

"No," she said. "You wouldn't get a snail's distance. Both you and that horse are spent."

She was bent over him as she let go of his arm and her shirt moved upward, stretching over her breasts and outlining a slender but curved body. She was older than he'd first thought, probably around twenty.

Frustrated by his own weakness, Pride sat against the bed, unable to summon the strength to try to hoist himself back onto the mattress, much less onto his feet and through the door. Drawing a deep breath, he caught a scent that made him sniff the air. The aroma of food drifted over him; he'd been oblivious to it earlier, concentrating only on reaching a standing, walking, maneuvering position.

He sniffed again.

"I have some stew," the woman said. "It's been cooking since yesterday, and it's probably burned some but . . ."

He could have eaten half a horse without pausing. "I'd be beholden," he said. Then he grinned weakly. "I'm already beholden, but . . ."

He noticed her eyes then. Dark brown. And . . . haunted. Sad. But not afraid, not the way she should be with a perfect stranger in her cabin, one that was gunshot and obviously running.

"Miss . . . or is it Mrs?"

"Susannah O'Callaghan," she said. "Call me Susannah. I think we're past fancy formalities."

True enough, he thought, glancing down at his chest and the bandage covering only part of it. "Your pa?" He tried to focus. "You said he would be coming." He'd thought she said it, anyway, but he wasn't sure. He'd been so tired and weak and hurting.

Her jaw set, and her lips trembled slightly. "That's right," she said.

But she wasn't a very good liar, and he realized no one was coming. How long had she been alone?

He didn't ask. Apparently she felt safer with the lie, safer from him. The thought shouldn't hurt, but it did. He'd never consciously hurt a woman in his life; hell, King had made sure he never hurt anything, period. *Don't be damned like I am.* He could still hear his brother's voice speaking the words.

So he merely nodded. "Smells good."

Susannah smiled then, and her face lit like a sky full of stars. She held out her hand again. He couldn't remember now how many times she'd offered it to him. Too many.

He took it, using her strength to pull himself up to sit on the bed.

But he didn't want to let go of her hand. It was small, warm, steady. Giving. He couldn't remember the last time he'd been touched that way.

King had been a good brother. Hell, he'd protected him, saved his life when they were both kids, fed him, made sure he had schooling. He'd taught him to use guns, and then had taught him not to use them. But neither tenderness nor gentleness had ever been part of his world.

"Mr. Gideon . . ." She said his name as she eased her hand away and he remembered she'd used it before.

"You know my name?"

"I . . . you . . . a poster dropped from your pocket when I took your shirt off."

He wondered whether that old poster had dropped or whether she had searched his clothes. From the flushed look on her face, he suspected the latter. He couldn't blame her, though. She would have been foolish not to look for signs of his identity.

Pride sighed. He didn't even know why he'd kept that old poster, particularly after King was absolved of any guilt in the incident that had led to its making. Except it was the only picture he had of King.

"I'll leave as soon as I get some food in my belly," he said, wondering why she had allowed him to stay this long. Most people didn't want any part of gunfighters—or their kin. With Keegan on his tail, he well understood why even the best of Samaritans would want to be rid of him.

She bit her lip, looking more uncertain than at any time since he'd first seen her. "I . . . have need of a gunfighter," she finally said.

"Gunfighter?" he echoed, wondering whether the weakness in his body also made him hard of hearing. Or simple.

"I don't have much money," she hurried on. "A few

small nuggets of gold, but you can have that, and I figure your life is worth something, and . . .''

"Whoa, there," he said, stopping the rush of words. "I couldn't whip a mad fly."

"But in another day," she said, "and with some food and rest . . .''

He tried to concentrate. He really did, but the biting hunger in his stomach, the ache in his head, and the burning agony in his shoulder made it nigh onto impossible.

"I'm not a gunfighter," he said, still befuddled with pain, and the totally unexpected conversation.

"The poster . . ."

And then he understood. That damned poster. She believed he was King. "I'm not—"

"Think about it," she said, cutting him off. Then she turned back to the fire and the pot that hung over the flames.

He stared at her stiff back as she stirred the contents, then poured some into a bowl.

He had to eat. He wouldn't get far without food—or rest. And then he would tell her. She had the wrong brother. The Gidcon who could have helped her was dead. And the one who was left . . . well, he had his own troubles.

Pride watched her as she moved gracefully, the shirt failing to conceal her lovely body underneath. Where was her man? Father? Husband? Protector?

And, most interesting of all, why in the hell did she need a gunfighter?

~ *Chapter Three* ~

Hⁱow does a person go about hiring a gunfighter?

From the look on his face, not the way she had done it. But he had to help her. He *had* to.

Susannah saw the denial forming on Gideon's lips, and she felt heat rush to her cheeks. Mortified by her stumbling attempt, she turned away and busied herself by finding a spoon for his bowl of stew. The stew was thick from cooking too long and it smelled burnt. Tears rushed to her eyes as she remembered making it yesterday morning—a year ago—while she waited for Pa to return from his claim. No more music, no more tales of the old "sod," no more laughter. The stranger—and his wounds—had served to dull the pain for a while but it came back, as sharp as ever. Pain. And anger. And even fear.

But she wouldn't run, not even if the gunfighter wouldn't help her. She knew how to use Pa's shotgun, which hung in its spot over the fireplace.

Blinking back tears, using a sooty hand to wipe away those that had escaped, she turned back to her patient. He was watching with green, secretive eyes.

She thrust the bowl into his hands and turned away again before he could see too much. She didn't want to expose her weakness.

"If you have only a dollar, Susannah, use it to buy a

*lace handkerchief rather than a meal. If people believe you
have money. they will give you money. If they believe you
are unafraid, when really you're terrified, they will respect
you. Perception, Susannah, is everything."*

She could almost hear her pa now. He'd said those
words so many times, and, God knows, he'd lived by them.

Susannah faced the man sitting on her pa's bed. He was
eating, his gaze on the stew which disappeared rapidly. He
ate as if he were starving. She heard him scrape the bottom
of the bowl, and she took the container from him, refilling
it without words.

He ate the second bowl, then drank a tin cup of water
she gave him. When he'd finished both, he sighed.

"That was mighty good, ma'am."

"The stew was burnt," she replied.

"Was it? I didn't notice."

Of course he hadn't, not the way he'd been shoveling
it down his throat. "When was the last time you ate?"

He looked surprised, and then puzzled. "I really
couldn't say."

"That long?"

"Yes, ma'am."

"Why?"

His eyes looked at her from under impossibly long, dark
lashes. "I'm being hunted."

"By a posse?"

"No, ma'am," he said, leaning back against the wall of
the cabin.

She knew what he must be seeing. The cabin was little
more than a one-room shelter. Her part was sectioned off
by a curtain, now drawn partially to reveal her own bed.

"You said your pa was coming?"

Susannah hesitated. For some crazy reason, she felt she
could trust him. Maybe because when she'd found him on
the mountain, his concern had been for her welfare, not
his own. Still, he was a gunfighter, a wanted outlaw, albeit

one she wanted to hire. But he couldn't be worse than Gallagher.

"He was killed yesterday," she said.

For the second time, she saw surprise, even shock in his eyes. "Yesterday?"

She swallowed hard. She had managed to avoid reality until now. She nodded.

"What happened?"

"He was shot. He made it back here to warn me. I'd just buried him when . . . Elijah took off, and I followed him. That's when I found you." She was rattling on. Probably making no sense at all, but then she saw something like compassion flicker through his eyes. Compassion and understanding. He held out his hand to her and without thinking she wrapped her fingers in his.

Empathy radiated from him, and it was her undoing. The tears she'd blinked away earlier started coming—hard and heavy, and unstoppable.

His hand tugged her, drawing her over to sit beside him on her father's bed. His arms went around her, holding her tight, as her body trembled, and she heard small whimpering sounds burst from her throat. The tears wouldn't stop; they came with a fury that equalled the tempest outside the cabin. She suddenly realized her arms were around his neck and he was holding her against his naked chest.

"It's all right," he was saying over and over again. "Let them come, you'll be better for it."

She no longer had a choice. She cried until she had no tears left, until she felt dry and hollow, and the aloneness overwhelmed her. She clung to him, to ward it off, even knowing he would soon be gone and she would truly be alone.

She felt his mouth touch her cheek, then her eyes, and she allowed it, needing that contact as she'd never needed anything in her life, needing that warmth.

Her gaze went to his, and she saw that his dark green

eyes glittered with moisture. And then he closed them, and his mouth pressed against hers, first with gentleness, then with a hunger that stunned her, a hunger she returned. A hunger, she realized, born of sorrow and need and loneliness.

However it began, though, the kiss soon turned tumultuous, like the lightning outside, like the thunder that resounded through the skies. As fierce—and sweet—as anything she'd ever known.

She forgot to breathe, forgot to think, forgot everything except the feel of his lips and the pounding of her heart. Their lips crushed together, and Susannah knew suddenly that he had also lost someone and had yet to mourn. His kiss was too desperate, too needing. Like hers.

Emotion thrummed between them like strings being played by a master fiddler, raw emotions echoing against one another while, outside, other forces of nature raged. Susannah felt her blood heat, then rush like a storm-swollen creek throughout her body.

His face was rough against hers, but his lips enticed even as they demanded, even as they parted hers and his tongue inched inside. She hadn't known a kiss like this before, had never known its pleasure or its agony.

Sensations blazed through her, like the lightning streaking through the forest, fostering wild fires that seared everything in their path. The mere touch of his hand on her face made her shudder with response, and her body was singing in ways she'd never experienced.

But more astounding, more frightening, was the depth of feeling she shared with him, two souls meeting, sharing, giving. She'd known him only a few hours, but she'd known him forever. . . .

How could that be?

Mindlessly, she lost herself in him, in the comfort of his arms, in the stirrings he created in her body. In an affirmation of life. He seemed to sense her surrender—no, not surrender, her need—and his tongue moved sinuously, sensually, deliciously, across and around her tongue in a primitive mating dance.

Her arms went around him, her fingers playing in the dark, curling hair at his neck.

He groaned and slid down on the bed, pulling her with him, their mouths still clasped together, their bodies now reaching for each other despite the clothes they wore.

Her body strained toward his, and she felt the bulge in his trousers. Pressure was building between them, the same kind of intense electricity that had permeated the air prior to the summer storm. She tasted the salty sweat on his face, heard his harsh breathing, felt the quickened beat of his heart, and raw need rocked her.

Their bodies moved together, strained together, became intertwined with a need that overwhelmed every other thought. His mouth left hers and moved across her face, placing small kisses like a trail of falling stars, each glowing fiercely as it burned its way into her consciousness.

His lips reached hers again, gentling, becoming more intimate. His fingers played at the back of her neck, and she felt a quickening deep inside, a craving for something she didn't understand but had to know.

"Susannah," he whispered. "So sweet."

And it was sweet. Whatever it was she was feeling was sweeter than anything she had ever known, more beckoning than the rainbow's end, more irresistible than heaven's call.

Or was it something sinful? She was against his body, her own fitting neatly into his crevices. He was filling her soul, her heart, chasing away the bewilderment, the terrible aloneness, erasing the fear, the unknown. He was strength, and she was greedy for it. Sin or not, she didn't care.

She moved, feeling the delicious abrasion of bodies, the natural reaction of one to another, the primitive need that made her body ache and her senses pound. His hand went to her left breast, caressing it through the cloth, and she felt it growing taut, full, tender.

"Susannah," he whispered again, the sound harmonizing with the tattering of rain against the roof, fading in the continued savagery of the storm inside and out.

But then she heard his sudden intake of breath as her body pressed against his shoulder.

His wound! How could she have forgotten that raw piece of skin, the pain that must be excruciating? She moved away—slowly, reluctantly, but her hand caught his and she wrapped her fingers around his fingers, unwilling to lose contact with his warmth, his magic.

"I'm sorry," she said softly.

"Don't be," he replied, drawing her hand upward and, with one of his own fingers, touching her chin with infinite gentleness. "You brought me back to life."

Susannah could only look at him, mesmerized by his words, his touch. He hadn't brought her back to life, he had brought her to life for the first time. She hadn't known she could feel like this, hadn't realized those vague longings inside could turn to something so exquisitely wondrous.

His hand, the free one, reached up and wiped away what she guessed must be remnants of tears, and that gesture returned the nightmare of the past day, the horror of her father's death. Guilt washed over her, erasing the new fine feelings, and she started to draw away.

"Don't," he said, his hand holding onto hers. "Don't feel guilty for being alive."

How did he knew what she was feeling?

She swallowed, her breath caught by a huge lump in her throat. "My pa . . ."

"Wouldn't want you to be alone," he said. "You loved him."

She nodded. "Of course."

His face changed, the green eyes darkening for a moment, and it occurred to her that her easy assumption of love was foreign to him.

Then, his gaze softening, he said, "Tell me about him."

She wanted to. She needed to. She had to keep Pa alive for a little longer.

"He was Irish," she said, "with a tongue that would tempt the angels from heaven, and dreams they would envy. Everybody liked him . . ." Her voice trailed off. Clearly, everyone hadn't liked him, or he wouldn't be lying out there under the mud.

She saw Gideon look around the bare, simple cabin, and she immediately felt compelled to defend Daniel O'Callaghan. "We've lived in fine places, real fine," she said, embellishing the truth only a little. Actually, they'd mostly lived in run-down boarding houses until Pa won this claim years ago.

When Gideon didn't say anything, she rushed on. "But Pa won this claim and he'd been working it hard. Making our fortune so he could build a mansion," she added defiantly, repeating the litany she'd heard so long—but never quite believed. It had hurt Pa that she hadn't, so she'd tried to convince herself.

His fingers continued to caress her face as he listened. "Didn't you ever get lonely?" he asked.

"Oh, we've always had critters," she said. "Pa was always finding sick and wounded animals and bringing them home. Elijah was beaten and starving when Pa bought him. He's never let anyone ride him but Pa, except last night. That was real strange, the way he let you stay on his back."

Gideon's eyebrows knitted together. "I don't mean animals, Susannah. People. Beaux."

"Beaux?"

"Courting. Haven't you ever been courted?"

She shrugged. "We've lived here since I was fifteen. One time I went to a mining camp with Pa, and an old miner . . . he, well . . . he tried to attack me. My pa nearly killed him." A shudder ran through her body, remembering. "After that, Pa went for supplies alone. We've been safe here until . . . until Gallagher and his men started claim jumping all up and down the creek.''

''Gallagher?''

''He killed Pa,'' she said. ''Pa told me just before he died. He said Gallagher would come here, and he told me to leave. But I can't. Not with Pa not having even a marker, I can't let Gallagher win and take Pa's dream as well as his life.'' She hesitated. ''That's why I need a gunfighter. You . . . you will help me, won't you? I have some money. You're famous, and—''

His hand stopped moving along her face, and he placed a finger on her mouth, hushing her.

''I'm not King Gideon,'' he said quietly.

''But you are. The poster—it's your picture.''

''It was my brother's picture.''

She stared at him, at the hard, bristled face that looked so much like the one on the poster. He *must* be lying.

''I'm not a gunfighter, Susannah. I don't even carry pistols, just a rifle I use for hunting food. And I'm running myself. I'll take you with me to someplace safe. But we'll have to leave soon, before the storm ends.''

Run? Run away from her father's murderers?

''No,'' she said flatly, taking her hand from his, almost jerking away from him. ''But if you're afraid, you can leave.''

Emotion flickered across his face at the contempt in her voice she hadn't tried to hide. He drew back, distancing himself from her, and all the warmth fled from the cabin. Susannah suddenly felt chilled.

''You're a Gideon,'' she tried again. ''I heard—''

''You heard my brother was a killer,'' he said coldly, ''that King Gideon didn't run from anyone. And he didn't. Not even at the last when he faced more guns that even he could handle. I watched him die, Susannah, after he went through ten years of hell, trying to put his guns away. And he couldn't. There was always a young gun wanting to prove his manhood, or a relative of that young fool seeking revenge. He didn't have a day of peace, and I saw him die bit by bit long before a bullet finished the job.''

Weariness laced Gideon's voice as he continued. ''King raised me from a pup. He looked after me for years, made sure I had teachers, although we were always moving. He always managed to find someone, some place. And he taught me everything there was to know about living in a desert or in high country.

''He tried to settle down a dozen times,' but some gunhand would come along and force a fight, and the law would order us to leave the territory. In all that time he never asked anything of me, not until he was dying. Then he asked that I never use a gun on a human being.''

Dark green eyes bore into her. ''My name is Pride, Susannah. Pride Gideon. And I made that promise to King. God knows, it hasn't been easy. He had enemies, and so I have enemies. But I won't break my word. Not because of Jack Keegan. Not even for you. If that makes me a coward in your eyes, then so be it.''

His words rang with passion and grief—and a belief she suspected she couldn't change. And with sudden insight, she suspected it had taken more courage for him to take the path he was following than it would to break his promise. But bitter disappointment soon overcame that generous appraisal.

''Who's Jack Keegan?'' she asked, desperate for more information, desperate to find some weapon that might make him change his mind.

''My brother killed his brother. A brother for a brother is the way he sees it,'' Pride Gideon said.

''Did he shoot you?''

Pride nodded. ''He's been on my trail for weeks. He got off a rifle shot yesterday morning, but then I lost him in the storm. He can't be far away.''

''Are you going to keep running?''

''I have an instinct for survival,'' Pride said dryly. ''Maybe I can lose him, head toward Montana. My brother and I captured some wild horses before . . . before he was killed. We'd broken and trained them, and a friend is keeping them for me. If I can make the north mountains, I can shake Keegan, send for the horses and start that ranch King always dreamed about.'' His voice softened. ''He would like that.''

Susannah felt hope drain from her. For a moment, she'd thought she might be able to shame him into helping her. Now she knew she couldn't. This was her battle. He'd already fought a private one of his own.

''Come with me,'' he said again. ''No amount of gold is worth either getting killed for or''—he hesitated—''killing.'' His hand reached out to her again. ''Killing does something to you, Susannah. I saw it destroy my brother. He lost a piece of his soul each time he used a gun until there was nothing left.''

''But he loved you.''

He hesitated, his jaw working, then he said, ''He felt *responsible* for me.''

Susannah felt he was holding something back. But then why wouldn't he? They were strangers, even though they'd shared moments of warmth.

''Come with me,'' he said again. ''Now.''

''I can't,'' she said. ''This is Pa's. He wanted me to have it.'' She wished she could explain better. The gold wasn't keeping her; God knew there was little left, if any. It was Pa. She just couldn't leave his dream to his killers. But she didn't think Pride Gideon would understand about dreams.

''You said he told you to leave.''

''But I can't,'' she said again. And she couldn't. She couldn't run from her father's murderers.

And regardless of what Pride Gideon believed, she could shoot, and she wouldn't mind killing the varmints that murdered her father.

''Go.'' She shrugged and got up from the bed. ''I have

some hardtack and jerky you can take with you. I'll be better off alone.''

Because she felt lost and alone she had meant the words to wound and, from the look on his face, she had succeeded. Unable to bear the effect of her own words, she went to the door and opened it. Rain blew in, soaking her, and thunder sounded in the distance. Though it was past dawn, the day was as dark as dusk. She shivered.

Where was Gallagher? And where were the men who sought Pride Gideon?

She shivered again. Despite it being summer, nights were cold in the mountains, and colder still during one of these storms. Pride would freeze out there.

So let him.

She'd been nothing but a tangle of emotions since she'd first found him, and never more so than now. With a resounding slam of the door, she braved the rain to make the trek to the lean-to. Checking Elijah and the horse was as good an excuse as any to avoid having to face Pride.

Pride knew he'd made one hell of a mess of the past hour. Damn, she'd even gone out in the rain to escape him. *Coward.* The word shone in her eyes even if she hadn't said it. But others had called him that and the label had hurt, particularly when he'd refused to face Keegan in a small mining town. Keegan had backed down then, because a town full of people were watching, but he'd vowed to kill Pride, gun or no.

Pride had had two choices: die or become like his brother. Any man who shot Keegan would become instantly famous—or infamous—and if his name were Gideon, God help him. Every would-be gunfighter in five states would soon be seeking him out.

So he'd run, though the personal price had been higher than he'd ever expected. And now, sooner than break his oath, he was refusing to help a woman who had saved his life.

He stood. The brief rest, w
some strength, though he wa
blood. The throbbing pain in his
unbearable. He took a step, then a
walk.

He paced around the cabin, testing
ing for a moment in front of a mirror. C
really him?

No wonder Susannah had mistaken him
the poster. Pain and weariness had added at
to his true age, and black bristles made him
brigand. He rubbed his hand along his cheek.
growth—or was it four? He'd lost track.

His shaving gear and another shirt were in his
bags. He would fetch them, change and shave, then
his way. The food and sleep had restored some of
strength, and he sure as hell didn't want to bring addition
danger down on Susannah, and his presence was sure to
do that. If Keegan knew she had helped him . . .

He cursed under his breath. He'd jumped from the fry-
ing pan into the fire, for sure. He kept trying to tell himself
he had no responsibility toward the woman, that, surely,
no one would go after her. But they would. He knew they
would. His illusions about the world had disappeared when
his own father had killed his mother in a drunken rage.

Pride closed his eyes, trying to figure a way out of this
mess. Even if Susannah agreed to go with him, they
couldn't make any kind of time with her on a mule, which
was all she appeared to have.

He opened the door but he didn't see her. She must have
gone to check on the animals again. The rain was still
heavy, the clouds still dense. The storm would last a while
yet. Keegan and his men would be bogged down someplace—as would the man, or men, who had killed Susannah's father. He hoped.

How much time did he have? Did she have?

Pride walked to the lean-to and stood just outside,

rets. Rain pum-
air. She, too,
ain, tendrils
around the
all, along
ame. He
he bags
horse

warmth and food had restored
still weak from loss of
shoulder was bad, but not
other. At least he could
his strength, linger-
d, was that horror
for the man in
east ten years
look like a
three days

the
the

he looked toward

ing he could think of better

e replied, her face too composed.

she had made decisions, decisions he suspected
ouldn't like. He'd seen that expression on King's face
too many times, always before a gunfight.

"Susannah—"

"I'll get some food for you," she said curtly. "Then
you can be on your way. Your horse is rested and fed."

He wanted to touch her again. He had only meant to
comfort her earlier, but he had somehow ended up taking
comfort himself. For a few magical moments, he had allowed himself to believe that he could have what King had
always wanted him to have: someone who cared.

But it was too late. For both of them.

Susannah finished tending the animals, then wiped her
face with a swipe of her arm. "I have to get ready," she
said with a dismissal that cracked his heart.

Ready to kill, ready to die.

She hadn't even lived yet. She hadn't been courted, or
loved, or probably even told she was beautiful. He'd
known as soon as he'd touched her how innocent she was.

Innocent and curious and filled with sweetness intriguingly cut by spice. Roses and thorns.

"How many men do you think will come after you?" he asked.

She frowned. "I don't know. Gallagher sometimes has four men with him, sometimes five. They've come by here several times trying to get Pa to sell his claim. Didn't want to give him anything for it, though."

"When will they come?"

"When the rain stops, I suppose. Probably went to Miss May's Sporting Palace in the mining camp after killing Pa. I heard killing does that to a man, makes him want a woman. But I guess you wouldn't know about that."

Pride stood stunned. "Where did you hear that?"

She shrugged. "I used to trail after Pa when I was frog high. Nobody ever paid attention to me, but there was nothing wrong with my ears."

There was nothing wrong with any part of her—except her obsession to go against unbeatable odds. And even that he understood. He'd wanted to kill the man who shot King. But then King's life would have been wasted. And he wasn't going to let that happen.

Pride fought himself. Every instinct he possessed urged him to help Susannah. Helping her, though, would mean betraying King. Unless he found a way to do it that didn't involve guns.

Pride shifted the rifle in his arms and stepped outside the lean-to. The rain pelted his upper arms, both cooling and irritating the burns on his shoulder. He tilted his head back, letting the water drip down his face.

Where are you, Keegan? How much time do I have?

But it didn't matter. He wasn't going anywhere. He couldn't shoot, but he also couldn't abandon Susannah.

Chapter Four

Susannah stole glances at Pride as he shaved. He seemed in no hurry to leave.

They had said little to each other since her return to the cabin. She had stopped for a few moments at her father's grave, wishing once more for some flowers to ease the ugliness of mud. When she had stepped inside, she'd found her reluctant guest shaving.

He had pulled on a shirt, which remained unbuttoned, and her gaze went to that magnificent chest again before moving upward toward the soapy face. She had seen her father shave, and paid it no mind, but watching Pride Gideon perform the intimate chore was something else altogether. Even his hands and arms moved with a sensuous grace that made her ache. She'd noticed it in the way he walked, too. In truth, he reminded her of a cougar she'd seen once in the distance. The sure, lithe movements—so aware, so cautious. Yet confident.

Yes, Pride had many of the instincts of a wild animal, but apparently not the instinct for killing.

As he shaved away the soap, wiping off the remnants with a towel, what emerged was a younger, less harsh countenance than the one on the poster. New beard had disguised a cleft in his chin, and the fine lines of a strong face. Pride Gideon was a very attractive man, though not what she would call handsome. His features were too stark, too rugged, to be labeled handsome. And his eyes were too piercingly green and alive for anyone ever to be comfortable under their scrutiny.

Yet, she had reveled in his comfort an hour ago, had shared intimacy and grief and desire. Unhappily, that desire was still strong, increasing in power every second she watched him. Her body tingled with it, with the aching want that began in her belly and spread to touch every part of her.

He's a coward, she kept telling herself. But the warning didn't work because the label didn't fit. He'd held his rifle with an ease that spoke of assurance. Nor had his face shown any fear as he'd spoken of the men chasing him, only a need to keep from killing and a conflicting desire to keep her from harm.

"You'd better go," she said with a harshness that made her voice unrecognizable, even to herself. She hadn't intended it to come out that way. "The rain could stop at any time."

He sighed, a lock of damp black hair falling over his forehead. "The rain should continue for a while," he said, "and my horse could use a few more hours rest."

"I don't want you here," she said. *Liar, Liar, pants on fire.* Both descriptions were true, she thought miserably, even as she tried to remember where she'd heard that rhyme.

He hesitated, dark brows furrowing together. "I can't leave you here alone."

"Then you'll help me?" Her glance went to the rifle propped against the wall.

"Not by killing," he said.

"Then you might as well leave. I don't have anything but this cabin, this land," she said.

"Damn it, Susannah, there's not enough gold on earth worth dying for."

"Certainly not in that creek outside," she agreed. "It's nearly played out, what little there was."

He looked stunned. "Then why . . . ?"

"Pa had a tendency toward exaggeration," she tried to explain. "We got a few small nuggets, but only enough for supplies. Unfortunately, Pa led Gallagher to think there was much more—a mother lode."

"Then tell him."

She shrugged. "He wouldn't believe me."

"Susannah!" Pride's voice was filled with frustration. "Then there's no reason to stay."

"There's every reason," she said bitterly. "For what it's worth, this cabin is my home. There's precious little gold, but it's all I've got. I have no place else to go." Her hands wrung together unconsciously. "And Gallagher won't get away with killing Pa."

"You can go to the law—"

"There's no law around here," she said. "Never has been, and everyone's scared stiff of Gallagher."

"Everyone, but damn fools," he muttered to himself.

But she heard him and felt her dander rising. Just because he didn't chose to fight for what was right, didn't mean no one else should.

"Go on," she repeated. "Run. I'll tell them you went in a different direction." She turned away from him, but her arm was seized and she was whirled around to face him.

"I have a damn good notion to tie you up and drag you out."

"I'll come back," she said stubbornly. "And you wouldn't get far with me riding Elijah, or with you and me riding double." She braced her feet and glared at him.

His expression said he would like to throttle her. He took a step forward, and for a moment she really thought he might seize her and throw her on Elijah. Instead, his lips crushed down on hers.

*   *   *

Pride had watched defiance and bluster cross her features, but it was the look in her eyes that finally defeated him. Bluster couldn't hide the fear, nor defiance the grief. Nor could her anger blunt the stark hopelessness of what she planned.

Even while he cursed the foolishness of staying, he respected the courage. He always respected courage, which made his own path difficult.

It takes more courage to live than to die, King had told him, and more guts to refuse a challenge then to accept one. Anyone could fire a gun. Anyone could die. Not everyone could learn how to live.

His brother never had. King had lived with death from the moment he'd killed their father twenty-one years ago when, in a drunken rage, John Gideon had beaten their mother to death and would have killed both of his sons, too. The scene returned to Pride in nightmares: his mother screaming, his father cursing, the sound and feel of a whip across his own back, then the explosion of a shotgun. . . .

He was going to make Susannah want to live, even if he had to seduce her to do it. And so he lowered his head, pressed his lips against her, hushing any protest.

She offered none. Instead, she kissed him back. The sounds of the storm outside increased in intensity. The rain pounded against the shutters, and a sudden clap of thunder announced the approach of another squall. Susannah clung to him as one particularly vicious—and loud—volley made the cabin reverberate. His lips moved from her lips along her cheekbones, tracing her skin with feathery kisses, trying to calm her trembling body.

His blood was hot, pulsing through him. Lightning flashed outside, illuminating the cabin, shaking the earth. He felt as though the very essence of that electricity had snaked along the ground and reached him, seared its way up his legs and settled in the core of him.

She felt it, too. He saw it in the widening confusion in her eyes, the fear turning to tumultuous excitement as his lips returned to hers. Their mouths met in an explosion as bright as any display nature could create.

The throbbing in his shoulder faded, replaced by a new, more exquisite pain. His arms wrapped around her, his hands exploring every intriguing curve beneath her clothing. Her body shuddered again, but this time he knew it wasn't fear, or cold.

Her arms snaked around him, and he felt her fingers creep upward to the back of his neck. Her lips opened to him, her tongue hungrily meeting his, and the desire pounding inside him pounded harder. His manhood swelled painfully, pulsing against her, stunning him with the force of his need for her.

He heard her moan, and he had to swallow a cry of his own as their bodies swayed together and seemed to fuse, even with clothes separating them.

He had always been a calculating lover, had learned to pleasure a woman, to take it slow and easy and give her satisfaction; and he knew it made his own enjoyment greater. But he'd never felt out of control before, like a volcano ready to erupt.

Pulling back, he whispered, "Susannah . . ." He heard the plea in his voice even as he realized how useless it was.

Outside, the storm raged on. In the shelter of the cabin, the warmth of the fire crawled along his spine. Or was it another kind of heat? He looked at her, held her gaze. He heard the catch in her breathing. And his hands started undressing her.

When had she decided she wanted this?

Almost from that first kiss, Susannah thought.

It no longer mattered whether Pride agreed to help her. She realized the odds against her, with or without his help, and she knew she didn't want to die without knowing what it was to be a woman. Didn't want to die without finishing what they'd started.

Expectation pushed her body into his as his kiss deepened, his touch sending increasingly urgent sensations cascading through her body. She felt tears again at the back of her eyes. Tears from too much emotion, too many feelings sweeping through her. Grief. Anger. Fear. Loneliness. Passion. And something more, some sensation she couldn't quite identify that had to do with tenderness and warmth. The fury of the storm—the driving rain, the thundering of angry skies—only intensified everything she was feeling.

She was lost, wandering through a dark forest of all those emotions, and Pride Gideon was shelter and comfort. As if he read her very thoughts, he gentled his attack on her senses, his kiss becoming tender, his lips touching hers with featherlike gentleness.

Susannah raised her gaze and saw the fire in his emerald green eyes. His hands started to unbutton her shirt, and she shrank inwardly, knowing what he would find underneath. No fluttery, feminine garment but a boy's undershirt. The expression in his eyes didn't change, though, as those questing warm hands lowered to her trousers, his hands lingering on her waist for a moment before undoing the buttons and sliding the trousers to the floor.

His hands slid up and down her body, touching her everywhere, his gaze devouring her. Her heart hurt and her body ached, as if the storm outside were being duplicated inside her, the tension building, feeding on every touch, his and hers. Her hands twisted through his thick dark hair, and her tongue tasted the delicious flavor of him.

She felt both bold and shy, alternating from greediness to wonder as his hands continued to inflame her. Yet despite the hot desire banking in his eyes, she felt the gentleness, even tenderness, of his every touch. She realized then that these moments were more than lust or passion or even escape from the horror of the past hours. She knew it when she touched his face, and felt wonder; when she saw the weariness in his face and the too-early lines around his eyes, and her heart ached. She knew it because she wanted to give him something, even though she wasn't sure what it was. Something more than passion, something more than satisfaction.

She swallowed hard with the discovery of new feelings, forcing breath beyond the fullness in her throat. Was this love? She had known him only hours, but he stirred her in ways and to a degree that no one ever had.

She closed her eyes, relishing what was happening to her body, her mind, her heart. She wanted to reach out and clutch this piece of life, this piece of unexpected heaven. She wanted to touch and be touched, to lust and be lusted after, to love and be loved. She wanted it all. Now!

His hand ran through her hair. "You're lovely, you know," he said, and his eyes confirmed the wondrous and astounding statement.

She stood there, with only the old red undershirt protecting her, but she *felt* beautiful. For the first time in her life, she really felt pretty, and wanted, and needed.

A clap of thunder rocked the cabin, followed by the crack of lightning as it touched the earth. She winced with the unexpectedness of it, and snuggled closer into arms that tightened around her. She felt his lips caressing her again, and then he was leading her to the bed.

Filled with both anticipation and nervousness, she looked toward the fire, newly fueled, burning brightly in the hearth. When she looked toward him again, his trousers were gone and he was unbuttoning her undershirt. His hands cradled her breasts for a moment, his gaze running over her body possessively.

Her own gaze faltered, fell to the ground, then slowly, shyly moved upward. She had never seen a naked man before, and she was awed by the sight. He was beautiful, all bone and muscle and sinew. And he was well named. There was pride in his bearing, in the tilt of his head, in the steadiness of his eyes.

She held out her hand to him, and he sat next to her, then guided her down, his hands caressing, seducing. She closed her eyes, her body melting like butter on a hot day. And need, so strong she thought she might burst, overwhelmed her.

She should be afraid, but she wasn't. She felt, instead, as if she were coming home, as if she were reaching a place she was always meant to go. Anticipation shimmered in her as his hands teased and stirred and stroked. When she thought she could bear no more, he moved his body atop hers, balancing himself on his good arm, his manhood teasing the most intimate part of her. His breath rasped against her neck, and she heard herself whimpering.

She was liquid heat, heat and light and need. Lightning seemed to flash between them, binding them as he entered her. She felt a stabbing pain and cried out, stunned by it as well as by the strange fullness his body being inside hers created.

He stilled and as he did, the pain faded. The fullness became welcome. Her body began responding to his, adjusting and clasping, and then his thrusts began again, slowly at first, then gaining a rhythm and speed that engendered a different kind of pain, an exquisite, insatiable sense of expectation. Her body was dancing in concert with his, writhing with pleasure as he drove deeper and deeper inside her.

She cried out as a convulsion seized her, then another, her body spiraling out of control, spinning, whirling, bursting with pleasure. She felt him collapse on top of her, his sweat mixing with hers, their bodies so intertwined they were one. And slowly, the sensations transformed again, tempering in force, leaving another kind of pleasure in their wake. The fire that had burned out of control mellowed gradually to warm and glowing embers.

Pride lay on the bed, panting, holding onto Susannah as quivers of satisfaction rolled through him. A sense of euphoria masked all other emotions. He'd never experienced anything like making love with her. Never.

Everything about her was perfect: the uncertain yet blinding smile, the smoothness of her skin and roundness of her body, her innocent yet erotic responses to him. Nothing could have been more of an aphrodisiac. His hand traced the lines of her face, and he smiled as her mouth caught a finger and nibbled on it.

"You taste good," she said with a contented smile.

"You feel good," he replied.

"Mmmm, so do you," she murmured. "Is it always like this?"

He kissed the tip of her nose. "No, darlin'. It's hardly ever like this, I think."

Her brows furrowed together worriedly. "Is it . . . can it be . . . better. For you, I mean . . . ?" she stuttered. "I can't imagine anything . . . any better."

He chuckled as he rested one hand on her breast, leaning over to kiss her slowly, lazily. Lovingly. "No," he said. "Nothing has ever been better."

The worry faded from her face. Her hand touched his mouth so tenderly his heart pounded against its rib cage. He loved that touch; even as it pierced him with its sweetness. He'd never quite given up on life, though it had been gray and bleak these past months, but he sure as hell hadn't been prepared for *this*. Love flooded him, made him raw and vulnerable.

Yet, he was a man without a future, and she was a woman determined not to have one. And he feared the hope flaming inside him could be as deadly as the storm going on around him. He looked at Susannah and knew he would do anything for her—except kill. Because more killing would only doom them both. They might have a day, a week, or a year, but they would live with guns at their back. Which wasn't living at all.

He couldn't do that to her.

She took his hand to her mouth and kissed the back of it. "Pride and King," she said. "Two unusual names."

"My mother," he explained softly. "She had high ambitions for us.'' He didn't remember much about his mother, and what he did remember was mixed up with what King had told him. He remembered softness, sweet smells. He remembered being held. At least he thought he did.

''Where is she?''

''Dead,'' he said flatly. ''She died when I was very young. I don't think our lives turned out as she expected, but then neither did hers.'' He couldn't keep the bitterness from his voice.

''What happened?'' she asked softly, real caring in her voice, and he found himself saying things he'd never told a living soul before.

''My father killed her. Beat her to death. He was a drunk. A mean drunk.''

Pride didn't look at Susannah—couldn't look at her—but for some reason he felt compelled to continue. ''After he killed my mother, my father turned on me. King killed him. He saved my life, then and other times. He was only thirteen himself, but he raised me, took care of me. He could have dumped me, but he didn't.''

''You stayed together?''

''Until I was eighteen. He'd taken a job with a rancher who was involved in a range war. He was a good shot, and he wasn't afraid of anything or anyone. Maybe because he really didn't care much about his own life once I was grown. But his reputation grew, and then he was always in demand because of his gun.''

''And you?''

''He didn't want me working with him. I usually hired on some place close as a wrangler. I was always good with horses. We'd meet occasionally. And then we heard about some wild horses in the mountains. I asked him to round them up with me, maybe start a ranch of our own with the proceeds.

''I think he was happy for the first time,'' Pride said. ''We spent two years in the mountains. Just him and me.

He would take some of the horses down once in a while and sell them. One time, his reputation caught up to him. A young gunny called him out and, just like always, he was forced to kill or be killed. Word spread about his whereabouts, and the next time we took horses down to sell, several would-be gunfighters were waiting.''

Pride felt his hand tense in Susannah's, and she used her thumb to caress the tension away. Gentle. Comforting. Accepting. She was all those things. But he couldn't continue. Not now. He didn't want to remember those last days with King or his brother's growing melancholy.

"You must have loved him very much," she said. "I think I would have liked him."

"Few did," he said. "Most people were afraid of him, and those who weren't thought him arrogant, even evil.'' Pride was silent for a moment. "He wasn't evil, though. He'd just learned to build walls around himself. Seeing our mother killed, shooting our father . . . it did something to him. I was too young to really understand, but he paid for that day every minute of his life."

She leaned over and put her head on his chest. His hand lost itself in the long tawny hair that spread like skeins of silk across his body. Perhaps, she *would* have liked his brother.

Lying peacefully with Susannah, he let himself drift for a time. But then, listening, he noticed that the rhythm of the rain had changed, lessened. Was it subsiding? How much time did they have left?

"Come with me," he said suddenly, his hand grasping hers tightly. "Now."

Susannah looked at him, those lovely brown eyes meeting his gaze directly. "I only have Elijah," she said. "If men are after you, we couldn't outdistance them."

Her voice was uncertain, though. She was thinking about it.

"We can ride double."

"I can't leave Elijah. Pa loved him."

"We'll take him with us."

She shook her head slowly. "We would slow you down."

Pride stared at her, wondered at her selflessness. He'd just made love to her, taken her virginity, yet she asked for nothing. The fact that she apparently accepted his explanation about King humbled him.

"I can't—no, I *won't* leave you here alone," he said.

"But you said—"

"I said I wouldn't use a gun. Maybe I . . . we can find another way."

"I won't hand over the claim," she said stubbornly. "Besides Gallagher can't afford to let me live now. He'll be worried I'll find a federal marshal and report Pa's murder, though God only knows where I would find one." She hesitated. "And the men after you . . . how many?"

He shrugged. "Six, last time I counted. Jack Keegan, two brothers, three cousins."

"Maybe they'll give up in this storm."

"Maybe," he conceded aloud. Privately, he knew Keegan would die first.

She was silent for a long time. The rain still pelted the roof, but not with the driving force of an hour ago. The thunder had also receded, growling now from a distance.

He brought her hand to his mouth, kissed it, then sat up. He was aware again of the pain in his shoulder, of the weariness in his body. Reluctantly, he pulled on his trousers, then stood and walked to the door, opening it and looking out. The sky was still dark; fat, clumsy clouds lumbered slowly overhead. It must be near dusk again, though it was difficult to tell.

He felt as if years, even eons, had passed since he'd awakened to Susannah's insistent demands. It seemed impossible, but in a matter of hours he'd learned how to love. And it seemed that amazing discovery had come too late.

Chapter Five

"Do you have any dynamite?"

Pride's question brought Susannah's gaze up to him in a snap. He was standing, framed in the doorway, facing her, and he looked dead serious.

"Dynamite?" she asked.

"That's right." His tone had lost all traces of tender sweetness.

Reluctantly, she rose from the bed and began pulling on her clothes, reality firmly reestablishing itself.

He, too, crossed the cabin, picked up his shirt, and put it on. Then, facing her again, he waited for her answer.

She nodded slowly, her thoughts churning. Why did he want dynamite? "Pa occasionally used it to blast boulders blocking the stream."

"Where is it?"

"Buried in a strongbox under a big cottonwood. He didn't want it near the cabin or Elijah."

"Show me."

She hesitated, then said haltingly, "I think you should leave."

He frowned. "I told you I'm staying."

"I don't want you to stay," she said. "I need someone who will shoot."

Pride went absolutely still, his green eyes turning to ice,

his back stiffening. "The dynamite?" he asked again.

"Why?" she asked. "Dynamite kills, too."

"It can, but there are other ways of using it." His voice was as cold as her eyes.

Susannah felt frozen in place, but she had to make him leave. "No," she said. "I want you to go. This isn't your battle."

"The hell it isn't," he said. "Some of those men out there are after me and if they suspect you helped me they wouldn't hesitate to kill you—or worse."

She *had* to find a way to get him to leave. He wanted her to go with him, but she would not endanger him by slowing him down—or by putting yet another band of murderers on his tail. Nor would she ask him again to use a gun.

She understood, now, why he wouldn't. Her heart had broken as he'd talked of his brother. She'd been willing to use a gunfighter, whose trade was life and death, but she couldn't use this man. And if he wouldn't pick up a gun, he would die. Lord, he'd been close to dead when she'd found him only because he wouldn't shoot back when someone shot at him.

She, on the other hand, would shoot to kill. She might have a chance against Gallagher, and she could throw Pride's pursuers off his trail.

She said the only thing she thought might work. "I can take care of myself. I . . . don't need a . . . coward."

A muscle twitched in his cheek. His hands clenched into fists. Then, he turned to the door and strode out, leaving her alone.

She moved almost blindly to the small, round table where she and Pa had eaten together. She'd never seen such utter devastation as she had seen on Pride's face. She might as well have thrust a knife into him.

She fought the urge to run after him, crying, "It isn't true! I didn't mean it." She wanted to tell him that she admired him more than any man she'd ever met. He was willing to stay here and help her, without weapons—to die for and with her—and she loved him for it.

No one had ever tried to take care of her before, not even Pa. Mostly, she had taken care of him.

But she had to get Pride out of here, and she'd only known one way to do it. The pain, though, ran as deep and bitter inside her as she suspected it did in him. It was a terrible thing to destroy a man's pride—particularly a man like him. And it looked as though she had succeeded. She would probably never see him again. The thought was excruciating. Her body still felt the warm effects of their lovemaking, and her heart was still filled with the new and unexpected joy of loving him.

She'd thought she'd known loneliness, but she hadn't. Not until this moment.

Pride had given her an idea, though—the dynamite buried a thousand feet away from the cabin. She knew how to use it. Pa had showed her, so she would be properly respectful of its power and destructive force.

Slowly, Susannah finished buttoning her clothes and plopped the floppy hat over her hair. Then, she packed Pride's few belonging into his saddlebags. She would take them out to the lean-to. She didn't want him to tarry any longer.

On her way out, she paused in front of the mirror. Her face was still flushed from lovemaking, but her eyes were bleak. Her hair was a tangled mess and the hat made her look like any down-and-out miner. She saw nothing at all appealing about herself. Biting her lip, she stepped outside.

She didn't see Pride, and when she reached the lean-to, she found his horse missing. Had he already left, even without his saddlebags and what few possessions he owned? Had her blow struck that deep?

She put the bags down in a dry corner, then went to Elijah who bellowed unhappily. She knew he must miss her pa. She stroked his neck several times, talked to him, but he stamped a foot impatiently and bellowed again.

Susannah gave him one last pat, then found the shovel she'd used to bury her father. Feeling more alone than ever, she walked past the grave to the spot where the dynamite was buried and started digging again.

Pride scouted the area. He moved quickly through the underbrush, avoiding the traveled trail.

Coward.

The word had gutted him. He'd heard it before. He'd heard it yelled by Jack Keegan in a street full of people, and it had hurt then. But that pain had been nothing compared to what he felt now. For a few moments, he'd actually believed Susannah understood his reasons, that she was one of the few who did.

Yellow belly. Coward. Words he'd thought he could handle. But he couldn't. Not coming from her, not from the woman who'd given him hope.

He didn't know why she'd allowed him to make love to her. Maybe she'd thought to convince him to use guns. Or maybe she . . .

Hell, who knew what a woman thought? He'd always avoided more than brief liaisons with women. Mostly, his name attracted the wrong kind and repelled the right kind. The simple fact was, though, he owed Susannah. He owed her for saving his life, if nothing else. And he was a man who always paid his debts.

He took off his hat, welcoming the frigid rain on his face. Maybe that would give him some sense. The rain had slackened, and he no longer heard thunder. The storm was moving off.

He should move off, too. She didn't want him. No one on God's earth wanted him—except Jack Keegan. And Keegan wanted him dead. But he couldn't leave her here alone, helpless, no matter how she felt about him.

Pride reached a high spot on the mountainside and looked down over the trail below. No movement. Not yet. But Keegan *would* come.

Pride started back down the incline, thinking. Keegan wouldn't be able to move at night, and neither would Susannah's enemy. They should be all right tonight, but tomorrow . . .

Once more he thought about taking Susannah, with or without her consent, and leaving that evening. But they would have the same trouble as Keegan traveling through these woods without moonlight.

He wondered how much dynamite she had, and he prayed it was still dry. He'd seen the confusion on her face when he asked about it, trying to puzzle out the difference between dynamite and guns, and why he would use one and not the other. Maybe he was splitting hairs, but dynamite wouldn't make a reputation like a shoot-out would. If he was lucky, no one would even know he was involved, or exactly what *had* happened.

And dynamite could frighten as well as kill.

He had another idea, too. Timing, though, would be essential to both defenses. Timing and vigilance.

He turned his horse and, carefully avoiding the trail, made his way back to the cabin.

Susannah covered her surprise by carefully averting her eyes from Pride when he came clumping inside the cabin. She'd thought he'd gone for good. He didn't look at her, though. Instead, his interest went to the box sitting in the middle of the room.

"I didn't know whether you . . . would come back," she said haltingly.

"I nearly didn't," he said.

Susannah winced at the raw bitterness in his voice. "I found the dynamite," she said.

"I see." He walked over to the box, stooped down to open it, and unwrapped the oil cloth from around the sticks of dynamite. "They're dry," he said tonelessly.

She pointed to a container inside the box. "Fuses."

He simply nodded. Then he went over to the cot, took

off his boots, and sat there for a moment. She saw pain flicker over his face and knew his shoulder must be hurting. He expelled a breath as he lay down, stretching across the bed. He had to be near dead with exhaustion, to say nothing of the lingering effects from blood loss and pain.

And she had called him coward.

She wanted to go to him, touch him, tell him she hadn't meant it, had only been desperate to make him leave. But his eyes were closed, and she knew he needed rest—and, besides, she still did hope to make him go. Didn't she?

She watched him for several moments, until she was sure he was asleep, then took her father's shotgun from its brace on the wall. She loaded it and placed ammunition next to the window, slipping the shotgun onto the floor next to the wall. She looked outside. The sky was edged with a cinnamon glow. The rain had stopped.

Anxiety clamored inside her. Her eyes kept cutting over to the large man sleeping in her father's bed. His breathing seemed heavy to her, but perhaps it was only her imagination. She remembered lying next to him, flesh to flesh, feeling his sex enter her . . . and she found herself turning liquid with need all over again.

"Hell's bells," she said under her breath. Maybe she'd better bake some bread. She had to do *something* to keep from going crazy.

Smoke. Fire. Heat.

Haunted by memories, Pride thrashed awake. He felt weighted down by mind-throbbing weariness and, as he forced his eyes open, he remembered everything—past and present.

He blinked several times. God, he was still tired, and his shoulder throbbed. How long had he slept?

The cabin was dim, but a fire roared in the hearth and the smell of baking bread filled the room.

He tried to focus and forced his feet to the floor. He wondered what time it was, but he had no timepiece.

Didn't matter, anyway. He needed to move. There were things to do. Yet his body felt so heavy.

His eyes searched the cabin again. Susannah wasn't there. Panic seized him for a moment, then he realized there were a dozen explanations for her absence, some of them very private. He rose to his feet, took a few steps, and felt strength returning, both to his body and his mind.

Pride walked to the door to see that night had fallen. The rain had stopped, but clouds still filled the sky, darkening the earth. He took a few steps outside and saw the smoke spiraling upward from the chimney.

Then Susannah appeared, seemingly from nowhere, her shoulders sagging slightly. He wanted to take her in his arms again, comfort her again, but she thought him a coward. And, besides, they had no time.

She almost bumped into him before her head jerked up and she stopped. She *was* tired.

"I was seeing to the animals," she said. "I think we should move them into the woods . . . just in case."

He nodded. "And quench the fire. The cabin will appear abandoned."

It was a poor hope, and he knew it. Anyone—especially the carrion that were after them—would stop at a cabin that showed clear signs of recent inhabitants, if for no other reason than to steal.

"I'll help you with the animals," he said. "Then you get some rest. I have a few things to do, and I'll keep watch."

"I . . . can't."

"You won't be good for anything if you don't get some sleep," he insisted.

She didn't protest any longer as they went to the lean-to. Susannah lit a lantern and led out Elijah while Pride took his bay. He let Susannah lead the way. She knew the mountains.

The air was still heavy from the storm, and he wondered whether another was coming. The mountain trails would be slippery for a while yet even without more rain, but he didn't think that would stop Keegan. What about Susannah's enemy? How desperate was he?

They walked a few minutes, then Susannah stopped a couple of hundred feet behind the cabin. "This is far enough. If anyone comes from this direction, Elijah will let us know."

They both looped the lead ropes loosely to trees. The ropes would hold the horses for a while, but the animals would be able to free themselves with a good jerk. Neither Susannah nor he needed to say aloud what he knew they were both thinking: that perhaps they wouldn't return to set the animals free.

After returning to the cabin, Pride took some of the hot bread Susannah offered along with a bowl of stew. Then, he piled the dishes up in the corner. "Get some sleep," he said.

She hesitated. He wanted to touch her, to kiss the worry from her eyes, and the unhappiness from her mouth.

Instead, he turned away, picked up the box of dynamite, and carried it to the table.

He heard her footsteps. Slow. Reluctant. Then the creak of a bed, the one behind the curtain. His shoulders relaxed, and he turned his attention to the dynamite. Tying several sticks together, he affixed the fuses to them, along with a piece of his red bandanna. When he'd completed seven packages, he listened intently to Susannah's breathing. It was soft and regular.

He pushed back his chair and rose. Brushing aside the curtain, he looked down at her. Her eyes were closed, and her body was curled up, her hands clutching a pillow. She was still dressed in the man's trousers and shirt, and she looked small and vulnerable and helpless.

A myth. She was anything but helpless. She was strong and brave to the point of foolhardiness. His heart twisted as he watched her.

Forcing his gaze away from her, he picked up the bundles of dynamite, quietly opened and closed the door, and headed for the lean-to, where he'd seen a shovel. He passed the new mound of earth, hesitated, then turned back to kneel for a moment. "I'll take care of her," he said.

Then, getting to his feet, he continued on. He had a lot to do.

Susannah woke to the first light of dawn creeping in the back window, which she'd left open to hear any alarm from Elijah. She hadn't thought she could sleep, but her eyes had evidently closed the moment she'd lain down on the bed.

The curtain kept her from seeing the rest of the room, and she wasn't sure she wanted to rise, to meet Pride's steady, cool gaze. She wasn't sure she wanted to face this day at all.

Why had Pride stayed? She knew she'd hurt him deeply. Yet he hadn't left her.

She clung to that.

Susannah rubbed her eyes. She was still wearing the same clothes she'd worn for two days. Her hair tumbled in snarls down her back. She looked again at the sun that punctured the curtain with one bright ray.

Sun! Suddenly, she was aware of silence, complete silence. No rain. No thunder. Not even the sound of birds.

She rose, threw aside the curtain. The cabin was empty. Even Pride's saddlebags were gone. Yet, her heart discarded the obvious conclusion. He wouldn't have left her.

Her gaze searched the cabin. Less than half of the dynamite sticks remained in the box. Then she saw her pa's Bible propped up on the table, a page sticking up from it. She read his writing once, then again.

I've gone scouting but should be back soon. Dynamite buried in seven places around perimeter of cabin, each with a piece of cloth sticking from it. If anyone approaches, fire toward the farthest piece of cloth near the cottonwood. If they keep coming, fire at one of the other pieces.

Susannah went to the door, noted the small red-checked pieces of cloth. *What if he doesn't come back?* What if he runs into the man he called Keegan? Or Gallagher, who would kill him sooner than risk having a witness when he killed her? Pride didn't have handguns, though he had a rifle. The question was whether he would use it on something besides game.

She pulled a chair up to the window and sat there, staring at the fluttering pieces of cloth. And praying.

Pride rode out at first light, leaving a nervous Elijah in the woods. Two trails led to the cabin: one went upward, climbing over a sharp incline, then fell to the stream below. The other led in the other direction, apparently toward the mining camp Susannah had mentioned. He set traps on both, stringing rope close to the ground, close enough to be hard to spot, but high enough to trip an unwary animal. A falling horse could well injure its rider and send other animals into confusion.

There was still no sign of riders when he returned at midday. Perhaps no one would come. If they didn't appear today, he would convince Susannah to leave with him, at least go to the nearest federal marshal. If she resisted, he'd tie her to the mule. He damn well wouldn't leave her alone, no matter what she thought of him.

He tied his horse behind the cabin with Elijah, who snorted a welcome, then stayed a moment to run his hands down his bay's neck, soothing him. He would bring both of the animals some oats after he talked to Susannah.

He dreaded this meeting. He had reached some decisions this morning; yet he wasn't ready to tell her. Her words still burned too deeply, far more painfully than the knife she'd used to close his wound.

Taking his rifle from its sling on his saddle, he looped the horse's reins around a branch, making sure the bay could jerk away if he really tried. He knew the animal wouldn't wander far and would come at a whistle.

As he walked toward the cabin, he gazed up through the trees. Bare patches of bright blue were visible here and there, but clouds still rode across the sky, only occasionally revealing the sun. He was hungry again, and pain continued to throb in his shoulder, but he felt stronger. The food had done its job, as had the brief rest.

As he entered the front of the cabin, he saw Susannah at the window, a shotgun in her hand.

"Can you use a rifle?" he said. He should have asked her whether she could shoot before he'd left her instructions about setting off the dynamite. Somehow, though, he'd just naturally assumed she could handle the shotgun.

She nodded. "Pa taught me. He had a rifle with him when he was shot, and I don't know what happened to it. We . . . I just have this."

The shotgun was old and probably had a kick like a mule. Pride shook his head and handed her his rifle. If she said she could use it, he knew she could. He knew her that well now. He would have liked, though, to have seen her shoot at something, but they couldn't risk someone hearing the shot.

Instead, he walked her around the sticks of dynamite, partially buried in the ground, each joined by fuses to the next. "Aim for that farthest piece of cloth first." He repeated what was in the note, wanting to make sure she understood. "That explosion should stop them for a while. If they start coming again, you aim for any one of the other six and they should all go off. I've connected them. It should scare the hell out of them, at least make them retreat and take some time to think about who might be in the cabin."

"And you?" she said.

"We have two guns between us," he said. "Not good odds against Keegan or that bunch you think is coming. You sure you don't want to leave?"

He saw the uncertainty in her eyes, but it quickly disappeared.

"I don't think we could make it," she said. "Gallagher will be coming from the mining camp. The men after you would be coming from the only other trail."

He studied her for a long time. At least, she wasn't staying for the gold. And she was right. They had a better chance here.

"What are you going to do?" she said in a voice wavering a little.

"I rigged a little warning system," he said. "I'm hoping like hell Keegan and your Gallagher get here around the same time."

Her brows knitted together. "Why?"

"I have an idea. I don't know if it's going to work, but if it doesn't, if they don't back off, I want you to go out that back window and take my horse. Ride like hell out of here. He's a fine animal, and he's rested now."

"What about you?"

"Don't worry about me. I've been running long enough to get myself out of tight spots."

She looked at him doubtfully. "Like two nights ago?"

"A brief setback," he replied with a small grin.

Biting her lip, Susannah dropped her gaze. Then, a few seconds later, she raised it to meet his. "I didn't mean what I said earlier," she finally whispered. "I just wanted . . . you to go. I was afraid for . . ."

"Me?" he asked incredulously. "You were *trying* to make me go?"

"Gallagher's *my* fight."

"And Keegan's mine," he said. "Do you think he would have just ridden on from here, if he thought you'd helped me?"

She smiled slightly, softly. "I think you're the bravest person I've ever met."

"Even if I don't wear guns?"

"Especially since you don't wear guns," she said.

Instantly, the pain in him eased. The dark, shaming words that had racked his soul since his brother's death faded into nothing. That she'd told him how she felt now, before he told her his intentions, meant everything.

Pride clasped Susannah's chin with two of his fingers, bent his head and kissed her long and tenderly. He was contemplating doing a lot more when, through the open cabin window, he heard a frantic neigh from a distance, then a short, sharp bark.

"Elijah," Susannah said, moving away from him.

He nodded. "Someone's coming. And if the mule heard, they're probably coming from the north. That means Keegan."

He started to turn, but her hand touched his arm, stopping him. "I'll be back," he said. "I'm only going to go start a little confusion . . ."

"Take the shotgun at least."

He shook his head. "It's too clumsy. Don't worry . . ." He stopped suddenly. "Hell, that was a damn fool thing to say." And he clasped her shoulders with both hands and looked her straight in the eye. "Close and bar the shutters on the back window. Don't open them unless you hear three knocks. And remember what I said about my horse. If you have to set off the second explosion, and I'm not back, fire some shots at them, then go out the back window and take my horse."

"No."

"Promise me," he said, his grip tightening on her.

"I can't."

"Do it for me," he said, willing her with his eyes, his mind, his heart, to say the words. "Do it for your pa, so someone will know what happened to him."

"Yes," she finally said, staring at him with her dark eyes misting with tears.

"Promises are meant to be kept," he said, leaning down and kissing her. "Everything will be wasted if you don't. Your father's life. My life."

Her arms went around him, and her lips clung desperately to his. He felt that desperation, felt the love in her. He felt ten feet tall.

He had to force himself to wrench away. His hand touched her cheek. "You are beautiful, Susannah O'Callaghan." Then he whirled around and went through the door before she could stop him again.

Chapter Six

Pride snaked up the mountain on foot, heading for a spot where he could overlook the trail. Elijah was still making his odd, barking sounds, and his bay was whinnying in response. The side of the mountain was slippery, and he had to grab at tree trunks as he climbed. Still, he moved quickly.

He wanted to get behind Keegan and his men. For a moment, he wished for his guns. King had taught him to use them long before either of them had realized the price of using them recklessly. He was a good shot and once had been nearly as fast as King.

But he didn't have his guns anymore. He'd buried them with King. All he had were his wits. *Find your own way, Pride,* King used to tell him. *You're smart enough, a hell of a lot smarter than me.*

If only things fell into place.

He had one thing going for him. Horse thieves hated other horse thieves who preyed on them. The former negated the latter's effort. And Jack Keegan was, among other things, a horse thief.

And Pride was banking on something else: that the men who killed Susannah's father would return, and return soon. They had left a loose end, and he hoped they felt that they couldn't afford to leave it long.

He stopped climbing when he had a good view of the trail. It had been eerily quiet all day, even the birds withholding their songs, and the squirrels their play. Was it tension from the storm? Or did the animals have an instinct for danger?

Suddenly, a man's voice—a curse—broke the silence. The noises increased rapidly, then, below, Pride saw four men on horseback and a fifth on foot, leading a lame horse. The man on foot was moving ahead of the others, apparently checking for other traps.

"It had to be Gideon." A familiar voice floated up to him: Keegan.

"But you hit him," another one said. "He probably bled to death."

"He's like his brother. Has nine lives. And I'm going to make damn sure he uses them all up."

Then they passed by him, and Pride could no longer hear their words. He followed silently, grateful for the soft carpet of pine needles, pausing as Keegan and his men halted. They'd seen the cabin.

The five men started up again, heading toward the cabin, and as they reached the spot where the trail leveled off and opened into the clearing, he heard a shot, then Susannah's voice.

"I wouldn't come any farther," she called to the men.

Her tone was strong, confident.

Then he heard Keegan. "We don't mean you any harm, ma'am. We're just looking for an outlaw."

A pause ensued, then she answered, "There's been no one by here,'cept my father and two brothers."

"Where are they? I want to talk to them!" Keegan's voice was authoritative.

"My pa's at our claim, and my brothers are hunting. Both should be back soon. You're welcome to wait out yonder by the trees."

"That's not very hospitable."

"Nope," Susannah hollered back, "but those are my father's instructions."

Keegan inched his horse forward, and a shot rang out, kicking up mud a scant foot from the horse's front hooves. He reared, and Keegan cursed again. When he had the horse under control, he dismounted, as did the others with him.

Pride let out the breath he'd been holding. So far, so good.

He listened as Keegan issued instructions. "Thomas, you hold the horses. Sam, you come with me. We'll see how close we can get. You two cover me," he said to the remaining men. "There's only a woman there."

"She shoots real good," one of his companions complained.

Pride said under his breath, "That's right, you bastards." Damn, but she had iron in her.

"I ain't going to give up on Gideon," Keegan said. "He has a way with women. Bet you anything, she's protecting him in there."

Keegan took several steps toward the cabin. Pride heard a shot, then another. She was aiming for the dynamite, but she'd missed. A third shot, and an explosion rocked the forest, sending Keegan and the other men scurrying for cover.

"Holy hell," he heard Keegan exclaim. The man holding the horses cursed as the animals reared and tried to escape. One, then another horse, broke loose and galloped down the trail. One of Keegan's men swung into the saddle and rode after them while the man named Thomas held onto the others.

"I don't like this," another man grumbled. "If she does have a father and brothers around, they probably heard that explosion."

"Wouldn't be no lady out here alone," chimed in another. "Let's get the hell out of here. Besides, nobody in their right mind would take Gideon in, not with his moniker.''

Keegan was silent. Pride understood his dilemma. Keegan was a man who liked the odds on his side and, right now, he didn't know what he was facing.

''We can't leave until Sam gets back with the other horses,'' he finally said. ''We'll watch the place until then.''

Pride smiled to himself. Susannah should be safe enough for the next few minutes.

He made his way up back through the woods, then found a tree overhanging the trail. If Sam found the horses, he would be coming back this way.

Pride climbed the tree, the strain sharpening the pain in his shoulder. He found a semicomfortable perch and concentrated on the sounds around him. Sound carried in the forest, and he would know if Keegan approached the cabin again. Susannah still had the ring of dynamite protecting her, and there was no way into the cabin from the back with the shutters bolted on the only rear window.

Time crept by. He knew minutes seemed like hours. Finally he heard the sound of hoofs, and a few seconds later he peered down from the cottonwood at the man called Sam—one of Keegan's cousins—who was returning with the runaway horses.

He prayed the gunman wouldn't look up and see him. But Sam had not forgotten the rope across the trail, and his gaze was directed toward the earth. Pride let him pass, then dropped down onto his back, knocking him off the horse. He hung on the man's back, not allowing him a look at his face, his arm twisting around Sam's neck, threatening to break it.

''Thanks for the horses,'' Pride said in a rough voice. ''Gallagher will appreciate them.'' Then, with his free hand, he took the man's pistol from his holster and hit him with it.

Sam slumped on the trail. Pride pushed him to one side.

He held the pistol in his hand for a moment, then tucked it into his belt. Not to take it was tantamount to leaving a calling card. Keegan knew his aversion to guns.

Pride swung onto Sam's horse and picked up the leads on the other two. Speaking softly to calm them, he left the trail, moving through the brush again. He planned to circle around Keegan and head south toward the other end of the trail—the direction from which Susannah expected Gallagher.

Susannah's palms were sweating. The first part of Pride's plan was working. She wished she knew the second.

Was he all right? She wished he had a gun. She wished she had more than the rifle and shotgun. The latter was lying on the floor next to her. She'd already reloaded the repeating rifle.

It had taken her three shots to hit the dynamite. Would it take her three more to hit the remaining sticks?

So many worries, so many thoughts, flitted through her mind. So many emotions. She was bubbling over with them. Fear. Love. Grief.

You are beautiful, Susannah O'Callaghan. She clasped those words to heart, knowing she would never forget them. She wasn't beautiful, but the fact that he thought so meant more than finding legendary El Dorado gold. If she were never to have anything more, she'd still consider herself among the luckiest people in the world: She'd had these hours, glorious golden hours, of loving and being loved.

"Come back," she whispered. "Come back, and I'll go anywhere with you."

She heard a gunshot in the woods, echoing across the small plateau where the cabin sat, and her heart stopped beating for a moment. He was alone, without weapons against at least five men.

Her gaze searched the perimeter of the clearing again, once more lingering over each bright piece of cloth. Another shot echoed through the trees, then a wild flurry of firing commenced. Her breath caught in her throat as terror clutched at her, terror that she might never see Pride again.

Susannah desperately wanted to go outside, but she knew she would only put Pride in danger. The gunman could use her to draw him in. No, she had to stay, dying an inch at a time.

Pride heard shots and suspected Keegan's men were spooked. They could have found the man he'd rendered unconscious, or they simply could have heard an animal in the underbrush. The shots, thank God, hadn't come from near the cabin.

He moved as quickly as possible through the underbrush toward the trail leading to the mining camp, still riding the captured horse and leading the other two. The bush was so heavy, the horses frequently balked, but he coaxed them onward. The route he was taking should make following a trail very difficult.

He came out on the path well below the cabin, just short of the ropes he'd placed across the trail. He stopped and listened for any sign of movement. Perhaps the man called Gallagher had given up, though it seemed unlikely from what Susannah had said. Whether or not Gallagher believed her father was dead, the storm had probably kept him from searching for a body. The violence of the storm had caught all of them unawares, and surely he had known that Susannah couldn't have left, especially without a horse, any more than he could come after her during the storm.

But now . . .

Damn it, where are you? Pride hunkered down in his saddle and waited. He would give them an hour, or until he heard dynamite blasts, and return to the cabin.

His hand touched the pistol in his belt. *Promises are meant to be kept.* He'd exacted the promise from Susannah that she would run if he didn't return, just as his brother exacted a promise from him.

He didn't know if she would keep *her* promise. But he knew he would break his in defense of her.

Suddenly, he heard voices, loud and boisterous and excited. He dismounted, tied the reins of one of the two riderless horses to a bush, and left the other as company. Then he led the one he'd been riding back into the woods, hoping, praying that one of the newcomers' horses would stumble over the rope. He didn't have to wait long. It was a repeat performance of Keegan's band's arrival. A horse whinnied in distress, and another snorted with fear. Curses filled the air, then a wild gunshot resounded. Pride smiled to himself. In a few moments, they should be very pleased to find two saddled horses. He doubted they would be willing to give them up easily.

Meanwhile, the wild shot should attract Keegan, whose men would be searching for their horses—and the men who'd taken them. With any luck at all—and it was damn well time for him to have some—Keegan and Gallagher would kill each other off, any survivors running for cover. His name, the Gideon name, would not be involved.

Pride waited, each minute seeming an eternity. He prayed for a moment, unfamiliar with the process but hoping, just hoping, he might be heard by someone. His one fear—that the two outlaw bands might join forces rather than fight each other—gnawed at him. Yet he knew these men; God knows he'd seen enough of their type. They were like ravenous dogs going after a last scrap of meat, tearing each other to pieces to get it. King had told him long ago that honor between thieves was a myth. Always watch your back, he'd said.

Then he heard the sound of galloping horses from up trail. His own horse snorted with warning, but the sound was drowned by the louder noise of surprised shouts, furious accusations and gunshots. He heard a scream, long consistent volleys of gunshots, then slower ones. The men who had survived the first confrontation had probably dismounted and were taking cover. The battle could last all day.

It had worked. He breathed normally again, yet he still felt a sense of urgency. He and Susannah had to get out, just in case there were survivors, though he doubted anyone would come looking for them. Keegan and Gallagher and their men would be too busy with each other. Pride mounted and cautiously moved through the brush toward the back of the cabin.

Her eyes still searching every foot of ground around the cabin, Susannah started at the sound of more shots, this time coming from downstream. She was so tense, so rigid, she thought she might break if she moved. But her faith in Pride kept her at the window.

The men watching the cabin suddenly disappeared, fading away. More gunshots crackled in the woods, then a cacophony of them broke loose. A pitched battle was taking place.

She had to fight herself not to go to the door, not to run toward the noise. Despair flooded her, despair and apprehension. *Where was Pride?*

He'd sworn not to use a gun. And she knew he would keep that vow. She'd learned that much about him during the short time she'd known him. Short? It seemed more a lifetime. Her life had started with him. It could well end with him.

Her hands were tightening on the rifle when she heard his signal at the back shutter. Three knocks. Putting the rifle down she rushed for the window, fumbling with the bar that locked him out. When she was finally able to open the shutters with trembling hands, he swung inside. Grabbing her in his arms, he held her tight for a moment or two, raining kisses on her face. Then, pulling her with him, he moved to the front window.

They stood there watching, listening. Nothing moved in

the clearing, but the gunshots continued below. The volume had lessened though, and so had the number of shots.

Susannah's fingers tightened on his. "I'm not even going to ask—"

"Don't," Pride said. "If any of them get away, they'll be blaming each other. No one will ever know about you or me." He was silent for a moment, then his head bent and his lips touched hers, softly, as his hand lifted to touch her cheek. "You're so damned gallant."

"For a man who doesn't carry guns, you have a lot of grit yourself," she said.

His eyes glittered, then he smiled slowly. "I think the better part of wisdom now is to run like hell. I just happened to find another horse. Will you go with me?"

Her heart somersaulted, and words crowded in her throat, nearly choking her. She finally managed a soft "Yes."

"Your father's claim . . ."

"It was nearly played out," she said. "If Gallagher lives, he can have it."

"I don't know what kind of future—" Her finger to his lips stopped the words.

He kissed them before continuing. "I do have some horses a friend is keeping for me."

"I don't care," she said, "as long as I'm with you."

He smiled, his green eyes dancing. She hadn't seen that smile before, nor joy in his eyes. She hadn't known he had a hint of dimples in both cheeks.

Pride kissed her again, this time hard and possessively. Then he said, "We can't take much."

"I don't have much. Just a few nuggets, a change of clothes, Pa's Bible." As she spoke she gathered her belongings. Hesitating a moment, she looked at him. "The dynamite?"

"We should blow it. It's too dangerous to leave around. Besides, the explosions will create even more confusion. But it's your home . . . ?"

"Not anymore," she said softly. "You're my home—wherever that is."

Pride grinned. "We'll head north to Montana and send for my horses. I don't think the name Gideon means much there." His eyes loved her for a moment, then he moved, picking up the rifle from where she'd dropped it at the back window. "You go out the back window and mount. Take whichever horse you want. Will Elijah follow?"

She nodded, pleased beyond words that he'd thought of the mule and understood what the animal meant to her. She reached up on tiptoes and kissed him long and lingeringly. "I love you," she said, then turned and bolted out the window.

Minutes later, she heard the explosions. And seconds after that, Pride was beside her, mounting his horse. She followed his lead as he moved stealthily through the bush, then she heard another explosion. A larger one. The cabin!

Pride dropped back to ride beside her, his hand taking hers, his eyes regretful and full of compassion. And love, so much love, she thought she could drown in it.

"I'm sorry, Susannah."

She looked back once at what had been her home. No one would find any evidence of either her or Pride. "I'm not," she said softly. There was lingering grief for her father, and she knew it would be with her for some time, perhaps all her life. She'd loved him; he'd been the center of her life as long as she could remember. But she also suspected he was smiling down at her. He would have liked Pride Gideon.

He would have admired Pride's way.

Susannah looked up at the sky through the canopy of leaves. The last of the thunderheads had disappeared, leaving only wisps of clouds and a bright glowing sun that sprayed the earth with golden rays.

One beam cut through the trees and caught Pride's face. "I think Pa's winking at you," she said.

His hand went to her cheek, and he leaned over, touching his mouth to hers. "I love you, Susannah."

The sunbeam moved then, seemed to wrap both of them in its warmth and light, and she knew indeed that Pa was watching, and approving.

STORMS NEVER LAST

 Vivian Vaughan

To Robert David
With his hand in mine
Storms never last.

☞ *Chapter One* ☜

Lindsey Mae Burnett stood in her open French doors on the third floor of the House of Fanciful Delights and let the humid wind blow against her skimpy clothing and through her ghastly short curls.

Inside her an ominous sense of disaster welled, disaster unrelated to the storm that brewed somewhere in the Gulf of Mexico. For Lindsey Mae was one step away from making the biggest mistake of her life.

A mistake, yes, she thought despondently, but an unavoidable one. She had agonized over the decision for days, searched her mind and this town for another solution to her dilemma. None existed, and now she was desperate.

Desperate. The word sounded weak when applied to what she was about to do. Indeed, nothing short of imminent ruin would have driven her to this room, to this profession.

Jittery as a June bug, when the wind slammed a shutter against the side of the house, she nearly jumped out of her borrowed satin kimono.

Across the room, March Sutton propped his denim-clad rear against the scarred dresser, boots crossed at his ankles, and watched her, fascinated. Except for the short hair, which any man knew was proof that a woman had been in the business long enough to contract lice from one of her customers, Lindsey Mae didn't look or act anything like your average whore. In fact, with proper clothing, a scrubbed face, and those black curls pinned up in a respectable hairstyle, she could pass for someone's innocent sister. Hell, it was probably his own jitters he sensed in her. He was fixing to have to kill his first man. But dang if she didn't act as jittery as he felt.

Could it be the storm? A week of stillness so sultry a man could hardly draw a breath had given way to high winds and rising bay water. A storm was brewing somewhere. He'd bet his saddle-weary bones on that. From the brick-dust cast of the sky, it could be a tropical cyclone. Which wouldn't affect him. With court winding up at five o'clock, he could take care of business and be long-gone before a hurricane hit town.

Not that folks around here worried much over a little wind and water. Certainly this house would withstand a hurricane. Sitting a couple of hundred yards back from the bay, the House of Fanciful Delights was one of the stronger structures in town.

March grinned to himself. If rising water drove folks away from bayside, they could take refuge here. Keep the girls busy. Storms would likely be good for business in a place like this. Lindsey Mae must be new to town.

Thinking to reassure her, he asked, "This your first—"

Her first . . . ? Lindsey Mae swirled to face the cowboy who preferred to remain anonymous. That wasn't unusual. According to Miss Fancy a lot of men refused to give their names. "Makes no nevermind," the madam advised. "This ain't no country club."

Wind whistled along the eaves and felt strangely cool when it hit her kimono, chilling the surface of her skin. But the sultry air did nothing to cool the sizzle inside her. Shutters continued to flap against the house. From somewhere down the street came other sounds she vaguely associated with a storm. Yet she identified nothing, for the noises mingled with the chaos that already churned inside her head. Desperately seeking control, Lindsey Mae summoned courage from her depleted supply.

"My first time?" she demanded. In movements that felt awkward, she threw back her shoulders like Willa Jean had taught. "Makes your tits look bigger, honey." Lindsey Mae shuddered at the thought. She was not eager to flaunt her bosom or anything else, but want to or not, she needed the money this job would pay. Experienced pay, not novice.

"I should say not!" she added emphatically. She *knew* what to do. She had paid close attention to instructions from Miss Fancy Delight and the girls. Understanding her dilemma, they willingly, eagerly even, shared wisdom gleaned from years of sordid experience. All of which, however esoteric, Lindsey Mae had committed to memory.

"I meant the storm," March corrected. He studied this wisp of a girl, intrigued. As though oblivious to the cheap lace curtains that blew into the room, she stood stock-still, while their wispy lengths wrapped around her like tendrils of a sea monster. Her skin was the palest he had ever seen, rendered almost translucent by the backdrop of stormy black clouds and unruly black curls that framed her face and looked soft as goose down. Her eyes were the size of blue moons. He wondered how they would look without all that kohl.

"Storm?" Lindsey Mae felt weak in the stomach. How could she have misunderstood? Lord 'a mercy, she wasn't good at lying or misleading folks. Her mother taught her to be honest and . . .

Frantically she rejected that thought. She was here. This was now. What she did in the next hour meant survival, escape . . . or catastrophe. She searched her mind for a way to cover her mistake. She couldn't get rattled now. She simply could not. Tossing her head of black curls so energetically two fuchsia bows fell out, she eyed the cowboy. "You've never done it in a storm?"

March squinted for a better look. Dang if this wasn't

the most peculiar whore he'd ever encountered. Why, she was doltish enough to rattle a college professor, which he certainly was not. On the other hand, he hadn't come up here for enlightened discourse. He'd come to relax his worried mind. Hell, he couldn't face Jeb Taylor with shaky hands and benumbed senses.

Ordinarily, he would have headed for the nearest saloon. But neither could he face Taylor half-crocked. What the hell, a witless prostitute might be the very thing to steady his hand.

He dropped to the iron-steaded bed and tugged off a boot, eyeing her suggestively over his shoulder. "Likely not as often as you, sweetheart."

His smirk unnerved Lindsey Mae. As did his composure. Even with the wind blowing on her, perspiration laved her skin. Willa Jean's kimono stuck to her back. While across the room her *caller*—Miss Fancy's term for customers—looked downright at home in the room of an upstairs girl. Which he probably was. He would know far more about how business was conducted than she.

She flinched when he dropped a boot to the floor. His forehead furrowed beneath a stray lock of damp brown hair. She focused on a bead of perspiration that rolled from his hairline and made a wet trail down his sun-browned cheek. Suddenly, she entertained the dreadful notion that he was about to order her out, to insist on someone more experienced.

Instead, he inquired, "Aren't you getting undressed?" When he waggled his eyebrows, the drop of perspiration fell from his jaw onto his blue chambray shirt. "Or am I supposed to do the honors?"

Undress her? The suggestion ignited a path of prurient flames that began in her breasts and raced to her stomach . . . and lower. Her gaze darted to his; she shrank inside the shabby fuchsia kimono, while Willa Jean's admonition to hold her shoulders back screamed in her ears. To hell with strutting bosoms. Lord 'a mercy! She wasn't that kind of girl.

Except for today. A gray stormy day, for the gray storm inside her. *Storms never last,* she admonished, recalling her mother's sage advice, which brought to mind her mother's last embrace, her dying words spoken in a soothing voice. Indeed, nature's storms never lasted in the Texas hill country where Lindsey Mae had been born and where she had grown up and lived all of her life so far—except the last six months.

There, the air was soft and sweetened with wildflowers, unlike this sultry gulf air that stung the skin with bits of sand and smelled of the sea and tasted of salt. And of disaster.

But she wasn't in the Texas hill country; would never be again. This was here, she admonished furiously, and this was now, and she had a job to do, an escape to effect. With that reminder, her determination returned.

"You aren't supposed to do anything with your guns on. I told you downstairs, I don't entertain gunfighters." Even if he walked out the door, she would stick to that. Gun-toting men had gotten her in the fix she was in now. She had no intention of tolerating another one, not even for an hour. Not even for the money she desperately needed.

"And I told you I'm not a gunfighter. And I'm not."

"Then you won't need your guns." She glanced pointedly to a hat rack in the far corner beside the dresser. "Hang them next to that carpetbag."

After he complied, she addressed the next hurdle. "Now I'll see your money. And none of those Confederate bills." She wouldn't get across the street with Confederate money, much less all the way to Alabama.

"How much?" Amused, March watched her consider. Her eyes narrowed in an unaffected way he recognized as intense concentration; her lips puckered in a little red *O* that he suddenly wanted to explore . . .

Lord 'a mercy! The way he looked at her! Why, it was downright embarrassing. Reaching deep within, she pulled forth another smidgen of courage. "Depends on what you want."

That brought March out of his trance. This upstairs girl was full of sauce, he'd give her that. "Might as well have the works."

"The works?" she echoed, while the cowboy's lopsided grin fired the roots of her short hair.

"Everything," he replied, as casually as one would ask for an extra splash of bay rum with his haircut and shave. "Beginning and ending with your speciality. What did you say that was?"

Speciality? Her gaze sought his. Warm, brown, mirthful, his eyes conveyed messages that dropped like lead balls to the pit of her stomach.

"Speciality?" she managed. No one had mentioned a speciality. On the other hand, specialities would surely fetch more money. Things might work out after all—if she could think of something the girls had described that would be considered a speciality.

Around a lump in her throat, she finally declared, "I'm very good at French kissing." Then remembered to add, "But it costs extra."

"Extra, huh?" The pink tinge to Lindsey Mae's cheeks had nothing to do with rouge; March would bet his summer's trail drive pay on that. "In that case, I'll have to inspect the wares."

"The what?" She wasn't sure which confused her more—his unexpected questions or the gentle teasing with which he delivered them. Having grown up in a house with four brothers, she was used to being teased. But the heat swelling inside her warned that this was teasing of a far different kind.

March watched her closely. Her small, straight nose wrinkled the slightest bit and her blue eyes turned the color of lapis. But instead of opening her mouth, she pursed those tempting red lips again. Even covered with layers of paint, that pert little mouth was beginning to have the desired effect on him. "Your tongue," he encouraged. "I'm particular about what goes in my ear."

"Your ear?"

"For starters."

Lord 'a mercy! She felt weak and dreadfully confused. His eyes didn't help. They danced upon her face, tripping her senses, catching her unawares. Willa Jean had been right about his looks, although at the time, Lindsey Mae had been interested only in the fact that her caller was a stranger to town and she would never have to lay eyes on him after today. This cowboy was uncommonly handsome, she admitted now. All sun-bronzed and muscled and those brown eyes that said they saw right through her pretense, straight to all the secret places inside her. He looked so . . . so normal. Like a real gentleman caller. He was supposed to look old and miserable and uninviting, instead of alluring and tempting and . . .

But she couldn't let him discover that. She must retain control. Miss Fancy said that was the only way to succeed. And she must succeed. She needed his money. All of it. "Actually,"—she shifted her shoulders in a failed attempt to strut her breasts as she'd been instructed—"I have several specialities. Just put all your money there on the dresser."

"All my money?" March had thought her naive but now reconsidered. If there was a method to her madness, it could well be to bilk customers out of their hard-earned cash. She wouldn't be the first woman to act sensual and thick-skulled to gain an end. "I took this for a respectable establishment."

Lindsey Mae gripped her hands in tight fists in an effort to conceal their trembling. Had she gone too far? Would he walk out now . . . before . . . "It is respectable," she assured him. "I meant, put it all there, and we'll sort out what you owe after you've sampled my . . . specialities."

The last word sounded tinny to her own ears, for her throat had tightened around it. She hoped he thought it was the wind.

She wasn't a very good liar, March realized, aggravated now. "It doesn't matter how many specialities you have or what they are, lady. I don't have anywhere near enough time for you to entertain up all my money."

He was that rich? Hope sprang to her quivering breast. "We'll see," she demurred, fighting to control the compelling temptation to look him in the eye.

He chuckled in spite of himself. Something about her was insidiously appealing. "In that case we'd better get started. I'm liable to change my mind quicker'n this storm blew up if you don't start showin' me some of those specialities. I didn't come up here to talk about 'em."

The threat did its job. Lindsey Mae tossed aside the fuchsia satin kimono so quickly he would have sworn in court she was a magician. And like magic, the sight of her sparked an astonishing reaction in him; not for its sexual nature, that he expected. But in other ways—he felt drawn to her vulnerability, found her naivete charming, even those sassy short curls had begun to grow on him. His hands fairly itched to play in them.

"And move away from that open door," he growled. In an attempt to draw his attention back to the physical nature of this encounter, March studied the way her chemise and pantaloons, damp with perspiration, clung to all the right places. His hands found a virtual garden to explore. "Unless you intend to divide my bill among every gawker on the street."

Discomfited, Lindsey Mae jumped aside, then glanced to the street, three floors below. Men rushed to and fro, but no one paid her any mind. Bay water had crept to within inches of the raised roadway. Overflow, folks called it. "Don't let it spook you," Miss Fancy had said. "Happens couple, three times a year."

In the six months Lindsey Mae had been in town, this

was the third time she had seen the wind whip bay water over the peninsula. Today it was whipping more than water.

Below her a lady's parasol collapsed. Down the street, a horse nickered and tried to run away with a wagon. Gusting wind ruffled the hair on a terrier, who was occupied with chasing his tail. After two days of a sultry stillness that sapped everyone's strength, the wind seemed to have brought life back to town. But it wasn't a refreshing kind of wind. It seemed almost as smothering as the mugginess that preceded it.

Truth known, the wind was frightening. And the sky looked downright menacing with its reddish yellow cast and billowing black clouds. A flash of lightning split the sky in a jagged streak, like a serrated knife would cut through a birthday cake. The devil's own cake, for sure. On a day like today, it wasn't hard to imagine the end of the world. Indeed, it was. The end of her world as a virtuous woman. She squeezed back tears.

Never in any nightmare in all her twenty-three years had Lindsey Mae dreamed of selling her body. But that was then, and this was now, and she had a job to do. She could worry about the consequences later, after she was safely away from this barbarous land and its gun-toting men and their insidious feuds. Suttons and Taylors! She was tempted to hate them both, even though it was the Suttons who had ruined her life. She couldn't be away from Texas soon enough. And not at all, if she didn't set about earning this cowboy's money.

She could worry about the storm later, if it was still around. Storms never lasted.

But what she was fixing to do would last forever.

Lord 'a mercy, she chastised. *Quit your bellyachin', Lindsey Mae.* Get it over with! Determination, or as she considered it, desperation, restored her sense of urgency.

She eyed the stack of bills the cowboy had stuffed into a lead-based hair receiver to keep the wind from blowing them off the dresser. Even wadded together, she could tell they amounted to a vast sum of money. Possibly enough to buy her passage to Alabama on the steamer *Louisa*, which was scheduled to leave port at four o'clock today. If she could earn that whole sum before then, she could leave town and never look back. Her courage once more inspired, she moved toward the bed. But her fingers were stiff as they fumbled with the tie on her chemise.

By now the cowboy had removed both boots. He stood up and began working on his clothing. Attracted against her will, she watched the forbidden ritual a second longer than was prudent, while a heated urgency took form in her belly and spread embarrassingly lower.

But her eyes seemed to have a will of their own, for no sooner had she glanced away, than her gaze returned to those large sun-browned hands with their sprinkling of brown hair and long, nimble fingers. With startling awareness, she realized that those hands would soon touch her skin. Her body sizzled at the thought. She pulled her attention away from the inevitable.

She was lucky. Unlike most men who came to this house reeking of salt from the sea and from their own perspiration, this cowboy was neatly dressed, his brown hair combed in an attractive flip to one side. He looked as though he might have come straight from the bathhouse. On the way upstairs, she even smelled bay rum. But she didn't feel lucky; her arms trembled and her legs felt absolutely weak.

Even so, something about him fascinated her. She watched him tug out his shirttails, watched the shirt fall open, revealing a muscular chest splattered with brown hair that looked soft as a baby's. When his fingers reached the button on his waistband, the heat inside her raced up her neck.

A clap of thunder sent shock waves through her. She jumped. This wasn't a good idea. She had never been so embarrassed in her life.

Get it over with, she scolded.

"You'll have to wash," she told him, anxious now to finish this disastrous encounter. Of course, afterward, she wouldn't feel any better. Except for the money, which would allow her to escape, she stood to lose much more than she gained. She had cried all night, once that realization set in. But she couldn't dwell on it now. Escape was too important. For better or worse, her decision was made.

"No one is allowed in bed until he's washed," she explained.

March watched her turn toward the washstand, where she poured water from the pitcher into a cracked bowl. Even with a rigid spine and tensed shoulders, she fascinated him. He wondered why. He had never been drawn to a prostitute before. Maybe it was his mind's way of handling the disastrous ordeal that awaited him at the end of the day. Loving a woman was infinitely more appealing than killing a man.

He admired her from the distance. She had the smallest waist he had ever seen, and this without aid of a corset. Roaming lower, his gaze lingered on her hips. They rounded from her waist and looked soft and inviting beneath the coarse cotton bloomers.

Compelled by Lord knew what, he rose and in two steps stood behind her. Heat radiated between them, inciting more than fascination. He reached for her waist, soft skin, hot enough to dry the damp cotton. With the span of his hands, he nipped her waist.

At his touch she turned to stone, then swirled to face him. Indignation ignited her blue eyes, before they dimmed to a smoldering nothingness. A drop of perspiration fell from her jaw, hit her chest, and rolled beneath the unadorned cotton chemise.

Of a sudden he wanted to buy her lace and silk. In the next instant he wanted to dip his head and lick the trace of salty perspiration from between her breasts, where he imagined it had come to rest.

She burst his fantasy by thrusting a wet cloth at him. "You have to wash . . . first."

"Why don't I kiss you first?" His question surprised even himself. Strangely, that was what he wanted at this moment—to kiss her. To hell with the cold, quick act he had come to this room to buy. He wanted to kiss her. To cover that sensual little mouth with his hungry lips and kiss her until they melted together, which event seemed inevitable, what with the heat that now enveloped them like a cocoon.

"Kiss?" She shivered at the thought, while his heated perusal sent flames racing down her already scorched spine. What would it be like, she wondered, to kiss him? To touch his parted lips with hers? Lips that moved toward her, reaching, inviting, tempting.

Enchanted now, March watched her blush. He knew when her searching eyes found an echoing response in his. He knew when she felt the same heated stirring deep in her belly that he did, because the moment she looked into his eyes, he quivered and felt her do the same.

Kiss him? Lindsey Mae ducked her head, lest he read her thoughts. Casting about for reality, she recalled Miss Fancy's list of services. "I told you kissin's extra."

"Add it to the bill," he said, still gripped by the insidious desire to kiss her instead of getting down to the business he had come for. "My money's on the dresser."

"No." She shook her head, resisting, when in fact she would very much like to know what those questing lips would feel like against her own. She strove to pull her mind away, to think of other things.

But other things were equally mindless. His hands, for instance. They spanned her waist like two horseshoes straight from the forge. Her practically *nude* waist. Desperate now, she sought composure by concentrating on the wind that buffeted the house. Or was it her own quaking flesh? Outside something crashed to the boardwalk, a sign, maybe. Urgency drove her. The sooner she got this over and him out of here, the better.

"Rules are rules. Wash first," she repeated, attempting to turn away. She knew what part of him he had to wash and she wasn't about to stand by and watch. Miss Fancy had explained the rules three times, and every time Lindsey Mae had blushed. But when she tried to pull away, the cowboy tightened his hold.

"What if I asked you to perform that little chore?" He watched her embarrassment turn fiery, felt it torch the startling fascination in his gut. What had begun in jest sounded like a dang fine idea. "I'd pay extra, of course."

Lord 'a mercy! Would she live through this gut-wrenching ordeal? "That isn't the way it works," she insisted through pursed lips. But was it? No one had mentioned that she might be required to . . . to *touch* . . .

Panic wormed its way through her roiling emotions. Something she once heard Willa Jean and a girl named Sissy laugh about came to mind. It would serve him right. Making her feel like a wanton. Asking her to wash his . . . his . . . With her eyes trained on his sun-browned Adam's apple, she summoned what she hoped was an authoritative tone and advised, "Saliva works best."

A strangled sound came from his throat. When she inadvertently glanced up, he was as red-faced as she felt. His teasing brown eyes had flamed into a conflagration.

Although March's body had no trouble deciphering Lindsey Mae's suggestion, spoken in her soft, seductive voice, it fairly knocked the wind out of him.

Who was this woman? She was unlike any prostitute he had ever met. Or any person, for that matter. One minute she sounded so naive he was certain she was just out of pigtails; the next, she talked bawdier than the mule skinners with whom he regularly swapped yarns. A titillating combination.

Was it by design? He decided to call her bluff. "Saliva, huh?" With one finger he tipped her chin so he could see her expression. "Yours or mine, sweetheart?"

Lord 'a mercy! What was he asking? That she spit on
... on ... Suddenly she felt dreadfully out of her depth.
How could she have thought this was a good idea? How
could she have gotten herself into such a mess?

More to the point, how was she going to get herself out
of it. Her head spun; the quaking inside her became first-
class tremors. She actually felt her body sway, as if she
might swoon. She, who never—

"Get dressed!"

Lindsey Mae suddenly felt abandoned. She grabbed the
dresser for support and struggled to clear her mind. Across
the room the cowboy lunged for his shirt. She watched
him stomp into his boots.

"Get dressed," he shouted again. "This place's fixin'
to go."

"To go?" Stunned, she realized it was the floor that
swayed beneath her, not her legs giving out. From the
street a cacophony of sounds took form—horses whinnying, dogs barking, men shouting, and clashes and clangs
so loud they set her teeth on edge. Rain beat against the
house. And above it all the wind wailed and roared, louder
and more unearthly than anything she had ever heard or
even imagined.

Dress? She glanced down at her nearly nude body. Yes,
she must dress.

Storms didn't unnerve March Sutton. Although he
hadn't been reared on the Gulf Coast, he spent many a
summer of his youth visiting his maternal grandmother in
New Orleans. Only folks who worried over tropical cy-
clones were newcomers. On the other hand, he didn't hanker to meet his end in a whorehouse in some podunk port
town.

His mother would never live down such an indignity!
She might have sent him to town to shoot a man, but that
was to uphold family honor. Dying in a whorehouse wasn't
likely to repair the dignity ripped from the Suttons by that

infamous, and to March's mind foolish, feud.

Behind him Lindsey Mae struggled into a once-white shirtwaist, which she buttoned with trembling fingers. The floor was bucking now; it felt like a herd of buffalo had taken up dancing in the parlor below. She strove to gather her wits. It was just a storm, after all. Storms never lasted.

Hastily, she pulled on dingy petticoats and a brown woolen skirt, then searched for her worn black boots. These were the only garments she owned.

From the hallway came sounds of scurrying feet, accompanied by female shrieks and male shouts. A loud crash of thunder sounded so close it shook the roof. When she glanced up, rain blew in through the open French doors. With one splash, it drenched her from head to foot.

"Come on, Lindsey Mae." March reached the hall door. "Get a move on."

Gripped by rising physical terror that surpassed her earlier inner trepidation, Lindsey Mae watched the cowboy tug fruitlessly on the door. While she tried to come to terms with this new reality, he grabbed her by the hand and pulled her after him in a dash for the gallery.

"What happened?"

"When the house shifted, the door got jammed," he shouted above the wind. "We'll have to go this way." He glanced at her; their gazes held. He saw terror in her blue eyes, but something else—trust? She hadn't wasted time dressing, he noticed with admiration. Her hand was rough, but small and warm, and he was struck by the immense comfort he received . . . just from holding her hand. Dang, he should have kissed her when he had the chance.

By this time, the curtains had torn away and tangled in his boots. He kicked through them, reached the gallery, and pulled up short. One look told him they were in trouble.

Two raised roadways bisected this low-lying peninsula, affording residents a way to get around during the frequent overflows. A good two feet of water now covered the road that ran in front of the House of Fanciful Delights; to either side, of course, it was much deeper, rising halfway up the first story of the mercantile across the street. Pieces of slate, planks, and other debris flew through the air like witches on Halloween. March watched a wooden barrel float past directly below them.

"Can you swim?" he asked.

"Yes." Confusion and terror swirled in her blue eyes. Her mouth remained ajar, and he wished again he had kissed her when he had the chance.

When he tried to release her hand, she gripped him tighter. His heart lodged in his throat. "Let me look around," he said lightly. "I'll find us a way down."

The only response she could manage was a nod.

"Get the bedsheets," he instructed. "Tie them together. We'll anchor one end to that iron bedstead and let ourselves down." Partway, he thought. Far enough.

Lindsey Mae went into action. With imminent disaster throbbing in her head, she tore the chenille spread from the bed and grabbed the sheets. For a moment she stood, arrested by what had transpired here—or by what had *not* transpired here. A fleeting sense of relief rushed through her. She hadn't been required to do what she set out to do on this bed—yet.

Hurriedly, she tore her mind from the past and dragged the sheets and bedspread to the open doors. On the gallery, the cowboy leaned over the rail, examining something below. He glanced back, smiled, winked.

Then, of a sudden, he was gone. While she watched him smile and wink, wishing she had let him kiss her, he fell. Just like that. As though a giant hand had reached up and snatched it away, one of the gallery posts blew off, the railing crumbled, and the cowboy with it. She gaped after him in horror for an instant while the wind seemed to hold him in place; then she came to life.

"Here! Catch!" But when she tried to toss him an end of the sheet, the wind blew it back in her face.

"Get back inside," he shouted on his way down.

The gallery floor went next, ripping away from the house with a noise that seemed to tear apart everything inside her. She was left to teeter on the threshold of a doorway that opened onto the roiling water—three floors below. Gripping the frame in tight fists, she braced her feet against the buffeting wind.

"Get back inside!" March shouted again.

Lashed by wind-whipped rain, yet unable to move, she watched him land amid timbers and barrels and a myriad of other debris. He struggled for balance in the swirling water.

"Here, catch!" Again she tried to toss him the sheet.

"Get back inside. Try the door again. Pound on it. Pull . . ."

Although most of his words were lost in the roar that separated them, she took his meaning. "I can't—"

"Go," he shouted. Then he smiled. "I'll be all right."

Her heart turned over. Was she watching this man die? Watching him smile his last smile?. He grabbed at a barrel that bobbled in the swirling water.

"Lindsey Mae," he called up. "I didn't mean to offend you. I was teasing. I would have washed my—" A sudden swell swept him under. Her heart lodged in her throat; he surfaced and tried again to grasp the barrel.

"Hold on," she shouted. "You'll make it."

"Go on, now. Get that door open."

"I can't . . ."

"Thanks, Lindsey Mae," he called, smiling again. The sight brought a tightness to her chest. "You're the prettiest thing these ol' eyes have seen in a coon's age."

Tears rolled down her face. Salty like sea spray and rain, she knew they were tears by the heated trails they traced down her cheeks. As she watched, horrified, a wave crested over the submerged roadway and swept the barrel toward a far corner of the splintering building.

"What is your name?" she shouted, before he disappeared. "I'll send word to your wife." *Lord 'a mercy!* She shouldn't have said that. He would think she'd given up hope.

"I don't have a wife," he shouted back. "Now, get the hell out of there. I'll be all right. Save yourself!"

Save herself? Yes, she must. Yet she stood, immobile except for billowing skirts and flying curls, staring after him. A myriad of emotions bobbled inside her. *No wife.* That hadn't been the only reason she asked his name, of course. She wanted to know it, needed to know it. Before she could question again, he shouted something else. Garbled by the wind, it sounded like a command issued by a stern general. No smile now.

"March!"

March? His abruptness jolted her back to reality. She might have escaped a fate worse than death in the bed behind her, but death itself stared her in the face if she didn't stop gawking after this nameless cowboy and get herself to safety.

"Okay, okay! I'll go!" Still she was unable to move. Mesmerized by the drama played out below her, she watched until the barrel bobbled around the corner and out of sight. Then, for a moment longer she stood, like at a recently covered grave, while tears coursed through the stinging sea spray on her cheeks.

Chapter Two

Preoccupied with the ignoble deed of selling her body, Lindsey Mae had paid scant attention to the wind and rain until the cowboy fell to certain death. Now, the magnitude of the storm struck her like a piece of flying debris.

Save herself, the cowboy had shouted. Yes, she must.

Blindly, she stumbled inside, only to find the hall door still wedged. Her shouts for help went unanswered. While she frantically pondered her next course of action, a great wrenching noise, louder than when the gallery floor collapsed, ripped through the room. It took her a moment to determine the source—one of two outside walls was being torn away.

Fear struck her like a falling wall stud. What had she gotten herself into? Fire and brimstone admonitions of circuit riding preachers from her youth denounced her. Had she called down the wrath of God by her sinful intentions? Intentions that had not even been realized.

Of course not. But as she dove into an interior corner behind the hat rack, she made a hasty pact. "Let me live, dear God! Let me live, and I promise never to *look* at a man again!"

Clutching her knees to her chest, she buried her face and prayed harder. But instead of dying away, the sounds became more terrifying—of nails being torn from wood, screeching down her spine; of timbers crashing around and above her.

At length, gripped by fright, she lifted her face and stared through the swinging carpetbag and the cowboy's guns into a jumble of ceiling beams that imprisoned her in a small triangular world, a world which was quickly being torn apart.

Even in her terror, the irony of the situation was inescapable. In seeking to flee death and destruction, she had stumbled directly into its violent path.

Albeit violence of a different sort. This natural disaster was a far cry from the manmade destruction from which she had run. Sutton killing Taylor; Taylor killing Sutton. In the last year alone her father and two of her four brothers had died by Sutton guns. The year before that the Suttons the same as killed her mother. Pneumonia took her mother's life, but only because the Sutton faction had the house surrounded in hopes of catching Lindsey Mae's father and Manny Clements. When the Suttons refused to allow her grandfather through to fetch Doc Wilson, her mother died of pneumonia—another innocent victim of that dastardly feud.

And the Burnetts were not even blood-related to the Taylors. Only friends.

Then six months ago the Suttons got wind of a secret meeting at Lindsey Mae's home. They stormed the house in the middle of the night. Bullets flew everywhere. Lindsey Mae hid under the bed and listened to the men curse into the blackness. Not prayers from their dying lips, but oaths, even from her father.

By this time Lindsey Mae had had her fill of gun-toting men who lived and breathed violence and whose every conversation was of who had been killed and who would be killed next.

The final straw came when her grandfather and two remaining brothers swore vengeance on her father's grave. At that moment Lindsey Mae knew if she was to survive this feud, mentally and physically, she must leave. And leave then.

So she ran, headed for her mother's people in Alabama, vowing to never watch another gunshot man die. But thanks to the lying, cheating mule skinner who hired her as cook, then ran off without paying her, she never made it to her destination. And now she was alone. Completely alone, with the awful truth that this storm would last forever, *her* forever. She prayed it would not be so.

Yet for endless hours, or so it seemed, she huddled in the corner, while rain and wind buffeted what was left of the House of Fanciful Delights. Eventually a measure of sanity returned, and she remembered to pray for her friends who lived by the bay. Destitute to a one of them, they would certainly be in more peril than she. They had saved her life when she first arrived in Indianola. She grieved that she was not able to help them now.

In time her fear became so great it filled every nook and cranny of her mind, and she became numb. With numbness, her thoughts returned to the cowboy.

She wished she had let him kiss her. Alone in the blackness of this night-day, she pretended she had. In her imagination, she kissed his lips and stroked his face and sifted her fingers through the brown hair on his muscular chest.

She imagined his lips, soft and warm; his face, stubbled; his heart, thrumming beneath her touch. Like hers did, thinking of him. She tried to conjure images of her mother in Heaven, which, she reasoned, should be comforting or at least reassuring.

But it was the cowboy's likeness that appeared time and again to ease her fears; the cowboy's hands she felt on her waist, firing her skin and bringing a begging ache to her breasts.

So successfully did she close out the storm around her, that when the dresser slid sideways, crushing her farther into the corner, she was hardly aware. Dazed, she lifted the hair receiver from her lap, felt the money.

His money. She squeezed a handful of bills in a tight fist. She would never earn this money now. The thought of it brought a tightness to her chest.

The cowboy had surely died in this storm, one more death added to the many she had known. Why hadn't she let him kiss her? Absently, she touched her lips. If she had known how things would turn out . . .

When next her reverie was broken, it was not by a sound, but by a sudden awareness. She sensed a change in the storm. Stiff with apprehension, she forced herself to look through the barricade of hat rack and ceiling beams. What was happening? Suddenly she knew.

All was still. Except for an intermittent shifting of debris, all was silent and still, so still she could scarcely draw a breath. The wind had ceased. The storm was over! Dare she believe it?

Gingerly, she touched her face, her hair, placed a hand over her heart, which beat a rapid cadence.

She was alive! Eagerness swelled inside her. Like an inhabitant of Noah's ark must have felt after forty days of rain, she wanted to jump up, to run to a window, to look outside.

But there were no windows; indeed, hardly anything was left of this room. Carefully, lest she shift the remaining supports, she wriggled out of her hideaway. The total destruction held her enthralled. One outside wall was gone and the other had fallen partway into the room. The bed on which she had planned the loss of her innocence was crushed beneath the roof of the house, the mattress torn. What feathers had not blown away lay clumped wetly together amid the debris.

A pressing need to escape built to excruciating levels within her. She cautioned herself to wait. To think. To plan.

What must she take? Reason held that once she left this room, she would never return. Since she didn't have anything except the clothes on her back . . .

The money. She stared at the cowboy's money, still clutched tightly in her fist. Of a sudden she jerked the wet carpetbag from the hat rack and stuffed the bills inside, telling herself he would surely want her to take the money. As she turned, his guns caught her eye.

She hated guns. She had sworn never to touch one again. But who knew what awaited her outside this room?

Allowing herself no chance to balk, she crammed the guns, belt and all, into the carpetbag. Quickly then, she climbed over ceiling beams and reached the door, which was gone; the stairs, which appeared intact. With great difficulty, she restrained herself from racing down them, forced herself to test each step, one by one by one by one.

Halfway to the bottom, a voice shouted up. "Lindsey Mae, is that you?" It was Miss Fancy. "Thank God, you're still alive. Are you hurt?"

"No." As though she walked through a dreamland, Lindsey Mae reached the foyer. She observed the disheveled madam without pausing.

"What about Willa Jean or Sissy?"

"I don't know. I haven't seen them . . . or *anyone*." The last word quivered from her throat. *Don't ask about the cowboy,* she thought, frantic that she might have to speak his fate aloud.

Tears brimmed in her eyes. She splashed through knee-deep water in the foyer, then wandered, benumbed, through a great jagged space where the front door had once been. Miss Fancy's pride and joy, that door, carved from mahogany by an itinerant tradesman.

Outside her breath caught at the destruction. Many of the buildings were little more than piles of kindling. On the road, water reached the ankles of her boots.

The air was deathly still and so heavy she doubted a bird could fly through it. She imagined it parting as she passed. Still, dense, and hot. Sultry. Stifling.

The only comfort, actually, was a circle of blue sky directly overhead. But even that looked ominous, for the horizon was still gray and stormy all around. As if in deference to the vast destruction it had caused, the force of the storm hung heavily in the dense air. Lindsey Mae felt as though she were standing at the bottom of a dark well, looking up to a faraway patch of blue sky.

Others had wandered out of hiding. They stood in stupefied silence beside destroyed businesses and dwellings. She paid them scant notice, except to observe their benumbed expressions. Was she as stunned as they? Likely, she decided, but she still had a mind for what to do. *Escape.*

Although her inner drive to board the *Louisa* and leave this demolished town behind bordered on madness, she knew she couldn't, not until she learned the fate of her friends—Ida and her children, Gordo, and Mister Simpson, whom most called Nevershed.

Gordo was an invalid and Ida Mahaney had five children, all with different fathers, none of whom had hung around to help shoulder any of the responsibility. Gordo and Ida's little Joey and Mister Simpson fished Lindsey Mae out of the bay one long-ago day. She could not leave here without seeing to their welfare. But the closer she came to the wharves, the worse the destruction, the deeper the water, and the greater her fears for these loyal friends.

Hurrying on, she decided to look for Ida first, then Gordo, then . . . Of a sudden, visions of the cowboy swam in the swirling water around her. Would she ever see him—

"Lindsey Mae!"

Her feet stumbled over her stalled heart. The cowboy! Had she conjured him? Tensed against horrors she could only imagine, she turned to find him standing in the road, very much alive.

Grinning broadly, his eyes searched hers and were as warm and wonderful as she had recalled. When he began to slosh toward her, something sweet and joyful caught in her chest. Her skin prickled suddenly inside her steaming clothes.

March took one look at Lindsey Mae and his whole world brightened. Then he was running, sloshing through ankle-deep water. Her shirtwaist was wet and clung to all the places he had seen and all those he hadn't, except in his imagination. Her skirt was bedraggled, but springy curls danced about her face. Even streaked with kohl and carmine, it was the loveliest face he had ever seen. Her shiny blue eyes told the tale—she was glad to see him, too. He reached for her.

She came into his arms. He pulled her to his chest, held her close, and tucked her head into the lea of his shoulder, against his wet shirt. He felt her heart beat strong against him; felt his echo the welcome . . . the need.

She inhaled deeply, drawing in the heady, masculine scent of the cowboy—a trace of bay rum, spiced with salt and masculinity. In her haste to throw her arms around him, she forgot the carpetbag clutched in one hand.

When it walloped him across the shoulders, he drew back and examined her with those teasing brown eyes she had thought never to see again. Her breath caught.

Just as she tightened her grip on the carpetbag, he pressed his lips to her forehead in a gesture so intimate her knees turned to jelly.

"You wouldn't by any chance have my money in that satchel, would you?" he whispered against her skin.

His money. Her knees stiffened right back up.

His money; her escape. She opened her mouth to explain, but all that came out was, "Why?"

When he tipped her chin, her breath caught at that lopsided grin. He was even more handsome than she recalled. He had a playful way about him that at once reminded her of her brothers and of something innately personal, something she couldn't put a name to, but which left her breathless.

"Because I have a sudden hankerin' to buy a kiss, but dang if I'm not flat broke."

Lindsey Mae's heart skipped when she thought about kissing those lips—truly kissing them—at last. But curiously, her boldness of earlier fled, leaving her unable to say what she felt. She wanted to tell him he didn't need to buy a kiss. She would give him one. Or buy one from him. Since she held all the money.

Money for her escape. Recollecting her purpose restored a measure of, if not sanity, at least determination. Regret weighed heavily in her limbs. She drew away, caught the carpetbag to her chest, and smiled.

"Good-bye," she said wistfully. "I have a lot of things to do before I catch the boat." March exploded.

"Before you *what?*" He was still reeling from the joy of finding her alive and unharmed and from his unexpected but nevertheless aching need to kiss her. She hadn't offered, though, and by some senseless logic, he didn't feel right taking something she sold for a living.

Which fact had troubled him while he clung to life and limb on that pitching barrel and later in the makeshift shelter of an old cistern. She didn't look like a whore. Absently, he wiped a streak of kohl off her pale cheek with the pad of a thumb. She shouldn't be one. But she was.

His touch fired emotions that mocked Lindsey Mae's recent pledge to never *look* at a man again. A pledge she felt duty-bound to honor, given to Whom it was made. Yet, at the time she made it, she believed the cowboy dead, and . . . "I'm taking the *Louisa*," she explained. "If it hasn't already left. It was scheduled to leave port at four o'clock, but maybe the storm delayed it."

"Hell, Lindsey Mae, no steamer has left this port in hours—"

"Good, then I'll be on my way." Regretfully, she thought, feeling her need to escape melt in the fire that flamed in the cowboy's eyes. But a promise was a promise, especially one to the Lord. She shouldn't even have noticed the fire in his eyes.

Besides, if she stayed here, all that awaited her was upstairs work. And after the cowboy . . . . "I'm awfully glad you survived," she told him.

"Thanks a lot," March retorted, miffed that she could consider leaving him so blithely. He caught her by the arm. "Listen to me, Lindsey. We've got to get somewhere safe. This is the eye of the storm."

She scanned the sky, noting once more dark clouds that roiled around the horizon. "It isn't over?"

"That was only the first side. The second side will be worse."

"Then I really must catch that—"

"Dang it, Lindsey Mae, we don't have time for me to explain a hurricane right now. We've got to get to safety."

She focused on his arms, strong and powerful beneath the torn chambray shirt. She recalled how he looked with his shirt unbuttoned, with the tails pulled out. She recalled his hands on his waistband, hands that would have been on her skin if the storm hadn't interrupted the worst mistake of her life.

But what if it wouldn't have been her worst mistake? What if it wouldn't have been a mistake at all? The pull of this man was stronger than the pull of a storm. Resistance seemed a thing foreign. If she didn't get away now, she would be lost. And she had, after all, made that pledge. "Go ahead. I'll catch the steamer."

"Dang it." March sighed. On second thought, maybe he would have to explain hurricanes right now. "No ship can leave this harbor, probably for days. And you can't make it to within a hundred yards of the wharves. They're under water, maybe even destroyed."

"Destroyed?"

"Kindling," he said bluntly, trying to make a point.

"Oh, no! They can't be. Not . . ." Frantically, she

scanned the harbor from left to right. "What about the people?"

"What people?"

"The people who live there. Did they get out? Did they drown? Where are they?"

"How the hell would I know? I've been riding a dang barrel all afternoon."

"And I've been huddled in a corner, while . . . Lord 'a mercy! I have to find them."

"Who?"

"My friends."

"Lindsey Mae, you aren't listening. We've got to get to someplace safe before the back side of this storm hits. We don't have much time."

"How much?"

He shrugged, exasperated. "Who knows? Depends on the size of the storm."

"I don't understand."

"Look, I promise to explain it some quiet day when we're sitting in our rocking chairs with nothing else to talk about. Right now—" Her startled expression halted his words.

Then he realized what he had said. *Sonofabitch!* Had the storm brain-dazed him? "Come on. I feel . . . responsible, sort of. If I hadn't wanted your . . . uh, services, you might have gotten out of there with something more than the clothes on your back."

"I didn't have anything more than the clothes on my back."

He eyed the carpetbag.

"And this old thing," she added, striving for nonchalance.

"Well, let me carry it. We've got to . . ." When he reached for the carpetbag she held fast. He cocked his head. "Why so protective? If you don't have anything other than the clothes on your back, why would you bring this heavy ol'—" He jerked the satchel away.

Life swooshed out of her when he opened it. She watched her escape evaporate before her very eyes. Served her right, she admonished angrily. Hadn't she promised the Lord above that she would never *look* at a man again? And hadn't she broken that promise the minute this ... this *cowpoke* waltzed into view?

"So you did bring my money," he was saying. "Downright thoughtful of you, Lindsey Mae."

"I intended to build you a monument."

He chuckled. "At sea?"

"What do you mean?"

"You were taking the *Louisa*. No doubt, with my money."

"Am," she corrected. "I am taking the *Louisa* as soon as this eye or whatever you call it is over."

"After the eye, sweetheart, comes the real storm."

Panic whirred inside her. Through the haze, she watched March remove his guns and holsters from the carpetbag. He surprised her by thrusting the rest back at her, money and all.

"Keep it for now," he said with a sly grin, while he buckled the guns around slender hips. "We can sort out your earnings later."

Any other time, she might have locked horns with him over that, but the sight of him wearing matching pistols banished every purient thought. Her stomach tumbled. He looked like her brothers, like her father. "I don't know what you need guns for," she said crossly.

"Looters?" he offered. "Or to defend a lady?"

She grimaced.

"I'm serious, Lindsey. Storms bring out the worst in folks. I wouldn't be much protection without weapons. Since lances and swords have gone out of style—"

"I don't recall asking you to defend me."

"I appointed myself. Come on." He reached for her arm, but she refused to budge. "Get off your high horse," he commanded. Then in a lighter tone, "I'll give 'em back after the storm. You can have 'em bronzed for my monument.''

"Guns on a monument? I know men who'd like that. I thought you were different."

"You thought right. I'm not a gunman. But I dang sure intend to defend myself . . . and you. So come on." He walked off a few steps, pulling her after him. Or trying to.

She dug her heels into the rain-soaked shell. "You expect me to change my plans just like that? I have friends who need me. And a boat—"

"You won't do friends any good by dyin' in this storm."

"I won't do them any good if I follow you! Who are you to make decisions for me? You who . . . I don't even know your name."

"March," he tossed back.

He infuriated her, but she sensed for all the wrong reasons. "Lord 'a mighty! Is that all you can do, issue orders?"

He turned with a weary expression. "March. That's my name. Want me to spell it? *M-A-R-C-H*."

"Oh." Somewhat mitigated, now that she knew he didn't shout commands at the drop of a hat, she nevertheless held her ground. "I'll make you a deal."

His brows shot up in that expression that set the roots of her hair on fire. "A deal?"

"Help me find my friends."

I'd rather have you safe, he thought, but refrained from voicing something so maudlin. "We don't have much time."

"Then stop arguing. I wouldn't ask, but they aren't able to help themselves, and they took me in when I had no one, and I have to find out what's happened to them, March, and . . ."

Her words, spoken in haste but with such passion, drew him to her. He stopped when she spoke his name, stunned by how much he liked hearing it on her lips. His eyes delved into hers, which burned like slow blue flames. He felt the heat from those flames clear to the toes of his soggy boots.

Again, he had to stop himself from kissing her. It was becoming quite a chore. "You're one crazy . . ." When the word *whore* almost slipped out, he cringed, finishing with, ". . . female."

She smiled and he thought for a minute the sun had come out. But it hadn't. It was her. She had that effect on him. Lord, help him. A waif of a prostitute, but dang if just looking on her didn't brighten his stormy day.

"Thanks, March." She took his hand and led him forward, and it was several minutes before he realized that she was leading him straight for the wharves which he had already told her were under water.

When he tried to object, she stopped him with, "That's where they live," and kept on sloshing through the murky water.

Lived, he thought. "They would have gotten out, Lindsey. Someone would have helped them."

"Maybe, but I have to be sure."

Within minutes a towheaded youth of ten or twelve, March judged, hailed them. "Hey, Miss Lindsey!" The boy looked like he had been wallowing with pigs. Mud plastered his once-light hair to one side, like a thick application of pomade. But he strode through the silt and water, undaunted. When he drew near, March saw that he was barefoot.

"Joey!" Lindsey Mae greeted the youngster with a warm hug that left March hungering for the same. "Where's your ma?"

"In the boathouse, Miss Lindsey. She an' the youngun's are clingin' to the rafters like chickens with a fox after 'em."

"The boathouse?" March questioned.

"It's a right handy place to live," Joey allowed. "Or

was till this overflow. Have our own fishin' hole right inside the house.''

March turned raised brows to Lindsey Mae.

"They took me in," she said by way of explanation, which wasn't an explanation at all.

Joey further confused the issue by adding, "After I helped Mister Gordo fish 'er out o' the bay."

Certain he was not ready to hear the details of that, March cast a wary glance skyward. "Let's get Joey to cover."

"After we rescue the others." Lindsey Mae spoke with a conviction that brooked no argument, but Lord help him, March thought, if her smile didn't still the storm inside him. "We'll take them to the courthouse," she added.

Reality smacked him like a fist to the chin. His hands went automatically to his guns. The jail adjoined the courthouse. Jeb Taylor was in that jail. Or had been. Jeb Taylor, the man he had come to town to kill.

"It's the strongest structure in town," she explained, hugging the boy again. "Oh, Joey! I'm so glad you're alive, all of you!"

"It was nip an' tuck there for a while," the child admitted. "That wind fairly tossed us to kingdom come."

When March tried to hurry them along, Joey stopped him with, "We'll need a boat, mister, 'cause Ma cain't swim, nor the younguns neither. Water's powerful deep 'round the shed."

March whistled through his teeth. In a gesture of futility, he glanced around. No boats in sight. "Looks like we're out of luck on that score." Where time was concerned, too, he thought grimly.

"Then I'll swim in and get them out," Lindsey Mae declared.

March sputtered and spewed and finally came out with, "Over my dead body."

Their gazes locked. He attempted to stare her down, but to no avail. At length, she smiled, and he thought she had given in. That's how little he knew about this woman, he realized when she suggested, "You do it, then. Before that eye catches up with us."

"Passes over," he corrected. "I have a better idea. Joey, come with me." He eyed Lindsey Mae. He couldn't leave her behind. No telling where she'd be when he got back. "You, too."

Finding the bathhouse took a bit of deduction, what with so many of the town's structures demolished. Once Joey learned their destination, he was fairly put out.

"I know I need a bath, mister," the boy argued when they trudged into the empty, but still partially standing, building, ". . . but don'tcha think we could save ma an' the youngun's first?"

"That's what we're fixin' to do, son. Give me a hand here, will you?"

In the end it took all three of them, pulling, prizing, and tugging to disengage one of the three wooden bathtubs from its moorings and haul it to deeper water.

"In you go," March ordered Lindsey Mae. Their eyes met, his determined, hers defiant.

"I can swim. I'll help push."

He should have known she would argue, he told himself, amused. "No need." He grabbed her by the waist, swung her over the edge, and set her down. But for a moment he couldn't turn her loose. His hands lingered on her waist, while their gazes held again, and fascination thrummed between them. He remembered holding her that way before and was certain she remembered it, too. Wordlessly, he unbuckled his guns and handed them to her.

That broke the spell. Her expression turned from sensual to cold in the time it would take a flash of lightning to slash the stormy sky. She glanced pointedly from the guns to the water.

"Don't even think it," he warned, wondering why guns evoked such an emphatic response from her. "Keep 'em dry. I was serious about defending you—and myself—and all your friends.''

They found Ida Mahaney and her younger children clinging to rafters, like Joey had said. The shed was half on land, half in water, and the roof had fallen in.

''Ma, Ma, I'm back,'' Joey called.

With more than a little trepidation, March squeezed through a small opening and found Ida nursing a baby. As though he had crawled headfirst into a coyote's den, he reversed direction and began to scoot backward through the narrow space. In his haste to exit the scene, he hit his head on a rafter.

''Damnation, Lindsey!'' he called, discomfited and angry for it. He'd seen women nurse babies before. Once or twice. It had certainly never had a sexual effect on him. Hell, there was nothing sexual about it. Everyone on earth was breast-fed at one time or another.

But everyone on earth had not spent the past few hours fantasizing about Lindsey Mae Burnett. March Sutton had. During the storm he held personal fears at bay by mentally undressing her. Leisurely. Hastily. Always provocatively. He touched her and fondled her and cherished her and . . . damnit . . .

''Lindsey!''

''I'm here.''

Awkwardly, he made room for her to squeeze past him. By this time Ida had covered her breast, but it was obvious what had been happening. Lindsey Mae's eyes found March's. She quickly dropped her glance, but not before he saw a touch of pink flush her cheeks.

''Lindsey Mae, child, where'd you come from? I thought sure we'd floated clear to Mexico.''

''You're still in the harbor.'' She laughed and the sound flashed down March's spine. ''Almost,'' she added. ''Hand me Little Bit.'' She took the baby, addressing the other wide-eyed children with, ''Wait'll you see what kind of boat we brought.''

Their frightened little eyes brightened, but, to March's surprise, they remained on their perches until their mother told them to scramble down.

Even then, Hoss was the only one who gave them a minute's worth of trouble. At five, he considered himself big enough to swim with Joey. March figured otherwise.

"Listen to Mister March," Joey told his brother.

"It isn't Mister March," Lindsey Mae objected. "It's Mister . . ."

March struggled to bring his mind back to the present. He had been studying the way Lindsey Mae looked holding Ida's baby. Studying and fantasizing and . . .

"Mister what?" she prompted.

Reality hit March another lick. He held her gaze, trying to read beneath the surface, afraid he had. Dang if she didn't have the most unsettling blue eyes . . .

"Uh . . ." He wasn't afraid to give his name to her, he reasoned, or even to these homeless folks. What could they do if they learned who he was and why he was in town?

It was more like he was ashamed, he realized with a jolt. He had come to town to kill a man. By nightfall he could be a murderer. The least he could hope for was that Lindsey Mae never connected him with such a deed. He wasn't sure why that mattered, but it did, more with every passing minute.

"Call me March," he responded abruptly. He should distance himself from her. The sooner the better. But the wind was already picking up. He couldn't leave her to fend for herself in this storm. Hell, she was plucky enough to go back to the wharves. He couldn't risk that.

"That's all right," Joey was saying. "I don't know my last name, either."

"You don't?"

"Naw. Susie nor Hoss nor me nor Little Bit. None of us has the same pa. Ma says it'd be downright confusin' to go about with different names. Ain't that right, Ma?"

Ida gave a wan sort of shrug, which March figured could

be embarrassment but suspected was plain ol' weariness.
She looked more worn-out than any person he had ever
seen, and he had a notion it didn't have all that much to
do with the storm. Her clothes and those of her children
were tattered and colorless. Her hair was mousy brown;
her face, weathered, leathery. She could lie down amid the
rubble of this town and no one would take the least bit of
notice.

All of which added one more burden to his worried
mind. Who was this woman? What was she to Lindsey
Mae? Lindsey Mae, with her bright eyes and ready smile.
The kohl and carmine had mostly washed away by now,
and he realized with a surge of pleasure that he had been
right. She didn't look anything like a prostitute. Especially
not holding Little Bit.

Then again, he had a feeling he didn't look anything
like a killer, either. He had to get away from her soon—
before he became one.

When they reached the raised shell roadway, he lifted
the children, one by one, from the makeshift boat, then
helped Ida to the ground. When he turned for Lindsey
Mae, she handed him, instead, the baby.

Before he thought not to, he took it. Then froze. A baby.
He had never felt so clumsy. He looked to Lindsey Mae
for help, but dang if she didn't start laughing.

"Laugh if you want," he retorted. "I'm not cut out for
this. I might . . ." The delight on her face stopped his
words and left him feeling something akin to lunacy.

Ida took Little Bit, but when March reached to help
Lindsey Mae alight from the tub, she had already climbed
out on her own. He stood there looking at her, empty
armed and hungering for her touch. Frustrated but not sure
why, he reached for the carpetbag and strapped on his
guns.

The courthouse, after all, was where Jeb Taylor would
be.

"Looters," he muttered at Lindsey Mae's incriminating glare.

Watching March belt on his guns, Lindsey Mae felt their earlier camaraderie wither. Men! They were all alike. They would rather fight than . . . than . . .

Than what? she chastised, furious with herself. Why was it so difficult to recall that pledge? It was, of all things, a pledge to the Lord. And He wasn't likely to take it lightly.

"After we help Ida and the children to the courthouse," she told March in a no-nonsense tone, "we have to find Gordo."

"Time's runnin' out, Lindsey."

"Then don't go. I'll take the tub."

"If you think I'd let you go out in this storm by yourself—"

Lindsey Mae bowed her neck, but before she could argue, Ida interrupted. "We can make it the rest of the way, child. Go ahead and find Gordo before the back side of the storm hits."

"Shout hallelujah!" March cried. "Someone around here knows what the eye of a storm is."

"You don't have to be sarcastic," Lindsey Mae countered. "Ida was born on the coast, and I wasn't. We'll meet you at the courthouse, Ida. Joey, help your ma with the youngun's."

"I will, Miss Lindsey."

"Miss Lindsey," March ordered, when she attempted to push the makeshift boat back into the water. "Just what do you think you're doing?"

"Going after Gordo."

"No, you aren't. The wind's pickin' up. Feel it?"

Although she wasn't about to admit it, Lindsey Mae did feel the wind, and it was more than a little frightening. Not that she would let March whatever-his-name-was know it. She had to find Gordo. And Mister Simpson. Driven by renewed urgency, she shoved harder.

March caught her shoulder. "Don't fight me, Lindsey."

When his touch sizzled down her arms, she jerked away. "I'm not. You're fighting me."

"I can't let you go. You know how bad it was before. The next time will be even worse."

"I can't leave him to die, March. He saved my life."

Frustration swept through March like a storm surge. "That's what I'm trying to do! Can't you tell? I'd bet all the money in that satchel you didn't fight him like you're fighting me."

"Then you would lose."

Her somber tone, combined with a look of despair in eyes that had moments before challenged him with sensual innuendo, sent March's spirits plummeting.

He watched her shove the tub into the water with dogged determination. Ignoring him, she sloshed in after it, unmindful of her sodden skirts. Of her life. Her black ringlets looked like little springs popping from her head. As though to tease him with what might have been, one remaining fuchsia bow peeked from beneath them.

Even as he watched, fantasizing, the wind gained strength. It molded her clothes to her body and made her look like a champion instead of a victim. He couldn't imagine her ever being a victim. She was a fighter. Suddenly, watching this diminutive, dauntless woman challenge the power of Mother Nature, March knew he would fight whatever battles she dragged him into.

But he didn't have to like it. "Where did he live?"

"*Does,*" she corrected primly. "He lives at the docks, in an old abandoned boat."

"Dang it, Lindsey, don't you ever give up on anything?" He recalled how she had almost jumped out those French doors after the gallery collapsed. If she'd been able to, she would have pulled him out of the water by the sheer force of her will. The sensuous blue thread of desperation in her eyes had almost done it. "I've never known anyone like you. Why, you're the most stubborn, pigheaded, thickskulled female I've ever encountered in all my born days.

You'd charge hell with a bucket of water. You take the cake, do you know that? You beat 'em all. Yes, you do. You—'' He stopped, mouth ajar.

She had started to laugh, really laugh, and the sound trilled down every tired muscle in his body. Like warm water and a brisk rubdown, her laughter renewed him. Her eyes danced. She looked at him with such compelling passion, that, for a moment, he, too, became oblivious to the world whirling around them. He wanted to kiss her. At the moment, that's all he wanted, all he ever wanted. Or the beginning of all he ever wanted.

Her. A prostitute.

And before the day was out, he could be a murderer.

"We also have to see about Mister Simpson," she was saying. "Most folks call him Nevershed. He lives up the way." Nothing tentative about her now, she was a bundle of pure, undiluted confidence. And why not? She had him lassoed and hog-tied, and dang if she didn't know it. Like a cocky belled steer, she was leading him to slaughter, and he was too smitten to protest.

He was past arguing. "How did you come to befriend every derelict in town?"

"They befriended me." That was all she said, and once again, her tone indicated that was all she intended to say. But it wasn't enough for March. It opened a Pandora's box of questions.

They found the wharf area a good fifty yards inland from where it had been at the beginning of this day. They even located Gordo's boat, what was left of it. A piece of hull with the words *Ol' Gordo* painted on the side lay beside a pile of unrecognizable debris that bobbled up and down in an unstable fashion. Lindsey Mae scrambled over it without giving one thought to her own safety.

March followed, his heart in his throat, his eyes alert. Hell, would he never get this woman to safety?

"Gordo!" she called. "Gordo, can you hear me?"

When March's toe struck something soft, he glanced

down, then froze. "Lindsey." Although the wind was rising steadily now, and he barely spoke, she heard.

In a moment she was on her knees in the rubble, tearing into the splintered wood with her hands. "Gordo! Gordo, say something! It's me. Lindsey Mae. I've brought help."

March knelt on the wobbly platform and placed a hand on her shoulder. "He can't hear; sweetheart."

"I know." But she scooped the man's head in her lap and buried her face in his wiry gray hair. He was an old man with bushy brows and weathered cheeks. March glanced farther—no legs. He hadn't lost them in this storm, but sometime earlier, for his trousers were knotted below both knees.

Who was this legless old man? What was he to Lindsey Mae, the prostitute with a heart of gold? Cliche though the description was, it could have been coined for the woman kneeling beside him.

He watched her shoulders quiver and felt the wind gust and rain pelt his face. They had to get out of here. She needed to grieve, but she also needed to live.

He needed for her to live. How much, hit him like the back side of the storm was fixing to. How could it have happened? He had known her little more than half a day, yet he felt like it had been forever.

Suddenly it made no difference that she was—had been—a prostitute. There was so much more to her than that. So much to admire and cherish . . . and protect.

"Lindsey, the second side of the storm is about to hit. It'll be worse than the first." Her shoulders shook harder.

He slid an arm around her, drew her gently against him. "We'd better go. The back side will drive this water out to sea. We'll be fighting it all the way in."

She shrugged off his arm. "You go. I can't leave him."

Rising panic mingled with a sense of desperation. "You said he saved your life."

"He did. And I won't leave him now. I can't."

"Then he saved it for nothing. Is that what you're saying?"

"No. I mean . . ."

"If you die down here you won't be doing anybody any good."

She raised stricken eyes to his. "Or any harm."

He held her grief-stricken, defiant stare and knew she was wrong. The depth of his feelings for her struck him hard in the gut, catching him unawares. Strange as it seemed, he'd bet the ranch it was real. "Don't I count?"

"You?"

He held her gaze, knowing that what he wanted to say was largely inappropriate at the moment. "You have my money," he quipped, resorting to flippancy. "And you haven't earned it yet." His reply startled her. Before she could recover, he tugged her to her feet and guided her off the stack of debris.

She glanced back once. "We can take him in the tub."

"Leave him where he is, sweetheart. He's an old seaman, from the looks of him. The sea claims their own."

"Yes. Yes, he would want that."

By the time they reached the road, the storm had returned in full force. Lightning flashed and thunder rolled with such frequency, March felt like he was back on the battlefield. Even though the objects being tossed at them were not bullets, in a direct hit they would be every bit as deadly.

Sight of the courthouse tore March's mind from the weather, for inside him raged a storm of a far different sort. It stood a hundred yards or so away, minus half a roof and many windows. A dwindling stream of refugees fought the wind and rushing water to climb to its second-story entrance.

The courthouse. The adjacent jail. Jeb Taylor. Maybe Taylor had already escaped and was long-gone. On the other hand . . . Worriedly, March searched each face, then finally stopped to check his pistols. His hands trembled, and he had a good idea why.

He wasn't afraid of Jeb Taylor. But he didn't want to kill him. Truth known, he never had wanted to kill the man. If push came to shove, he dang sure didn't want Lindsey Mae to see him do it.

The area around them looked like Georgia after the war. Every other structure, or thereabouts, had been leveled. Those that still stood, canted on wobbly foundations and were submerged in several feet of water.

March hurried on, searching left to right, right to left. No, he didn't want to kill Jeb Taylor. But neither did he want Taylor to kill him. The gusting wind continued to rise. Not even a Taylor would be fool enough to make a move in this kind of weather.

When Lindsey Mae tripped, March caught her and they continued along the shell road, arm in arm, sloshing through water, struggling against rising wind, dodging an assortment of debris—fence posts, window frames, even furniture.

He held her close to his side and couldn't help thinking about how she looked in her pantaloons and chemise . . . and wondering what he would do, should Jeb Taylor appear, how he could avert a killing and still uphold his promise to his mother.

As if she felt his dilemma, Lindsey Mae tightened her hold on him. And in that instant March knew that Jeb Taylor and his own promise to his mother were the two least important things in his life.

"Come on." He gathered her closer. "Let's run for it." He pointed to a path littered with enough debris that they might have a clean shot at the courthouse. "Watch out for nails."

Two steps later, she tripped again. "It's this skirt," she said. "It's sopping wet."

He stopped, started to scoop her in his arms, then froze. Not fifty yards ahead he saw Jeb Taylor. March had been watching the few stragglers slog up the steps. When he stooped to lift Lindsey Mae, his eye arrested on a lanky man with a light-colored handlebar mustache that looked as limp as the starch in Lindsey Mae's shirtwaist.

Head turned against the wind, Taylor shouldered his way down the steep steps. Into the water. Not out of it. Into the storm. Not away from it. Directly toward March and Lindsey Mae.

Woodenly, March set her down. Regret tightened in his chest. Why hadn't the man made his escape earlier? Why had he waited until now, until this moment?

The inclination to let Jeb Taylor slip into the storm became overwhelming. *Let him go,* reason cried. *Let him go.*

But his mother's plea spurned such cowardice. "If that man is not convicted of his crime, you must mete justice," she had insisted. "His kin killed your father and your brother and got away with it. Now he's murdered your uncle. Every Taylor who's come to trial has been acquitted. This one must not go free."

"Matching killings, this thing will never end," March had objected. The feud began shortly after the war and was ugly from the first. March left the area, rather than become involved.

"Matching killings?" his mother had cried. "You're all I have left. If you'd been here earlier, maybe . . . maybe . . ."

"I couldn't have prevented their murders, Mother."

"Please, son. It's your duty. Go down to Indianola and put an end to that family's evilness."

So here he was. And there was Jeb Taylor, escaping. Preoccupied by the storm, no one else paid the man any mind. A natural disaster like this tended to reorganize priorities. Even March's. But his mother . . . Surely, March thought, if he called out someone would respond.

With a sickness in his gut, March stepped away from Lindsey Mae. "Jeb Taylor!" His hands hung heavily over his guns.

Taylor hesitated, glanced his way.

"Stop that man," March shouted. "He's breaking jail. Stop him."

Taylor leaped the rest of the way to the water-covered ground, ducked a piece of flying slate, and sprinted to the side of the building. He reached into his shirt as he ran. For what? A gun? Of course. One way or another, Taylor would have taken a gun from someone. March drew. Aimed at the man's legs. Fired.

Missed. Stopping to take aim, Taylor fired once in March's direction, then dashed around the building and out of sight.

Jeb Taylor missed. So had March. Damn! He had gone through hell and a hurricane, and he let the man get away. No one else seemed to care.

Then he heard the wailing, a keening that came from somewhere near and grew louder and more unearthly with every note. "Lindsey!" His heart stopped beating. "Did he hit you?"

Her eyes were wild, made even wilder by flying black curls and the storm's gathering darkness. "I knew it! You're a gunfighter and . . . and a liar! I knew—"

"I'm not a gunfighter." March shoved the gun back in its holster.

Lindsey Mae spun away, slogged through the water. He caught up with her. Jerked her around.

"I'm no damned gunfighter."

"Then why were you shooting at . . . at that man?"

"That man was Jeb Taylor."

"I know who he is."

"Then you know he's on trial for murder. He was escaping and—"

"That's no concern of yours."

In a decision quick as the lightning that flashed around them, March decided not to tell her how much concern of his Jeb Taylor really was. Jeb Taylor, cold-blooded murderer of his uncle. The jury had been on the verge of acquitting him. Now he had escaped into the storm.

"I'm a citizen. Citizens are expected to see the law up-held."

"Spoken like a gun-toting man. Mob justice, that's what it is."

"Where's the mob?" March flung his gaze skyward, to the storm-tossed clouds. His eyes returned to hers just as a jagged flash of lightning sliced across the warring heavens. "Tell me that, Lindsey. Where's the dang mob?"

"You're the mob. You and every man like you. It doesn't take . . ."

Sick at heart, March spun away to gather his wits. Just then a window frame came flying through the air directly toward them. Without a moment's hesitation, he turned to Lindsey Mae, seized her around the waist, and spun her away. The frame glanced off his shoulders and fell harmlessly to the side.

She struggled to free herself. Then she started kicking. "Let me go! I don't want any part of . . . of a murderer!"

"Dang it, sweetheart, gettin' you outta this storm is becomin' a downright chore. You're harder to corral than a rangy ol' mossy horn."

They didn't make the courthouse. Where Lindsey Mae had not been fazed by huddling in a third-floor corner while a building blew away around her or by rushing headlong into the bay in search of homeless people, March's firing at an escaped prisoner was her undoing.

It didn't make one iota of sense, not to him, unless he considered it a delayed reaction to everything that had happened in the last several hours, which March decided must be the case.

By the time he calmed her down enough to lift her in his arms, the wind was so strong he had trouble keeping his balance. The second time a combination of water and wind almost toppled him, he realized they would never reach their destination.

He chose the sturdiest structure within range, a house partially off its foundation, with a couple of missing walls and only half a roof. Several feet of water on the ground floor forced them upstairs. With each step, he expected the staircase to collapse.

Even so, it felt good to have the rain and wind off his back, and Lindsey Mae out of the storm. Gaining the second floor, he found a selection of furniture, since most of the residents' furnishings had obviously been carried up there out of the water.

Wearily he chose a sofa and eased himself down, still cradling Lindsey Mae in his arms. He had a notion, he might just hold her forever.

For a while he sat in wet clothing and soggy boots, mindless. He tried to concentrate on the storm, at least enough to determine whether they were in imminent danger. The wind howled around the unstable walls and whistled through open spaces in the roof, reminding him of the proverbial wolf. It wouldn't take many huffs and puffs to blow this house down. With that thought, he roused himself, stretched Lindsey Mae out on the sofa, stored his guns and belt in her carpetbag, and went to investigate.

The sofa appeared to be in the safest place, against an inside wall. It was the roof that concerned March—he didn't hanker to have it fall in on them. After a moment's deliberation, made all the more urgent by the way the house rocked and rattled in the gusting wind, he dragged some fallen timbers and a mattress to the sofa. From them he fashioned what he hoped would be a secure nest with an opening just wide enough for him to crawl through.

Lindsey Mae had turned her back to the outside and lay so still he thought she had dozed off, until he lay in the dark beside her and heard her sobbing.

The sound filled him with sadness. Yet, hadn't she earned the right to shed a few tears? What she'd been through in the last few hours, would have spooked a seasoned ol' cowpuncher.

Strong didn't begin to describe this woman. Pride swelled in his chest when he recalled how she fought for his help to save her homeless friends, help she hadn't needed. She proved that and then some. Lindsey Mae Burnett would do to ride the river with, dang if she wouldn't.

And the sight of her holding Ida's baby. That was something March wouldn't soon forget. It touched places inside him he hadn't known existed. An unfamiliar longing gripped him now, just thinking about it.

But her crying . . . he had never known what to do with crying women. His usual response was to back off. But this was Lindsey Mae. So he scooted closer, slipped an arm around her, and nuzzled his face alongside hers. "We'll be safe here, sweetheart."

She must have heard his claim for the lie it was, for she began to sob harder. In an effort to comfort her, he turned her by the shoulders until they lay face-to-face. But the proximity misled his body, which made instant demands for closer contact. He ignored them, best he could.

"How'd you come to know Gordo and the others?" he asked, partly to take her mind off the storm, mostly to take his mind off kissing her. Something told him that once released, his desire would run wild. And the middle of a dang hurricane was no place to initiate the kind of activities his body had in mind.

"Gordo kept me from drowning myself in the bay," she told him. When she spoke, she blew little puffs of warm breath into the lea of his shoulder.

But heated though parts of his body were, her implication chilled March. "I thought you said you could swim."

"I can. That's why I was having trouble drowning myself."

"On purpose?"

"Of course, on purpose."

For a moment nothing inside their sheltered nest moved, not even his heart. He couldn't imagine anyone being down enough to want to take his own life. Even his mother, who had lost so much, never considered giving up. She would fight back with her dying breath and expect March to fight with her.

The Lindsey Mae Burnett he saw in action today would do the same thing. Of course, today she had been fighting for the lives of others. Why had she given up on herself? Sensing this wasn't the time for so personal a question, he asked instead, "How'd Gordo manage that? Without legs, I mean?"

"He called Joey, and Joey called Mister Simpson, and together they jumped in and dragged me back to land."

March didn't know what to say. He stroked her back through layers of wet clothing. Inside their barricade of boards and mattress, the air was still and steamy. His body was on fire for her. His heart felt like it might break for her. "Why?"

"Because I came here to escape death and killing."

March blanched, recalling his own reason for coming to Indianola—to kill a man. He hoped she never discovered that.

After a while, she continued. "I had taken a job cooking for a mule train in exchange for enough pay to get me to my mother's people in Alabama. When we arrived here, the damned mule skinner ran off without paying me one red cent. All I got from him was lice from sleeping in the wagon with those mule skinner's filthy clothes. He left me stranded, with shorn hair and not a dime to my name."

March tousled her short curls and couldn't squelch his relief that she had come by her lice in an innocent way. But, of course, that wasn't the end of the tale. "So you turned to entertaining men?"

"Not at first. I couldn't find a job for a while. I had no way to live; I knew no one in town. After Joey and Mister Simpson fished me out of the bay, Ida got me a job cleaning house for Miss Fancy. Ida cooks for her, time to time. But the pay would never have gotten me to Alabama."

March let his fingers play in her damp hair. Against his

will he was curiously drawn to a line of questioning he would rather not pursue. "So you decided to work for Fancy in other ways?"

"I tried."

"You didn't . . . uh, *like* it?" *Why was he torturing himself?*

"You were my first customer and the storm—"

His hands stilled an instant before his heart caught in his throat. "Your first? You mean you've never . . ."

"You didn't know?"

"How would I have known?"

"I was so . . . ignorant. And clumsy."

March's mind whirled like a top spinning out of control on hard-packed earth. He buried his lips in her curls and willed his breathing to steady. "If that was clumsy, sweetheart, I'll take clumsy every day of the week."

When she went stiff against him, he realized she hadn't taken his teasing as a compliment. Teasing, hell. It was the gospel truth. The sweet gospel truth.

She wasn't a prostitute. And he wasn't a murderer. Jeb Taylor escaped in the storm, and March was free.

Free to do what he had only envisioned until now. Anticipation quivered through his arms as he burrowed his fingers in her still-damp hair, pulled her head up, and stared into the blackness that was her face.

"Broke as I am, I was fixin' to ask to borrow back some of my money. Now, I'll ask instead . . . for a kiss . . . freely given."

Kiss him? Lindsey Mae shied from the idea like a skittish colt. But hadn't it been right there in the front of her mind all day? Hadn't she longed to feel his hands, his lips, his . . .

Suddenly lying in his arms wasn't as soothing as it had been. Stretched out beside him, she became embarrassingly aware of every place their bodies touched. And—Lord 'a mercy!—of all the places where she craved his touch.

An acute ache of longing and foreboding fought for

dominance within her. Kiss him? He was everything she longed for. Everything she had run from.

His hands tightened on her head. When she started to squirm, he shifted a leg over her sodden skirts.

"Hold still a minute," he whispered. "This won't hurt. Guaranteed."

"No . . ." The breath caught in her throat. A strangled sound escaped. Then, in the darkness, his lips touched hers. Skimmed them. It felt like lightning skipping across water. The house shook, and for a moment she was reminded of when the storm hit the House of Fanciful Delights. This time she was certain it was her heart.

He held her so close, she felt his heart thrash against hers. His warm breath on her face sent shivers down her spine. His lips found hers with the accuracy of a homing pigeon.

That's what it felt like, a homing. A returning, but to a place where she had never been. A place so exotic she had never even imagined it; so exhilarating she never wanted to leave.

He angled his head and scooped her into a tighter fit, and opened his lips over hers. They were hot lips, wet and demanding.

But instead of relieving the ache that gnawed inside her, his seeking, questing lips spread that ache like honey. The force of it caught her by surprise. As did her eager response. Like the professional she had pretended to be, she slipped her arms around his neck, flattened herself against him, and matched his kisses, ardor for ardor.

Just when she thought she would surely die from such sweet intoxication, March's tongue darted through her open lips, where it delved and probed and caressed and teased. Without a single thought to the impropriety of her actions, Lindsey Mae found herself mimicking this wet, sensual dance.

When she pulled back to breathe, he traced her lips with

his tongue. "You were right," he murmured against her face.

Her mind was mush. She struggled to think. "About what?"

"You're very good at French kissing."

"I am?"

Chuckling, he nudged her lips apart once more.

"I haven't even touched your ear," she reminded him, while her fingers sifted through his hair.

"Ears don't have all that much to do with it," he admitted.

On impulse she ran a finger around the rim of one of his ears, only to feel a tremor race through his body.

"Then again . . ." he moaned.

"What did I do?"

"Ah, sweetheart, you fire my blood and you don't even know it." He cupped her breast and massaged her through the damp shirtwaist and wished he could feel her skin, taste her skin. But the unrelenting wind and rain that pounded and shook the remains of this house were proof that the storm had not run its course.

As of one accord, their lips sought the other's again, insistently drawing and pulling, until Lindsey Mae felt as though her soul were being pulled forth.

March's hand slipped from her breast down her side. He cupped her wet skirts and pressed her bottom to his. She felt his need through their clothing, and somehow knew it was as great as her own intense yearning. A yearning that grew with every stroke of his lips, his hands. She felt as though she were weeping inside for something unknown, yet desperately sought. A fulfillment. A closeness. A oneness. Emotions buffeted her with the strength of the storm that rocked this house.

All lucid thought vanished. While the storm played outside, she felt safe and secure here in March's arms. She never wanted to stir. March, so gentle, so . . .

Like claps of thunder, remembered gunshots ricocheted

suddenly through her brain. March, who shot at men with such alacrity it must be a way of life. As if to reinforce her memory, her hand slid down his chest, over his ribs, and rested on his hip. No guns now. But tears stung her eyes, remembering.

"I'm not a dang gunman, Lindsey Mae," he whispered against her face.

"You shot at Jeb Taylor."

"I did. But I'm not a gunman."

Her lips found his. She kissed him once, twice, then avidly again, as though the strength of her passion could obliterate the truth.

"Lindsey . . ." In the middle of his plea, a singular sound rose above the rest and exploded through the mattress barrier. In an instant he swept Lindsey Mae beneath him, covering her body with his.

"What . . ." She struggled to rise.

"Stay still, sweetheart."

The sofa began to move.

"What's happening?"

"I don't know. Just stay still."

"No! You'll be hurt . . ."

He cradled her face in his shoulder and buried his face in her hair and held on tight, while the sofa became a bucking bronc. Like many a bronc ride, this one ended with a jarring impact. They were still on the sofa, he realized, and he still held Lindsey Mae, while around them all hell broke loose.

By the time things settled down, Lindsey Mae had begun to squirm. Braced on his hands, March allowed her breathing room, but little else.

"What happened?"

"I'm not sure. I think the floor may have fallen in beneath us."

"Lord 'a mercy!"

He chuckled. "To put it mildly." Then he turned serious. "Are you all right? Feel anything broken?"

"No. You?"

"Only a few rattled bones." He settled back, pulled her loosely to his side, and willed his heart to settle down, too.

"I was frightened," she admitted in a small voice.

"Me, too," he whispered against her hair.

"I thought you might . . . die . . . protecting me."

He drew his lips across a strand of her hair, felt it curl inside his mouth, and knew he had never cared so deeply for another person. "It'll take more than a hurricane to get rid of me, sweetheart." And, dang if he didn't mean every word of it.

Soon afterward the wind ceased. When they looked out, daylight had arrived.

"Sun's out," March proclaimed.

Piles of rubble rose around them. Yet, they lay in each other's arms as though it were the most natural place to be.

Lindsey Mae stirred first. "We don't even know whose house this is."

"Was." He stared through her with a faraway look that brought an instant heaviness to her stomach. "Glad it wasn't ours."

What an astonishing thing to say! "Yours and mine?"

He kissed her nose but refrained from kissing her lips just yet, letting his want from her build anew. "Sounds far-fetched, huh?"

"Lord 'a mercy!"

"You like the idea, though?" Unable to resist longer, he kissed her lips, a tender, sweetly wet morning kiss. "Kinda?"

"Hmmm." She felt safe and secure here in his arms, and thoroughly loved. She wondered how silly he would think that, should she say it. But wasn't he being rather foolish, too? It was the storm, she reasoned. Shared danger tended to bind people together. That must be the explanation, yet the intensity of her desire surprised her still, and of his. Even now, she craved his touch, his kisses. It was more than a little frightening.

March saw his hunger reflected in her eyes. He also saw her reticence. Reticence, hell, it would be downright stupid of her to feel any other way.

In spite of the stupidity, however, he continued to kiss and caress her. His hunger seemed an endless torment. "We don't have to get married this morning," he murmured against her face. "How 'bout we give it till sundown?"

She smiled. How easy it would be to forget what kind of man he was. Easy—and dangerous. March was the kind of man she ran away from home to escape. She must not forget that.

" 'Course by then, I'll be plum wore out from wantin' you," he teased, except he wasn't teasing at all. He nipped her neck and moved lower, kissing her chest through her bodice, and she wanted more. Much more.

But she didn't tell him, for as every other time during the long night when she had been tempted to give all to this man, she remembered the deliberate way he had drawn his guns and fired at Jeb Taylor. With or without a last name, March was a replica of the men she had left home to escape.

Unable to reconcile her conflicting emotions, Lindsey Mae scrambled from the sofa. Crossing what was once a room took a little more agility, since the floor was littered with rubble.

Self-conscious now, she smoothed her shirtwaist and fluffed her tattered skirt, the only one she owned, and crossed to where she could view the town, or what was left of it.

"Storms never last," she whispered, staring aghast at the leveled town. While inside her, her own personal storm raged on.

March watched her survey the damage. Rising, at length, he buckled on his guns and went to her side. When he took her shoulders in his hands, she flinched. "Tell me why you're so spooked when it comes to guns," he asked quietly.

She drew a deep, quivering breath. "That's what I ran away from."

"What?" He wrapped her in his arms from behind and propped his chin on her head.

"Guns. Men who use guns."

"All men use guns, Lindsey."

"Not all men kill each other."

"No. Most try to sidestep such confrontations. Are you talking about last night? About Jeb Taylor?"

"Jeb Taylor. I know him."

Wary, but unsure why, he turned her to face him. "Lots of folks know him, Lindsey. That doesn't make them afraid of guns." Then, as though it had dropped from the clear, stormless sky of this new day, an entirely new thought struck him. His heart stood still. "Did Jeb Taylor kill someone close to you?"

"No."

March relaxed. A heartbeat later, she broadsided him with, "The Suttons killed my family."

It was his turn to flinch. She might have gut-shot him, so great was the shock, the pain. "Suttons?"

"Surely you've heard of the feud. They call it the Sutton-Taylor Feud."

"I've heard of it." But he didn't want to have, not then or now or ever again. Neither did he want to ask. But he had to know.

"Who . . . ? I mean, who . . ." He couldn't form the question. He wasn't sure he could listen to an answer.

"Who was killed? My father and two of my brothers. By William Sutton and his murderers. My mother, too, in a way."

"But you're not a Taylor! Your name is . . ."

"My father and Creed Taylor were friends. It's as simple as that. Friends. I don't ever want to see any of them again. Not ever. They're brutes, all of them. My family and the Taylors and the Suttons.''

While she spoke, her voice rose and she started to tremble. March pulled her to his chest, held her tightly, and by sheer force of will kept from crying himself. He had never felt so helpless; never had life seemed so hopeless.

He still wasn't ready to throw himself in the bay; but the way things stood, it would take something just short of a miracle for him and Lindsey Mae to . . .

To what? Hell, he'd known her less than twenty-four hours and here he was thinking about spending his life with her.

Had been.

But the thought of it still fired him inside and out; the impossibility of achieving it left him weak. He threaded his fingers through her short curls and lifted her face.

"We can leave here. Leave everything that hurts you behind. I'll take you far away. To the Pecos. That's where my ranch is. Way the hell away from here. I'll take care of you, Lindsey Mae. I promise I will.''

She ducked her head. He felt her eyes on his guns.

"All right," he barked, aggravated, not with her, nor even with himself, but with the untenable situation.

But was it untenable? Couldn't it be changed?

She was running away. Why couldn't he? Why couldn't they? Hell, they could go beyond the Pecos. This time he would leave his name behind.

And these damned guns! Of a sudden he unbuckled them and moved her aside. Raising his arm, he was ready to pitch them to kingdom come. Damned if guns hadn't done exactly what she said, destroyed lives, futures, hope.

He sought the bay and had to look far into the distance, for overnight the back side of the storm had carried all the water it had previously swept inland, back to sea.

It was far, but not far enough. He studied her anxious face. "I could throw these things to the depths of the sea, but it wouldn't solve anything, sweetheart.'' He handed them to her. "Keep 'em. First place we come to, I'll trade 'em in on a shotgun."

The guns weighed in her hands in equal proportions to her lightening heart. Hastily, before he could change his mind, she stowed them in the carpetbag with his money.

"I wasn't trying to steal your money," she said, contrite. "I thought you were . . ."

"Dead?" He took her in his arms. "Well, I'm not. So hang on to our money, we'll need it to outfit ourselves for the trip. Soon's we get to someplace with goods to sell."

Lindsey Mae felt like she should pinch herself. Dare she believe all this? She had gone to bed alone and lonely and had awakened in love. She couldn't be gullible, taken in by someone she had just met. She didn't know anything about March. Not even . . . She grinned, a little shy to ask at this late date.

"I don't even know your last name," she said.

The guilt that dropped anchor in March's heart would have sunk a ship if there had been any left afloat in the harbor. "Maybe I'm like Joey. Maybe I don't have a last name."

"Everyone has a last name."

"But not everyone has you." He drew her close and kissed her, knowing the truth could shatter this new and fragile relationship, unwilling to take the chance, just yet. He would tell her, someday. After they built a stronger relationship, a love so solid she would accept him for himself, not reject him for his name.

"Promise me something," he whispered against her face.

"What?"

"That you won't ever try what you did out at that bay again."

"To save someone?"

"To take your own life."

"Oh, March, you have to understand. I didn't know what I was doing. It was like I'd run to the end of the earth and there was no place else to go, no way out.''

"There's always a way out.''

"For you, maybe.'' She scanned the rubble. "For men. Men have control over their lives. Or they know how to reclaim control. Women don't have a chance.''

"I'll take care of you, sweetheart.''

"That's what I mean. Women are dependent on men, and when those men die or leave or turn to violence, the women are left destitute.''

"I'll teach you to take control.''

She grimaced.

"I will. I don't want you dependent on me, Lindsey. I've never had anyone dependent on me. Except once.'' He thought of his mother and the way she had almost manipulated and cajoled him into committing murder. Duty, she had called it. Well, no one owed anyone that kind of loyalty, not even one's mother. "Stick with me, sweetheart. I'll teach you to take care of yourself.''

His lips descended. Hers rose to meet them. Anticipation quivered deliciously through her body. But no sooner had they embarked on what promised to be the wettest, most passion-inciting kiss yet, than they heard someone stumble toward them through the rubble.

Lindsey Mae moved quickly out of his arms. She spied a stout old lady who stood fists on hips, surveying the wreckage. "Grandma Bill!'' Wading through silt, she embraced the woman. "I didn't realize this was your house. I'm so sorry.''

"Ain't we all, honey. Ain't we all.''

March came up behind her. "We thank you for the refuge, ma'am. We'd been down by the bay and couldn't make it back to the courthouse.''

"Gordo . . .'' Lindsey Mae cleared her throat. "He's dead.''

"Lordy mercy.'' The old woman shook her head. "An' how many more?''

"No telling. We helped Ida and the children get out.

But I didn't have time to check on Mister Simpson."

"You mean ol' Nevershed? Why, honey, he rode out the storm in grand style."

March scoffed, certain no one had ridden out this storm in grand style.

"Saw him jes' a while ago," Grandma Bill claimed. "Climbin' outta a cistern that'd floated his way. Stayed snug as an oyster at the bottom o' the bay."

Lindsey Mae placed a hand on the old woman's arm. "We'll find him. He should be told about Gordo. We . . . we couldn't bring in Gordo's body."

"Jes' as well, honey. Ol' Gordo'd be mighty uncomfortable in a dryland grave. The sea's been his home all his life. Why, I never knowed no one other'n a fish to be so at home on the water."

"The children will miss him. And his stories." Lindsey Mae included March. "Gordo had a story for every constellation in the sky at night and every cloud by day. Ida's children know more mythology than anyone on the peninsula from listening to him." When she squeezed back tears, March nudged her with a hand.

"Let's go find Mister Simpson."

Outside the air was so still it was hard to draw a full breath. And silent. The silence seemed as heavy as the air. The only sounds came from shifting piles of debris, and an occasional exclamation from dazed citizens.

But most were stunned into silence. Walking in pairs or groups, they seemed unaware of folks around them. When anyone spoke, it was in the hushed tones heard at a funeral.

"How many people do you think died?" she asked once.

"Likely no one will ever know."

"After we find Mister Simpson, I need to see Miss Fancy and the girls. The house was in such bad shape before the lull, it might not have withstood the second blow."

March surveyed the leveled peninsula that less than

twenty-four hours earlier had held a thriving town of six thousand inhabitants. "It's hard to believe," he muttered. "Hard to believe."

·Harder still to believe was the woman at his side, the strength of his feelings for her. It hit him suddenly, how much he could have lost—to the storm and by killing Jeb Taylor. Dipping his head, he kissed Lindsey Mae full on the mouth.

When he lifted his lips, she felt lost in an expression too loving to be true. It was too soon, much too soon to feel something so strong, so permanent. Too soon.

Or was it? With trembling fingers she brushed a lock of tangled hair off his forehead. She recalled the fear that had gripped her while their sofa flew through the air, and the joy she felt afterward, learning that he was unharmed. And with her. Together they . . .

"Hey, Lindsey Mae!"

She turned at the shout, ready to greet a friend. Then her heart stopped. *Jeb Taylor!* Intuitively, she clutched the carpetbag to her bosom. The carpetbag in which she carried March's guns. Lord 'a mercy!

"I didn't recognize you last night, Lindsey Mae." Jeb Taylor strolled toward them, a smirk on his lips. It dawned on her then that she had kissed those lips.

Her first kiss. At a party when she was only thirteen. They played spin the bottle and he kissed her. Until last night she hadn't known that it wasn't a kiss at all. Not a real kiss.

He stopped ten paces away, legs spread, hands hovering at his waist. *Arrogant,* she thought. Then he spoke.

"Lindsey Mae, what the hell're you doin' with that damned Sutton?"

Chapter Three

Sutton? Lindsey Mae looked from side to side, confused. She glanced to March for help. His expression broadsided her like a piece of wind-hurled debris. Suddenly her head filled with a roar. Her body began to tremble. She was back in the storm.

Her storm.

This one, she sensed would certainly last forever.

March reached for her. "Lindsey, I—"

"Don't." She stumbled backward, stunned. "Just don't."

"I had nothing to do with that feud, Lindsey. You've got to believe me."

Her gaze darted from March to Jeb Taylor, then back to March. March *Sutton!* Betrayal stripped her of all sense. She felt naked, vulnerable. The sultry air pressed in on her. She struggled to breathe, to think.

"That's why I left the country," March was saying, "to keep from getting caught up in it. You've got to believe that."

She had heard it said that hope and despair were two sides of the same coin. Now she understood. Moments before she had been filled with hope. Now she felt as if that coin had been tossed in the air, and all hope lay face-down in the silt at her feet. Believe him? "How could you ask me to believe you? You lied to me."

"I never lied to you."

But suddenly it was as clear as bay water after the sand had settled. A stranger in town. Quick with guns. Like her father. Her brothers.

Like all the men she had run from, all the men she had loved.

And like all the times before, her pain was so intense, she wanted to run from it. Run. Away. Far, far away.

But this time, there could be no running away. This man had betrayed her in the deepest, most personal way. This time she must stay and fight. "Then why are you in town? Why? At this particular time?"

"He came to kill me," Jeb allowed with a sneer. "Or to try to. An eye for an eye, ain't that right, Sutton?"

No! She wanted to refute Jeb's claim, but it made too much sense. She could hardly force herself to question March. But she intended to hear it from his lips. Lips that had . . .

"You came to . . . to *kill* Jeb?" she demanded.

"My mother sent me." His voice sounded strange, familiar, yet not. "To see justice done."

"Justice!"

"I changed my mind, Lindsey. *You* changed my mind. Last night, yesterday, all of it. Please, listen . . ."

The truth crashed like felled buildings inside her. Finally she was angry. "You couldn't wait to jump into the fray, could you? You and your guns. You lied . . ."

"I never lied to you," he repeated.

"It's the same as. You didn't tell me the truth. Not even after I told you . . . everything . . . you lied."

"Lindsey." He reached for her again, but she shrank away. "Please don't, Lindsey. I was going to tell you. After—"

"After what? A sundown wedding? You didn't want to

marry me. You wanted to flaunt me in their faces. To use me. Well, I found out in time.''

But she hadn't found out in time. Despondency swept through her. Men and their promises! ''You betrayed me, March Su—'' Her throat tightened over the name. She struggled to get it out. When she succeeded, it was to spit at him. ''March *Sutton*.''

''I didn't betray you, Lindsey. I swear it. I was going to tell you. I knew how you'd react, and I wanted . . .'' March clinched his jaws. ''Dang it, Lindsey Mae, I wanted us to have a chance.''

Jeb Taylor had heard enough. ''I didn't come to listen to no lover's spat,'' he shouted into the tense, still air. ''Go for your guns, you yellow-bellied Sutton. If you came to town to shoot me, by God, start shootin'.''

Lindsey Mae's mouth went dry. The air was so still and sultry, she thought she might choke on it. Her body was wet again, but with perspiration now. Perspiration and grief.

She spun away from March, stared through a haze at Jeb. He looked about as mean as a man could get. Fear pulsed through her anger. She swung back to March, who stood tall and straight, like a general. His eyes were focused on Jeb Taylor; he revealed no emotion. His hands, hands that had caressed her with profound, sensual promises, hands that held Ida's baby with such gentleness, now rested at his hips, loosely, casually, as though he did this every day.

Lord 'a mercy! Was he just going to stand there and let Jeb shoot him? She glanced around for help. People had gathered. Fanned out on either side of the combatants, they stood in foot-deep silt left by the storm. No one stood in the roadway behind either man.

Terror raced up her spine, screamed from her throat. ''Won't somebody help?''

No one moved. The scene around her might have been a photograph of storm survivors, so still did the people stand amid the rubble of this town. Lindsey Mae gripped the carpetbag tighter. Something sharp and hard pressed into her chest. *March's guns.*

His attention was riveted on Jeb. "Don't tell me you've started shootin' unarmed men, Taylor." His voice was strong, steady. By contrast, everything about her seemed ready to shake apart.

"Unarmed?" Jeb spat to the side, licked tobacco juice from his bottom lip. "When'd a Sutton go anywhere without a gun?"

March shifted his gaze, found Lindsey Mae's, held hers. It was the most desperate look she had ever beheld. But there was no fear in it, only . . .

Since he fell in love with her. That's what he was thinking. She knew it. He stopped wearing his guns because he loved her. The idea was startling, absurd.

Far-fetched, like he said earlier. But she knew as well as she knew this town had been destroyed by the storm, as well as she knew her family and his had died in this feud, she knew it was true.

March Sutton loved her. She turned to Jeb. His hands hovered above his gun butts. She watched his fingers flex. His eyes were the coldest she had ever seen. Like flint, and filled with hatred, the kind of hatred she had always imagined seeing in Sutton eyes.

But she had never seen hatred in March's eyes, only warmth and love and a gentle teasing that set her afire. Even now, March didn't seem to hate Jeb Taylor, not like Jeb hated him.

Realization struck her like the back side of the storm. Jeb intended to shoot March in cold blood.

Panic sped through her. He couldn't. She couldn't let him.

She loved March Sutton. She would love him no matter what his name was. He had been right not to tell her his name earlier. If she'd known, she would never have given him a chance. *Them* a chance.

A chance Jeb Taylor intended to take away.

"He's telling the truth, Jeb," she cried.

Jeb scowled. A sickly grin tipped his mustache.

Lindsey Mae tore open her carpetbag. She dug inside for March's guns. Pulled them out.

March's guns. They felt like anchors in her trembling hands. For an instant she wavered. She hated killing. And men who killed. She had vowed never to love another man who wore a gun; never to hold another dying head, never to stroke another cold dead brow; never to cry over another man's grave.

But this was March.

And she loved him. She couldn't let him die without a chance to defend himself. With gritty determination, she thrust the guns toward him, her arms stiff and trembling.

His gaze locked with hers, and she saw it there again. His love. Relief swept through her; like honey it soothed her anguish and coated her fear. She willed herself not to cry. March loved her. She hadn't imagined it. It hadn't come from the depths of her own fierce need. March Sutton loved her.

Moments passed, tense moments, while she held the guns and he stared at her. Finally, he shook his head. "Put 'em back."

"But he's . . ."

"I promised you, Lindsey. Put 'em back."

Jeb shouted from the other side, "Get outta the way, Lindsey Mae. I'll deal with you later. This Sutton's gonna pay for all the lives he an' his have stolen from us."

Lashed by fear, Lindsey Mae's mind reeled. The back side of the storm. Her storm. The back side was always the worst, March claimed.

And they had seen it was true. If Jeb killed March, her life would be as ruined as this flattened town.

Without further ado, she dropped the guns where she stood and hurled herself into March's startled arms. "Deal with me now, Jeb Taylor." She clung to March. His heart thrashed against her, telling her he wasn't as calm as he had pretended. Nevertheless, with both hands he tried to set her aside. Somehow she withstood his greater strength.

"If you shoot him," she screamed at Jeb, "you'll have to shoot me first. He's unarmed, and so am I."

Seconds passed, minutes. It seemed like longer than both sides of the storm put together, like forever, before she felt anything but March's strong arms around her and his heart thrashing against her, while fear stung her back with the promise of Jeb Taylor's bullets.

When at length March nuzzled her head with his chin, she lifted her face, still weak with terror. His warm brown eyes were so hot they melted her. Gradually she began to hear voices, murmurs that turned into drones, into a general clamoring.

"The sheriff's hauling him away," March explained. "Thanks to you."

"To me?" She turned slightly, for to move farther was impossible, since March had tightened his hold. From the corner of her eye, she watched a cluster of men shove Jeb in front of them up the raised road.

"Not a man of them was brave enough to take him until you threw yourself in his path."

She didn't believe that. Neither could she understand the confrontation. "Why did he think he could confront you in the middle of town?"

"What town?"

She sighed.

"I reckon he figured with everything blown away, including the jail, folks wouldn't pay any mind to one more killing."

One more killing. March's. But he was alive. They were together. She felt safe in his arms. *Right,* in his arms. His smoldering expression raised her temperature by degrees.

"Why didn't you tell me?" she whispered.

"Because I would have lost you." He kissed her then, or she kissed him. She wasn't sure who initiated it, but it was the best kiss yet . . . both exciting and inciting.

But one question remained. One desperate question. "Your father?" She was relieved when he understood.

"His name was Samuel."

Samuel. Tears of relief spilled from her eyes. Fiercely, she squinched her lids together and buried her face in March's chest. His father hadn't killed hers. Or her brothers. On this day of such terrible tragedy, that, she knew, would have been the hardest of all to bear.

"Come on," he urged at length. "Let's get out of here."

"Where?"

"Pecos River?"

"With you?"

"Always, sweetheart."

She smiled. He took it for reticence.

"I know it's soon, Lindsey, but dang, I've never felt this way before." He searched her face. "I have a notion you haven't, either. If it doesn't work out, I'll bring you back."

"Here?"

"Wherever you want. To your brothers."

"Neither of my brothers will ever accept you." As always thoughts of the feud brought a deep sadness.

"That's their problem." After a while he added, "Time heals wounds, Lindsey. After this feud is over, after things settle down, we'll do what we can to change their minds."

But nothing could diminish their rising spirits now. They continued, arm in arm, up the raised road, oblivious to everyone except themselves until they passed the House of Fanciful Delights. Or what was left of it.

"Lindsey Mae!"

Miss Fancy Delight and Willa Jean stood in front of what had once been a gaudy whorehouse parlor. Only a wall or two remained. Lindsey Mae felt a surge of relief, seeing them alive.

"Where're you headed?" Fancy called.

"To the Pecos," March replied without breaking stride.
"That's a long walk."

He laughed. "Longhorns make it every year. I reckon
we can, too." At Lindsey Mae's doubtful grimace, he
grinned. "Soon's we find a place, we'll buy us a couple
of horses." He glanced pointedly at the carpetbag. "You
still have your money, I hope?"

"Your money," she corrected.

"*Our* money." March raised a brow. " 'Less you expect me to pay for all those specialities you promised earlier."

Specialities? Lord 'a mercy, that seemed like a lifetime
ago. What did he expect? She felt less than stupid in the
romance department, especially since she discovered that
French kissing didn't involve sticking her tongue in his
ear. An aching hunger traversed her, just recalling the intimate way he had teased her lips apart and played inside
her mouth. What else did she have to learn?

Anticipation vied with trepidation and was on the verge
of winning, when little Joey overtook them.

"Miss Fancy sent 'em," he explained the bundle he
thrust in Lindsey Mae's face. "Said the blankets might be
wet still, but if the matches are dry, you can build a fire
and dry 'em out."

"If there's a place left on earth where the kindling's
dry," March mused.

Joey tagged along. "Where you headed?"

"Pecos River," March told him.

"Can I come?"

"No."

Lindsey Mae was less direct. "What would your ma do
without you?"

The boy shrugged. "I'd sure like to get her outta here.
An' the young'uns, too."

Lindsey Mae turned to March. March rolled his eyes.
She grinned and hugged the boy. "Let us go ahead and
get settled, Joey. As soon as we find a place for you to

live, and work for your ma, we'll send for you.''

"Honest?''

"Honest,'' March responded heartily.

Joey raced back to tell his ma the news. Lindsey Mae and March trudged on. They stopped once to rest, while they ate stale biscuits and jerked meat provided by Fancy Delight. Not until sundown did they get out of the hurricane's path of total destruction. Even then, signs of the storm were everywhere.

Finally, with the sun sinking below the horizon, March stopped beside a felled cottonwood. "Why don't we camp here? That stream yonder looks like it might be more fresh water than salt.''

Lindsey Mae stared at the stream in the distance and fidgeted. "March, I . . . I have something to tell you.''

"What?'' He dropped Fancy's bundle to a patch of grass beside the tree, eyed her speculatively. "More secrets?''

"Maybe a lie. A white lie,'' she hastened to add.

"A white lie. Now why would you tell a white lie?''

"Not tell, told. Something I said earlier. Before the storm.''

"Before the storm?'' He grinned. "Ready to pick up where we left off?''

Lord 'a mercy! She'd been right to worry. He expected more than she could give. He expected specialities . . . and she had none.

"I, uh . . .'' *Quit your stammering,* she chastised. *Get it over with.* She tossed her head, pursed her lips, and admitted, "I don't have any specialities.''

For a moment, he just looked at her with that lopsided grin that fired the roots of her short hair—along with other places. "No specialities?'' He took her face in his hands. His expression sobered. His eyes smoldered. "Dang it, sweetheart, if you had any more specialities, my blood would be boiling.''

She grimaced, certain there was more to all this than she was aware.

March recognized her uncertainty. "Leave the specialities to me." He kissed her forehead, then stepped aside and reached for the bundle.

It didn't hold what Lindsey Mae longed for, fresh clothing. But the two blankets were fairly dry, as were the matches. He pulled out more biscuits and jerked meat, then a bar of soap. She fell to her knees. "A comb."

He laughed. "Bring a woman a comb and her problems are solved."

"Not entirely." She still doubted her ability to please this man who did so much to please her. "At least we can bathe."

His grin would have caused the sun to swoon from the heavens, had it not already done so. "Share a bath? From a woman who claims to have no specialities?"

"Share . . . ?" Mortification spread through her like a wildfire. "Not together!"

His brows waggled wickedly. "Together or not at all." But in the end he let her go ahead while he put together a fire and draped their blankets nearby to dry more completely.

She found a partially secluded pool around a bend in the river and disrobed quickly. First she washed her clothes. Scrubbing hastily, she rinsed her skirt, shirtwaist, and underthings, then tossed them over a low-growing shrub, where she hoped they would dry some by the time she finished bathing.

At least they wouldn't smell like the storm. The water was deliciously cold and relaxing. She lathered her body, then her hair, scrubbing her scalp and short curls with her fingernails.

When she came up from rinsing, her breath caught. There was March. In the water, just beyond arms' reach, submerged to his shoulders. His eyes smoldered with resolve.

Panic sped through her, leaving a fiery trail. Even

though she could see little of him, she knew, just knew, he was naked.

Suddenly she wished she weren't. He had seen her in pantaloons and chemise. Even wet, they would be better than nothing at all. Striving to conceal her shyness, she tossed him the soap and hoped he kept his distance.

He caught it with one hand. Although she tried to turn away, she was unable to keep from staring. Her stomach turned to a mass of quivers when he raised an arm, revealing ropy muscles and an intriguing patch of brown hair under his arm.

"What's this?" He wasn't looking at the soap in his hand. His grin was for her, the grin that fired the roots of her hair. She thought suddenly that it always would.

"Dang it, woman, you've been trying to get me to wash ever since I first met you."

Lindsey Mae fought to gather her wits. She wanted to join in the fun, regardless of how mortified she felt, so she lifted her chin, and in an authoritative voice replied, "At least we found fresh water, so I won't be required to spit on you."

"Spit on . . . ?"

She could tell he was confused. In the next instant, her meaning must have dawned, for he grinned that grin again and advanced through the water with purposeful strokes. "Is that what you meant when you mentioned saliva?"

She nodded, holding her ground, although everything in her wanted to duck beneath the surface and swim away. Everything except her thrumming heart and rapid pulse and tingling skin and the fiery need that burned in the pit of her stomach.

Then March reached her. Like an eagle on his prey, he swooped down, gathered her in his arms, and carried her off toward the riverbank.

"Put me down," she squealed, although in truth the touch of his hands on her bare skin was the most wonderfully sensual thing she had ever experienced. "I don't have any clothes on, March."

"Neither do I." He winked, shaking his head in mock despair. "Spit on me? Dang if you don't need a few lessons, sweetheart. Lucky I came along when I did."

With that he lowered his lips, and while administering the wettest, most mind-boggling kiss so far, he carried her to a blanket spread beside the fallen tree. When she reached for a corner to cover herself, he stopped her with a hand to her wrist.

"It's too light," she protested feebly.

He kissed her short and sweet. "The better to see you by." His eyes left her face. She watched him inspect her—all of her—while her heart thrashed loud enough to be heard in China.

She knew when his gaze touched her breasts, for she felt his eyes upon her, actually *felt* them. She watched the tilt of his head and knew when his gaze traveled lower. Unable to bear both the embarrassment and the longing that had begun to lap at her lower regions like the bay at high tide, she squeezed her eyes tight and pressed her thighs together.

But sightless, she felt the glory of his touch as he brushed her breasts with hot fingertips, her belly with a flat palm, and lower with threading fingers, searching fingers, fingers that touched places no hands had touched before.

"Look at me, sweetheart," he prompted.

The urgency in his whispered plea could not be denied. She opened her eyes to a gaze so loving she wanted to stay lost in it forever. He kissed her lips, again short and sweet. With tender prodding, his tongue parted them and dipped inside.

Her stomach tumbled; her breath caught. He lifted her hand, which was limp and practically useless, or so she thought until he placed it on his chest.

Mesmerized, she curled her fingers in the downy-soft hair. A moan left his lips, surprising her.

"See what you do to me?" he questioned softly. "That's one of your specialities."

While she contemplated his meaning, he moved her hand lower, pressed it against his belly button, then lower. She began to resist. He tightened his hold.

"A little farther," he urged. "Let me show you . . . what you do to me."

Aquiver with a startling mixture of curiosity, trepidation, and spiraling desire, she tried to relax her arm, and partially succeeded. She knew what was coming.

She didn't know what was coming.

She had no idea what was coming! Her gaze found his, just as he fastened her hand around the softest, hardest, most intimate part of a human being she had ever touched or imagined touching. For a moment she couldn't move.

She thought she might die, but wasn't sure of what. Fright? Shock? Or the wanton desire that flowed like lava through her already burning body. But while those thoughts crossed her mind, she felt him throb within her fist!

She tried to look away, but his simmering gaze held hers. She must positively glow!

"See? You do have specialities." He spoke in a low, throaty voice that stirred the melting honey inside her. Before he finished, she felt another throb. With each throb, he seemed to grow in size!

Lord 'a mercy! Should she let go? Or should she hold on forever?

He lowered his head and kissed her, deep and wet, a kiss that reached into her heart and caressed her very soul. Timid, yet determined to give to him in return, she slipped her tongue through his parted lips.

Of an instant, he removed her hand and placed it around

his neck, mumbling something that sounded like *slow down*.

She must have misunderstood. He couldn't want to slow down. She felt like a team of runaway horses had taken charge of her senses. She let her hands play through his damp hair.

And he let his play, too. Over her skin, on her breasts, across her belly, and lower, sweetly, agonizingly lower, between her thighs and into her sizzling core.

She had never felt so loved. Or so frantic to love in return. When he kissed her again, she slipped her tongue inside his mouth and felt his pleasure, then her own, as he tugged gently on her tongue, caressing it with his mouth.

"That's how it's done, sweetheart," he whispered.

"What?"

"Washing. No spitting allowed."

While she considered his meaning he moved above her. She felt him nudge, then probe hotly, finally finding his mark. He entered her slowly.

She held herself still, experiencing, savoring.

"Next time you can wash me first," he murmured.

First . . . ? Understanding dawned. At least she thought it did. She had never heard of anything so wanton, not even from Miss Fancy Delight and the girls. Lord a' mercy!

"Or the time after that," he amended, letting her get used to his ideas, as he let her get used to the feel of him inside her. Then he thrust fully into her.

She stiffened; he held her gaze.

"Okay?"

She drew a shaky breath, inhaled the scent of him, the scent of them. "More than okay. I didn't know it would be so wonderful."

He grinned. "Hold on. We're not done yet."

Slowly, rhythmically, he began to move inside her. With each stroke she expected the end, but each stroke only produced a greater urgency. She wrapped her arms around his sweat-laved shoulders and held onto him, desperately craving release. At the same time, she never wanted the exquisite pleasure to end.

"Will it last forever?" she murmured.

"Are you ready for it to end?"

"Never." In confirmation she lifted her hips and moved with him, up and down, up and down. He chuckled weakly against her.

"Never's a little long for me, sweetheart. Your specialities have just about throw'd an' tied this ol' cowpuncher." Her eyes glowed, and he recognized the pinnacle, for he had reached it, too. With one final thrust, he carried them heavenward.

She felt as though she were spiraling toward the sun, carried on the spinning heat of a cyclone. One minute the earth was flying around her, the next, the sun seemed to explode in the heavens. A miracle, that's what it was.

March collapsed on top of her. He rolled them to the side, held her tightly.

A miracle. Awed by the profound intimacy of what they had shared, she thought back to their first meeting. "This is what I almost sold you."

He felt the dismay that sounded in her voice. He settled her against him. "No, sweetheart. What you gave me just now could never be sold—or bought."

"What we *shared*."

By now the stars had come out. She lay cradled in his arms, letting the cooler air of night dry her body. Star patterns reminded her of Gordo and all the stories he told and all the stories he would never tell. The storm had ravaged the peninsula, taking lives and property. Only she and March had gained from it. Or had they?

Bracing on an elbow, she faced him. "I may be in trouble," she confessed.

"Trouble? Who with?"

"The Lord?"

"Above?" March rolled his eyes. "You mean you don't believe in"—provocatively, he traced her bare hip—"all this good stuff before marriage? You, who was just a storm away from becomin' an upstairs girl?"

"That isn't it. I, uh, during the first part of the storm, I made a promise to God."

March raised a brow. "So what'd you promise? To join a convent or something?"

"If He let me live, I promised to never look at a man."

March chuckled. "Why, Lindsey Mae Burnett, how could you have promised such a thing? You knew I was comin' back for you."

"I did not. Besides, I thought you were dead," she reminded him.

"In that case I guess you'd've had to join a convent"— he kissed her just long enough and wet enough to make his point—"'cause I wouldn't have been able to enjoy heaven with you down here *lookin'* at all those other men."

"You wouldn't?" By now she had caught on. She trailed a finger around the ridge of his ear, eliciting a delightful shudder. "You would've had your pick of all the angels in heaven."

"I don't want even one angel, Lindsey Mae. I'm in love with you." She saw the truth reflected in his warm brown eyes.

"In love." Her desire for him built anew at his admission. "Is it possible to fall in love this fast?"

His expression turned solemn. "If I tell you what I think, will you promise not to laugh?"

"Promise."

"I think we've always been in love. It just took us a while to find each other."

"A while," she agreed, snuggling against him. "And a storm."

Eventually, she stirred enough to say, "In that case I don't guess God will mind that I broke my promise."

"I'd bet the ranch on it, sweetheart."

ONCE STRUCK

 Lynn Michaels

To Cindy Tady and Jan Kenny
research assistants extraordinaire (and darn good
writers, too)
For telling me more than I ever dreamed
there was to know
about wheat farming and mules

Chapter One

The buzzards were beginning to circle. Old Blue's carcass was still warm, and already they were floating in high, lazy spirals. Two of them. A mating pair, most likely.

Peach MaCauley sat watching them from the hill overlooking her forty acres of ripe winter wheat. Her hands were splattered with blood, her ears still ringing from the report of the Colt pistol she'd used to shoot Blue.

She wanted to cry, but it was too hot for tears. So hot she could scarcely breathe, even in the shade of the drought-yellowed hackberry tree behind her. The sweat on her back had long since stuck her brother Will's faded gingham shirt to her shoulder blades.

Blue's stablemate Red grazed nearby. The reins of the harness Peach had cut him out of with the Confederate bayonet Will had brought home from the War trailed the brittle, heat-killed grass. She needed two mules to pull the reaper, but Blue still lay in the field where he'd fallen. Peach was too stunned and stricken and Red too exhausted to move him.

The Colt lay beside her in the dusty grass, its barrel finally cool. So was Peach's horror and her panic. She wouldn't stick the gun in her mouth and pull the trigger like Will had almost a year ago. She'd get this crop in— some way, some how—then she'd sell the two-hundred and thirty acres her grandfather had hacked out of the Nebraska prairie. Her father had turned the farm into the showplace of Lynch County and Will had nearly driven it back into the sod with his gambling and drinking. Then she'd take Aunt Bethel up on her offer to come live with her in Omaha.

But not sitting here watching the buzzards circle Blue's carcass she wouldn't. Peach took a deep, determined breath and pushed to her feet, gritting her teeth at the throb in her head and the shriek of her muscles. She'd slept only five hours in the last two days, but she'd managed to cut and bind fifteen acres before Blue stepped in the gopher hole that snapped his right foreleg.

Her future hinged on the twenty-five acres of uncut wheat stretching before her, top-heavy and nodding in a stifling breath of wind. Selling the farm would pay the last of Will's debts. Selling the wheat would buy her independence. Without it, she'd land on Aunt Bethel beholden for every scrap of food she ate.

Peach would sooner rot in the field with her wheat than take charity, but she had no choice. It was beg or borrow another mule or a team of horses—or end up a poor relation. Peach was glad her parents were dead. She tightened her hands into fists and almost wished Will was alive so she could shoot him herself.

Some folks said the hill Peach stood on wasn't a hill at all but an Indian barrow. "Find a few arrowheads," her father had said, with a wink and a grin and a slow shake of his head. Peach still carried the one he'd given her in the pocket of her trousers: Will's trousers, cut off and rolled above her boots and cinched at the waist with a frayed scrap of rope. She carried the arrowhead for luck, when half the county said nothing good would ever come of it.

They still said the same thing about Kit Taggart.

From her vantage point, Peach could see the Taggart place and a fair portion of northeastern Lynch County.

Most of the fields still rolled ripe and uncut beneath the scorching midafternoon sun, but Kit Taggart's hundred acres lay flat and stubbled against the heat-whitened sky. His wheat was already in, sold at a tidy profit and loaded in a railcar on the Lynchburg spur.

"Bought hisself a fancy team of hosses and one of them newfangled headers," Jed Tyler had told her just yesterday, when he'd stopped by on his way to the thresher, his wagon spilling over with bundled wheat shocks. "Sure as it ain't rained since May Day, Miz Peach, your brother Will, God rest him, and every other fool crazy enough to get near Taggart with a pack of cards in his hands paid for 'em."

Peach knew better but she hadn't said so. His drinking and gambling debts were the only ones Will had paid— he'd left her saddled with the rest. She hadn't found a single IOU written to Kit Taggart, but a fistful made out to Ben Wilkins, Junior, Will's so-called friend.

Peach could see the thresher from here, on the Wilkins place at Three Corners. She could also see a fresh load of trouble Kit Taggart didn't need. Or deserve.

The pall of dust and wheat chaff kicked up by the eight-horse team that powered the thresher was the only cloud Peach had seen in six weeks. Wheat ripened early in dry weather, which suited her fine—the sooner she got out of Lynchburg, the better—but it made harvesting twice as hard, for the wheat grew short. Peach had read about the newfangled header in *Prairie Farmer* journal, had marveled at how wide and close to the ground it was said to cut, how easily it caught stunted wheat a reaper rolled right over.

What Peach wouldn't give for a header. And what she wouldn't give to forget she'd once felt the same way about Kit Taggart. She'd been fifteen and foolish. Too young to be drawn into the moonlit shadows behind the church at the Fourth of July Social, backed against a hickory tree and kissed the way nineteen-year-old Kit had kissed her.

He was thirty-one now, she twenty-seven, but just as foolish as she'd been all those years ago, standing here moon-
ing over a boy who'd gone off to war and come back a
man. A hard, barb-edged man by all accounts.

Peach hadn't laid eyes on Kit since he'd come home to
Lynchburg a year ago, scarce a month before Will shot
himself in the barn. At first she'd hoped—no, she'd
prayed—that he'd come calling, but he never did. She
wondered if Will had warned him off, as she suspected her
father had that long-ago summer just before the War. If
the town tabbies had told him the MaCauleys had fallen
on hard times. If he'd ridden by and seen for himself the
sagging fences and empty pastures where curly red steers
had once grazed by the score.

She'd waited for Kit to call after the Fourth of July
Social, but he'd never come. Her father had told her Kit
Taggart didn't covet her near as much as he coveted the
MaCauley land. She wondered if he was right. And some-
times, late at night, she still wondered if he'd turned Kit
off.

"Right busy feller, young Kit is," Jed Tyler had told
her soon after Will's funeral. "Says he's gonna clean up
that place a'his and make it pay. He's a Taggart, sure
enough. Dumb as rocks, the whole lot of 'em."

Rocks weren't dumb. Rocks were tenacious. Kit Taggart
had plowed and planted, fertilized and cultivated, replanted
and stocked the pastures his drunken father had let collect
trash with fat-rippled Aberdeen calves.

"Hardly ever sleeps," Jed had told her a few months
ago. "Cain't no how, he says. Too much to do."

Peach wondered if Kit had dreams like Will, if he woke
up hollering and sweating and shaking and if that's why
he didn't sleep. She wondered where he'd been since the
War, how he'd come by the fortune he'd spent restoring
his fields, raising new barns, tearing down the sod house
he'd been born in and building a proper one.

The rest of Lynch County wondered, too. Kit Taggart,

they said, was no better than he oughta be, no matter how much money he had stuffed in his pockets. And didn't they know how he'd come by it? Didn't he carry his father's dice, and didn't he rattle 'em like loose change when folks stopped to talk to him, a hard, slanted look on his face?

Weeds were not allowed in Lynch County—in field, farrow or society—and most folks considered Kit Taggart a weed. Those same folks still treated Peach like a belle of the county, even though Will had gambled away her dowry and her hands were rough and calloused. It wasn't right and it wasn't fair, but in Lynchburg, Nebraska, where change came slowly, if at all, that's how things were.

Peach knew it, and so did everybody else. Then why on earth, she wondered, had Kit come back? Why, when he could have started fresh someplace—anyplace—else? And why, Peach wondered, was she standing here fretting about Kit Taggart and letting Red wander off?

With a sigh, she swooped her wide-brimmed straw hat off the ground and turned to catch Red. Mulelike, he threw his head up and wheeled away, dragging his reins just out of her reach.

"Damnit, Red, c'mon now." Peach struck out after him, her voice and her stride firm. Honey might catch flies, but not a weary mule. "We're done for today, I swear."

Red swung his head around and blinked at her around his blinders, gave an off-key mule whinny that was more donkey bray than anything else, and trotted away over the hill. Peach sighed again, slapped the dust off her hat, plunked it on her head and trudged after Red. The parched grass crunched beneath her boot soles and sweat sprang on her upper lip as soon as she cleared the shade of the hackberry tree.

At least she didn't have bad weather to worry about. No rain to rot the shocks she'd bound by hand, no hail to flail the grain off the stalks. Or so Peach thought, until she crested the hill. She saw it then and her heart nearly stopped—a bank of thin, smudged clouds creeping up the southwestern horizon.

"If you don't like the weather here'bouts," ran one of the oldest jokes in Lynch County, "just wait five minutes and it'll change."

It was only a slight exaggeration. The winds that tore year-round out of the Rocky Mountains could bury western Nebraska waist-deep in snow between breakfast and the noon meal. Thunderstorms flared up quick as a just-struck match. In her lifetime, Peach had seen temperatures plunge thirty degrees in an hour, barns exploded by lightning, cows struck dead in the field by hail the size of her fist.

Sometimes, the soaring dome of hot air that formed over the Nebraska prairie in high summer stalled the storms in the foothills. Sometimes. But not this time. Peach felt it in her bones, tasted the perfect, bitter irony of it in the back of her throat. She'd worked so hard since Will died to salvage this crop and her dignity. For the past two nights—from dusk, when she fed and watered her exhausted mules, until it was too dark to see—she'd cut sections the reaper had missed with her grandfather's cradle, a long-handled scythe with curved fingers to catch the cut stalks. It weighed half as much as she did and looked for all the world like the clawed, skeletal hand of the Grim Reaper.

The image made Peach shiver, but she pushed it away. She wanted to scream, wanted to throw herself on the ground and beat her fists, but she didn't. She caught Red instead, led him back into the shade, stripped him of his harness but left his bridle, grabbed a fistful of reins and scrubby mane and swung herself up on his thin, bony back.

The wind gusted through the hackberry, scattering a handful of dead yellow leaves under Red's nose. He lifted his head, twitched an ear and flared his nostrils. He smelled it same as she did, the faint metal tang of rain. Of ruin and doom if she didn't get a move on.

With a sharp kick, Peach wheeled Red and clucked him into a trot, her jaw set against his tooth-jarring gait and the panic welling inside her. What little money and every ounce of strength she had she'd invested in this crop. She would not lose it.

She was a MaCauley, by God, and MaCauleys—except for Will—never quit.

Chapter Two

The wind raced Peach to Three Corners, tugging at Red's mane and the loosened tendrils of hair she'd pinned under her hat. The image of the Grim Reaper haunted her. So did the single glance she took over her shoulder, at the long gray fingers of cloud uncurling across the sky like an opening fist. Peach didn't look back again, just set her jaw and dug her heels into Red's flanks.

His withers were dark with lather by the time she reached the rocky stretch of pasture on the Wilkins place where the thresher stood. The wind had blown away most of the dust and chaff, still the four men unhitching the eight-horse team from the sweeps that turned the bull-wheel and powered the thresher wore kerchiefs tied over their noses and mouths.

So did Jed Tyler, flinging sacks up to Ben Wilkins, Senior, who stood in the bed of Jed's wagon to catch them, and the two sewers stitching up the last of the wheat-filled bags. One of the sewers was Jed's carroty-haired son, Tad, fumbling with his thread and paying close attention to the master sitting beside him on a pile of done-up sacks.

The flash of the other man's broad, sharp-edged needle in and out of the rough burlap bag between his knees swelled a lump in Peach's throat. Her father had won blue ribbons in sack sewing three years straight at the Lynch County Fair.

An expert sewer could earn three dollars and fifty cents a day and close a 140-pound sack of wheat with twelve swift stitches. Less than a dozen and the sack would leak at its half-hitched edges and spill precious grain.

Whoever this man was, he was an expert. Peach recognized the rest of the men, by their hats and their muffled voices calling to each other, as neighbors she'd known all her life, but the sewer was a stranger. Hired by Ben Senior, most likely, from one of the harvest gangs that worked their way across the Nebraska prairie every summer.

A stiff gust of wind snapped the back of Peach's shirt and sent Jed's hat skipping away under the wagon wheels. He tossed the sack he carried up to Ben and chased it down. He saw Peach as he turned around and hollered at Ben, who tugged off his kerchief, jumped down from the wagon and waved as he came toward her with Jed.

Peach waved back, her hand freezing when she saw Ben Junior, who everybody called Bud, come trotting over from the sweeps. She hadn't seen him since she'd all but beggared herself to pay the last IOU Will had written him.

Gallantly, Bud had offered to settle for land rather than cash, the prime forty acres where she'd planted her wheat. Peach had sold her last three cows to Jed's wife, Lily, instead, to pay the debt and buy seed for this one last season.

She watched Bud catch up with his father, jerk his kerchief aside and whisper in his ear. Ben glanced at the ground and wiped a hand over his mouth. When he looked up, his eyes didn't quite meet hers.

"Afternoon, Peach. What'er you doing up there on Red?"

"Blue broke a leg. I had to shoot him."

"Darn shame." Ben shook his head. "Sure do wish I could help, but with this bad turn in the weather coming—"

"S'all right, Ben," Jed put in quickly. "Don't you fret, Miz Peach. Got me a spare plow mule you're welcome to."

"No you don't, Jed." Bud pushed his hat back on his headful of dark hair and slid a cool, squint-eyed smile up at Peach. "You just promised it to Clem Parker. Remember?"

Jed looked startled, then swiftly away. "Reckon that's so," he mumbled, his face turning as red as his hair.

"Like Paw said." Bud laid a hand on his father's shoulder. "With this bad turn coming, we're pooling our resources. Gonna work in teams to get everybody's crop in before it hits."

"Well, that's fine," Peach said to Ben Senior, a sigh of relief in her voice. She hadn't spoken to Bud since she'd paid him off last summer and she didn't intend to ever again. "I've only got twenty-five acres."

"You'll have to wait your turn," Bud said curtly.

Peach stiffened on Red's narrow back and glared at him. "Well, of course I do."

Bud's smile widened. "Explain it to her, Paw," he said, his fingers squeezing his father's shoulder.

One side of Ben's mouth twisted. With pain or distaste, Peach thought, or maybe both. He shrugged Bud off, took a step forward and laid a hand on Red's damp neck.

"These men all have families to feed. Their wheat comes first. It's the only fair way, Peach. Surely you see that."

Peach saw a lot of things. The way Ben still couldn't look her in the eye, Jed staring ashamedly at the ground. Every man on the threshing crew watching her, even the stranger sewing sacks. Until she jerked up her chin and they all ducked their heads. All but Bud. The gleam in his eyes made her shiver. So did the bank of soaring, dark-bellied thunderheads beginning to pile up on the horizon.

"I'll tell you what I see, Ben." Peach pulled Red a snorting step back, his long ears flattening against his head.

"My turn coming last, if it comes at all. I see my wheat rotting in the field and Bud at my door, thinking I'll be desperate enough to accept his generous offer to buy my place for a fraction of what it's worth."

"Your place ain't worth squat," Bud said, a confident, jeering edge in his voice. "Will seen to that."

And you helped him! Peach wanted to shout, but didn't. She couldn't without bursting into tears. Instead she tightened her grip on the reins and leaned over Red's withers.

"Here's what you'll see, Bud, if you even *dare* to set foot on my place. My father's Sharps buffalo rifle. Loaded, cocked and pointed right between your eyes."

Bud's smile vanished. His face washed an ugly shade of red and he started toward her. "Why you high and mighty—"

"Hold it right there, Junior."

Only one person had ever called him Junior. Last, behind the Lynchburg school when Bud said his father was a no-good cracker. Peach had been there to hear it and witness the vicious, bare-knuckled fight that followed. She could hardly believe she'd heard it. Not here, not now.

Neither could Bud. She saw it in the slow widening of his eyes, the startled backspin he made to face the stranger rising from the stack of wheat sacks. Only he wasn't a stranger. Peach knew who he was before he tugged off his green bandana. He was Kit Taggart.

A boy no longer, but a man. Taller than Peach remembered, shoulders broader. His brown denim trousers dusted gold with chaff, sweat gleaming on the wedge of sun-browned chest she could see in the unbuttoned gap of his white chambray shirt. He pushed his hat back as he stepped away from the sacks. What she could see of his hair, once the color of ripe wheat, looked as dark as the glower on his face.

"Hellfire!" Bud rounded on Jed. "I told you to hire a sewer, not a damn cracker!"

Peach caught her breath, but Kit only tipped his head to

one side, gave his hat a one-fingered push and grinned suddenly. Like a fox in the chicken house.

"That's what I done," Jed shot back. "Best man with a needle I've seen since Sam MaCauley, God rest him."

"Mighty glad t'have him," Clem Parker added, leading a pair of chestnut horses away from the sweeps. "Ain't spilled a single kernel of grain."

He stopped just short of where Bud stood, still quivering with fury. A tall, raw-boned man, who obviously didn't owe Bud any money.

"Don't much care who he is or who he sprung from," Clem finished, nodding at Kit Taggart. "No offense."

"None taken," he replied mildly and returned the nod. Unruffled, apparently, though Peach could have sworn she saw something flicker in his gaze. He hadn't so much as glanced at her, not once. He never took his eyes off Bud.

"We had a deal." Bud shoved himself in Jed's face. "You'd pay the sack sewer and we'd call it square."

"Call *what* square?" Ben Senior asked sharply.

"Never you mind, Paw." Bud stabbed a finger in Jed's chest. "I don't call this square. I say you still owe me."

"That's enough." Ben pulled his son off Jed. "What's this about?"

"Nothin', Ben. Nothin' at all." Jed glanced nervously at his son, Tad, a lanky fourteen-year-old listening avidly with his head cocked to one side. Ben followed his gaze and frowned. "Later then," he said.

So quietly Peach almost didn't hear him over the faint rumble in the wind and the thud of Bud's boot heels on the hard-packed ground. He'd spun away from his father and Jed, and was stalking toward Kit.

"Clear out!" He waved his arms like Kit was a steer he could frighten. "And don't ever show your face here again!"

"*Bud!*" Ben thundered. "You hold up!"

He didn't, until Kit raised a hand. Then Bud flung up his fists, but all Kit did was open his palm.

"I'm owed a day's wages," he said. "Pay me and I'll be gone. Just as soon as you apologize to Miss Ma-Cauley."

Surprise shot Peach straight up on Red's back. She thought they'd all forgotten her, especially Kit. She wished he had, wished she'd never come.

"Apologize?" Ben gave a short, nasty laugh. "What for?"

Kit smiled. A hard, barb-edged smile. "For behaving like a cracker, Junior."

Peach hadn't known what cracker meant that day in the schoolyard. Her father had explained it to her after. Or tried, hemming and hawing until he'd given up with a gusty sigh and said, "Frankly, it means a Taggart."

Clem Parker and a couple other men snickered. Jed grinned. Peach sat still on Red's back, holding her breath and waiting to see what Bud would do. So did Ben, his fingers twitching nervously, his mouth a thin, pinched line.

"You got more gall than sense, Taggart."

"Pay me and apologize."

"The hell I will," Bud said, and spat in Kit's hand.

His gaze didn't flicker, it leaped like a flame. So did a muscle in his jaw. Bud took a wary, ready-to-swing step back as Kit's left hand shot up. Not to wring Bud's neck as Peach expected, but to jerk off his bandana. He used it to wipe his palm, then ground it into the dust with one foot.

"I said pay me and apologize to Miss MaCauley."

"When hell freezes," Bud said, and hurled a fist at Kit.

He ducked the punch and stepped to one side. Bud lunged after him, off balance and stupid with rage, his arms milling like the empty sweeps turning slowly around the bull-wheel in the steady blow of the wind. Bud lost his hat and nearly his footing as Kit dodged him a second time, and then a third.

"Damn you, Taggart!" Breathing hard, Bud spun after him, his jaw clenched as tight as his fists. "Fight me!"

"Not today, Junior. Too damn hot."

With a mad-bull bellow, Bud hurled himself at Kit. Jed's boy, Tad, saw what was coming—so did Peach—and scrambled out of the way as Kit stepped aside and let Bud's momentum carry him, face-first and falling, into the piled sacks of wheat. He landed with a dusty thump, flung himself over on his elbows and glared up at Kit.

"I'll kill you, Taggart." Bud's voice was shaky and breathless. The glitter in his eyes made Peach's heart thump. "I swear to God I will."

"I expect you'll try, Junior." Kit took off his hat and wiped sweat off his forehead with the back of his hand. "Do me a favor and pick a cooler day."

He put his hat on and turned away toward the sweeps. Bud pushed up on one hand, grabbed the wickedly sharp sack needle and sprang after him.

"Kit!" Peach shouted.

Needlessly, for he'd either heard or sensed Bud's lunge and thrown his left arm up and back. Nose-first, Bud plowed into his cocked elbow and keeled over like a felled tree, sprawled on his back and unconscious.

"Lord A'Mighty." Ben wiped a hand down his face. "Wait till Taggart's gone, Clem, then toss some water on him."

"Sure thing," Clem replied, smothering a grin as he trotted off toward the water cask near the thresher.

Peach was shaking inside and out, but Kit just kept walking unhurriedly toward the sweeps where the saddle horses were tied. She watched him collect a big sorrel with a creamy mane and tail, expected him to mount and ride off, but he turned and led the horse in her direction. His boots were as dusty as his trousers, his shirt sweat-stained, but still he looked—well, a damn sight better than she must, filthy, windblown and sunburned in Will's old clothes.

And still Kit Taggart didn't look at her. He looked at the reins in his hand, glanced at Ben and Jed, squinted up at the thin skeins of cloud sweeping across the sky. Peach felt her heart sink. It was time, she decided, to gather what dignity she had left and go home. She clucked to Red and dug in her heels. He backed a step and balked.

"Please, Red," Peach whispered into his long, cupped ear. "This is no time to remember you're a mule."

She kept thumping him, but Red refused to budge. Peach gave up, ducked her head and looked at her hands, wrapped so tight in the reins they'd turned blue. She eased her grip, felt the blood rush back into her fingers and scald up her throat, heard the slow, thudding approach of Kit's sorrel and Ben's quiet aside to Jed, "Send your boy home. Then you and me'll have us a talk."

"Ain't a thing to talk about, Ben. Just a misunderstanding 'tween me and Bud, that's all."

Peach had lost count of the times she'd heard that from Will, the times she'd threatened to tell Ben about Bud's card and dice games. The times Will had promised he'd never go back, all the times she'd trusted and believed him.

It was her own fault she was sitting here on Red's tired old back, bone-weary and begging and nearly penniless. Her fault, her pride that had kept her quiet about Will's weakness and Bud's secret games.

A deep, sweet ache for Will sprang inside her and brought tears to her eyes. She blinked them away and peeked up at Jed, backhanding sweat from his upper lip. If she were a man, she'd backhand him herself. For spreading lies about Kit that blamed him for Bud's shady doings, and then using him to buy back his markers.

"I'll tell you, Ben," Peach said and did, keeping her voice low so Jed's son wouldn't hear, her half-lifted gaze on Ben's thunderstruck expression as he turned to face her.

She told him about the ramshackle old hay barn just over the rise in this very field. She told him quickly, ignoring Jed and his angry, shame-faced glare, lifting her voice just a bit over the drawing-closer clop of Kit Taggart's horse. She told him everything she knew about Bud's illicit, clandestine games, then she ducked her head, heard Kit's horse snort and stop, and wished she could disappear.

"Who's gonna pay me?" Kit asked bluntly.

"I will," Jed replied nervously. "Ain't got that kinda money on me, but I'll see you get it."

"You know where to find me." Peach heard leather creak and breathed a sigh of relief. He'd mounted his horse, he was leaving. Or so she thought, until Kit Taggart added, "So do you, Miss MaCauley."

⤳ *Chapter Three* ⤳

Nothing could steal the loveliness from Peach Ma-
Cauley's face, though the harsh Nebraska sun had tried its
damnedest. Tiny lines feathered the corners of her eyes,
but they were still blue as cornflowers, still framed with
thick, dark lashes. And they still hit Kit Taggart like a fist
when her chin shot up and she blinked at him, startled and
wary. So hard and so quick that his knees went weak.

Weak enough to give his stallion Buck ideas. He snorted
and danced, but Kit had a bellyful of showing off. From
himself as well as his horse. With a rough tug on the reins,
he hauled himself and Buck back in line. Once struck, he
reminded himself. Once struck, twice shy.

"I beg your pardon?" Peach MaCauley said to him.

Cautiously, her eyes so blue they made him ache, and
only half-lifted from the worn leather reins wrapped
around her bloody hands. Her nails were ragged and broken, the tips of two fingers split. Friction cuts from binding
wheat.

"I said you know where to find me," Kit repeated, "if
you want help getting your wheat in."

She wanted it, all right. He saw it in her face, almost
felt the sharp prick of tears that sprang and jeweled in her
lashes. Wanted it, but knew she couldn't afford it. So did

Kit, but he wasn't after money. He was after Peach MaCauley.

This wasn't the way he'd planned it, but he decided it'd do. He'd planned to approach her last summer, at the church Fourth of July Social—the perfect irony he'd thought—until her brother Will had shot himself. He'd postponed it then, out of respect for her mourning, busied himself fixing up his place and biding his time.

Lily Tyler had told him Peach never missed a church social. She was always there, Lily said, even though she scarce had a decent dress left to wear. She said it while she skimmed cream off the milk given by the three Jersey cows she'd all but stole from Miz High and Mighty MaCauley. She'd made a point of telling him that, too.

He'd wanted to drown Lily Tyler in her damn milk, felt a twinge of conscience remembering, but pushed it away and told himself Peach MaCauley owed him. She owed him what she'd promised with her mouth and her body pressed tight against his that long-ago night behind the church. He intended to have it, have her, and be free once and for all. Free of the obsession that had drawn him back to Lynchburg, free to live the rest of his life as far away from here as he could get without Peach MaCauley and her blue eyes haunting him.

He owed her for the warning shout; if she hadn't called out to him, he might be the one sprawled in the dirt, though he doubted it. What dodging his father's fists hadn't taught him, the War had, and Junior was nothing but a bully.

Scratch one, Kit knew, and you found a coward. He'd learned how to take a beating from his father; from the War, how to fight back. He'd taught himself not to dwell on things he couldn't change, and to *never* owe anybody for anything, so he'd repay Peach MaCauley by bringing in her wheat.

"Never you mind what Bud said, Miz Peach," Jed Tyler piped up stoutly. "That mule o' mine's yours."

And Junior said he had gall. Kit watched Peach draw

herself straight and glare down at Jed Tyler. The High and Mighty Miss MaCauley, with tendrils of honey blond hair fluttering around her ears, not the work-worn ragamuffin who looked like her skinny mule ate better than she did.

"For how long, Jed?" she asked him. "Till Bud wakes up and tells you what to think?"

"Aw now, Miz Peach—"

"Thank you, Mr. Taggart." Her gaze shifted from Tyler's sheepish face to his. "I'd be grateful for your help."

"Think what you're doing, Peach." Ben Wilkins came out of his daze and frowned at her. Kit wondered what Peach had said that had struck him dumb. "Think what folks'll say."

"I don't give a damn what folks say." She gave her mule a sharp tug that pulled his head down and shifted his weight onto his rear quarters. "I'm going to harvest my wheat."

"If you throw in with Taggart," Ben told her coldly, "you'll be on your own."

"I've been on my own since Will died." Peach gave her mule another sharp yank that tucked his head too close to his chest and started him gnawing on his bit. Kit doubted she noticed, angry as she was, her eyes hard and glaring at Wilkins. "I'll be back with my wheat, Ben. My father paid his fair share for that thresher, so I'd best be able to use it."

She wouldn't have to, but this wasn't the time to tell her he'd bought a thresher with the header, steam-powered, that would separate her wheat in half the time it took this old horse-powered rig. It was time to get Miss High and Mighty MaCauley out of here, before her mule tossed her off his back or Bud Wilkins tossed her off his land.

"Let's really give 'em something to talk about," he suggested, his voice a taunting drawl. "Invite me to supper."

She glanced up quickly, from Ben Wilkins's face to the gray-tinged clouds scudding from west to east—nothing to worry about, not yet, just feelers sent out by the storm while it made up its mind which way to go—then caught her bottom lip between her teeth and shot him a questioning look.

Kit's heart thudded hard remembering the flutter her breath had made in the back of his throat when he'd caught her lip in his own teeth. Twelve years ago, yet the memory was so vivid he could almost feel her mouth trembling on his, could almost taste the tang of apple cider on her tongue.

" 'Spect it'll hold off another day," he told her.

"Wouldn't trust him if I was you, Miz Peach," Jed Tyler put in belligerently, squaring off on him. "Wondered why he brung his wheat in so early. Reckon he can read the weather like his paw done. Ain't that so?"

"I reckon my old man," Kit said, leaning on his saddle horn menacingly enough for Tyler to scramble back, "would've told you black was white if you offered him enough whiskey."

It was how Fess Taggart had made his living, feeble as it was, witching water and foretelling the weather. The only things he'd had a knack for, besides drinking himself blind and beating Kit and his mother senseless before she'd died.

Folks around Lynchburg had paid Fess Taggart in whiskey. All but Sam MaCauley. He'd paid in chickens or vegetables. Those were the only times Kit had eaten halfway decent. He'd despised his father, but he'd always gone with him to witch water for Sam MaCauley. To admire Peach up close, and make sure Fess didn't trade his supper for a jug of cheap whiskey.

"Thought you'd turned out better'n this, Taggart." Ben Wilkins tipped his weathered face up and glared at him. "Sneaking onto my place and now shaming Peach."

"Shaming!" She cried, her voice so shrill that Buck tossed his head and snorted, her hands twisting the reins so tight that her mule's eyes bulged. "How dare you!"

"I didn't sneak onto your place." Kit nudged Buck forward and caught the mule's bridle, surprising Peach into relaxing the stranglehold she had on the poor thing. "I walked on, bare-faced, with Jed," he finished, shifting in his saddle to glance down at Ben Wilkins. "If you'd looked at me, you'd'ave known who I am. Junior did, when he bothered. You didn't ask my name. You asked could I sew."

Ben Wilkins had never looked Fess, or anybody else he considered beneath him in the eye, and he didn't now, just shook his head and said, "Can't figure why you came here."

"For the money," Kit Taggart replied bluntly. "I don't do anything unless I'm paid, and paid well."

Peach couldn't pay him at all. Leastways not until her wheat was in and sold. She wondered if Kit knew, if Jed had told him. She considered the expression on Kit's face and decided no; felt her heart skid, calculating how much money she'd have left once she paid him—at thirty cents a bushel, not much—and her cheeks flame as it struck her how long it had been since Ben Wilkins had looked her in the eye. Not since Will died, for sure. Maybe not since the scarlet fever had taken her parents three years ago.

Ben had barely glanced at her, Peach recalled, when he'd come to buy her last saddle mare so she could afford to bury Will. Not at all when he'd bought her calves to save her the work and expense of feeding them. She'd been grateful for the money then. Now she was furious. And mortified.

"I'm not even a weed to you, am I, Ben?" Peach demanded, her voice shaking. "I'm just a carcass you've been picking at. You and Jed and all the other vultures in Lynch County."

"A weed?" Ben blinked at her, his gaze fixed on her chin. "What in thunder are you talking about?"

He hadn't the faintest notion, but Kit Taggart knew. She saw it in his eyes—still a clear, steady brown, even in the shadow of his hat brim—and the gleam in their amber-flecked depths. It was avarice, or she was blind. Or heat struck. His hand, still firmly gripping Red's bridle, was nothing more than a greedy talon. He was no different than Jed, she realized, no better than Ben Wilkins.

There's nothing left, Peach wanted to shout at him, but took a deep breath instead to still her panicked breathing. Kit Taggart thought she was dead and done for, thought all he had to do was wait for her to stop kicking to move in and strip the last of the meat off her bones.

Well, Kit Taggart thought wrong. She was a MaCauley, by God, and she'd prove it. She'd show him. When he let his gaze drift from her face to her throat, to the wild hammering of her heart she could feel against her breastbone, she knew exactly how. Her body was all she had left, and she'd use it—even though the thought made her stomach clutch—to get her wheat harvested and herself out of Lynchburg.

"I'd be pleased to give you supper, Mr. Taggart. Six sharp. And don't worry." Peach ducked her head, lifted just her eyes to his face. "You'll be paid for your trouble."

Kit had a sudden, dry-mouthed feeling she didn't mean money, glanced up from the pulse fluttering in her throat, saw the tilt of her head, the shimmer in her eyes through her lashes, and knew she didn't. So did Ben Wilkins and Jed Tyler. The glimpse he had of their shocked expressions from the corner of his eye told him so.

"Six o'clock," Kit repeated, stunned and on his guard, wondering what in hell she was doing. "I won't be late."

"I didn't think you would." She smiled, letting her gaze rake defiantly over every single man on the threshing crew as she squared her jaw and her shoulders. "Now if you'd kindly let go of my mule, Mr. Taggart. I have a jam cake to bake."

By God, if she wasn't thumbing her nose at 'em. Wilkins and Tyler and the whole of Lynch County. He shouldn't let her, and he wouldn't. Still he wanted to laugh, even as he let go of her mule, nudged Buck up beside her and murmured in her ear. Her small, perfectly shaped ear.

"Have a care, Miss MacCauley. I'm not worth cutting your throat with these fine folks."

"Of course you're not," she whispered back, flicking him a look cool as butter in the springhouse. "But getting my wheat in and myself out of Lynchburg to my aunt Bethel in Omaha is. Do I make myself clear, Mr. Taggart?"

Well, this was a surprise.

"Yes, ma'am, you do. In that case"—Kit straightened in his saddle and said loud enough for everyone to hear—"your mule's favoring a leg. Best take the weight off 'im."

Alarm sprang in her eyes, but he winked at her and it was gone. So was his breath, when she winked back. A picture leaped in his head of the new house he'd built and Peach in his kitchen baking her jam cake. Peach in his bed winding her arms up to him, her eyes soft, her lips parted and inviting. . . . Kit forced himself to shake off the image and take a breath. Peach MacCauley could break his heart, if he had one.

"Be pleased to take you home," he said, fixing a picture of the MacCauley place firmly in his mind.

"Thank you, Mr. Taggart," she replied graciously.

Once struck, Kit reminded himself—steeling himself—as he leaned out of his saddle to pull her up behind him. He meant to slip his arm around her waist, but she drew his hand over her hip and cupped it there, like she had that night behind the church. Sometimes in his dreams he still felt the soft, sweet curve of her flesh beneath his fingers.

Now he felt only the hard, sharp press of bone as she grasped his saddle horn and used the leverage of his body to swing herself off the mule. Buck had never much cared for carrying double, but she weighed so little he hardly flicked an ear as she settled herself behind his saddle and wrapped her arms around his waist.

Kit laid a hand over hers and caught the mule's reins, settled back in his saddle and felt her breasts press against him, full and firm, despite her thin, knobby wrists. Desire shot through him, and a wash of guilt. Then a flare of gut-burning anger as Junior gave a low groan.

Peach had warned him with her father's Sharps rifle, turned Ben Wilkins white as fresh-milled flour with whatever she'd said to him. He'd stepped in something here, something deep and smelly. Kit could feel it sucking at him, threatening to pull him in deeper. But only if he let it.

He lifted his hand from Peach's wrists, swiftly, and gave Buck his heels. Whatever was going on here, it had nothing to do with him. Nothing at all. He wasn't rescuing Peach MaCauley, no matter how it looked.

He felt eyes on his back, watching, and a shiver up his spine, brushed it off and told himself it was only the tickle of Peach's breath. Nearly convinced himself, too, until Junior hollered behind them, his voice sounding thick and drunk, "I'll get you, Taggart! See if I don't!"

Peach's arms tightened around him. Kit resisted the urge to pat her wrists reassuringly and nudge Buck into a trot. Wouldn't do to look like he was running, like he took Junior seriously, but he frowned and shrugged off another chill.

They didn't speak until Ben Wilkins's pasture lay well behind them. Until Buck, trailing the mule, ambled to a halt at Kit's tug on his bit, out of sight and earshot below a rise where the road picked up. East was Lynchburg and his farm, west the MaCauley place.

Southwest the storm was still thinking things over. It seeped across the horizon like a big gray cat contemplating a mouse, below a soaring bank of thunderheads shot with silver where the sun broke through. The sky was half cloud—thin, high and ragged—half blue-white hot, the wind still gusting and stifling, laced with a faint purring rumble.

"Do you truly think," Peach asked worriedly, "that the weather will hold another day?"

"Said so, didn't I?" Kit kept his voice matter-of-fact. As if he knew what he was talking about and not just hoping, as if the feel of her tight against him wasn't driving him crazy. "Where's the mule you shot?"

"Still in the field. Red and I couldn't move him."

"I'll tend to him 'fore supper."

"Thank you, Mr. Taggart." Kit felt her shift behind him and slide her leg over Buck's left side. "And thank you for helping me make such a graceful exit."

"Hold up," he said, kicking his right foot free of the stirrup. He wasn't sure he could trust himself to touch her, but the gentlemanly thing to do was dismount and help her. So he did, dropping Buck's reins on the ground so he'd stand, wiping his hands on his denim trousers before he lifted them up to her and said, "I wouldn't call it graceful."

"Really?" Peach wrapped her hands around Kit's forearms, felt his hands close on her elbows, a ripple of muscle and strength as he braced himself and eased her off his horse. She landed lightly on her feet, grateful for his firm but gentle grip. She wasn't sure she could stand this close to him without it. Not without her knees trembling. "What would you call it?"

"I'd call it a spit in the eye exit."

"Good." A dimple he'd forgotten she had flashed at one corner of her mouth. And a hint of relish. Or was it malice? Either way it made Kit uneasy enough to add, "Maybe asking for trouble, too."

"Even better," Peach said, hoping she sounded brave and tough. In truth, she felt silly and helpless with Kit looming over her, a stern frown on his square-jawed face.

And drawn to him, like she always had, to his quiet manner and sorrowful eyes. More than anything Peach wanted to fling herself into his arms like she had that night behind the church, when they'd come upon each other in the darkness, Kit on his way to the privy, she on her way back. And she intended to, once she'd bathed and washed her hair, put on a dress and given him supper.

"As I recall, Mr. Taggart," Peach said, "you're partial to chicken."

She was hoping to flatter him, but his deepening frown said she'd failed. So did his tightening grip on her elbows.

"If you remember that," he said, a sharp edge creeping into his voice, "then you oughta recall that what Junior lacks in brains he makes up for in pure damn meanness."

"I do, indeed, Mr. Taggart." Peach lifted her chin and her elbows out of his grasp, stepped back and caught Red's trailing reins. "Do you prefer biscuits or dumplings?"

He looked like he'd prefer to choke her. For a moment Peach feared he might, but he caught her by the arms again and pulled her roughly against him.

"This is what I prefer, Miss MacCauley," he said, and brought his mouth down on hers.

Hard and angry, meaning to startle some sense into her, just as a sudden gust of wind snatched at her beat-up straw hat. Her right hand flew up to catch it, thrusting her breasts against his chest. She gasped, or maybe he did. His pulse leaped, her eyes sprang wide with surprise. So did her lips, so suddenly he felt the startled, fluttery gasp she made in the back of his throat.

Exactly as he had all those years ago, only now there was no handy hickory tree to back her up to so he could revel in Peach MacCauley. He swept his arms around her instead, dragged her against him and slanted his mouth, let her feel what he wanted, how badly he wanted it.

And Peach did, clutching her hat in one hand and Kit's shirtfront in the other. A surge of relief, a rush of awareness at how big and strong he was, how easily he could take what she wanted so dearly to give him—but couldn't afford to—so she shoved him away and lifted her chin, biting her lip so it wouldn't tremble.

"That's what I prefer, Miss MacCauley," he said, his

voice deep and taut. "What

"For dinner, biscuits or du
my wheat in . . ." Peach's voice
bravery failed her. She bit her lip
sucked an unsteady breath and said,

Dear God. She hadn't meant mone
ined it. If he had a heart, Kit thought, it
with joy. Instead, his hands were trembli
mouth, as he gently lifted her face and caug
at the tears clinging to her lashes.

"For supper," he said softly, "I'll take dump

are you offering?''
...plings. For helping me get
...and her feeble attempt at
...arder, ducked her chin,
... ''Myself.''
... He hadn't imag-
... would be bursting
...g. So was her
...ht his breath
...lings.''

...nto the pot for
...u and heat-stroked thing
...cn worried the meat would be
...ots woody from lack of rain. The onion,
...fresh from her garden, cut like a rock.

There was no milk for the jam cake, so she used water and an extra egg, a bit more nutmeg and cinnamon. No butter for frosting, either, so she baked a single layer, spread with blackberry preserves and sprinkled with sugar.

There were no potatoes from the heat-killed vines, no beans from the bolted runners she'd pulled down weeks ago. The corn relish she'd put up last year would have to do.

Even with the dumplings she mixed in an earthenware bowl and covered with a flour-sack towel, it was a meager repast. Good thing Kit Taggart wasn't coming for the food.

Scrubbing the kitchen table kept Peach's mind off what he *was* coming for. But when she swept the floor, it seemed the corn husk broom hissed at her—whore, whore—with each stroke. She ignored it and kept on sweeping, out the door, across the porch and down the steps, a stiff gust of hot wind catching the house dust and mingling it with the dirt blowing in swirls across the yard.

Her chin started quivering as she laid the table with the

lace cloth she'd crocheted over the winter with the last of her thread, and the remnants of her mother's English bone china, the few pieces she'd hidden so Will couldn't sell them. When she set out the silver saltcellars, her mother's most cherished possessions, her hands began to shake.

If Kit Taggart was wrong and the weather didn't hold, the cellars would have to go. So would her dream of placing them on her own table someday and telling her children how Great-grandma MacCauley had carried them sewn inside the hem of her apron, all the long, hard way by ox-drawn wagon from her father's house in Pennsylvania.

Until today, she'd had no idea what her children would look like. Now she couldn't picture them with eyes any color but amber-flecked brown, couldn't see herself sweeping her fingers through hair any color but ripe wheat blond. Which was silly, and a sure-fire invitation to heartbreak.

Kit Taggart's intentions were not honorable. If they were he would have come calling. He'd said it plain enough—he wanted her and he wanted dumplings for supper. And who could blame him, Peach thought, catching a glimpse of herself in Granma MacCauley's mirrored sideboard. She wasn't Sam MacCauley's pretty little Peach anymore. She was a dried-up old prune.

Candles. That's what she needed. Candlelight would soften the lines around her eyes, fill the hollows in her cheeks. Not to mention save on her dwindling supply of lamp oil. Quickly, Peach fetched her mother's brass holders from the sideboard, swallowing a lump in her throat as she fixed them with tapers and set them on the table.

She'd meant to keep these, too, but if the weather broke, she'd have to sell them. She would if it came to that. But not to Lily Tyler, damn her, who oggled the brass sticks and hinted how nice they'd look in her parlor every time she set foot in Peach's house.

Maybe she was foolish to want to keep these few things. Maybe it was best to sell the whole lot and start fresh in Omaha, but Peach couldn't bear the thought of having nothing to remember her mother by, or her father.

His Sharps rifle hung over the fieldstone kitchen fireplace. Peach thought about taking it down and loading it, until she saw the time on Granma's china clock, ticking placidly on the walnut mantel Sam MaCauley had built to hold it. Almost five, past time for her to wash and change.

Never mind the gun, and never mind Bud Wilkins. If his nose wasn't broken, it was certainly still throbbing. The image made Peach smile as she hurried out of the kitchen and up the parlor steps to her bedroom. Mean as Bud was, he didn't worry her overmuch. He was a coward, and cowards ran in packs like wolves.

If she kept nothing else, Peach swore she'd keep Granma's clock. If, as a ten-year-old, her father could ride all the way from Independence, Missouri, with the clock on his lap, the wagon bouncing so hard over the rutted trail that his knees had been bruised for weeks and not complain, then she could sell her body—or her soul to the devil—to get her wheat in and herself out of Lynchburg.

She might die shamed and a spinster, but she wouldn't die *poor* and shamed and a spinster. She'd have *some* money and the memory of what it was like to be loved by Kit Taggart. And that, Peach told herself, would be enough.

Her last best dress was a blue silk plaid with lace collar and cuffs. The same dress she'd put on the day after the Fourth of July Social when she'd waited all day by the parlor window for Kit Taggart to call. She'd had pretty, real pearl earrings to wear with it, then, but Will had sold them long ago with the rest of her jewelry.

She couldn't bear the thought of wearing it now, hung it back in her clothespress and picked a broadcloth skirt, once a deep nutty brown, now faded with work and washing, a blue gingham bodice and an apron she'd dyed red with pokeberry. Much better, Peach decided, eyeing the no-nonsense ensemble laid out on the bed, more suited to the occasion. This wasn't a seduction, after all, it was a business arrangement.

Please God, let the weather hold, Peach prayed. If it didn't, she had no idea what she'd do. The thought made her fingers twitch nervously on the rope tie at her waist, and her eyes flutter shut as she savored the memory of Kit Taggart's kiss. She could still feel his mouth on hers, how strong he was, how safe and protected she'd felt wrapped in his arms, how tired she was of being alone and afraid.

Please, God, let me have this one chance to be loved. Peach prayed, drawing a deep breath as she opened her eyes. For luck, she fished her arrowhead out of Will's trousers and tucked it in the pocket of her apron.

She'd forgotten she still had Will's bayonet, until she sat down on the side of the bed to take off her boots and saw it tucked inside the right one. She pulled it out and put it on the dresser, tugged off her wool socks, gathered up stockings darned where it wouldn't show and garters, a clean chemise and drawers, a towel and hairbrush, her last precious bar of rose soap and hurried downstairs.

In the kitchen she picked up the iron kettle she'd left steaming on the back of the stove with a knitted hot pad and carried it outside. It was heavy and spit boiling water that left a trail of drips and splashes down the steps, across the yard, and around the west corner of the porch where Sam MaCauley had built a washing area enclosed by the house and a screen of two six-foot-high board walls.

He'd planked a floor and a shelf where Peach put the kettle, her soap and brush and towel, drove pegs where she hung her clean underwear. The rain barrel was bone dry and dusty. Peach picked up two buckets and headed for the well.

The sun was starting down, but it was still blistering hot, the thin gray fingers of cloud stretching across the sky flushing a dull, gritty orange. So far Kit Taggart was right—the weather was holding. Still Peach couldn't bear to look at the storm blooming like a bruise in the southwest, and turned her back on it as she primed the well pump and cranked the handle until her arms ached to bring up two buckets of water with silt enough in them to plant potatoes.

It was a good thing she was selling out if the well was drying up. Lynch County hadn't seen a decent dowser since Fess Taggart drank himself to death six months after Kit enlisted. Could he really witch weather like his father, Peach wondered, as she lugged the buckets behind the screen. Or could he just witch her, with his amber brown eyes and hard, demanding mouth?

In spite of the heat, she shivered as she shucked off Will's clothes and poured half the hot water into an enamel basin. She washed twice, rinsing between with well water, toweled off and put on her clean under things. Then she bent forward and emptied the kettle over her head, sighing at the soothing rush of the now-tepid water, picked up the soap and scrubbed her hair with handfuls of rose-scented suds.

Peach felt almost human when she finished, almost like a woman. She spent so much time in Will's trousers her stockings and garters felt odd. Odd enough to make her smile and start to hum as she flipped her wet hair back and picked up her brush to comb out the tangles.

"Well, well," Bud Wilkins said, the jeer in his voice snatching Peach's breath. "Ain't this a pretty picture."

Horrified, she snatched the damp towel over her chemise to cover her breasts and whirled around. Bud stood watching her with his hat pushed back and his arms folded, his gaze raking her from head to foot. The narrow-eyed smile on his face froze the blood in her veins.

"Get off my land, Bud, before I throw you off."

"Now how you gonna do that?" He grinned, taunting her. "March me off with your hairbrush?"

It was the only thing she had that even remotely resembled a weapon. She still clenched it in her hand, tight against her chest with the towel. Why hadn't she loaded the gun, or kept Will's bayonet? Kit had warned her, or tried to, but she'd been in such a hurry to bake the jam cake. Fat lot of good it did her now.

"If you're gonna make threats," Bud said, shaking a finger at her, "then you best be prepared to carry 'em out."

His nose was swollen nearly double. It made his eyes look smaller and meaner, and Peach's heart thud with dread.

"Kit should've hit you harder," she said, clutching the towel and the brush tighter as she lifted her chin. "He'll be here soon. He's coming for supper."

"Six sharp, I know. Jed couldn't wait to tell me. 'Magine he's told half of Lynch County by now. Your fine family name is mud, Miss MaCauley. So's your reputation, takin' up with the likes o' Taggart."

"I'm shattered. Now if that's all you have to say—"

"I'd expect Taggart t'be late, if I was you." Bud tugged his watch out of his vest pocket and sprang it open. "Yep. Half past five. Jed oughta be at his place by now, makin' sure he's late enough for you and me to have us a talk."

Oh God. She'd forgotten Jed had overheard her invitation to Kit. Peach swallowed hard and sucked a shaky breath.

"Get off my land," she said through gritted teeth. "I have nothing to say to you."

"Sure had plenty to say to my paw. Had me a good thing goin' in that old hay barn till you shot your mouth off."

Bud snapped his watch shut, so suddenly Peach jumped. Her teeth were chattering. From cold, not fear, she told herself, from her wet hair dripping down her back.

"You should'a kept quiet, Peach." Bud tucked his watch in his pocket and started toward her, a menacing gleam in his narrowed eyes. "Now I'm gonna make you wish you had."

Chapter Five

The buzzards led Kit to the dead mule. Five of them flew off the carcass, squawking indignantly, when he drove the header, pulled by his team of bay Morgans, into the field. Made the most sense, he'd decided, to have it in place and ready to go at first light. Buck trailed behind, saddled and tied to the header.

The sun was going down, the wind falling off. Kit could almost feel the storm drawing and holding its breath. He glanced up at the sky, just beginning to flush a dull, gritty orange. It was so hot he could hardly breathe, so humid he could almost drink the air. When this storm hit, it was gonna be a humdinger.

He parked the header in the shade of the hackberry tree and untied Buck. The stallion snorted and rolled his eyes, nervous and sweating from the racket the header made. Kit led him away, loosened his girth and hobbled him to graze.

The buzzards circled overhead while he unhitched the Morgans, the gelding Babe and the mare Belle, and led them into the field. The carcass reeked to high heaven, but Kit cooed softly to his team, and except for a snort from Babe, and Belle twitching her withers, they allowed themselves to be hitched to the reaper and pulled it out of the field. A more sensible, even-tempered breed Kit had yet to see. Small and nimble-footed but strong as oxen.

He hobbled Babe and left him to graze with Buck and slipped Belle into a single pull harness with a drag hook. The mule lay where he'd fallen in the harness Peach had cut him out of, his right foreleg snapped in two. Kit doubted the leather could be mended, but he stripped the harness anyway and attached the hook.

With a single, clucking, "Giddap!" Belle dug in and dragged the carcass out of the field. The buzzards squawked again and flapped in tight, agitated circles.

"That's right, boys." Kit glowered at the big, ugly black birds. "No easy pickin's here."

He made sure by dragging a good-sized brush pile over the carcass. With the spade he'd brought, he filled the gopher hole with dirt and gravel scraped out of a close-by, dry creek and capped it with a rock he stamped flush with the ground. He found the second entrance to the burrow dug into the creek bank and left it be. No need to put Mr. Gopher out of his house, so long as his front door didn't pose a hazard.

He also found a three-sided shed on the far north end of the field. Built against the foot of the hill it looked deep and wide enough to house the reaper, which was probably its function, and the header. He rehitched the Morgans and moved both machines into the shed.

In a far corner, he found a bedroll made of three folded blankets and two threadbare quilts, all freshly shaken and neatly folded. Peach MaCauley had been sleeping here. He could almost see her crawling onto the blankets, too exhausted to drag herself back to the house. How in hell, he wondered, had she managed all this time on her own?

The buzzards trailed him as he went back for the harness and led Babe and Belle to the hackberry tree, their shadows flickering ahead of him over the top heavy wheat. Hot as he was, his shirt sweat-stuck to his back, Kit shivered as he tossed Blue's harness into the shade. It landed with a dusty and distinctly metallic clunk. Curious, he kicked it aside, and frowned as he picked up a long-barreled Colt pistol.

Most likely the one Peach used to shoot the mule. He opened the chamber and spun it. Empty. He was sure the gun was Will MaCauley's. Kit had one like it, issued with his uniform when he'd joined the Fifth Iowa Cavalry. Will had served with the First Nebraska, at Fort Donelson and Shiloh, later at Fort Kearny, chasing Indians off the Nebraska frontier. Reasons aplenty to make a man shoot himself.

Kit wondered if Peach had loaded Sam MaCauley's Sharps rifle, wished he'd thought to remind her. Another shadow flicked past him, creeping a chill up his back. He glanced up, squinting, at a lone buzzard liting high in the hackberry tree, a dark, spread-winged silhouette against the bruised silver clouds soaring above the crest of the hill.

Kit hated buzzards. He'd seen too many of them in the War, hovering over battlefields and hospital tents where men lay sick and dying.

"Damn scavenger," he muttered, shaking off the chill.

His ears were buzzing, almost ringing. They had been, he realized, since Peach had ridden onto the Wilkins place. Now his guts were jumping, every nerve in his body jangling like a pair of loose spurs.

He hadn't felt like this since Gatlinburg. Sometimes he still dreamed about it, but not often—he'd learned to wake himself up—but he'd felt this same way before the fight commenced, his ears buzzing, his skin trying to crawl off his bones. For no apparent reason, he'd thought, until the Rebs had come leaping and hollering out of trees.

He'd known then that something was wrong, just like he knew it now. He couldn't figure out what it was, until he heard the thud of hoofbeats and turned toward the dry creek, in time to see Jed Tyler come bursting out of the tree line riding a lathered chestnut and leading a rangy brown mule.

The ring in Kit's ears rose to a roar. He shook his head

to clear it and stepped away from Belle to meet Jed.

"Hellfire, you're a hard man to find." Tyler reined his horse and the mule, swept his hat off and a sleeve across his forehead. "Been at your place near an hour—"

"Why?" Kit cut him off sharply.

"Bud Wilkins sent me." Tyler sucked a breath and clapped his hat back on his head. "To make sure you was late to supper so's he could have a word with Miz Peach. Only I didn't like the look on his face, so I come to fetch you."

Kit didn't have to ask who'd told Junior Peach had invited him to supper. It was written all over Jed Tyler's face.

He tucked the empty Colt in his belt, wheeled toward Buck and tightened his girth, removed his hobbles and swung into the saddle, gathered the reins and gave Jed Tyler a hard look. "How'd you know I was here?"

"I didn't. I give up waitin' and come along myself. Wanted to fetch this mule to Miz Peach anyhow."

Made sense. Tyler had come from the right direction.

"Junior won't like you loaning her the mule."

"Don't much care," Tyler said stoutly. "The look that come over Bud when Ben finished chewin' him out scared me, and that's a fact."

"If this is a lie, Jed, I'll make you eat it."

"It's the truth. I swear."

"Can I trust you to fetch my team up to the barn?"

"You bet." Tyler nodded grimly. "Be right behind you."

"You better be," Kit said, and kicked Buck into a run.

The house lay about a half mile away, across the flat expanse of pasture beyond the hill some folks still said was an old Indian barrow. If Junior so much as laid a finger on Peach, Kit swore he'd see it used as a grave one more time.

At a gallop Buck plunged over the crest of the hill and raced, straining at his bit, through dry, knee-high grass toward the farmstead. Kit could see the barn, a weather-beaten gray shimmer against the vivid red sunset. A good sign. A red dawn boded ill. So, Kit feared, did the thunder in his ears. He could see the roof of the house now, the chicken coop, the privy and two sheds—and a lone horse tied to the barn corral. Junior's white-faced black gelding, but there was no sign of Junior. Or Peach.

Much as he wanted to ride in like the Furies of hell, Kit didn't. It was never smart to spook a coward, especially a coward who might be carrying a gun. He dismounted downwind of the gelding, dropped Buck's reins so he'd stand and pulled his Winchester carbine from his saddle holster.

The wind kicked up again as he slipped up to the barn and peered cautiously around it. The house stood about sixty yards away across a patchy stretch of shriveled grass. The door was open. He thought he heard voices, but couldn't be sure over the racket in his head and the buffet of the wind swirling dust devils across the yard.

Bracing the Winchester against his shoulder, Kit crept forward. Midway between the barn and the house he paused and shook his head. His ears popped and cleared and he could hear again. The faint whistle in the wind cutting around the corner of the house, Peach's shallow, thready voice.

"I won't keep quiet anymore, Bud." Kit turned his head, straining his ears to pinpoint her direction. "Not and let you ruin Jed and God knows who else like you ruined Will."

"Will ruined himself. Couldn't play cards worth a damn."

"Not with a marked deck he couldn't."

"You lyin' bitch!" Junior shouted, and Kit placed him—around the house, west corner.

He wheeled, cocking the Winchester, heard the cartridge click into place, a ringing *thwack!* and a yowl. Junior staggered into his gun sights, hands clapped over his nose, from behind a board screen jutting past the corner of the house. In drawers and chemise, Peach leaped after him, her wet hair flying as she swung a hairbrush two-handed at Junior's head.

The blow caught him on the left ear, hard enough to knock off his hat and make Kit wince at the crack. Peach hit him again as he wheeled and tried to run. He stumbled and fell, and Peach dove on his back, raining blows on his shoulders.

Grinning, Kit lowered the Winchester, eased the hammer down, and took his time loping around the house. Maybe she'd whack some sense into Junior. She gave a startled yelp when he looped an arm around her waist and pulled her, kicking and swinging, off Bud Wilkins.

"This just ain't your day, is it, Junior?" Kit said.

Bud Wilkins groaned; Peach went still and stiff. Kit put her down, and she darted behind the screen. A second later she reappeared with a damp towel draped over her shoulders, fire in her eyes and a blush as vivid as the sunset staining her cheeks. She held the towel closed at her throat with one hand and the brush half-raised in the other, ready to coldcock Junior as he dragged himself to his feet.

"Now get the hell off my land," she said fiercely, "and don't come back."

Wilkins swiped his hat out of the dirt and swung unsteadily around to face them. His face was almost purple with rage, his nose swollen and the welt on his left cheek a perfect imprint of the back of Peach's hairbrush. He glared at her, then Kit, his eyes black and glittering with hate.

"Damn Jed Tyler and his big mouth," he said, slapping his hat on his leg as he stalked past them toward his horse.

Peach followed Wilkins across the yard, and Kit followed Peach, keeping his eyes fixed on her tangled hair. Over the top of her head, he saw the rifle in Junior's saddle holster. He raised the Winchester and drew back the hammer.

At the loud click it made, Wilkins wheeled in midstride and gave him a furious glower. Kit smiled and cradled the rifle across his body, the barrel resting in the curve of his elbow.

"You ain't seen the last of me." Junior untied his gelding, mounted and glared down at them. "Neither one of you."

"The lady," Kit said firmly, "asked you to leave."

"Some lady." Wilkins snorted derisively, gathered his reins and turned his horse away from the corral fence.

Before Kit could make a move toward Junior—he intended to yank him out of the saddle and knock his teeth out—Peach caught his arm and stepped in front of him.

"Let me," she said, swinging the brush with all her might at the gelding's gleaming black rump.

It connected with a resounding crack. The horse whinnied with fright, leaped into the air and bolted, knocking Junior back in the saddle and his feet free of the stirrups. Grabbing the saddle horn and swearing a blue streak, he bounced like a ball as the gelding thundered away in a haze of dust.

"And don't come back!" Peach shouted. Then she drew a breath, clutched the towel tighter and turned to face him. She had a smudge of dirt on her nose and another flush washing up her throat. "If you'll excuse me, Mr. Taggart, I'll get dressed and make the dumplings."

"Yes, ma'am," Kit said, gallantly shifting his gaze away from her. *Please God, be quick about it,* he thought, *I'm only human.* "I'll fetch my horse and wash up."

"Take your time," she said, nodding as she turned away.

Kit drew a deep breath and snuck a peek over his shoulder in time to see Peach climb the porch steps, shake back her hair and lift the brush to comb out the tangles. He noted the sway of her hips in her dusty cotton drawers and felt his mouth go suddenly dry.

He heard a harness jingle, turned and saw Jed Tyler on

his chestnut, leading his mule and Babe and Belle across the field. Kit let his breath go in a gusty sigh and started toward him, with a grin and a slow shake of his head.

What a fool he'd been to even wonder how Peach MaCauley had managed to survive on her own.

Chapter Six

The chicken *was* stringy, the carrots woody. The dumplings were tough, and the jam cake tasted like stale nutmeg. Peach was so mortified she could hardly meet Kit Taggart's gaze across the table. At least the dismal meal looked all right in the dim glow of the candles. The air was so still the flames burned straight up with hardly a flicker.

Kit Taggart had no sense of taste. Or so Peach thought, until he swallowed his last forkful of cake, wiped his mouth with his napkin and complimented her on the coffee. She wasn't sure if she wanted to laugh or cry, but murmured a thank you and rose to refill his cup.

The coffeepot trembled as she carried it to the table. She'd been quaking inside and out since Kit Taggart had walked into her house, in a blue chambray shirt and brown leather vest, with his wet hair combed back from his high forehead. It was bone dry now, long enough to brush his shirt collar, and darker than she remembered. It gleamed a deep, burnished gold in the candlelight. So did his straight nose and chiseled features, his freshly shaved square jaw and his amber-brown eyes.

A blind man, Kit thought, could see how badly Peach was shaking. It was too much to hope being alone with him was the reason. Most likely she was still shaken from her run-in with Junior. So was he, drawn tight as a bow-string remembering the few glimpses he'd stolen of thin white cotton and delicate lace.

She could have served him mud pies and he would have eaten them, but he couldn't tell her that. The best he could do, as she dipped the pot over his cup and it wobbled precariously, was close his hand gently over hers. She jumped like a startled deer and splashed coffee on the crocheted cloth.

"I'm sorry." She put the pot down and mopped the spill with a napkin. "How clumsy of me."

She looked like an angel with her pinned-up, honey blond hair glowing like a halo in the aura of the candles. The sun had gone down, but it was still hotter than hell, the long prairie twilight beyond the open door and the window over the tin sink a gritty, oppressive gray. Kit figured he'd spent enough time in hell, between dodging his father's fists and the War, to recognize an angel when he saw one.

"My fault," he said. "I didn't mean to startle you."

"Oh, you didn't. Not one bit. I'm just—"

Lying through her teeth. Kit knew it before she sat down and looked at him across the table.

"I'm not a very good liar, am I?"

"I've heard better."

"I'm sorry, Mr. Taggart. I—"

"You used to call me Kit."

"I'd be pleased to again, if you'd call me Peach. You've never called me anything but Miss MaCauley."

Sometimes in her dreams she still heard his ragged, "Oh, God, Miss MaCauley," after she'd kissed him timidly in the dark behind the church, could still feel his hands hot and questing on her body when he'd backed her against the hickory tree. She wanted to feel his hands on her again, so much that she ducked her chin, afraid it might show in her eyes.

"That's how I was taught to address my betters."

"I've never thought myself better than you." Peach shot her gaze up and met his squarely. "Not when we were younger and certainly not now."

"Is that why you kissed me behind the church?"

"Yes." Even in the candlelight he could see her face flame. Was it maidenly demure, he wondered, or regret?

"I never would have touched you, no matter how much I wanted to. And I wanted to. I still do. You're the reason I came back to Lynchburg."

Peach couldn't have been more surprised if he'd said he loved her. But he hadn't. He said he wanted her. It was what she'd hoped for, what her future depended on. Still she felt her heart crack, and sat straighter in her chair, determined not to let it show.

"Then why," Peach asked, "didn't you call before now?"

He'd tried calling twelve years ago, the day after the church social. He'd spent the morning polishing his only pair of boots, brushing his one good suit of clothes, only to be turned away by Sam MaCauley. Kindly but firmly.

He thought he was over the rage and shame, but remembering the glint in Sam MaCauley's eyes, he felt the sting of it again, still hot and bitter as bile in his throat. He supposed it was possible Peach didn't know, though he couldn't see how. *Ask her,* he told himself, but he couldn't. His pride, and the risk of being rejected again, was too great.

"Because my intentions aren't honorable," he told her. "I thought I'd made that plain. I thought you understood."

"Oh no, I . . . I mean . . . yes. You made it plain. I understand perfectly." Peach shot to her feet, gathered a stack of dishes and fled to the sink. The pump hadn't worked since her father died, but she was so shaken she grabbed the handle and started cranking it. "It was a silly question."

"Then why did you ask it?"

The pump shrieked and spat a cloud of dirt and rust all

over the dishes. Peach sighed with dismay and turned to face Kit Taggart. He'd stretched his long legs under the table and sat watching her with his arms folded.

She'd wanted to know if he was going to break her heart, and now she knew. But she couldn't say it, not and have any pride left. Kit Taggart could take her body, but not her dignity, and she'd be damned if she'd hand it to him.

"Since my feelings are not engaged," she said, putting her heart and soul into the lie, "I simply wanted to assure myself that yours aren't either."

He'd thought so, still it cut deep to hear her say it, to realize he was nothing but a means to an end. The only way she had to get her wheat in and herself out of Lynchburg.

"You needn't worry. I don't have any feelings."

He said it with a smile. A hard, barb-edged smile that twisted Peach's heart. Lucky you, she thought.

"Then we have an agreement?" she asked.

"Yes, ma'am. My services in the field." Kit paused, let his gaze drift down her body. "For yours in the bedroom."

Her first instinct was to shrink into a chair, but Peach held herself straight, back against the sink, and let Kit Taggart look. She felt his gaze cling at her throat and her hips, lift and linger on her bosom.

He rose from the table and her heart leaped. He came toward her and her knees began to quake. He stopped in front of her, and she gripped the edge of the sink behind her.

"One night, Miss MaCauley." His gaze traced her mouth, the curve of her jaw. "One whole night from dusk to dawn."

"One night, Mr. Taggart." Peach lifted her chin and said firmly, "Once my wheat is in."

"Once your wheat is in. Here's my hand on it."

He offered his right hand, and Peach offered hers, still hugging the sink with her left. Kit Taggart raised it to his mouth and pressed a kiss to the inside of her wrist.

He felt her pulse flutter, his thunder. When her lips parted and quavered, he bent his head toward hers. Her eyes lifted to meet his, a deep lustrous blue in the shadowed candlelight, bottomless and dangerous. Once struck, Kit reminded himself, and took her mouth, hard and swift, in his.

She shivered and sighed, tasted like blackberries and coffee and smelled like roses. He wanted to crush her against him, but didn't, just stroked her wrist with his thumb, her tongue with his. She moaned and swayed and he caught her against him around the waist.

He was nearly deaf from the roar in his head. His blood pounding through his veins, Kit thought, until a gust of wind billowed through the door, so humid it felt cool—cool enough to brush a chill up the back of his neck—and stiff enough to snuff the candle flames.

Peach blinked and tore her mouth away from Kit's. Her lips were throbbing, her heart pounding. It took a moment for her eyes to adjust to the dimness and focus on the frown on his face. The whine in the wind made her shiver. So did the quick jerk of Kit's head toward the door.

"Think I'll check my horses," he said, already moving away from her.

A little too quickly for a man who simply wanted to check his horses. Peach hurried after him, the wind catching her skirt a step past the door and whipping it around her ankles. Kit was already in the yard, his face tipped up as he turned in a circle. Peach raked back wisps of hair worked loose from her pins, looked up and felt her blood run cold.

Colossal white clouds sailed from west to east, from the ragged, inky blot of the storm to as far as she could see. The stars looked huge in the indigo sky, blazing so close to the ground that Peach imagined she could reach out and touch them. If only she weren't rooted to the porch with dread.

It was night, yet it looked like day, the milky clouds reflecting the glow of the three-quarter moon. A hunter's moon, still low in the sky, a stark, silver disk beaming through the clouds racing past its pockmarked face.

Kit had never seen such a sky, hadn't a clue what it meant. He listened for a rooster to crow, which meant rain before dawn, but the scrawny old bird he'd seen pecking around the coop while he'd washed up remained silent.

He drew a breath through his mouth. The temperature had fallen some, but the wind was still warm and humid, thick and dusty on his tongue. He wondered if he'd imagined the chill that had swept through the house, until Peach came down the porch steps chafing her arms.

"I've never seen the sky like this. Have you?"

"Once or twice," he lied, wishing he'd paid more attention when Fess talked about the weather, trying to remember if he'd ever said anything about the significance of a daylight sky at night. "Sure is pretty."

Peach thought it was terrifying. So was the flush she could still feel from Kit Taggart's kiss, and the distant flash of lightning she saw: a dull, silver flicker in the vast black depths of the storm. One thousand one, Peach counted, her lips barely moving, one thousand two—

"We won't hear any thunder," Kit said. "The rain is still too far away."

Peach glanced at him sideways. He was looking at the storm, not at her, his hair fluttering back from his forehead in the wind. She couldn't see how he'd known she was counting, unless he could witch more than weather. The thought made her chill and rub her arms.

"How can you be sure?" she asked.

He wasn't, but he couldn't tell her that. She was jumpy enough, her eyes huge and overbright, like the eerie glow of the sky. He could almost feel the gooseflesh she kept rubbing on her arms, and something else he couldn't put a name to, something out there just beyond the range of his senses. Like the Rebs in the trees. All the signs were there; the ringing in his ears, the twitch in his nerves.

"I c'n always tell when it's coming on me," Fess had told him once, in one of his rare sober moments. "Starts in my ears, like a million bees buzzing in my head. Gits louder and louder till them bees is crawling up and down my bones, till ever inch of me's jumping like a flea-bit dog."

He was beginning to understand why his father drank. He only wished he knew what was setting him on edge. He stared hard at the ugly black mass of the storm, sensed it brooding and seething, sucking up all the hot wet air, building itself up for an almighty blow. But not yet. He knew it, though he didn't know how, and that unnerved him.

So did the glimpse he had from the corner of his eye of Peach and her curiously tilted head. He could almost hear her thinking, wondering if she could trust him, if he had a clue what he was doing. He wheeled away from her because he didn't, with a curt, "I'm gonna check the horses."

If there was anything wrong, anything untoward, his team and Buck would sense it. Kit found a lantern on a peg inside the barn door, lit it with a match from his pocket that he struck on his boot heel. The mules paid him no mind, but the three horses wheeled their heads toward him over their stall doors, blinking in the light and wickering as he rehung the lantern and walked toward them.

Babe and Belle were calm as lake water on a still day. Buck snuffled deep in his chest as Kit rubbed his neck and tugged straw out of his mane. He'd been down, sleeping.

"What beautiful horses," Peach said, her voice close enough to startle Kit and turn his head over his shoulder.

He hadn't heard her come into the barn, but she stood behind him stroking Babe's muzzle with one hand and Belle's with the other. The Morgans wickered and sighed.

"Old Buck's a good one, too," Kit said, scratching the stallion's ears. " ' 'Cept he snores."

Buck snorted and butted him in the chest, pushing him back a step or two. Peach laughed. Kit turned and saw her leaning against the post between Babe and Belle's stalls, her eyes soft and glowing in the flickering lantern light.

"And how do you know that, Mr. Taggart?"

"I've slept with him." Kit bent his elbow on Buck's stall door and smiled. "I've spent more nights with this horse than a man married ten years has spent with his wife."

"In the War?"

"Nope. Mostly in Texas and Kansas. Some in Iowa and Colorado. Gets damn cold there at night, even at the peak of the wheat harvest. That's how I made the fortune the fine folks of Lynch County keep speculating about. Got lucky in a few card games, bought a couple herds of beef in Texas and drove 'em up to Wichita at a nice profit with some fellas from the Fifth Iowa, but mostly I worked damn hard sewing sacks from here to Texas and back again."

"I thought as much," Peach said, a frown on her face. "I can't prove it, but I'd wager Bud Wilkins started all the gambling talk about you."

"Let me guess," Kit replied. "To cover his own tracks?"

"Yes." She drew a deep breath and told him about Junior and his secret games in the old hay barn, about Will and his IOUs, the marked decks he could never prove.

"You told Ben Wilkins all this today?"

"I couldn't stand it anymore. Not when I saw Jed lying his head off in front of his son."

There was no point saying she should have told Ben a long time ago. He knew why she hadn't; he understood pride better than most. She'd kept quiet when she could have helped herself, spoken out only to save someone else.

"You're damn lucky Junior left his rifle in his saddle."

Her chin shot up, sharply and suddenly. "Surely you don't think—"

"I don't know what I think, but I'm staying the night."

Her eyelids took a startled leap and he added quickly,
"Out here in the barn."

She bit her lip and looked away from him, then swiftly
back with a troubled frown. "All right," she said, "if you
think it's best."

"I do," Kit said firmly, "just in case."

"I'll fetch you a quilt and a pillow."

"Some shells for the Colt, too, if you have them." She
started toward the door, but stopped and gave him a surprised look. "I found it in the field."

She nodded, said, "I have a few," and hurried on her
way.

Kit stepped into the doorway and watched her cross the
yard. His nerves were still jumping, but eased some once
he saw a lamp flicker on in the house.

You haven't seen the last of me, Junior had said, yet
Kit hoped to hell he had, knew damn good and well Junior
didn't have sand enough to face him. He went into the
barn for his Winchester and returned to the doorway to
wait for Peach. He felt better with the rifle cradled in one
elbow, still he frowned as he glanced up at the sky and
saw a ring around the moon, a ring with no stars in it. A
ring with no stars, Fess always said, meant rain within
twenty-four hours.

What the hell, Kit wondered, was Junior up to tonight?

Chapter Seven

At first light Kit found out what Junior had been up to. By the look of the header, most likely with a sledgehammer.

Smashed beyond repair and glittering with dew, it sat in a twisted heap in the three-sided shed at the bottom of Peach MaCaulcy's wheat field. Where the tines weren't bent they were snapped clean off, the wooden platform that caught the stalks and held them for binding pounded into splinters. Sam MaCauley's old reaper sat next to it untouched.

The rage and hate it had taken to destroy the header worried Kit more than it angered him. So did the glimpse he had of Peach from the corner of his eye, her clenched fists quivering as she spun away from him toward the wagon, tossed back the canvas sheet he'd put in the bed and picked up the Sharps rifle she'd taken down from the wall and loaded.

"Don't go flying over there," he said, striding toward her. "That's exactly what Junior wants us to do."

"I don't care." She turned to face him, holding the heavy, short-barreled gun across her body. At close quarters one of its .50 caliber cartridges could blow a man in half. "If I don't hang I'll go to prison, but I *won't* go to Aunt Bethel a poor relation."

Peach MaCauley was not the least bit hysterical. She was perfectly calm. And perfectly serious. A half-starved waif in her dead brother's clothes with nothing left to lose.

Marry me, Kit wanted to say. He'd lain awake half the night murmuring it to himself, smelling roses in her hair, tasting blackberries on her lips. If he thought she'd say yes and not spit in his eye he would've dropped to one knee.

"Settling the score with Junior will keep," he told her. "Your wheat won't. That's why he wrecked the header."

"Why not the reaper, too?"

"He wants us to kill ourselves trying to beat the storm."

She glanced up at the sky, a flat, dull gray between the dawn flush above the trees along the creek and the crest of the hill. Kit didn't bother to look. He could hear the storm howling in his head, still faint and far away, but already itching and crawling along his nerves.

Peach let her breath go in a gusty sigh and dropped her gaze to the scuffed and worn-thin toes of her boots. "We don't have a prayer without the header, do we?"

"Depends," Kit replied, "on how much time you're gonna waste deciding whether or not to blow Junior's head off."

Her chin shot up and her eyes went wide. "You mean you're not—" She bit her lip and spun away, put the Sharps back in the wagon bed and flipped the canvas over it.

"I'm not a quitter, Miss MaCauley. I gave my word, and I intend to keep it. And I sure as hell don't intend to let Junior win."

"How do you suppose," she asked, keeping her back to him, "that Bud knew the header was here?"

"I suppose Jed Tyler snooped around and found it before he brought my team up to the barn."

"I'm beginning to think Jed's as bad as Bud."

"Worse. You never know which side of the fence he's on."

"Leave Jed to me," Peach said. "I'll fix him."

All she had to do was tell his wife what she'd told Ben Wilkins. Picturing Lily Tyler lighting into Jed with the broom she used to keep her chickens and her children in line made Peach smile. Until she heard an owl hoot on the still morning air, a surefire sign of rain.

So was the dead limb on the hackberry tree that cracked suddenly and fell with a thud. Kit felt the impact in his clenched jaw, saw the leap of panic in Peach's eyes as she wheeled toward him. It was there for just a moment, then vanished as she drew a deep breath and met his gaze squarely.

"Well, Mr. Taggart. We'd best get to it, hadn't we?"

"Yes, ma'am," he agreed grimly, "we'd best."

While Kit pulled the reaper out of the shed and hitched the Morgans, Peach unloaded the water cask and buckets, the sandwiches she'd made and the rifle, and put them under the hackberry tree. Then she climbed into the wagon and drove Red and Jed's brown mule into the field to collect the shocks she'd bound yesterday. The morning fog burning off around the trees on the creek bank was rising rapidly. Another sign of rain. Certain and soon. *Please God,* Peach prayed, not at all sure what she was praying for anymore.

The sun disappeared almost as soon as it cleared the tops of the trees along the creek. For a while it gleamed through the overcast, a dull, silver disk, then vanished behind the heavy gray clouds. They'd cut nearly an acre by then, Peach driving the reaper and Kit following behind, cutting what she'd missed with the cradle and binding it into shocks.

His hands were already chapped and irritated from rust sores on the grain. He stopped to pick briars out of his stinging knuckles and rolled-up shirtsleeves, swept off his hat to swipe an arm across his forehead, and saw Peach picking her way toward him through the cut stalks, a tin cup dripping water in her hand.

Between the top of her bowed head and the crest of the

hill, Kit could see the clouds beginning to dip and darken. The faint breath of wind stirring the wisps of hair worked loose from the pins under Peach's straw hat was still hot and sticky. A good sign for them, a bad sign for the weather. The longer the storm held off, the worse it would be.

"Your turn on the reaper," Peach said, handing him the cup. "My turn with the cradle."

Kit took the water and drank. It was tepid and gritty, Peach already pale and drawn with fatigue. Even more than she needed a new well, she needed to forget this wheat crop and marry him. One night from dusk to dawn wasn't enough.

It would never be enough. He'd realized it as he'd tossed and burned thinking about her on his pallet in the barn, felt it, with a sharp pang, as he watched her press the back of one wrist to her upper lip. Once struck, twice shy, hell. Once struck, *forever* struck.

She might say yes. If for no other reason than to escape being a poor relation. She didn't love him, but he could live with that. So long as he never had to see her like this again, dead on her feet and worn thin with overwork. So long as she was his—all night, every night—for the rest of his life. He'd ask her, but he'd wait until her wheat was in, so there'd be no mistaking his proposal for pity.

The wagon was nearly full. Another half load of bundled shocks dotted the field around him. Kit slanted a look at the bruised clouds, breaking up into wind-driven furrows, felt a shiver and a fresh howl in his ears.

"You stay on the reaper," he said, handing her the cup. "I'm gonna fetch what we've cut up to the barn."

Kit looked back when he reached the wagon and saw Peach staring bleakly up at the sky. She rushed toward the reaper as he climbed onto the seat, otherwise he might've gone back, swooped her up and carried her off to the nearest preacher.

When he drove the wagon around the foot of the hill

and got a good look at what was coming, he damn near did. The storm stretched from south to north across the entire western horizon, black and terrifying as a nightmare, flickering with flashes of lightning, skirted by drifting veils of rain. Far enough away that he couldn't hear thunder. But not for long, Kit gauged, and slapped the mules hard with the reins.

When the wagon rumbled into the yard, he saw Buck standing in the corral, head down and tail to the wind near the barn. Not a good sign. Neither were Peach's scrawny chickens, pecking around the yard with their feathers ruffled. Quick as he could, Kit pitched the shocks into the barn and shooed the chickens into the coop.

Buck would have no part of being stabled. He dug in his hooves and threw up his head in the barn doorway, snorting and rolling his eyes. Kit saw nothing amiss, yet he felt it, a slow, *I'm-watching-you* crawl up the back of his neck as he turned away from Buck and his gaze caught on a flock of crows flapping way, way up against a patch of silver in the midnight gloom seeping across the sky.

Crows flying that high meant wind. Lots of it and soon. He grabbed a lead off a hook inside the barn door, clipped it to Buck's halter and tied him to the back of the wagon.

He tethered the stallion to the three-sided shed at the bottom of the field and went back to raking and binding, gritting his teeth at the scream in his muscles and the howl in his head. He made two more trips to the barn before the gnaw in his stomach told him it was midday or better.

At the foot of the hill Kit parked the wagon and waved his hat at Peach. She nodded and drove the reaper to the edge of the field. If he hadn't been there to meet her, she would've fallen on her face as she swung off the seat and caught his arms. The tremble in her fingers gave him a nasty stab of guilt. If he wasn't such a coward, so afraid of rejection, he wouldn't have put her through this.

"Go sit down," Kit told her. "I'll water the stock."

He didn't try to help her, just followed as she made her

stiff, shaky way to the hackberry tree. He poured her a cup of water, filled the buckets and carried them to the mules and the Morgans. Peach's cup was empty when Kit dropped down beside her on the brittle, dusty grass, the storm still howling in his head.

He shook it off, filled her cup and handed her a jam sandwich. She drank but laid the sandwich aside. So did he, his appetite gone, his stomach jumping with unease, though he couldn't say why. The Morgans seemed calm enough lazing in their traces, Buck grazed placidly at the bottom of the field, and the sky didn't look any worse.

When Peach sighed and leaned back against the tree, he looked at her and watched her lashes flutter shut, her too-thin wrists resting on her drawn up knees. The friction cuts he'd noticed yesterday were raw and weeping.

In all his years on harvest gangs, Kit had never seen any man work as hard as Peach. She'd damn near kept up with him, but she was done-in. So were the mules, restive and tugging at their harness. If he hadn't set the brake, they'd be halfway to the barn with the wagon by now. Sometimes, Kit thought ruefully, a mule had more sense than a man.

"How many acres have we cut?" Peach asked tiredly.

"Ten." Kit looked away from her. "Maybe twelve."

"I figure it closer to eight."

He started guiltily and glanced at her. Her eyes were open, a tired smile creasing the dimple he'd forgotten she had. He wanted to kiss it and the patch of sunburned skin he could see in the unbuttoned throat of her gingham shirt.

"You're the kindest man I've ever known, Kit Taggart, but you're as rotten a liar as I am."

"I still say it's closer to ten."

"And stubborn, too."

She said it with a weary laugh that roared like thunder and echoed in his ears. He didn't pay it any mind until the sky went suddenly dark as a blown-out candle, his ears popped and cleared and he heard another rumble—low, menacing and all too real—and shot to his feet.

So did Peach, wide-eyed and shivering in a sudden, fierce gust of cold wind that hissed through the branches of the hackberry and blew her hat off. It spun away in a swirl of dead yellow leaves as she ran out from under the tree, past the wagon and into the field behind Kit.

The howl in Kit's head rose to a shriek as he spun around and caught Peach against him, bracing her against the wind. The trees on the edge of the field tossed and whined beneath the racing black storm front, lightning flashed, thunder boomed. A chill of sheer dread laced up Kit's back.

"Here it comes," he said grimly, the wind buffeting Peach against him, a flood of gooseflesh shooting up her arms. "You get the horses into the shed. I'll get the mules."

The wagon groaned and rocked in another vicious gust of wind. Peach knew she should move, but all she could do was stare, awestruck, at the immensity of the storm rumbling and flashing overhead. Kit hadn't said they were done for, but she knew it by the blackness of the sky, felt it in the cold bite of the wind through Will's old clothes.

"Let's go, Miss MaCauley," Kit said urgently, "before we all get blown away."

He gave Peach a push and she went, breaking into a shaky run toward the reaper and the Morgans. He started toward the mules, took two half-running steps and staggered back three as an almighty blast came howling over the hill. Peach went tumbling to her knees. The canvas sheet covering the bundled wheat ripped loose from its tie hooks, caught on the wagon seat and hung snapping and flapping over the backs of the mules. They reared and plunged, rocking the wagon and spilling shocks, the grain winnowing off the heads in the icy gale driving like needles at Kit's eyes.

He swung his head away and flung himself at the wagon, grasped the front wheel and saw Peach struggling to her feet. Over the roar in his head and the mad flap of the canvas, he heard a splintering crack. He thought it was thunder, until he felt the wagon shudder, caught the brake handle and it snapped off in his hand.

The wild-eyed mules bolted in opposite directions, jerking the front end of the wagon off the ground and flinging Kit off the wheel. He grabbed the canvas and yanked it free as he stumbled backward, tripped over the stubbled wheat stalks and fell, hard enough to see stars. He rolled up on his knees, shaking his head and gasping for breath.

So did Peach, floundering to stand, her hair lashing at her face. She raked it out of her eyes and pushed herself up, Will's shirt and trousers whipping and snapping in the wind. A hellacious crack of thunder boomed, another fearsome gust of wind spun her back toward the wagon.

She couldn't see Kit, just the mules pitching and dragging the wagon forward and sideways, the left side wheels off the ground. She couldn't hear the warning scream she gave over the shriek of the wind, but she felt it tear up her throat and cold fingers of rain drumming on her back as she ran toward the mules.

Kit heard her, just barely, glanced up and saw the wagon listing and rolling toward him, and flung himself clear as it crashed over. The tongue splintered in a crack like thunder—or maybe it was thunder—and the mules broke free.

Much as she wanted to, Peach knew better than to try to catch Red. She dodged him as he plunged past with Jed Tyler's brown mule, the shattered tongue bumping the ground behind them, then she ran for the wagon, sobbing for breath in the driving, frigid rain.

Please God, take the wheat, she prayed, *take everything I have, only please let Kit be all right.* She pushed her streaming hair out of her face, and saw Kit fighting the wind for the canvas sheet as he came around the back end of the overturned wagon. Peach sobbed with relief and raced toward him.

He wobbled on his feet, but held out one arm and caught

her against him. He was soaked and shivering with cold—
so was she—but he was alive. Peach clung to him until
he sucked a deep breath and pulled her away from the
wagon.

"The horses. Hurry," he said raggedly, stuffing the
wadded up canvas under his arm. "Get Buck into the shed.
I'll fetch the team."

Peach raised her face, wiped rain and tears out of her
eyes and felt her heart seize. The eerie green sky roiling
behind the black storm front meant hail. And ruin for her
crop. Ice pellets the size of chickpeas were already slashing
at the wheat. She pulled away from Kit, ducked her head
against the hail striking and stinging on her shoulders, and
ran toward the shed and Buck.

The stallion danced and wheeled and tugged at his
tether, the end of it wrapped around a spike driven into a
weathered board. A hailstone the size of an apple struck
Buck on the rump just as Peach reached him. He shot up
on his hind legs, pulling the lead taut enough to rip the
board out of the wall. Peach could just hear his frightened,
angry bugle over the hail ricocheting off the roof of the
shed.

Before the stallion had time to realize he was free and
bolt, Peach darted under his pawing front hooves—praying
she wouldn't slip—and caught the rope. Backing quickly
away from Buck, she unwound it from the spike and tossed
the board away. The stallion came down with his teeth
bared, took a nip at Peach, but followed her tug on his
lead.

She turned Buck into the shed, wheeled to help Kit, and
staggered as a hard, icy blow struck her between the shoulders. Stunned and breathless, she grabbed the wall of the
shed. A jagged hailstone the size of her fist plopped at her
feet, already melting in a pool of rain.

It hurt to breathe, but Peach forced herself, looked up
and saw Kit running toward her between Babe and Belle,
his hands clamped on their bridles, the sheet thrown over

his head and theirs. The hail beat a hollow drum on the canvas, crunched beneath Kit's boots and the horses' hooves.

A resourceful man, Kit Taggart. Not quite resourceful enough to save her fifteen acres of wheat, but he'd tried. She'd give him that. And she'd give him what she'd promised. Peach's throat tightened and tears swam in her eyes. He deserved something for his trouble. Lucky he was only interested in her body. She had nothing else left.

The hail was slowing up, drifting away on its tattered veil of green cloud. The dark, heavy sky and blinding rain closed behind it. Her wheat was soaked and shredded, beaten flat against the ground and covered with ice. Everything she'd worked for, so hard and so long—gone in less than five minutes.

The saltcellars would have to go, and her mother's candlesticks. But *not* to Lily Tyler. Maybe Granma MaCauley's clock, too, and the Sharps rifle. She'd left it under the hackberry tree, Peach remembered, stepping out of the way as Kit hurried Babe and Belle into the shed.

"Here." Kit whipped the canvas off the Morgans and tossed it to her. "Shake this out."

While Peach did her best to shake the mud and ice off the heavy, rain-soaked sheet, Kit pushed the header out of the shed to make more room. Peach gathered in the canvas and watched the wreck thump and rattle away down the slight incline on its bashed-in wheels. Bits and pieces of it fell off and plopped into the mud.

"I'll reimburse you for your loss, Mr. Taggart." Peach knew from advertisements in *Prairie Farmer* that a header cost nearly three hundred dollars. The sum made her stomach clutch but she vowed she'd pay it—somehow—as she lugged the canvas toward Kit. "Just as soon as I sell the farm."

"Keep your money, Miss MaCauley." He took the sheet from her and edged outside, squinting in the rain running off the roof and splashing on his boots. Sure

enough, there were nails driven along the edge of the over-
hang. ''I plan to take the price of the header out of Junior's
hide.''

''We haven't any proof he did it.''

They would, and soon. Kit felt it in another *I'm-
watching-you* crawl up his back but didn't say so, just
hooked one edge of the sheet over the nails. Peach Ma-
Cauley had had enough bad news for one day. Her face
was gray, the hollows in her cheeks and under her eyes
vivid as bruises.

''Junior's a bully and a braggart,'' Kit said, grunting as
he hung the water-logged canvas. ''If he hasn't already
told half the county, Jed will, and then I'll have him.''

And do what with him, Peach wanted to ask, but didn't.
She felt chilled to the bone; not from the wet and cold
seeping through Will's clothes, but the gleam in Kit's eyes,
the muscle working in his jaw. She was suddenly glad
she'd left the Sharps out in the rain, that Kit had left his
Winchester in the barn.

''If the header hadn't been in my shed,'' she said stubbornly, ''nothing would have happened to it. It's my responsibility. My fight with Bud.''

''Not anymore, Miss MaCauley.'' Kit finished hanging
the canvas and stepped inside the shed. The sheet only
covered half the opening. The bottom edge fluttered in the
wind and rain still howling across the field, but the corner
where Peach had laid out her bedroll was dry and protected. ''It's *our* fight now.''

⮞ *Chapter Eight* ⮜

*O*ur *fight.* How good that sounded, how safe and protected it made Peach feel to think, for just a moment, how
wonderful it would be if only Kit meant it. If only they
had a future, if only he only wanted her for more than one
night.

But he didn't, and dwelling on it would only break her
heart. So would gazing at him standing in the shed doorway, a determined scowl on his face, his hair dark and
dripping with rain, his soaked denim trousers and muddy
shirt clinging to him like a second skin.

"You are kindness itself, Mr. Taggart," she said
briskly, turning away to catch Belle and strip the mare of
her harness. "But I can't let you involve yourself in my
problems."

Rain hammered the roof, springing a leak that splashed
on the toe of her left boot. Peach felt water dripping from
the cuffs of her rolled-up trousers and Kit's gaze on her
back.

"Why can't you?" he demanded.

"Because I can't afford your help," she replied, struggling with the rain-swollen straps and harness buckles. "I
don't have any money."

"I'm not interested in money," Kit said, rounding Belle's other side and startling Peach into glancing up at him.

She ducked her head almost instantly, but not before he saw that her lashes were wet. With rain, Kit wondered, or tears? "I thought I'd made that plain."

"Oh, you have, Mr. Taggart." Peach tugged on the buckles, felt them come free at last and pulled the soaked harness off the shivering Belle. "Very plain."

"Then what's the problem?"

He didn't understand, and there was no way to make him understand but to tell him. And what difference did it make? He'd seen her in her drawers and chemise, which was about all Peach figured she'd have left once she'd paid everything off. She tossed the wet harness aside and squared her shoulders.

"I can't afford to be dependent, Mr. Taggart, even for a little while. Dependent on you, my aunt Bethel, or anyone else. I'm alone in the world, and with no dowry, most likely I will be for the rest of my life. I'd best get used to taking care of myself and solving my own problems."

"Marry me and you won't have to," Kit blurted.

And could have kicked himself. Peach recoiled as if he'd slapped her. Lightning struck close-by in a splitting crack of thunder, startling the horses and making them snort, illuminating the fire and the hurt in Peach's eyes— those beautiful blue eyes that had drawn him back to Lynchburg.

"I don't need your help," she said, spinning away from him to work on Babe's harness. "Or your pity."

"I don't pity you, Miss MaCauley. I love you."

He said it so quietly Peach wasn't sure she'd heard him right over the rain pelting the roof. She undid the buckles on Babe's harness and tossed it aside with Belle's.

"Then you're a liar," she shot back angrily. "I asked you especially—"

"Yes, ma'am, I'm a liar," he cut her off. "And a brute to work you so hard when I knew we hadn't a prayer of beating this storm. I wish to God I'd asked you to marry me this morning, but I'm a coward. I was afraid you'd say no.''

He was still afraid she'd say no. So afraid that when the shed trembled in a clap of thunder he did, too. He tried to tell himself it was only the cold weight of his sodden clothes, but he knew better. Peach didn't say anything, just stood with her back to him, unmoving, next to Babe.

The gelding swung his head around and nudged her, and still she didn't move. Until Buck poked his nose over Babe's withers and blew, ruffling her damp, tangled hair. Then she sagged against Babe and pressed her forehead to his neck.

"Then why didn't you call?" She asked, her voice muffled in the gelding's mane. "I waited all day. I put on my best dress and sat in the parlor, but you never came."

She hadn't known. *She'd waited for him.* For him, Fess Taggart's son. If Sam MaCauley wasn't dead, Kit swore he'd kill him for the heartbroken warble in Peach's voice.

"I did call." There was no other way to say it. "Your father sent me away."

"I wondered." She lifted a hand and twined her finger's in Babe's mane, as if she needed something to hang on to. "I suspected as much, too. I always have."

"I should've stayed in Lynchburg. I should've stayed and found a way around your father. I would have, if I hadn't been so damn proud."

"I know about pride," she replied wearily. "It's all I've had to live on since Will died. I've tried to eat it every way but fried, and it's not very filling."

"It won't keep you warm on a cold winter night, either."

Peach's heart was thumping against her breastbone. Did he truly love her, or had he just said so because he thought she wanted to hear it? She did want to hear it—Oh God, how she wanted to—but even more, she needed to believe it.

"What did your dress look like?" he asked.

"Blue silk plaid with a lace collar and cuffs. I still have it. I almost wore it last night."

"I brought you flowers I picked along the way. Queen Anne's lace and cornflowers as blue as your eyes. They would have looked real pretty with your dress."

"Very pretty," Peach murmured.

She could almost see the Queen Anne's lace, as frothy as her collar, and the cornflowers as blue as her eyes. Of all the things she'd lost, the jewelry Will had sold and her mother's china, she ached the most for this bouquet she'd never seen. A sob choked Peach and tears swamped her. She threw her arms around Babe, buried her face in his neck and cried for the blooms she'd never held to her nose, the sweet, warm scent of summer she'd never breathed but could almost smell.

"I'll bring you flowers every morning." Peach felt Kit's hands on her shoulders, one of the worn-thin quilts from the bedroll wrapped around her. "I'll build you a hot-house. You can have Queen Anne's lace and cornflowers year-round. Even roses. I can give you anything you want. I'm begging, I know, but I—"

"Don't, please." Peach spun around and pressed her fingers to his mouth. She felt his lips tremble and his hands as he gathered the quilt around her. "I'm a liar, too."

He gazed at her, puzzled, a wary gleam in his somber brown eyes, until he realized what she meant. Then she felt his sharp breath against her fingers, his grip tighten and the quilt bunch around her shoulders.

"What did you lie about?"

He held her so close Peach could see tiny flecks of wet chaff caught in his eyebrows. She stretched up on her toes and pressed a kiss to his lips. Lightly, shyly, the way she had twelve years ago in the dark at the Fourth of July Social, smiling as she wiped a smear of mud off his chin.

"How much I love you," she said, the whiskers he hadn't taken the time to shave that morning bristling against her fingertips. "How much I always have and always will."

"Oh, God, Miss MaCauley." Kit didn't groan it as he had that night behind the church, he breathed it wondrously, his voice unsteady, the amber flecks in his brown eyes glowing. "Will you marry me?"

"Yes," she said, her eyes shining. "Oh, *yes*."

And just as he had all those years ago, he kissed her back. Slowly this time and gently, slipping an arm around her to hold the quilt, cupping her face in one cold, shaky hand as he bent his head and brought his lips over hers.

Peach felt the scrape of his whiskers but no hard, barbed edges. Only tenderness. Sweet and aching, welling up inside her and fusing her mouth to his. He loved her. She felt it in the quaver of his lips, the checked strength and care not to scratch her in the slant of his mouth. He'd come back to Lynchburg because he loved her, but she'd been too stubborn and scared to listen. What a fool she'd been. What a lucky fool Kit wasn't too proud to beg. Peach flung her arms around his neck, a joyful sob shivering up her throat.

Kit felt it and raised his head. Her mouth was trembling, but she was smiling, and the rain was still pounding on the roof. So was his pulse and Peach's heart. He could feel it, and the soft fullness of her breasts against his chest.

She loved him. Peach MaCauley. The prettiest girl in Lynch County. She'd waited for him. He still couldn't believe it, and said, "I wish I'd known you'd waited for me."

"I've *been* waiting for you," she said, "all these years."

She hadn't realized it until this moment, yet Peach knew it was true and felt her eyes fill with tears. The heart Kit could've sworn he didn't have almost broke. He drew a deep breath and said firmly, "Best not to think about that."

"Especially since we can't change the last twelve years."

"But we can sure as hell spit in their eye." Kit gathered Peach and the quilt closer. "We can get married just as soon as it stops raining. As soon as I can fetch my wagon and drive us into town."

"Oh, Kit." Peach laughed and arched her head back to look at him. He lowered his gaze and caught a glimpse of the soaked lace edge of her chemise clinging to the damp swells of her breasts through the gaped front of her shirt. "We've got three horses. We don't need a wagon."

"I thought you might like to get married in a dress." Kit lifted his gaze. Reluctantly but gallantly. "Maybe in blue silk plaid with a lace collar and cuffs."

"Oh, I would." She sighed and shivered. "If I don't catch my death in these wet clothes."

"Then you'd best take them off."

"At last," she said, her smile and her eyes gleaming with mischief. "I thought you'd never ask."

"Miss MacCauley!" Kit gave a whoop of laughter and swung her into his arms. Quilt and all, one arm beneath her shoulder blades, the other beneath her knees.

So quickly and effortlessly Peach yelped and clutched at his shoulders, laughing as he spun her in a circle and carried her across the shed. Belle snorted indignantly and wheeled out of the way.

Lightning flashed and thunder rolled, but Peach barely heard it above Kit's deep laugh. The wind howled and rain pounded on the roof. Another leak sprang and splashed on her forehead. Kit kissed it away and murmured in her ear, "We should wait until we're married."

Wistfully, for God knew he didn't want to. Still he meant to be a gentleman, and merely set her down on the edge of the bedroll, but she tricked him, tripped him—a wicked gleam flashing in her blue eyes—and sent them tumbling onto the blankets, laughing and rolling in each other's arms, until Peach gave a yelp of pain and Kit shot up on one elbow.

"Did I hurt you?"

"Of course not." She drew up her right knee and the cuff of her trousers and plucked a bayonet out of her boot. "Will brought this home from the War. I always carry it with me in the field. Never know when you'll need a good, sharp knife."

Kit took it away from her and cocked an amused eyebrow. "I don't think you need it now, d'you?"

"Not unless you plan to make me wait." Peach caught the front of his shirt and pulled his mouth toward hers. "I've *been* waiting for twelve long years."

And she wouldn't wait any longer. The eager, open-mouthed kiss she gave him said so. Kit groaned and tossed the bayonet aside, rolled on his back and pulled her with him, fumbling for the buttons on her shirt and the rain-swollen rope at her waist. He kissed her and tugged, nuzzled her and pulled, but the knot held fast.

"Let me." Peach pushed up on her hands, breathless and straddling him, her hair a damp, tangled mane of honey blond curls. She undid the rope, the last of her buttons and tugged Will's shirttails out of her waistband.

"Let me." Kit peeled the shirt past her shoulders, his breath and his gaze catching on the high, round fullness of her breasts sculpted in damp, clinging cotton. He cupped one in each hand and watched Peach's lashes flutter shut as he circled her nipples with his thumbs.

And mistook their peaking for desire, until she caught her bottom lip to keep her teeth from chattering and gooseflesh flooded her arms. He chuckled then, drew the quilt over her shoulders, folded her into his arms and chafed her back with his hands.

"I'll be w-warm in a minute," she said, huddling beneath his chin. And never cold again. Or lonely or frightened. Peach sighed and snuggled closer, Kit's strong, steady heartbeat thudding in her ear.

"You deserve better than this anyhow." He kissed her temple and sighed. "Of all the places I've dreamed of making love to you, I never dreamed of a damp, muddy shed in the middle of a thunderstorm."

Peach raised her head, bent her left arm across his chest and leaned her chin on her wrist to look at him. "I dreamed about you, too," she said, brushing her lips across his chin.

Slowly back and forth, the prickle of his whiskers stirring a flutter deep inside her. His nostrils flared as he caught her mouth in his and rolled her over. She curled her arms around his neck, felt his hand caress her breast, and parted her lips on a sigh as his thumb hooked the edge of her chemise and tugged her nipple free.

He broke the kiss and bent his head to suckle, wincing as a cold drop of rain dripped in his ear. Another splashed in the hollow of Peach's throat. She started and wiped it away, felt the hammer of her pulse and made a moue of disappointment as Kit pushed up on his elbow and glowered at the leaks springing everywhere from the roof of the shed.

"Damn rain," he said, shaking his head as another drip splashed between his eyes.

"It's all right." Peach cupped his cheek and turned his face toward her. "We have all night to be together. Tonight and every other night for the rest of our lives."

She smiled, her eyes soft and shiny, and so did Kit, picturing her in his bed, his ring on her finger, her lips and her breasts swollen from his lovemaking. He leaned forward to kiss her and felt a chill of dread, a slow, *I'm-watching-you* crawl up the back of his neck.

"You're cold, too," Peach murmured, rubbing his cheek.

"A little. Button your shirt and wrap up in the quilt." He caught her hand, kissed her palm and rolled away from her.

A little too quickly for comfort, just as he had last night.

Hastily, Peach did up her shirt, shrugged the quilt over her shoulders and pushed up on her knees. The roof was leaking like a sieve, the canvas sheet flapping in the wind, a chill buffeting through the cracks in the walls.

The horses, huddled together for warmth in the far corner, were snorting and milling restlessly. Kit slipped among them, shushing and stroking. Peach got to her feet and hurried up beside him, slipping in the mud squishing underfoot.

"What's wrong?" she whispered, her heart pounding.

"I don't know." Kit frowned and shook his head.

He laid a hand on Buck's neck and felt the stallion tremble as he tossed his head and bugled. A metallic clang from outside, and a whinny muted by a rumble of thunder answered. Wishing he'd taken the time to fetch his Winchester from the barn, Kit crossed the shed, jerked the canvas sheet aside and found himself looking down the big-bored muzzle of Sam MaCauley's Sharps buffalo rifle.

"Be real careful, Taggart." Bud Wilkins grinned at him, squinting in the rain dripping off the brim of his hat. "I do believe the powder's dry enough to fire."

Chapter Nine

The click of the hammer drawing back froze Peach's breath in her throat. From where she stood between the Morgans, behind Kit and a little above him on the sloping, muddy floor of the shed, she could just see the rain-glistened barrel of the Sharps pointed at his chest and the gleam of Bud's right arm encased in a wet yellow slicker.

"Never 'spected to find you here," she heard him say to Kit. "Though I did wonder why you wasn't around to stop me when I set fire to Miss High and Mighty Ma-Cauley's barn."

"Damn you, Bud Wilkins!" Peach flung the quilt off her shoulders, pushed her way between Babe and Belle and slid across the shed.

She might've fallen in the mud at Bud's feet—or better yet, scratched his eyes out—if Kit hadn't caught her in one arm, pulled her tight against him and given her a warning, calm-down look.

"Keep your drawers on, Peach. You still got a barn. The wood was too wet to burn, but your wheat was sure nice and dry. Too bad." Bud flicked her a glance and tsked, but the Sharps never wavered from Kit's heart. "I know how much you were counting on that money."

"Not anymore, Junior," Kit said. "You wasted a match."

"How's that?" he asked, but Kit didn't answer.

Neither did Peach. Bud's gaze narrowed on Kit's arm over her shoulders and the fistful of his shirt she clutched in one hand. She was shaking with cold and fear, but willed herself not to let Bud see it, just notched up her chin as a slow grin spread across his face. His nose was still swollen, the imprint of her hairbrush on his cheek as bruised as the sky rumbling and flickering with lightning.

"Two lovebirds," he jeered. "Congratulations, Miss High and Mighty MaCauley. Or should I say, Mrs. Cracker?"

"Mrs. Taggart," Kit said sharply. "And tip your hat when you say it."

"Awful brave, ain't you, for a man with this old monster pointed at his heart?"

"Won't fire, Junior. Powder's too wet."

"Care to wager on that, cracker?"

"Stop it!" Peach flung herself in front of Kit. Bud Wilkins was a bully, but she didn't think—and she fervently prayed to God—he wasn't a murderer. "You burned my wheat and smashed the header. You've gotten even. Now go home and leave us alone."

"Oh, Peach." Bud tsked at her again, a nasty chuckle in his voice. "I haven't even started to get even."

He half-turned his head over his shoulder, giving her a glimpse of another man in a slicker and dripping hat bent over the header with a rope. The other end was tied to the horn of the saddle on Bud's black gelding. Peach knew who the accomplice was before Bud shouted at him, raising his voice above the whine of the trees tossing in the wind.

"C'mon, Jed! Get that damn rope tied!"

"Gimme a minute!" he hollered back, glancing up at Bud. "Cussed thing's wet and slicker'n a greased pig!"

Through the sheeting rain Kit couldn't see Tyler's face, but he recognized the fear in his voice. He'd heard it too many times in the War to mistake it. He wished he'd taken the time to investigate when Buck had balked at the barn door, wished he'd paid attention to the slow, *I'm-watching-you* crawl that had plagued him all day.

"Get the hell up here!" Junior thundered at Jed over a boom of the real thing. "I'll do it myself!"

He took an angry step backward and slipped a little in the mud. The muzzle of the Sharps swung to the left, giving Kit space enough to push Peach behind him and clamp his hands on her wrists to keep her there.

"I thought you said," she hissed furiously in his ear, struggling to break his hold, "that this was *our* fight!"

"Not anymore," he shot back in a low voice. "Not since you stepped in front of a loaded gun."

"The powder's too wet—"

"Maybe it is and maybe it isn't. Now hush up. I plan to marry you, not bury you."

One last time Peach tried to wrench free and gave up. She was so angry she could scream, so frightened she could cry, but she wasn't about to let Bud Wilkins get away with whatever he had planned. She was a MaCauley, by God, and MaCauleys never quit. Except for Will, she thought, and remembered the bayonet.

"Kit," she whispered.

"Shhh!" he hissed sharply.

"Get a move on, Jed!" Bud bellowed. Peach peered around Kit's right arm and saw Jed break into a sloppy run. His face, already pinched with cold, turned even paler when Bud shoved the Sharps into his hands, none too gently, and said, "Keep these two covered."

"Hellfire, Bud. There's no call for this. I never—"

"You'll do what I tell you." Bud whipped his slicker back, drew and cocked his pistol and shoved it into Jed's chest. So quickly Peach gasped, and Kit squeezed her wrists. "Or your family'll pay."

"Anything you say, Bud. See?" Jed leveled the Sharps at Kit and Peach, his hands shaking so badly the barrel wobbled. "Just relax, all right?"

"That's better." Bud eased off the hammer and reholstered his gun. "Now mind these two while I finish up."

"You bet." Jed stepped aside as Bud stalked past him. "Best be quick. I don't like the look of this sky."

Neither did Kit. The trees edging the field were bent nearly double, the wind so fierce the rain fell sideways. Lightning flashed and thunder rumbled almost nonstop.

"I believe Junior's gone crazy, Jed," Kit said to Tyler and nodded at Bud fighting the wind and the rain to tie the rope on the header. "But I figured you had sense enough to stay home in a storm like this."

"I was home, puttin' up my stock when Bud rode in," Jed replied nervously, glancing at Bud, then at Kit. "Lily asked him in and gave him a glass a beer. She didn't like it when he said he wished he'd seen your face when you found the header, but she kept quiet until he said he wasn't done with you and Miz Peach. Lily said she wouldn't hear such talk and next thing I know, Bud's got his gun pointed at her head."

A colossal boom of thunder shook the shed and made Peach start. Jed, too, and Kit. Buck bugled, the Morgans wheeled and whinnied, and Bud's gelding bolted. Bud managed to catch the end of the rope and drag him back to the header, shouting curses Peach could just hear above the shriek of the wind.

"What could I do?" Jed eased back on the hammer of the Sharps and lowered the barrel. "My youngun's was cryin' and Lily scared t'death. I said I come along and help him."

"You want outta this, Jed?"

"Hell, *yes*."

"Fetch the bayonet, Peach. Keep low and be quick about it before Bud gets that rope tied and looks up here."

Peach spun away, slipped and fell but kept moving toward the bedroll on her hands and knees with her heart pounding in her throat, and back with the bayonet in her teeth. Out of breath and covered with mud, she struggled to her feet behind Kit and slipped the bayonet into his left hand hilt first.

"How we gonna do this?" Jed asked.

"Try to take him by surprise," Kit replied. "If you slip and bump him, I can get behind him before he pulls his gun."

"I can help," Peach put in, wiping the mud off her hands on her trousers. "I can—"

"No, you can't," Kit cut her off. "As for you, Tyler, switch sides on me again and I'll put this bayonet through your heart before Junior puts a bullet through mine."

"Hey, Taggart!" Bud shouted. "Watch this!"

The wind caught her hair as Peach stepped out from behind Kit. She tugged it away and saw Bud walking the rope hand over hand toward his horse. As much to keep himself upright, it seemed to her, as to test the knot.

"You got any thoughts about fixin' this thing?" Bud hollered, grinning at them over his shoulder as he swung up into his saddle. "Better learn to swim!"

He kicked his horse hard and the gelding began to pull, dragging the wreck through the mud toward the creek. No longer bone dry, but a racing torrent of foaming dark water trying to leap its banks.

"I didn't know Bud meant to do this," Jed said.

"S'all right." Kit sounded calm and unruffled, but Peach saw a muscle leaping in his jaw. "He'll pay for it."

The header left a deep, ugly gouge across the field littered with bits and pieces of itself. Near enough to the bank to make Peach cringe, Bud swung his horse to the right and turned the header parallel to the creek. He dismounted, picked up a stout oak sapling, and used it as a lever to roll the header over, ever closer to the racing water. Once, twice, then he stood back to take a look. One more roll and he'd have it.

Peach didn't want to watch and turned her head away. Over the wind-bent trees along the bank, upstream and around a deep bend, she saw an uprooted walnut tree plunging toward Bud. At least twenty feet of trunk, spreading green crown and roots, already rolling sideways and bumping the banks as the swift current swept it along. Bud wouldn't see it until it turned the bend. And not at all unless he turned around.

"Kit!" Peach grabbed him and pointed, cupped her hands around her mouth and screamed, "Bud! Run!"

He didn't hear her over the wind. Or Kit, either, running toward him and shouting at the top of his lungs. Jed was hollering, too, and shoving the Sharps into Peach's hands as he bolted after Kit.

The weight of the gun and the fierce wind sent her staggering backward into the shed. She kept her feet, shook back her wet hair and blinked at the rifle in her hands. What better way to find out if the powder was dry enough to fire. Peach raced outside into the rain and the wind, raised the Sharps to her shoulder, swung the barrel clear of Kit and Jed and Bud, pulled back the hammer and pressed the trigger.

It went off like a cannon and knocked her flat. Stunned, and her head roaring, Peach sucked breath into her lungs and rolled onto her side. She saw Kit nearing the creek and waving his arms, and Bud, his mouth falling open in a scream she couldn't hear, spin upstream and throw his arms up to ward off the gnarled root ball hurtling toward him.

It was too late to scream, too late to do anything but fling her head away and pray for Bud. The muddy field and the black sky lurched and spun. Peach swallowed thickly and squeezed her eyes shut . . . opened them and saw Lily Tyler bending over her in a yellow slicker with a red wool shawl over her head, a worried frown on her broad, freckled face.

"Lily." Peach blinked the shed walls into focus, realized she was stretched out on the bedroll with her mother's old quilts tucked under her chin. She couldn't believe she'd fainted. "What happened?"

"Knocked yourself silly," Lily retorted, "shootin' that damned old gun of Sam MaCauley's, God rest him."

"No, no. I—" Peach's voice caught. "I mean—Bud."

"He's alive." Lily's tone gentled. "Can't move his legs. Not yet, anyhow. Ben's gone to fetch his wagon. Sent my Tad for him once Jed and Bud rode off. Ben got here right after me. He helped Jed and Kit fish him out of the creek."

"Thank God." Peach sighed, wincing as she tried to move her right shoulder. "I thought he'd drowned for sure."

"Come close, pinned like he was against the bank by that big old walnut tree. Took both mules to pull the tree off him."

"Red came back?"

"'Course he did. Him and Jed's old flea-bag, Sam, come wanderin' in, draggin' the wagon tongue soon's the rain quit. Damn shame about the tree. Lost a fine crop of nuts there."

Lily tsked and shook her head. A thin ray of watery sun slanted through a hole in the roof that hadn't been there before the storm. Lily took off her slicker and unwrapped her shawl from her mass of pinned and frizzy ginger hair.

"I'm glad Bud didn't hurt you. And grateful," Peach said though it galled her, "that you spoke up for me."

"*And* your intended," Lily added, folding her shawl.

Damn Jed and his big mouth, Peach thought. "I love Kit," she said fiercely, "and I mean to marry him, Lily. No matter what you or anybody else in Lynch County thinks."

"I'll tell you what I think, Peach MaCauley," Lily replied, her voice tart but her pale blue eyes twinkling. "I think you're a mighty lucky young lady."

"No, ma'am, Miz Tyler," Kit said, leaning on one shoulder in the shed doorway, dripping mud and smelly creek water but smiling at Peach. "I'm a lucky man."

"That's for damn sure." Lily sniffed at him, and winked

at Peach. "How 'bout a glass of cider? Fetched a jug with me from home."

"Thank you, no, Lily. I don't want cider."

"What would you like? Glass of water?"

"Nothing to drink, thank you," Peach said, smiling back at Kit. "I'd like to get married."

Chapter Ten

The wedding took place two days later in Lily Tyler's parlor. Lily insisted, after she'd bustled Peach and Kit home with her, bathed them, fed them and given them clean clothes. To soothe her guilty conscience, Peach was sure, until Lily produced Mary MaCauley's wedding dress. The gown of lace-trimmed blond silk Peach had hidden away in tissue paper but Will had found and sold.

Since Lily had three girls beside Tad, Peach didn't quite believe her claim that she'd bought the dress from Will intending all along to give it back to Peach. Until Kit offered to pay her for it and Lily threatened him with her broom.

"You can stay with us till then. And well you should." Lily gave Kit such a pointed look he felt the tops of his ears turning red. "But it's your wedding," she finished, shooing Jed and the children outside, "so you decide."

"I've waited twelve years," Peach said hesitantly to Kit. "I suppose I can wait two more days."

He wanted to tell her he couldn't wait two more minutes, but looking at her sitting in Lily's rocking chair with her mother's dress spilled in her lap, the silk shimmering in the glow of the kitchen fire, he didn't have the heart.

"After the day you've had, you deserve a fine party,"

he said gently. "And like Lily said, it's your wedding."

"It's *our* wedding," Peach shot back, her eyes—those beautiful blue eyes that had drawn him back to Lynchburg—blazing as bright as the flames in the fireplace. "Unlike *our* problem, Mr. Taggart, which you took upon yourself to solve without consulting me. If you think I intend to live my life being told when to hush up, why you can just—"

"Hush up." Kit dropped to his knees in front of her, grinned and gathered Peach and her mother's wedding dress into his arms. "And kiss me."

She did, laughing, her mouth soft and shivery. Not with cold, this time, but desire. For him, miracle of miracles.

"Oh God, Miss MaCauley," he groaned raggedly in her ear. "It's gonna be a long two days."

But worth every second to see Peach in her mother's gown, her bosom flushed and pink above the glowing blond silk neckline, the bruise on her right shoulder left by the Sharps rifle almost faded. To kiss his bride, and taste the same ache that had kept him awake for the last two nights, to feel it trembling through every sweet inch of her.

A fair portion of Lynchburg society attended, with the exception of the Wilkins family. Bud still couldn't walk, Peach heard it whispered at the punch bowl. A shame, sure enough, but no surprise, considering his wild, reckless ways. The talk made her frown, until she saw Kit coming toward her, so tall and handsome in a fine blue suit and snowy white shirt that her throat swelled with pride that he was hers.

"Some folks," he whispered in her ear, just a hint of bitterness in the wry twist of his mouth, "will go anywhere for a free meal."

The bride and groom danced to Clem Parker's fiddle, ate the fine, fat pig Jed roasted in a pit and licked Lily Tyler's sponge cake off their fingers. Each other's fingers, in a quiet corner of the kitchen, between small, hot kisses, until the parson cleared his throat behind them and said he thought it was time they took their leave.

Which they did in grand style in a well-sprung buggy with brass trim and a red leather seat pulled by a prancing Babe and Belle. A dozen or so young Lynch County bucks chased them on horseback halfway to the Taggart place, whooping and hollering and firing their pistols in the air. The sun was starting down when Kit turned the buggy off the road, between railed fences and rolling green pastures, where Buck grazed with a pair of pregnant mares. He raised his head at the rattle of the buggy, whinnied and came to trot along the fence with Babe and Bette.

The house he'd built himself sat atop the rise just ahead, its white clapboard walls flushed gold in the fading daylight. Peach sighed, stifled a yawn, and laid her cheek on his shoulder.

"Tired?" He murmured, kissing the top of her head.

"Not a bit." She sprang up and gave him a bright smile.

"You will be," he promised, the gleam in his amber brown eyes brushing a slow, lush shiver up the back of her neck.

Halfway up the rise, Peach saw the reason Kit had refused to let her see the house until now. Her breath caught and tears filled her eyes. She blinked them away and stared, dazed and speechless, at flower beds ringing the kitchen porch steps, edged in stone and overflowing with Queen Anne's Lace and cornflowers.

Kit stopped the buggy and set the brake, wrapped the reins around the handle and looked at Peach. Her chin was quavering, her thick, dark lashes jeweled with tears.

"Welcome home, Mrs. Taggart," he said softly.

"Oh, Kit." Peach pressed her lace-netted fingertips to her lips, looked at him and the proud, pleased smile on his face, and burst into happy, laughing tears. "I've never seen anything so beautiful in all my life."

"Neither have I," he said and kissed her, tasting the salt in her tears and the cider on her tongue.

Just as he had all those years ago in the dark behind the church. But she was his now. No longer Miss Peach MaCauley, but Mrs. Kit Taggart. His bride. His wife. His to love and cherish and laugh with, make babies with and grow old.

Once struck, forever struck. Praise God.

He broke the kiss and sprang out of the buggy. She laughed as he swooped her up in his arms and looped her arms around his neck. He grinned and raced up the steps, through the kitchen and the parlor and up the stairs, into the bedroom. He set her down beside the bed, kissed her and cupped her face, his heart hammering at the shimmer in her eyes.

"I'll tend the horses," he said, his voice deep and out of breath, "and be right back."

"I'll be right there," Peach murmured, sliding her gaze toward the bed. "Waiting."

And she was, lying calm and still with her hands at her sides in the middle of the goose down mattress. Perfectly, gloriously naked, her breasts and belly glowing in the soft, lavender twilight filtering through the lace curtains Lily Tyler had put up the day before, the gold wedding band he'd slipped on her finger glinting in the fading light.

"Welcome home, Mr. Taggart," she murmured, her arms lifting, and her breasts, already peaked and rosy, as he bent one knee on the mattress and kissed her without touching her.

Her eyes were soft and shimmering when he raised his head and his hands to his trouser buttons. She touched him there, shyly. He caught his breath and her hand, raised it to his lips and kissed her fingers, sucked them one at a time into his mouth, teasing them with his tongue while he opened his trousers and took off his shirt.

With a soft moue, she slid her hands up his chest, raking lightly with her nails, breathing in quick, shallow pants. When he swung away to sit and take off his boots, she curled around him like a cat, her hands hot and questing, his heart thundering at her touch. He yanked off his boots, stood and faced her and shucked off his trousers and long johns.

"Oh, Kit," she breathed huskily, her gaze sliding slowly up the length of his body, a soft smile creasing the dimple at the corner of her mouth. "This was worth the wait."

"Had enough waiting?"

"More than enough," she murmured, rolling onto her back.

She opened her arms and parted her lips and her legs. He sank into her mouth, her embrace, almost but not quite inside her. She shivered and moaned, her breath fluttering in his throat. He took her tongue first, deep into his mouth, felt her pelvis arch and her hips spread and pushed partway into her. Her breath seized and he freed her mouth, pushed up on his hands and gazed down at her, the pulse hammering in her throat, the deep, luminous sheen in her eyes.

"Oh, please," she whispered shakily. "Don't stop."

"I haven't even started," he said softly, leaning back on his knees and cupping her breasts.

She arched again and caught her breath as he brushed her nipples. First with his thumbs, then with his tongue, nuzzling and nipping until she moaned and clutched his wrists.

When his mouth closed on her right breast, Peach thought she'd die of ecstasy. When he sucked and stroked with his tongue, she forgot how to breathe. When he moved to her left nipple, she shivered and arched against his mouth, pushing more of her breast into his mouth. He groaned and deepened the slow, exquisite suckle.

When she thought she couldn't stand another slow, stroking tug without screaming, he freed her nipple and raised his head. He smiled and leaned over her with his weight on his elbows. Peach sighed and shifted beneath him, arched her back, lifted her hips, felt him push and slide into her as far as he could, felt him shudder and suck a deep breath.

"I love you so much," he said raggedly, "I'd rather die than hurt you."

"*I'll* die," Peach murmured in his ear, "if you don't."

He laughed and raised his head so he could see her face, said one last time, his voice deep and shaky, "Oh, God, Miss MaCauley," and made her his in one quick, hard thrust.

She winced, and then she smiled, her eyes shining. "Mrs. Taggart," she said proudly. "And tip your hat when you say it."

ANITA MILLS
ARNETTE LAMB
ROSANNE BITTNER

*Join three of your favorite storytellers
on a tender journey of the heart...*

Cherished Moments is an extraordinary collection of
breathtaking novellas woven around the theme of mother-
hood. Before you turn the last page you will have been swept
from the storm-tossed coast of a Scottish isle to the fury of
the American frontier, and you will have lived the lives and
loves of three indomitable women, as they experience their
most passionate moments.

THE NATIONAL BESTSELLER

CHERISHED
MOMENTS

CHERISHED MOMENTS
Anita Mills, Arnette Lamb, Rosanne Bittner
_____ 95473-5 $4.99 U.S./$5.99 Can.

Only in his dreams has Burke Grisham, the once-dissolute Earl of Thornwald, seen a lady as exquisite as Catherine Snow. Now, standing before him at last is the mysterious beauty whose life he has glimpsed in strange visions—whose voice called him back from death, and the shimmering radiance beyond, on the bloody field of Waterloo. But she is also the widow of the friend he destroyed: the one woman who scorns him; the one woman he must possess...

A Glimpse of Heaven

Barbara Dawson Smith

"An excellent reading experience from a master writer. A triumphant and extraordinary success!"
—*Affaire de Coeur*

KAT MARTIN

Award-winning author of *Creole Fires*

GYPSY LORD
_____ 92878-5 $5.99 U.S./$6.99 Can.

SWEET VENGEANCE
_____ 95095-0 $4.99 U.S./$5.99 Can.

BOLD ANGEL
_____ 95303-8 $5.99 U.S./$6.99 Can.

DEVIL'S PRIZE
_____ 95478-6 $5.99 U.S./$6.99 Can.

MIDNIGHT RIDER
_____ 95774-2 $5.99 U.S./$6.99 Can.